Legion

of Strangers

Legion of Strangers

The Vivid History of

a Unique Military Tradition—

The French Foreign Legion

BY CHARLES MERCER

Holt, Rinehart and Winston

NEW YORK   CHICAGO   SAN FRANCISCO

Published simultaneously in Canada by Holt, Rinehart
and Winston of Canada, Limited.

Library of Congress Catalog Card Number: 64-13707

Grateful acknowledgment is made to The John Day Company, Inc., New
York, N.Y., for permission to quote briefly from *Doctor at Dienbienphu* by
Paul Grauwin; and to Charles Scribner's Sons, New York, N.Y., for permission
to quote from "I Have a Rendezvous with Death" and *Letters and Diary of
Alan Seeger* by Alan Seeger.

First Edition

Designer: Ernst Reichl

85669–0114

Printed in the United States of America

To

Herb Jaffe

With Gratitude

Contents

1	The Mystique	3
2	The Country Without a Name	12
3	A Spanish Adventure	22
4	March or Die	32
5	Dark and Bloody Ground	44
6	Dubious Friends in High Places	55
7	*"Bonjour, Ma'moiselle"*	71
8	To the Halls of Montezuma	83
9	End of an Era	99
10	Sahara	113
11	The Fort in the Desert	137
12	"We Have Fought a Thousand Years"	151
13	The War Against Women	164
14	Of Men and Mules and Empire	180
15	Cheap and Dirty?	188
16	Appointment in Morocco	198
17	"A Rendezvous with Death"	208
18	The World of Abd-el-Krim	230

19	The Beguiling Wound	241
20	A Troubled Stepchild	256
21	"So That Honor May Be Saved"	277
22	The Dead Cause	303
23	At Aubagne	320
	Acknowledgments	325
	Sources	327
	Index	335

Legion

of Strangers

I

The

Mystique

As DRUMS ROLLED AND TRUMPETS BLARED, the lines of white-capped soldiers braced smartly to attention. Then General Charles Ailleret, Chief of Staff of the French Army, tugged sharply at a cord and a white shroud fluttered to the ground, revealing a huge bronze globe guarded by the bronze figures of four soldiers.

Thus, on April 30, 1963, there began a new, and perhaps the last, chapter in the long and turbulent saga of a strange fraternity of men —the French Foreign Legion.

The scene was Camp de la Demande in the French town of Aubagne, near Marseilles. There the Legion had established its new headquarters after quitting its principal base of more than a century at Sidi-bel Abbès in Algeria. It was far from being a routine transfer of a routine troop unit, however. It was, rather, a move fraught with the sadness and reluctance of men who had been forced to abandon their home, for the French evacuation of Algeria dealt a heavy blow to Legion morale.

The Monument to the Dead, which General Ailleret unveiled, had been painstakingly transported from Sidi-bel-Abbès to Aubagne in the previous October. Other trophies and relics of the Legion, garnered over the course of its 132 years of fighting and travail, had been moved with the Monument. The most important, especially on that thirtieth of April, was the wooden left hand of Captain Jean Danjou, a hero whose name in Legion annals bears the aura of a saint. A century previously, on April 30, 1863, Danjou had been killed when his company of 46 Legionnaires withstood a day-long assault by an army of 2,000 men at Camerone in Mexico until, at the climax of the battle, the 6 remaining Legionnaires mounted a bayonet charge into the heart of the massed Mexicans. Each year the thirtieth of April is faithfully observed as the Feast of Camerone by every Legion unit. Officers read the story of the battle to their men and all are served the best food and drink available.

On the centenary Feast of Camerone at Aubagne in 1963 men of nearly fifty nations, wearing the white kepi of the Foreign Legion, stood at attention while the ceremony progressed. No one could read the thoughts masked by their tanned, weathered, immobile faces. Certainly, some were deeply imbued with loyalty to the Legion. Certainly, too, others were seeking a way out of it. It is equally certain that most were embittered by the belief that an age finally had ended, that they had come to a time of no more wars. And what is the use in being a Legionnaire if there is no fighting to be done?

One who studies the history of *la Légion Étrangère*—the Foreign Legion—is struck by the astonishing mystique it has developed since its founding by Louis Philippe, King of the French, in 1831. Nothing like it has ever occurred in the history of mercenary troops and it rarely has been equaled by soldiers of one nation fighting for a common nationalistic cause. In certain respects the mystique bears resemblance to that of a strenuous religious order.

It is expressed by the Legion's motto, *Legio Patria Nostra:* The Legion Is Our Fatherland. Although the Legion always has fought at the behest of the French Government, loyalty to France is sec-

4

ondary to loyalty to the Legion. A man may openly express contempt for France or the French people, but if he is a loyal Legionnaire, it does not matter.

A recruit in the Legion is thoroughly indoctrinated with the mystique. It is an integral part of his arduous training and its purpose is to make him believe that the Legion is his home, his family, his nation. His past is forgiven and forgotten. He is offered the opportunity of a new life in which he can find virtues he may not have displayed before. The Legion tries to make him feel that he has the chance of a fresh beginning, a catharsis, the hope of regeneration, if he wants it. He is exposed to the philosophy of men who have lived more intensely, venturesomely, and with a greater sense of solitude than most experience. In effect, the Legion says to him that life is fleeting and death close, that it is better to die well than to live badly. Thus good becomes synonymous with courage and death, while evil becomes synonymous with cowardice and life.

A Legionnaire who accepts the mystique obeys orders unquestioningly, adjusts to a parochial life of limited freedoms, and faces death unhesitatingly. It is not surprising that the Foreign Legion always has appealed to men with suicidal tendencies and that suicide always has been one of its chief problems. Nor is it surprising that the Legion has had to close its eyes to that limited form of suicidal escape from the realities—alcoholism. Heavy drinking is the tradition, the pride, the abomination, and the besetting vice of the Foreign Legion. It has no regulations against drinking, provided a man can manage to perform his duties. In fact even today, at some posts, work is suspended on payday because of the prevalence of drunkenness.

The Legion's mystique has, indeed, been potent. It has resulted in thousands of heroic acts and scores of military victories. It caused the Legion to become the most decorated French military unit of World War I. Like some visible banner, the mystique has led the Legion through wars in Algeria, Morocco, Tunisia, Spain, Mexico, the Crimea, Italy, France, Germany, Austria, Norway, West Africa, East Africa, Central Africa, Libya, Syria, Madagascar, Turkey,

Greece, Serbia, Indochina and Formosa. It has inspired hundreds of thousands of men of 101 nationalities to endure frightful ordeals at slight pay, and for little idealistic reason, in the interests of a foreign power which few of them admired.

Although many men have given the mystique of the Legion their wholehearted assent, many others have dissented vigorously. Often a dissenter has undertaken what is the cardinal sin in the eyes of the Legion hierarchy: desertion. A man who tries to desert the Legion before he has completed his five-year term of enlistment is punished swiftly and ruthlessly. The Legion will not divulge precisely how many men have succeeded in deserting, but the total runs into many thousands over the course of the years.

All manner of men have been attracted to the Legion for all manner of reasons. It is impossible to find a craft, trade, profession, or way of life that has not been represented among the wearers of its white kepi. Members of royalty and a great variety of nobility have served in the Legion. On occasion the professional musicians in its ranks could have formed an outstanding symphony orchestra. Poets and priests have marched and fought alongside pimps and perverts. A Spanish bishop, serving as a private, used to play the organ in the chapel at Sidi-bel-Abbès; drink had been his undoing, and he had to be well lubricated with alcohol in order to play effectively. Once, during the Rif War in Morocco, when a Legion battalion had been badly mauled and was without medical aid, three physicians in the ranks disclosed their former profession and tended the wounded. Although poverty is the rule for nearly every Legionnaire, at least one American millionaire enlisted as a private during World War I. Once, a general, reviewing a regiment in Syria, was struck by the military bearing of one private. He asked what his occupation had been before enlisting. "I was a general, *mon Général*," replied the private who had been a major general in the White Russian Army.

Prince Aage of Denmark, a first cousin of King Christian X, served as a captain in the Legion for many years, and concluded that many men join it because "life is a torture" to them. Tortured or not, men of all sorts they have been, both brutal and kind, heroes

6

and villains, from all walks of life, enlisted for all sorts of reasons. Many who had lived badly died well. Some who had lived well deserted in the fear that they would die badly.

For more than a century after its founding the Foreign Legion drew many of its best soldiers from the lost causes of Europe. Whenever might triumphed, some of the defeated found their way into the Legion. Generations of freedom-loving men who were suppressed in Italy, Poland, and Spain joined it. After the Bolshevik Revolution in Russia, thousands of White Russians flocked to it. After the defeat of Germany in World War I, large numbers of German ultranationalists poured into it. As Hitler's swastikas engulfed Europe, the Legion became the refuge of Jews, Austrians, Czechs, Poles, Hungarians, Serbs. Of course not every lost cause is a good one. After Hitler and Mussolini were defeated, the Legion became a refuge for Nazis and Fascists. But whether a man was an anarchist or a monarchist or a democrat made no difference to the Legion; what mattered was that he was willing and physically able to serve and fight.

Yet the ranks of the Legion always were a far cry from being filled with men seeking political asylum. The vast majority of men are concerned more by personal than by political affairs. With some notable exceptions, the Legion usually has enlisted men who are poor or rootless or personally harassed.

A recurrent story with the same theme has been told about generations of Legionnaires. Most recently in the twentieth century it concerned an Italian who had joined the Legion and was asked what sort of man Mussolini had been. "He wasn't so bad," the Italian replied, "but you should have met that wife of mine."

Despite claims of romantic fiction, Legionnaires agree on one thing: many a man has joined the Legion in an effort to try to forget a woman he hated, but rarely to forget a woman he loved. Almost invariably a desire to escape from something has been the motive that led men to sign the Legion's five-year pledge of service—escape from a wife or parents or a way of life.

Germans always have been attracted to the Legion. So have Swiss, even though their Constitution forbids them to enter the military service of any foreign power except the Swiss Guard of the Vatican in Rome. Throughout the Legion's long history it always has had large complements of Spaniards and Italians, and it has been said that there never was a Legion company without at least one Belgian serving in it.

Although the French are prohibited by law from joining the Legion, thousands have served in it. All have assumed a different name and nationality upon enlisting, a choice the Legion always has given each recruit. Some have been motivated by political reasons, wishing to serve France while being opposed to the government in power. Many others, finding their status as citizens endangered for legal reasons, have sought the prize the French offer all Legionnaires who have served honorably for five years: full French citizenship.

Contrary to general belief, relatively few British and Irish and even fewer Americans have joined the Legion. The English historian, D. W. Brogan, has remarked dryly that "a very high proportion of those few wrote books; a very high proportion also desert; some do both."

Anglo-Saxons who joined the Legion seem to have ignored or been unaware of dozens of reminiscences published in English by former Legionnaires. Most written by enlisted men condemn the Legion and reject its mystique. Most written by officers extol it. Dozens of reminiscences published in French, German, and other languages follow the same general pattern. When studying these writings, one is sometimes reminded of a remark attributed to Trotsky: "You can usually approximate the truth by a comparison of the lies."

Most English-speaking peoples' concept of the Foreign Legion stems from romantic fiction and films which contain shoddy emotions, banal situations, and glaring inaccuracies of fact. The first novel which purported to be about the Legion was published in 1867 by a plain but passionate Victorian lady named Marie Louise de la Ramée, who wrote under the pseudonym Ouida. Her *Under Two Flags* is one of the all-time best sellers and has been filmed

8

many times. It did not matter to her readers that she confused the French *Chasseurs* with the Foreign Legion; in the public mind the Legion became fixed as the most outrageously romantic body of men who ever took up arms.

In this century came the commercially successful and factually inaccurate romances of Percival Christopher Wren. Among his mistaken notions was one that the Legion's punishment battalion was the infamous *Bataillon d'Afrique* which is composed of French criminals who have a choice of serving in Africa in that military labor unit or in France as convicts. More amusing was Wren's insistence that women had served in the Legion, thereby indicating that Legionnaires don't bathe or take physical examinations. No woman ever had served in the Foreign Legion when Wren was writing *Beau Geste* and *Beau Sabreur*.

But, as a matter of fact, one woman later *did* serve in the Legion—and without masculine disguise. She was an English woman, Miss Susan Travers, who was accepted by the Legion's 13th Half-Brigade as an ambulance driver before it embarked for Norway in 1940. No writer of romance ever has imagined anything to equal Miss Travers' adventures with the 13th in Europe, Asia, and Africa throughout the course of World War II.

The Foreign Legion is an outstanding example of the triumph of a way of life over the literature written about it. Despite millions of published words of blame and praise, of truths and half-truths and downright lies, the Legion has remained essentially the same for more than a century. Politics and the changing social currents of the world have been the determining factors in its enlistments, its casualties.

The story of the Legion is essentially the story of the rise and decline of the French overseas empire. For the Legion did more than any other military organization to create that empire and then fought a bloody, heartbreaking series of hopeless battles to preserve it.

One can view the story through the eyes of a Don Quixote or a

9

Sancho Panza. In truth, both viewpoints are necessary in order to understand it thoroughly.

A Don Quixote might see the Legion as have ecstatic crowds of Parisians when its crack units have paraded down the Champs Élysées. The Legionnaires' slow and sinister desert step is indeed something to behold. With arms straight and fingers outstretched, the men move forward in a ghostly glide to their marching song, *"Le Boudin."* Like all the favorite Legion tunes—"Figuig," "The Wooden Trumpet," "Into the Desert"—the music is haughty, wild, melancholy, exalting the pride of men who for years have been cut off from a life as others know it.

Ah, say the romantics, isn't it grand! The gallant foreigners who die bravely for France. The men who have lived back of beyond, fighting in the lonely desert posts and the hilltop fortresses. Life must hold a greater savor for men who have endured constant danger on the threshold of death.

But a Sancho Panza, plodding in the ranks, does not see it so. He remembers the blisters and the blood in the boots, the thirty-five-mile march in blazing heat as he staggered under a hundred-pound burden. The roads built and the roads repaired. The desert battle against hopeless odds. Always being the first to advance and the last to withdraw. The thirst, the hunger, the loneliness, the heat of the day and the cold of the night, and that time in the *bled* when the man suffering from *le cafard* ran insane with a flashing knife.

French public opinion is divided on the Legion, as it is on almost everything. Some citizens feel it is disgraceful that their country should hire foreigners to fight its battles. But their feeling has made little impression on the various French governments of the past 130 years. With a certain logic that may seem cynical, French governments have viewed the question in this manner: There are foreigners who wish to fight for us and we have battles to be fought. Is it not true that for every foreigner who dies in battle, the life of one Frenchman is saved?

This "logic" is the result of a long tradition in France which many French military historians ignore. It is not widely known that over the course of centuries the French have employed more mercenary soldiers than any other Western nation. Its Foreign Legion is only the last in a long line of mercenary units.

As early as 886 the King of France hired a Scottish bodyguard. For centuries the Scots were the favorites among the detachments of various nationalities who served as part of the French Royal Household troops until, in 1400, the Scottish contingent was 7,000 strong. Gradually the Irish replaced the Scots as favored mercenaries; by 1714 there were seven Irish regiments in the pay of France. Other nationalities were used freely, too. At various times the French service hired units of English, Germans, Swiss, Poles, Spaniards, Swedes, Italians, and Dutch. During the Revolution more than 700 Swiss Royal Guards fought to the death, defending Louis XVI from the mobs in the Tuileries. Then, after wiping out the royal mercenaries, the French Revolutionary Government faced about and hired units of foreigners to fight for it. Even the great Napoleon Bonaparte employed as many foreigners as he could obtain, and at one time almost half of his army was composed of foreign mercenary units.

Today the future of the most renowned mercenary unit in the world, the Foreign Legion, appears in doubt. The overseas empire it helped to create and maintain has been transformed into sixteen free nations, all self-governing and most of them co-operating with France. As a result, the Legion's stepparent, the French Army, seems to be dubious as how to employ it.

In fact the future of the Legion always has been in doubt since the first months of its inception, and such uncertainty is not peculiar to the Legion. It has been, rather, the prevailing state of mind of military bodies throughout recorded time. For who ever did know precisely what the morrow might bring?

2

The Country

Without a Name

ALTHOUGH THE EMPIRE of Napoleon Bonaparte was only a fond
memory, Frenchmen still dreamed of military glory. One of the
dreamers was the last of the Bourbon kings of France, the fat and
bigoted Charles X, who had succeeded Louis XVIII to the throne.
At last, in the spring of 1830, Charles believed he saw the opportunity
to give some substance to his dreams by sending a military expedition into what a Frenchman called "the country without a name"—
Algeria.

Charles wanted to do *something* that would reflect creditably on
the Bourbons in those dull days following the fall of the Napoleonic
Empire. As Emile Bourgeois observed wryly, "For lack of a conquest on the Rhine, he started with all speed an expedition against
Algiers."

French school children are told that the expedition was sent because an irritable character named Hussein, the Dey of Algiers,

struck the French consul with a fly whisk. There was a bit more to it than that—though not much. Two Jewish merchants named Bacri and Busnach, who had been supplying North African wheat to France for a number of years, were unable to collect a considerable amount of money owed them in the city of Algiers. So why not send a "punitive" expedition to the coast of North Africa with the purpose of collecting debts and flexing a flabby Bourbon muscle?

The expedition of 37,000 men which landed at Sidi-Ferruch on June 14, 1830, had some comic aspects. It was led by the most unpopular soldier in France, the Comte de Ghaisne de Bourmont, who had deserted to the enemy three days before Waterloo. In his initial proclamation Bourmont addressed the Algerians as Moroccans, though they were several hundred miles away. During the first two weeks after he reported his landing, Bourmont sent no further messages to Paris and received only two from his government. The first contained instructions on sending plants and fossils to a museum; the second asked him to ship home sixty camels at all possible speed.

On July 5 the French Army entered Algiers. While Bourmont was wondering what to do next, Charles X was toppled from his shaky throne and went into exile. The House of Bourbon was replaced by the House of Orléans in the person of Louis Philippe, who is remembered as the Bourgeois Monarch. He was penurious, but not thrifty. He was shrewd, but showed that he knew it. He had little respect for his fellow humans, and most of them reciprocated with little respect for him. His strength depended on the support of the French bourgeoisie whose fear of a republic was greater than their love of Louis Philippe. It was not surprising that such a man often tried to kill two birds with one stone.

Europe was in ferment as Louis Philippe cautiously inched himself onto the throne of France. Italians were revolting against the despotism of Austria and the Papal States; the Poles rose against the Russians; the Belgians sought independence from the Dutch; democratic-minded citizens of the numerous German states were fighting suppression. After might had prevailed, thousands of the

13

defeated left their homes in exile. Then, as now, there was no more popular place to become an expatriate than Paris. The exiles swarmed into the city by the thousands, and they were, as the Duke of Wellington said on a more crucial occasion, "a damned nuisance." Most were penniless and nearly all were brawlers. But many also were brave, experienced soldiers.

Meanwhile, the conquest of the principalities strung along the North African coast was not proving to be the quick and glorious adventure that some Frenchmen had anticipated. The Arabs no sooner were put down in one place than they rose in another. Disease, too, was taking a heavy toll of the French expeditionary force. Several advisers urged Louis Philippe to call off the whole thing. But the House of Orléans had as great a need for military victories to boost its prestige as the House of Bourbon had had. Louis Philippe reasoned that victories in North Africa could be made to sound impressive, while defeats could be overlooked. As he cynically expressed it, "What difference does it make if a hundred thousand rifles fire in Africa? Europe doesn't hear them."

During the first year of his reign he saw one of those opportunities to kill two birds with one stone when a Belgian adventurer who called himself the Baron Böegard made him a proposal. Böegard offered to enlist the fractious exiles who brawled through the streets of Paris into a *"Légion Étrangère"* and lead them to North Africa to aid the French forces there. Wishing to rid Paris of the troublesome exiles and wanting to offset the losses of French soldiers in North Africa, Louis Philippe required little urging to accept the plan. Thereby he added one more to the long list of mercenary units which had served France.

On March 9, 1831, Louis Philippe signed the royal decree forming *"la Légion Étrangère."* Its initial strength is not positively known, but probably numbered about 3,500. Eventually men of all national backgrounds were integrated in units of the Legion, but in its original formation seven battalions were segregated by nationality. The first battalion was composed of Swiss-Hohenlohe veterans; the others were made up respectively of Swiss, Germans, Spanish, Italians and

14

Sardinians, Belgians and Dutch, and Poles. Their first flag was a tricolor enscribed with the words *The King of the French to the Foreign Legion* and showed a bronze cock resting a talon on a globe marked *France*.

Impressive though the Legion's flag was, its advance guard had a depressing appearance when it reached North Africa. These Legionnaires arrived before Louis Philippe had officially signed the decree, and the French writer, Camille Rousset, happened to be on hand in Oran to watch them come ashore. He said:

"On February 9th [1831] the curious crowd which came daily to watch the embarkations and landings was stunned, amazed and stupefied to witness the arrival of a group of about 300 individuals. It was a real masquerade. To clothe this mob, whose ranks contained men of all ages, from sixteen to sixty and more, it seemed that the bottom of the army supplies had been scraped thoroughly to procure the oldest rags. It was a grotesque sight; the men would have been the delight of a circus crowd. But their heads high, their banner in front, their drums beating to the rhythm of the famous war song *'La Parisienne,'* they proudly paraded through the crowded streets of the city."

For a long time the Legionnaires must have felt that they had, indeed, come out to a masquerade. The fabulous treasures of Africa, described to them when they enlisted in Paris, simply did not exist in the pestilent coastal cities, which swarmed with flies. The beautiful dreams of a King of the French could become a nightmare for his soldiers.

The simoon blew. It rained. The rain stopped. The sun burned down on rock and sand. The simoon blew. The supply of wine was short. The women were not willing. The simoon blew.

Heavy woolen French infantry uniforms arrived to replace the motley in which Legionnaires had started their great African adventure. Attired in baggy red pants and long blue high-collared tunics, they went out on liberty to see the sights of Algiers, Bône, Oran. Sweating in their woolens, they staggered through the glaring heat, following narrow, winding streets that ended in blinding white

15

walls. They stared at Arab women swathed in white cotton to the peepholes for their eyes. They discovered the ancient smell of the East that must have become familiar to Alexander the Great after he ventured out of Europe: a blend of ages-old excrement, the acridity of urine, the ammonia of animal dung. They learned to smoke sweet Arab cigarettes and in fetid little Mohammedan shops they learned to eat *kuskas* and *galettes,* leathery pancakes served with honey. And on balconies high among the minarets of mosques Mohammedan priests walked slowly to and fro in flowing white robes calling the faithful to prayer: *"La illah Allah! . . . Wa Mohammadou yasou! Liah!"* Only God is God and Mohammed is His Prophet.

Penned up in the coastal cities by a people who showed no inclination to accept Western civilization, the Legionnaires suffered terribly from disease. Typhus, typhoid, cholera, syphilis, and an incurable amoebic dysentery took a toll of them. And yet, incredibly, fresh recruits from Paris swelled the ranks of the battalions. Already the Legion had begun grinding out its infallible law of supply and demand: feeding on the ferment of Europe and expending on the frontiers of world empire.

The French and their Legionnaires lacked many things in North Africa. But none was more trying than their lack of knowledge of the land and its people, and their lack of a definite idea as to what they were doing there.

Algeria, a country four times the size of France, was a miserable place then. It was the scene of disease, poverty, and some of the worst plagues in history. Beyond the coastal plains and central valleys, which have been made to blossom, rise the dark and craggy Atlas Mountains, and beyond them stretch thousands of square miles of the Sahara Desert.

In the fourth century a barbaric Asian tribe called the Kabyles snatched the area from the fringes of the old Roman Empire and in the seventh century they were in turn conquered by Arab followers of Mohammed. Successive waves of Arab invasion, which washed on into Spain, established Arabic as the language and Islam as the religion. Algeria was a battleground when Spain fought the Ottoman

Turks for control of the Mediterranean. After the Spaniards were defeated, it became a Turkish pirate state, the rich and infamous Barbary Coast, which gradually was weakened by repeated blows from the maritime powers. Its nominal heads were officials of the crumbling Ottoman Empire whose mercenary soldiers, the Janizaries, enabled them to control the principal ports and monopolize trade in grain and olive oil, the chief exports.

In the 1830's and 1840's about three million persons lived in Algeria. About 80 per cent were nomadic Arabs grouped in tribes of varying size and ruled by chiefs and religious leaders. In summer they lived in tents and grazed their sheep and goats on loosely defined tribal domains; in winter many settled in mud huts and tried to raise grain on thin soil which they scratched with primitive plows. For all these people life was a harsh ordeal. Crops failed more often than they succeeded; disease took a constant heavy toll; tribes warred frequently. Only the superstitions of Islam made the famine, disease, and warfare tolerable.

Another 10 per cent of the population were the Kabyles, descendants of the original inhabitants who had fled the Arabs of the plains and lived in mountainous areas near the coast. The Kabyles were more accomplished and less superstitious than the Arabs, whom they disliked. Besides raising grain and livestock, the Kabyles had planted fig and olive trees and developed a thriving artisan business in tiles and jewels.

In no sense were the peoples of Algeria unified except in the practice of religion. The Arabs living in the coastal cities accepted the French invasion somewhat indifferently and were contemptuous of their nomadic country cousins whom they called Bedouins. They were, incidentally, even more contemptuous of the Foreign Legionnaires, whom they called "the Bedouins of Europe."

Occasionally the Legionnaires were prodded out of the atrophy of garrison life and sent out on an unpleasant mission, to take a town or crush some recalcitrant tribe that usually faded away through the heat glare and into the hills. The bones and sinews of this land rose gauntly through its flesh like those of a starving man. It was a coun-

17

try such as the Europeans of the Legion never had marched and fought in before. And they marched and fought by standards approved on the plains of France. Their packs were cumbersome, their uniforms had been issued by someone who apparently anticipated a blizzard any noonday. They took up defensive positions in squares, attacked frontally, and when they had to withdraw, they leapfrogged back by sections. The failure of the Arabs and Kabyles to fight according to approved Christian military rules was a source of great irritation to them.

The man who called himself the Baron Böegard did not last long in Algeria. The next commander of the Foreign Legion was a Napoleonic veteran named Colonel Bernelle, who was renowned for his explosive temper and his loud, formidable wife. Madame Bernelle appears to have been the only woman who ever terrified the Legion. She considered it created for her personal convenience, using its troops as servants and making sure that its youngest and handsomest officers were members of her husband's staff. One Legionnaire who was ordered to weed her garden in Algiers received fifteen days in the guardhouse because he came upon her in "informal" attire. When the Colonel took to the field, Madame Bernelle donned trousers and rode with him astride a mule.

A Legionnaire on whom Madame Bernelle made a lastingly unfavorable impression was a young Frenchman, Sergeant Achille François Bazaine, who was destined to become a marshal of France and play a strange and tragic role in the history of his country. A native of Versailles who had failed to pass the entrance examinations to the École Polytechnique, Bazaine enlisted in the army as a private and then transferred to the Foreign Legion in the hope that it would bring him advancement. Diligent and capable, the broad-shouldered young Bazaine was commissioned a second lieutenant from the ranks in 1835. That summer he marched inland from Oran with the Poles and Italians of the Legion in a French column commanded by General Trézel. They were seeking Abd-el-Kader, who had organized the dissident Arabs of western Algeria against the French.

Besides being a highly competent military leader, Abd-el-Kader was

18

a myth adored by the romantic-minded who haunted the salons of Paris, for he was said to be young, handsome, learned, chivalrous, both a poet and a great horseman, of the blood of the Prophet himself; Byron in a burnoose, no less. But to the leaders of France's colonial venture he was a very real person. The most vexing problem to them after coming to North Africa was that they never could discover who was in charge there. If only they could find *the* enemy, they could beat him—or at least negotiate with him. Finally they decided Abd-el-Kader must be in charge because he was powerful, belligerent, and ambitious. Abd-el-Kader, flattered by such attention, treated with them. Through their good auspices he obtained arms with which he turned around and waged war against those infidels —the French.

Many in the force that marched in search of Abd-el-Kader were having their indoctrination into the ways of Moslem warfare. Distant horsemen kept them under surveillance as they marched. When they bivouacked at night, the initiates suddenly discovered the unpleasantness of guard duty in the chill darkness of enemy country. There would be a shriek and the sergeant of the guard would find that one of his sentries was missing. Soon there would come the bloodcurdling screams of the missing sentry. A few moments later his severed masculine parts would be tossed into the glow of firelight. Not long afterward his head would follow. The Arabs always insisted that such acts were performed by their women rather than by themselves. But the practice never endeared Abd-el-Kader to soldiers of the Legion. They said he might be young, handsome, and learned, but he was not chivalrous. Such atrocities would scandalize the Paris drawing rooms where he was adored.

Abd-el-Kader attacked Trézel's column in a defile with 6,000 cavalry and 1,300 foot and hacked up the Polish Legionnaires unmercifully. Arab flintlocks proved evenly matched against old Napoleonic muskets. In the excitement a trumpeter blew the retreat. Trézel extricated his column with difficulty and turned back to Oran. Then the Legionnaires and their French comrades learned a lesson concerning what would be characteristic Arab tactics in North Africa

19

for more than a century: invariably they launched their strongest attacks on a retreating column. Before Trézel reached Oran he had lost a fourth of his force of 2,500. His losses would have been much greater if the Legion had not held off the attacks on the rear. Bazaine, wounded and cited for bravery in the rear-guard action, was promoted to first lieutenant and rewarded with the Legion of Honor.

At about the same time the 2nd Battalion of the Legion was assigned a special job by the Commandant of Algiers where it was stationed. He ordered the battalion, commanded by Captain Droualt, to build a road from Douèra to Bouffarick, a distance of about forty miles through fever-infested swamps and across rocky hills. Presumably the job was assigned to the foreigners because it was a nasty one.

The 2nd Battalion was composed of Swiss, traditionally a thorough and patient people. Laboring carefully and persistently, putting aside picks and shovels occasionally to fight off tribesmen who harassed them, they built a magnificent road in two months. The French hailed it as a masterpiece of engineering. They were further impressed by the fact the Legion had lined the road with trees and dug several wells beside it. The 2nd Battalion had set a precedent, and in military life the one thing scarcely anyone can beat is a precedent.

The French are a logical people, though not all other peoples always find them so. They are inclined to deify their logic; as the poet Charles Péguy once wrote: " 'It will be a nuisance,' God said, 'when there are no more Frenchmen. There are things I do that no one else understands.' " Although hundreds of thousands of Legionnaires have asked why in God's name they had to build so many roads, the French understand why. Because the 2nd Battalion built such an excellent road from Douèra to Bouffarick.

Thereafter the Foreign Legion was regularly employed in building roads in North Africa—hundreds and thousands of miles of roads. While building roads, the Legionnaires naturally involved themselves with problems of drainage, with planting trees and digging wells. It is no wonder that in times past Legionnaires often carried shovels instead of rifles when on parade. Their achievements as builders have led many people to think erroneously of the Legion

20

as some sort of vast labor battalion. To which many a disgruntled Legionnaire would have replied that it certainly was.

But it has been much more. Nearly all men join the Legion in order to fight, and few have had their wish unfulfilled. Certainly not the first who enlisted for a glorious adventure in North Africa. Although most probably soon decided there was nothing glorious about it, a change was in the offing. Louis Philippe had thought up a new adventure for them.

3

A Spanish

Adventure

FOR GENERATIONS the history of Spain involved the inability of its rulers to govern well and a widespread Spanish unwillingness to be governed badly. From this clash sprang the sparks of frequent civil war. The chaos of Spanish politics was further complicated by repeated intervention. Britain and France, especially, never seemed able to resist the temptation to try to straighten out matters in Spain.

When Louis Philippe formed the Foreign Legion, Ferdinand VII, a cruel and cowardly man, had been the King of Spain for many years. His repressions of the mildest so-called liberal reforms had been so brutal as to appall even Louis XVIII of France and the Czar of Russia, neither of whom ever was accused of harboring democratic ideas. Still childless when his third wife died in 1829, Ferdinand took as a fourth wife a cousin, a plump and dark-eyed Neapolitan Princess named María Cristina. A year later, to the surprise of nearly everyone, she bore Ferdinand a daughter who was named María Isabel

Luisa. When Ferdinand died in 1833, his daughter succeeded to the throne as Isabella II with María Cristina as Regent. Almost at once Ferdinand's brother, Don Carlos, who coveted the crown, rallied supporters in the northern Basque region and Spain was plunged into civil war.

Tough Basques and Catalans formed the core of the Carlist armies. Madrid and the cities of the south supported the Regent's Government. Bad as had been the Government of Ferdinand in its persecution of all liberalizing reformers, it was generally believed in the south of Spain that rule by Don Carlos would be even more despotic. With the curious facility of mankind for exaggeration, the label of "liberal" was tagged to the Regency of Isabella II, even though neither María Cristina nor her daughter ever really accepted the principle of representative government.

Britain sent a force to support the Cristinist Government against the Carlists. Louis Philippe was not to be outdone, but he was parsimonious of French lives. In the early summer of 1835 he ordered the Foreign Legion into Spain to join the Cristinists.

The Legionnaires grouped at Oran that August. New enlistments swelled the ranks that had been decimated by disease and the tribesmen of Algeria. They numbered about 4,100 men, and they appear to have been in great haste to leave North Africa, for they forgot to take their flag. At the last minute someone remembered it, and the Legion flag was thrust through a porthole as the last transport weighed anchor. Besides their flag, they took with them several cases of cholera.

A few days later they landed in the Balearic Islands, their staging area before entering Spain. Although Bernelle was burdened with a quick temper and a domineering wife, he was a good officer who introduced into the Legion a significant innovation which still exists. Finding that men grouped by nationalities had little incentive to learn French and thus were not commanded efficiently by their French officers, Bernelle mixed his Legionnaires in five battalions. Never before in the long history of mercenary fighters had such a plan been effective for any length of time. Yet it worked for the Legion. Men of different nations tended under the stress of march and combat to try to outdo their comrades, as if each felt he was a representative of his native country.

They landed at Tarragona in Spain, marching up the narrow streets of the ancient walled city whose architecture—Phoenician, Roman, Arabic, and Christian fretwork—reflected centuries of conquerors. Diplomatically the Legion's band played Riego's Hymn, the anthem of Spanish liberalism, while the Tarragonians roared, *"Vivan los Extranjeros! Vivan los Argelinos!"* Madame Bernelle rode in the procession astride a mule, wearing toreador pants and followed by a buxom maid in similar costume.

A British officer who observed the arrival of the Legionnaires described them as a "really magnificent body of men. . . . Never have I witnessed finer troops who from their appearance, organization and discipline gave a higher opinion of their power to contend with all the difficulties and fatigue that were to be met with in such a war."

It was, indeed, a war of great difficulties and fatigue, as warfare always has been in Spain. The land wills it so. No one ever has improved on the description of Strabo, the Greek geographer of the first century, in likening Spain to a vast stretched oxhide; a rough and tawny land, lying taut and dry in the blazing sun. South from the great wall of the Pyrenees flow dark, serrated chains of mountains broken by arid, twisting valleys. This was the area of Carlist strength, from the Basque country on the Bay of Biscay south to the Ebro River and eastward into Catalonia.

For the Cristinists, penetration of the mountain fastnesses held by the Carlists posed problems of supply, reinforcement, and communication which they never overcame satisfactorily. It was a war of hit and run, of actions by relatively small units of men who seldom were certain what lay beyond the next ridge. It was warfare of a kind in which the Legion already was becoming adept.

The Spanish clerics inveighed against the Legionnaires as depraved men, but Spanish girls were bold and Spanish wine was not at all bad. At first the Legionnaires liked Spain, but soon, as they became familiar with the cruelty that has always characterized its civil wars, many began to loathe it. To the *aguadores* of Asturia, dressed in coarse duffel and leathern skull caps, as to the beggars of La Mancha, wearing tattered blankets, life was cheap. When it was learned that one Carlist leader killed his prisoners with a lingering thrust of the bayonet, an indignant Cristinist Government replied by shooting his mother—with the result that the Carlist executed four women in filial retaliation.

Each of the five Legion battalions which marched north from Tarragona into Catalonia that September was composed of eight companies, in the pattern of French Infantry of the Line Regiments. But the Legion was superior to regular French infantry in that each battalion had two elite companies of picked men—one of *grenadiers* and one of *voltigeurs.* The *grenadiers* were the commandos of their day, selected to be shock troops because they were bigger and tougher. The *voltigeurs,* light and swift, were employed in advance scouting and flank skirmishing. The remainder of the battalion was called "the infantry of the center."

A Legionnaire was armed with a long, muzzle-loading musket of limited range and virtually no accuracy. Customarily the first rank knelt and fired a volley, and then the second rank, standing, fired a second volley over the heads of the first. Since reloading took so long, the Legionnaires usually charged with the bayonet after one volley. Their bayonets were long, carefully honed, and had a tendency to bend out of shape when driven into the body of an enemy. When the Legion landed in Spain, its elite companies also were armed with sabers. But these disappeared rapidly and never were replaced as standard equipment.

The disappearance of the saber was one of several permanent changes in Legion equipment and uniforms which resulted from the Spanish campaign. A haversack and wine flask, both worn on the side, were added and retained for nearly a century. A leather waist belt with a large cartridge case which was worn squarely in front also was added and eventually led to the Legionnaires being called "the Leather Bellies."

The Legionnaire who arrived in Spain wore red pantaloons, a

blue jacket and greatcoat, heavy boots, a light cloth cap, and a black leather stock which fitted his throat tightly. *Grenadiers* wore red epaulettes, much larger than those worn by Legionnaires today; the epaulettes of the *voltigeurs* were yellow, and those of the other companies blue.

During the travail of the war in Spain, when both the French and the Spanish refused to replace the Legionnaires' uniforms, dire necessity resulted in changes that still were apparent in the Legion uniform decades later. The red pantaloons gave way to white, the beret became standard headgear, the black leather stock was replaced by one of blue cloth. Before many months had passed in Spain, men's boots had worn out and they were wearing sandals.

To Colonel Bernelle's distress, he had to break up his battalions in Catalonia in order to conduct effective guerilla warfare. The companies splayed out in the mountain valleys, marching on through the red Spanish dust under a burning blue sky as they sought out the redcaps of Navarre. Bazaine, now an acting captain, was trapped with 100 men in a hilltop town on the Segre by 3,000 Navarrese. But he held out for a week until relieved by two Legion companies which had learned of his plight.

The Legion companies received few supplies and no pay. When supplies failed to reach them, they lived off the country. This, like all guerilla warfare, was frustrating and pointless to the forces which were supposed to represent law and order. Disease took a greater toll than did Carlist bullets; amoebic dysentery, typhoid, and typhus were the causes of numerous graves. Desertions rose as some disgusted men decided that the other side was better than the one for which they were fighting. Before many weeks had passed it became necessary to reconstitute the five battalions into four.

Around New Year's Day, 1836, the Legion was ordered to quit Catalonia and march to Vittoria, about two hundred miles to the northwest. In that area the main Cristinist Army under General Espartero had worn itself out in a drive to take Pamplona, the capital of Navarre, and wanted reinforcements. Up the Ebro Valley marched the Legion. In the rain and snow of winter the red Spanish dust had turned to gluelike mud. The Legionnaires slogged through it, their uniforms in tatters, their haversacks containing little besides crusts of bread, their pockets still empty of pay. Yet when they entered Vittoria on January 15, members of the British force, wrapped in warm sheepskin coats, marveled at the precision of step and military bearing of the Legionnaires clad in rags. They marveled, too, at Madame Bernelle upon her mule, surrounded by a bearded guard.

The next day, in a snowstorm, the Legion marched out with the Cristinist Army against strong Carlist positions dug into the hills. The attack was ill conceived and worse co-ordinated. After suffering heavy losses the Legion bivouacked in the snow for three days. During the lull a church was looted. General Espartero ordered the Cristinist unit believed responsible to be paraded without arms; when no one in the unit would confess, he had ten men taken at random from the ranks and executed. Although the Legionnaires were accustomed to strict discipline, they were shocked and disgusted by such cruelty.

Meanwhile Bernelle fought the Legion's battle for pay, clothing, supplies, and reinforcements with a steady stream of vituperative letters to indifferent ministers in Paris and Madrid. Ignoring his demands and finally tiring of his letters, the Government fired him from command. The Legion gave him an emotional send-off, not unmixed with sighs of relief at the departure of his loud, stingy, tattletale wife.

Then came groans of despair at the appointment of a new commander, Major Lebeau, who had an acid manner and the military bearing of a scarecrow. Stringy whiskers and sheepish eyes beneath a battered hat distinguished his features; he disdained epaulettes, but was forever tripping over a pair of enormous spurs on his down-at-heel boots; his favorite weapon was a Turkish scimitar which hung from his belt by a bit of dirty cord. Lebeau lasted scarcely any time and was succeeded by an outstanding officer, Colonel Conrad.

A cheerful little Napoleonic veteran from Strasbourg, who spoke five languages with equal ease, Conrad had won the affection of the Legion by telling off Madame Bernelle when she attempted to interfere with his duties as regimental adjutant. He had, of course, been bounced for such incivility. But now he had bounced back. He was the model, the very epitome, of what a regimental commander should be: personally fearless, always lucid in his commands, utterly devoted to the welfare of his men. By the sheer strength of his character he checked the steady trickle of Legion desertions. Perhaps Conrad's greatest contribution to French arms was the lasting impression he made on Bazaine, whom he made his chief of staff and treated as a son. Throughout his long military career Bazaine appears to have tried to act as Conrad might have under similar circumstances.

In May, 1837, when the Legion attacked the ancient town of Huesca, Conrad galloped ahead of his men on a white charger with his cap raised on a cane. That, thought Bazaine, was the way to lead troops. In that battle the Legion lost nearly a fourth of its remaining force.

The next month the Legion fought its last battle in Spain. Despite the fact that it had received heavy replacements during the preceding months, it was reduced to a bare battalion in strength. The scene of the battle was an olive grove near a town in Aragon called Barbastro. A Cristinist general noted for losing battles and marching against strongly fortified positions with bands playing gave the order to attack a powerful force led by Don Carlos himself. While both sides fumbled vaguely, the Carlists caught the Cristinists in flank by sheer accident. Suddenly the Legion came face to face in the olive grove with a foreign legion which Don Carlos had raised, partially from those who had deserted the French.

Perhaps the chief lesson of war is that it brutalizes those who fight in it too long. There seems to be no other explanation of the horror let loose within sight of the church spires of Barbastro as the smoky shadows of the olive grove became a screaming holocaust of struggling men. Although both legions served bad masters and might well have shaken hands, they fought with rage. Pole sought out Pole, German sought German, Italian searched for Italian and they fought one another fiendishly.

There was little chance for load and fire. When their bayonets bent and broke because of cursed faulty steel, they swung clubbed muskets. When musket stocks broke, they fought with fists and knives and stones, with gouging thumbs and stamping heels. Conrad, cap aloft on his cane, was everywhere among his gasping, shrieking, frantic men. When at last he fell with a bullet through the temple, Bazaine lifted his body and, with tears streaming down his face, carried it from the olive grove. It was, some said, the only time in his life that Bazaine cried.

Then he returned to the grove where men still murdered wounded fellow countrymen who had chosen to fight on a different side. Neither side won. The battle simply died away as men fell in their tracks from exhaustion. It was the end of both legions in Spain.

Bazaine got Conrad's body into a carriage, and a few score of exhausted Legionnaires formed an honor guard around it. A drum tapped slowly as the tattered, blood-stained column staggered south. No one except Bazaine knew where they were going. But they marched on through blinding heat, across the red-rock wilderness where the lonely sentinels of ancient Roman watchtowers still stood on barren hilltops. Coming to the yellow Ebro, they followed it toward the sea until they reached Saragossa, where Conrad had once told Bazaine he wished to be buried.

There they crossed over a bridge and passed the red-tiled cupolas of the Pilar. In the shadow of the great tower of the Seo they held a memorial service for Conrad and buried his body. A Legionnaire with a broken hand found a hammer and a chisel and cut the name on a stone. None among them had any poetic eloquence to convey how they felt. But one remembered a line that seemed dignified and fitting. And so the Legionnaire steadied the chisel in his broken hand and cut the words *Sic transit gloria*.

The next morning Bazaine led his Legionnaires again in search of any comrades who remained. At last, in Pamplona, they found a few. Altogether the Legion then totaled less than 400 men. In the course of time the original force which entered Spain had been reinforced by about 4,000 more Legionnaires. Thus, of approximately

8,000 Legionnaires who had fought in Spain, all had been lost to combat, disease, and desertion except those few huddled miserably in Pamplona.

They had not been paid in more than a year. Louis Philippe said it was the responsibility of María Cristina, who replied that it was his own responsibility. But Louis Philippe had abandoned his old Legion and had begun raising a new one and sending it to Algeria.

One who becomes a marshal of France is ambitious. Bazaine knew that the old Legion had ceased to exist and believed there was nothing to be gained by rotting in Pamplona. So he had himself transferred to a regular French regiment.

A different attitude was taken by a few French officers whose names unfortunately are not remembered. For, as a result of their initiative, there occurred a phenomenon that was to characterize the Foreign Legion in later crises. Deserted by all responsible authority, lacking a common language or sense of patriotism to a native land, such a group of men might be expected to disband and disappear. Yet they did not. Though they had come together as strangers and had often quarreled among themselves, war and suffering had made them brothers. Officers and men drew together in the strong bonds of desperation. They had marched into trouble; they would march out of it.

One autumn morning 159 remaining Legionnaires formed ranks in a street of Pamplona. The drummers tightened their drumheads and brought their sticks down sharply as a trumpet raised doomsday notes. At the head of the column rose a tattered banner enscribed with the faded words *The King of the French to the Foreign Legion.*

A voice rang out: *"Marchons!"*

And they did march. They marched north toward France.

They marched through narrow valleys, among mountains that rose ever higher ahead of them. Many limped and stumbled; nevertheless they marched. They marched for six days until they came to a Carlist town called Jaca, twenty miles south of the French border.

30

There they surrendered their arms and begged food and twenty-four hours to rest. It was refused them.

They marched on, up a narrow winding pass, with the snow-capped summit of Pic du Midi d'Ossau, 9,500 feet high, soaring on their right. They marched through the pass and down into the green valleys of France. At last they reached Pau where people leaned out windows and wondered about these men who looked like beggars, but marched like soldiers behind a strange tattered banner.

The Legion virtually had been wiped out in a war that brought no lasting benefits to anyone. The rebellion led by Don Carlos eventually was suppressed and he was exiled. María Cristina, who married a handsome guardsman and had several children, later was forced into exile, too. Isabella II was as wayward as her mother; she married an impotent man and bore various lovers nine children. As a result of her erratic interventions in political affairs, though not of her philandering, she lost the throne in 1868 and took up a gay life in Paris. Louis Philippe did not last in power as long. Because he indulged in a complex plot involving the marriage of Isabella, he weakened the Anglo-French partnership—which indirectly cost him the French throne in the stormy year of 1848.

But as the remnant of the Legion recuperated at Pau, Louis Philippe did not foresee his own political demise. He sent word that any survivors of the old Legion who wished to join his new Legion would be welcome. And he added a gesture typical of his nature: officers of the old Legion, regardless of experience and rank, would be accepted as sergeants in the new Legion.

Perhaps history is principally the story of mankind's resilience to outrageous fortune. Of the 159 Legionnaires who had marched out of Spain and across the Pyrenees, 63 re-enlisted in the Legion and were shipped back to Algeria.

4

March
or Die

FAME HAD ELUDED Thomas Robert Bugeaud at the age of fifty. Yet the energy and intelligence he applied to unpleasant tasks were to make him a marshal of France and win him a dukedom before he died.

A pocked, red-haired, irascible man, Bugeaud enlisted as a private in Napoleon Bonaparte's Imperial Guard at twenty and rose through the ranks to a distinguished colonelcy. The overthrow of Napoleon left him, like countless other officers, unemployed and embittered. Retiring to the country, he cultivated the land and a cantankerous disposition. When Louis Philippe was elevated to the throne, Bugeaud won a seat in the Chamber of Deputies where he quickly made more enemies than friends. There, too, he began to interest himself in the problems of Algeria—and thereby he was to make his name memorable in the history of France.

Sent to Algeria in a subordinate capacity, Bugeaud soon distinguished himself for energetic leadership. In 1840 he was appointed governor general and spent much of the next six years in the field fighting Abd-el-Kader and his followers. Before Bugeaud became governor general the policy of the French Government in Algeria had been vacillating; Bugeaud made it positive. Under him energy succeeded slothfulness.

Bugeaud quickly saw that the French Army and its subordinate Foreign Legion, penned in seaboard garrisons, were withering away from disease and inactivity. Realizing that the pacification of Algeria required different tactics, he instituted "flying columns"—or *colonnes* —of troops who would move swiftly, as self-sufficient units, and strike hard.

Generations of Legionnaires have known little, and probably could not care less, about the career of Thomas Robert Bugeaud—how he was named Marshal of France in 1843 and rewarded with the title of Duke of Isly after he defeated Abd-el-Kader at Isly a year later. Yet these generations of Legionnaires lived the arduous, and sometimes agonizing, life Bugeaud had prescribed. As a result, Algeria was conquered in a few large battles and hundreds of forgotten bloody skirmishes.

As the Legion grew, a fixed process of indoctrination came into being. It was the custom of the Legion to launch its recruits into a depressing atmosphere. Apart from reasons of economy, the purpose appears to have been psychological. A recruit must learn he is *Monsieur Zéro*. The Legion is all; the individual nothing.

Once a man had signed his own or a false name to a commitment of five years' service, a sergeant took away his passport with the remark, "You won't be needing this any more." After a physical examination recruits were sent to Marseilles.

For a century, until World War II, the reception center in Marseilles was Fort St. Jean, an ancient and sinister-looking fortress overlooking the harbor. Its tiny windows were barred, its cubicles had no drains. Usually it was so crowded with recruits that men slept on straw in the corridors. But to recruits of more recent times the grimmest reminder that they were in the Foreign Legion was found in the central hall of the fort. Enscribed there on a whitewashed wall was a terse statement by General François O. de Négrier, one of the Legion's renowned officers:

"Vous êtes soldats pour mourir, et je vous envoie là où l'on meurt."

"You are soldiers in order to die, and I'm sending you where one dies."

During World War II, Fort St. Jean was destroyed by bombs and the Legion transferred its reception center to the equally gloomy atmosphere of the twin fortress of St. Nicholas.

In its earliest years the Legion accepted almost anyone who wanted to join it. Boys of sixteen rubbed elbows with men of sixty. During those years some unquestionably enlisted in order to escape prison or hanging. Gradually, however, standards were set and improved until a man underwent a thorough physical examination and a careful security check.

He must be between the ages of eighteen and forty-two—a rule that still is broken today. He must be at least five feet two inches tall, but lightness of weight does not matter. Experience taught the Legion that a lean man makes a better foot soldier. Experience also taught it that a flat-footed man can march as far and fight as well as one with perfect arches. Nor does it matter to the Legion that most men assume false names upon joining. When honorably discharged, a man is urged to resume his correct name. But upon entering, it is his privilege to use any name he chooses.

After World War I the Legion kept pace with the extraordinarily efficient police systems of Europe. Its own internal security system became one of the best in the world. While waiting at Marseilles every recruit today is fingerprinted and his body minutely measured by the Bertillon System. Thus, when a man gives a false name, he does not protect himself from an intensive scrutiny of his police record. Since France has extradition treaties with most nations, a man sought for a major crime who tries to enlist in the Legion almost invariably is detected and extradited to the scene of his crime.

Concerning men who have committed minor criminal offenses there appears to have sprung up an understanding between the police and the Legion. Men who might have received a year or two in prison if convicted of theft or a similar offense sometimes apparently have been allowed to escape into the Legion on the theory of good riddance and in the hope the Legion might reform what a prison could not. Beneath its intolerance of seemingly minor infractions of discipline, the Legion sometimes displays extraordinary tolerance of more significant matters. If a man is trying hard to be a good Legionnaire, the Legion will go to great lengths to protect him from persons in his past life who try to hound him. But if he is a bad Legionnaire who tries to desert, he is disciplined ruthlessly.

Before the Legion's principal bases were removed from Algeria, recruits were shipped from Marseilles to Oran, and thence to Sidi-bel-Abbès.

The Legion's 3rd Battalion established the base on a plain about sixty miles south of Oran in 1843. It was carrying out the orders of General Bugeaud who had directed the Army and the Legion to set up depots at several points in Algeria to supply their "flying columns." The depots became known to troops as "biscuitvilles" in dubious honor of the dry fodder which was the principal food of the Western world's fighting men for more than a century.

When the 3rd Battalion selected the ground for a "biscuitville" it was the site of the lonely grave of a religious hermit named Sidi-bel-Abbès, which means "Lord, the Happy One." After a series of Arab attacks, the Legion was ordered to fortify Sidi-bel-Abbès in 1845. As invariably happened, the Legion produced its experts from the ranks —draftsmen, masons, carpenters, and other craftsmen. It is said that one Legion company turned out five qualified architects. Within the next few years the Legionnaires constructed the fortified barracks blocks which still were in use in 1962. They went on to construct a school, a church, a police station, and several other buildings as a town began to grow about the post. When the Legion marched away in 1962, Sidi-bel-Abbès was a thriving city of about 80,000 persons with boulevards lined by silver beech and plane trees.

Until the Legion left it, Sidi-bel-Abbès may have contained more bars and cafés than any city of its size in the world. It also contained one of the most celebrated red-light districts in Africa. The Village Nègre—as red-light districts are called in North Africa—was a small city within a city. Surrounded by an eight-foot barbed-wire fence, its twisting, narrow streets were lined by about 500 buildings which included brothels, bars, restaurants, and venereal disease treatment stations. Its prostitutes were said to include every conceivable nationality and race with the possible exception of the Eskimo. In its brothels any man who could pay the price had his choice of an extraordinary variety of women: Nordic blondes; almond-eyed, small-breasted Vietnamese girls; statuesque Negresses and Mauresques, as mulattoes are called in Algeria. Unprintable songs were sung about the wonders of the prostitutes in the Village Nègre.

But it was a long time before recruits arriving in Sidi-bel-Abbès had an opportunity to enjoy the pleasures of its bars and brothels. As they marched up a wide street, they saw ahead of them the high white walls of the Legion's headquarters and its flag fluttering from a staff. They passed through a great arched gate with the words *Caserne de la Légion* inscribed on its lintel while smartly uniformed Legionnaires stood at attention in sentry boxes on either hand. Then they found themselves on a wide parade ground in front of trim white barracks and buildings.

In more recent times not all were yet members of the Legion, however. Another careful physical examination almost invariably culled men from the ranks of each arriving contingent. In the last century everyone went to the rifle and shovel work of infantry training. More recently, as Legion units were diversified and mechanized, there was an effort to place men where their special skills could be most effectively employed. But whatever a man's eventual specialty, the Legion trained him thoroughly in route marching. It never forgot its slogan of "March or die!"

After a brief stay at Sidi-bel-Abbès, most recruits were sent to an infantry training depot such as that at Mascara, which was located in hilly, thickly wooded, semitropical country. There, living fourteen men to a room in four-story barracks, the recruits underwent what has been called the most rigorous basic military training course in

36

the world. Instructions were in French, and a recruit who did not understand it was given instructions in his own language until he learned French commands. For the first sixteen weeks he was not allowed to leave the post.

One aspect of the training—marching—was especially arduous. The distance a man must go and the weight he must carry on the march were increased steadily—ten, fifteen, twenty, thirty miles a day in excruciating heat and without water. Then the route was changed from roads to the hilly countryside and finally to thick underbrush where men often had to cut their way through. Such training went on for weeks and months.

At the end of it, said former Legionnaire Ensio Tiira, "The men were as tough and well-trained a bunch of fighters as you might find anywhere. They hated the Legion. They didn't like each other. But when it came to a fight they would give and take with anyone. Unconsciously a sort of *esprit de corps* had built up among us. The Legion represented toughness and the men were proud to be tough, physically and in their way of life, in their talk and in their behavior."

Tiira, a Finnish sailor who left his ship in a French port and impulsively joined the Legion, deserted on the way to Indochina. With a fellow Legionnaire, a Swede named Ericsson, he escaped from a troopship in the Indian Ocean aboard a life raft. He told of his experiences during a month adrift at sea in a gripping account entitled *Raft of Despair*.

The testimony of innumerable men about the Legion is similar to that of Tiira who said, "I hated it. And I'll make sure I never set foot on French soil again. But it does know something about taking men and turning them into fighters."

The Legion learned how to make extraordinary fighters of ordinary men through long years of experience under the most trying physical conditions. Basic to everything else a Legionnaire had to do was his capacity to march. Failure to march meant death. And well into the present century marching meant that a man must carry the

37

heaviest pack borne by any soldier in the world—more than 100 pounds.

For many years until the advent of khaki the Legionnaire's uniform was heavy and colorful. He wore laced boots and white duck trousers lashed at the ankles by leather gaiters. Over his shirt he put on a heavy blue military cloak known as the *capote*, its tails buttoned back so that his legs were free for an untrammeled gait. Around his waist he wound a *ceinture*, a blue woolen sash about four yards long which gave his body firm support on the march and warmed him in the cold nights of the desert. Attached to his cap was a thin linen neck cloth, the *couvre-nuque*, which buttoned onto his cap and protected his neck, ears and cheeks from blazing sun and blasting winds. Until World War I he was not issued socks because they aggravated blisters; he bound his feet in strips of linen sometimes called "Russian socks."

A Legionnaire's equipment, called the *tenue de campagne d'Afrique*, would sound incredible to soldiers today. Besides his rifle and bayonet he carried between 200 and 400 rounds of ammunition and a two-liter flask. In his knapsack were two complete extra uniforms. Tent canvas and a blanket encircled the knapsack in a long roll and tent stakes were fastened to the sides. On the top of his pack he lashed his metal mess plate and fuel for the bivouac fire. Besides all these things he carried a shovel or pick or one of the company's large copper cooking pots.

Laden with this equipment, he had to be able to march at least fifty kilometers (thirty-one miles) a day at a pace of five kilometers an hour for days—even weeks—on end.

Erwin Carlé, a German who served in the Legion early in this century, has given perhaps the most graphic description of what marching meant to the individual Legionnaire:

It is always drummed into the Legionnaire that he is intended for nothing else in this world except marching. If the pangs of hunger are gnawing at his stomach or thirst parches his tongue, that is so much the worse for him, but is no sort of reason for not marching on! He may be tired, dead tired, completely exhausted—but he must not stop marching. If his feet are bleeding and the soles burn like fire, that is very sad—but marching pace must not be slackened. The sun may burn until his senses are all awhirl, he must go on. His task in life is to march. The greatest crime he can commit is to fail on the march. There is no such thing as an impossible marching assignment for the regiment of foreigners. Each individual is inoculated with the one idea, it is hammered into him, that he has to march as long as he can control his legs. And when he can no longer control them, then he must at least try to crawl.

When a Legion unit was on the march, meat rations were abandoned and men subsisted exclusively on rice, macaroni, and hard biscuit. A march usually began about one o'clock in the morning and continued with hourly halts of only five minutes until the day's distance had been completed.

Carlé described vividly his first day on a march of nearly four hundred miles to a remote post. His experience was that of thousands of men after Bugeaud devised his "flying columns."

Milestone after milestone passed by and the jokes ceased very soon as the marching regiment settled down to business. Silently the regiment tramped onwards. The knapsack pressed heavily: heads went down and shoulders bent low to spread the heavy weight on the back; the gun straps cut into the shoulders until one's right arm was almost lame and the painful prickly feeling caused by the non-circulating blood had grown permanent.

After the first ten kilometers a shrill signal whistle sounded and the whole company wheeled off to the roadside to rest in line for five minutes. The men kept their knapsacks on their backs and at once threw themselves at full length on the ground. Later on I did the same. The halt was so short that one lost priceless seconds in taking off and strapping on the knapsack, seconds only, but even seconds are precious for the marching Legionnaire.

Five minutes is but a short span of time, but never in my life has a time of rest seemed so delicious, so beneficial, so reviving as when I lay stretched out on the hot African sand for those pitifully short five minutes.

The company wheeled into column again and trudged forward on the endless road, whose straight sameness was only interrupted by the milestones. With each mile it became quieter in the marching rows. The legs and backs were strained to the utmost, and a word spoken appeared a waste of energy. One seemed to be a machine, marching on mechanically behind the man in front when once put in motion; each man was sufficiently occupied with himself. If anyone in utter weariness took a step to the left out of marching line, he got an oath hurled at him—you were so tired that even the slight touch of your comrade swaying out of line was an extra burden for your tormented body.

When the morning mists and the bitter cold of the dawn were followed by the hot, burning sun, we had accomplished a march of forty kilometers, and the time came when our legs refused to do any more. When the signal sounded for rest, we fell down helpless, and when we started marching again, it looked as if a crowd of invalids and old men were slowly wandering down the road. The worn-out legs revenged themselves for the hard usage they had received. During the halt the flow of blood was hemmed in the limbs. Standing on one's feet again, one felt sharp, stinging pain in the soles. Every step was torture. For five minutes afterwards I crawled along as best I could till I became once more an unfeeling automaton.

Carlé's company achieved its goal of fifty kilometers by eleven o'clock in the morning. But a Legionnaire's day was far from ended. Then began the work of bivouac in enemy country, a relentless ritual for survival that existed in the Legion for nearly a century.

A company was marched onto the selected campsite with its three sections in files and with intervals in the files between each squad which consisted of a corporal and five privates. At the command to halt, everyone stopped and the corporals raised their bayonets. After the company adjutant had straightened the lines, the corporals thrust their bayonets into the ground. Over the equally spaced bayonets the squads raised their tents, each man supplying a part of the tent from his knapsack.

Then came a cry that the Legionnaires dreaded: *"Aux murailles!"* It meant that a wall must be built around the campsite.

Men exhausted by the long march crept under the broiling sun, clawing rocks of twenty pounds and more from the flinty earth and lugging them back to the lines of the proposed walls. There twenty men designated as masons, using mud for mortar, cemented the rocks together. At regular intervals a space was left, and outside each egress another short wall was built.

Custom decreed that the height of the walls reach the breast of the tallest man in the company. If at first he stooped a bit to accommodate his toiling companions, he took care to stand erect and have the wall measured carefully once the company had undergone the terrors of a night attack. It appears to have been the custom for the company adjutant never to say when the walls were sufficiently high. He simply muttered, *"Bien!"* Sometimes he merely whispered it. But always one or another Legionnaire was listening carefully and passed the word.

Legionnaire Bennett J. Doty, an American who served in the Legion many years after Carlé and recalled the same ritual for survival, said that, after the work was done, "We returned to the wall and made our [rifle] loopholes, our *créneaux*. Each man made his own *créneau* according to his height, his conformation, his taste, or even his caprice, and after that it was his loophole, no one else's. Woe to him who, in the confusion of a night attack, made for the wrong one. Each man his own *créneau*, that's the rule of the Legion."

Meanwhile scouts had carefully reconnoitered the countryside for any sign of enemies. If danger was detected, sentries were doubled within the little mud and stone fort.

By sundown the quiet of exhaustion settled on the camp. All but the sentries sank into sleep, huddled together in their small tents, heads resting on their knapsacks. Each squad brought its rifles into its tent where the corporal strung a long chain through the rifle trigger guards and attached the chain to his own wrist. It was a necessary precaution, for the most careful sentry duty never could prevent Arabs from slipping stealthily into a bivouac to steal the rifles they coveted. Sentries had standing orders to challenge an Arab only once at night and then to fire.

Provided the fort was not attacked, the company rose at one

o'clock in the morning. After destroying their fort, to make certain an enemy never used it against them, they marched on through numbing cold under glittering stars.

Carlé likened his five years in the Legion to "500 years." Before enlisting he had migrated to the United States where he worked as a newspaper reporter in St. Louis and was sent on special assignments to Latin America. Returning to Germany, he quarreled with the girl he loved and "in despair" joined the Legion. His story had a happy ending, however, for after he left the Legion he went back to Germany, married the girl, and wrote numerous books on a wide variety of subjects. But there were many times during his Legion experience when he thought he would not live out the day.

On the long march of sixteen days, which he describes, the suffering of the men became more acute after they entered the true desert and depended on oases wells for a scant supply of dirty water that doubled up many of them with painful dysentery. He said:

At night, when starting on the march, the field flasks were filled. The distribution of water was conducted under sharp supervision. Every man got two liters of dirty, muddy water. Company orders warned us to save up half a liter for tomorrow's "soupe." On camping next day every Legionnaire had to give up half a liter of water to the mess of his company for cooking purposes. Whoever had emptied his field flask during the heat and weariness of the march and was unable to deliver any water only got a handful of raw rice given him; he had to get it cooked as best he could.

This is one of the many brutal rites in force on these marches and there is method to it. Contrary to most of the Legionnaires I have always seen the necessity for the hard marching discipline. Troops that have to march in such droughty country must be able to economize their water rations. This is a simple law of necessity.

There is another brutal feature on the Legion's marches: cruel at first sight but it is really kindness to the men. A Legionnaire who faints on the march is tied to the baggage cart. A pole is pushed through the sides of the cart at about the height of a man's arms and the Legionnaire roped to it by the shoulders. The pole keeps him in a standing position—the cart rolls on. He either has to march or he is dragged along the uneven ground.

Seeing the thing done for the first time I was filled with indignation at the apparent brutality of this torture. But afterwards I understood. In the wars of the South the fighting value of the Foreign Legion depends solely on its marching capacity. Very often the ambulance is not able to follow. If a Legionnaire remains behind the company in the desert, if only a kilometer, he is irretrievably lost. Hundreds and hundreds of men incapable of marching have found a terrible end in this way. The Arab women, who are far more cruel than the men, soon surround the helpless man, who suffers a painful death after being horribly mutilated and disfigured.

Separation from the troops means death. This was not only the case at the time of the great Arab mutiny (1871), which affected the whole of Algeria, but it is the same today. Peace between the French and the Arabs down in the far south of Algeria is a myth. At the small military stations on the borders of the Sahara, little skirmishes are a daily occurrence. When the station is alarmed and the thirty or forty men garrisoned there set out to pursue the pillaging Bedouin tribes, every Legionnaire knows well that now he must march, or if he cannot march any more, he must die. March or die!

Thus, after Carlé contracted amoebic dysentery on his company's long march, he was ordered to keep going. He recalled:

But the others were no better off. They marched with open wounds in their feet; with blisters between neck and shoulder blades where the straps of the heavy knapsack pressed; with eyes enflamed by the sun; with severe bronchial trouble; with bleeding and festering sores on their thighs. Many limped and most marched wellnigh double, sunk together —a miserable, pitiful sight. Surly, silent, raging with bitterness, pictured in the hard lines of the face and in the tired eyes, we stomped onwards. The only words heard were curses.

Our nerves strained to the bursting point. Over the whole troop lay the strain of over-exertion, bodily and mental nerve-sickness.

43

5

Dark and
Bloody Ground

IN THE LAST CENTURY the Algerian frontier was the scene of savage fighting such as characterized the American frontier in its darkest early days. As in America, Europeans settled among hostile peoples who had lived on their lands for centuries and responded to encroachment with barbaric acts.

For decades the role of the Foreign Legion in Algeria was like that of frontier fighting forces in America. In small, remote garrisons Legion units tried to keep restless tribes in a state of reasonable passivity. They had to be able to march long distances quickly and strike hard at an enemy of vastly superior numbers. They had to inspire respect and even terror in their nomad enemies. And, when things were quiet, they had to build roads and bridges in order to strengthen the ties of the new country.

General Bugeaud had little formal training in history and the classics, yet in manner and thought he was a Roman such as Julius

Caesar would have understood. He wished to colonize Algeria with groups of French veterans and their families in the way that Rome had developed its vast empire. But the French were not enthusiastic colonizers. To Bugeaud's profound disappointment he saw Algeria being settled by what he called "the agricultural scum of the European countries." Like many an architect of empire, he died a disenchanted man, in 1849.

The French did not flock to the arid soil of Algeria. The first settlers were 400 Rhinelanders, who arrived in 1832 after sailing from Le Havre for America; tricked by a crooked French sea captain, they were put ashore in Algiers against their will. Maltese, Italians, Sicilians, and Spaniards followed. A Government survey of 1954 revealed that more than half of the one million Europeans then living in Algeria issued from non-French stock.

If the numerous Arab tribes and the Kabyles had taken up arms in a common cause against the French at an early stage, France might not have conquered Algeria. Abd-el-Kader came close to unifying the resistance of native Algerians against France. But he failed for the same reason that the American Indian leader Pontiac failed in his confederation against the white man: few Arabs or Kabyles could believe for long in the validity of any group larger than their own tribe. So the Arabs and Kabyles of Algeria, like the Indians of America, fed themselves into the chopper of conquest bit by bit.

The Legion marched and fought to make life secure and commerce prosperous for the settlers. Yet the *colons* despised the Legionnaires almost as much as did the Arabs—though for different reasons. To an Arab a Legionnaire was a bad enemy; to a European he was an impossible friend. He became known to the settlers as a heavy and belligerent drinker, as one who would carry away anything portable in sight. No respectable woman would be seen in public with a Legionnaire. In the days when women's skirts were sufficiently ample for expressive gestures, it was said that every respectable colonist woman held her skirt aside when she met a Legionnaire. It was the colonists who coined the phrase, "Dogs bark when the Legion passes." Upon which a noted Legion commander, General Paul

Rollet, once remarked laconically, "Who could care less that dogs bark when the Legion passes?"

Certainly Legionnaires learned not to care. They became accustomed to being despised and despising others. They became accustomed to dirty jobs and raw deals. They became accustomed, in some campaigns, to casualties running as high as 90 per cent.

The extraordinary fact about the Legion is that it created a military tradition and an *esprit de corps* second to none. When its units went into battle, the men in the ranks who seemed to hate everyone and everything suddenly became magnificent. Why? They lacked the usual incentives that create good soldiers. They were not fighting for country or family or political ideals. They were not fighting for money or booty of any value. They were not fighting for love of France. Often they did not even seem to be fighting for love of the Legion.

If the mystique of the Legion had worked its magic on a man, however, he might possibly be fighting for some finer and more gallant image of himself than he carried in his heart. Nothing could fire a man's image of himself and inspire him to heights of valor more than the example of a valorous officer, whether he was a lieutenant or a general. The role of leadership, principally by French officers, undoubtedly was one of the most important elements in creating the spirit of the Foreign Legion.

In garrison life at larger posts enlisted men saw little of their officers; training and discipline were left largely to the noncommissioned grades. It was the theory of the French Army that familiarity between enlisted men and officers in garrison bred only contempt. But in battle, when men became familiar with the cool courage of a good leader, they were inspired to emulate and, in some instances, even to adore him.

It was evident at the siege of Constantine, the powerfully fortified Kabyle citadel east of Algiers which French forces invested for a second time in 1837. With the expedition marched a battalion of the Legion, 500 strong.

The shining minarets of Constantine soared from a rocky plateau which was surrounded on three sides by a gorge nearly 1,000 feet deep. Its ruler was the Bey Hadj-Ahmed, a cruel and lecherous man who had brought certain refinements to the staid entertainment of the East; he always insisted that his slave girls dance for him naked to the accompaniment of a slave orchestra whose eyes he had blinded with hot irons. His Kalif, Ben-Aissa, who took command of the defenses, was more gallant.

As the French and Legion forces grouped before Constantine, Ben-Aissa sent a message to General Damrémont, their commander: "Should the Christians run out of gunpowder, then we shall let them have some of ours. If they have no more bread, then we shall share ours with them. But as long as one of us remains alive, they will not take Constantine!"

A few days later Damrémont was killed by a sniper's bullet and the command evolved on General Valée. French artillery shells bounced off the walls of Constantine like marbles. Food supplies ran so low that the French and the Legionnaires killed and ate the artillery horses. After every stratagem had been exhausted, Valée decided on a frontal assault along the one accessible route to the citadel.

It was what Ben-Aissa's Kabyle sharpshooters and Turkish artillerymen had been waiting for. As the long red and blue lines curled out across the plateau, artillery zeroed a murderous fire on them. The lines withered, shrank, fell back. Again they came on, stepping over their dead and screaming wounded until the lethal fire stopped them once more. Although a few sappers managed to blow a break in the walls, they were buried in the explosion and the infantrymen could not press on to take advantage of the hole.

Then Valée regrouped his attack in an order of battle that was to become familiar in Algeria and many other areas of the world when French arms were on trial. In the van he placed the remnants of the Legion battalion. As they advanced, bending into the hail of fire, their officers fell with them.

But suddenly one dashed ahead. He was Captain Leroy Saint-Arnaud, who had said when he joined the Legion, "I shall be remarkable or die." It was a moment of all or nothing, a moment when Saint-Arnaud literally sprang onto the stage of history from which only death would remove him. A more typical Legion hero could scarcely be imagined. He was thirty-six years old then, a wolfishly handsome man who apparently had no future. Gambling, women, and wine had been his undoing in Paris; creditors had hounded him until he found refuge in the Legion. As a gambler he understood all or nothing; as a man he had nothing to lose but his life.

Sword winking in the roiling smoke, Saint-Arnaud plunged into the breach. Turning, he roared words that would become immortal to Legionnaires: *"A moi, la Légion!"* And the handful who had survived the murderous Kabyle fire went with him through the break in the walls. It was the turning point in the battle for Constantine. And it was the turning point in the career of Leroy Saint-Arnaud.

Behind the Legion spearhead the French regulars poured into the city. Constantine finally was taken after fierce house-to-house fighting. Of the 500 Legionnaires who had marched against it, less than fifty survived.

The Legion's role in the Battle of Constantine restored its reputation. Ironically, despite the great suffering, ill treatment, and heroism of the Legion in Spain, the new Legion came to Algeria tarnished by the Spanish adventure. Its battalions were forbidden to have elite companies and for a time it appeared the organization might deteriorate into a labor unit. But the Battle of Constantine changed the mind of the French high command about the Legion. Its *grenadier* and *voltigeur* companies were restored and its morale soared.

For every scene such as that at Constantine, however, there were a dozen ordeals such as the terrible sixteen weeks at Miliana. For courage always did involve far more than a grand gesture in a fire-raked breach.

Miliana was a miserable outpost in the hills which Abd-el-Kader had left a smoking ruins in 1840. Then he disappeared with his elusive *Smala,* as his moving capital was called. Though the constantly roving court, army, and officials of the Emir included 30,000 men, women and children with their flocks and arsenal, the French and the Legion never had caught up with it. Occasionally they had glimpsed the dust and elements of the *Smala* at a distance, like a mirage in the sky, but they never could come to grips with it.

Early in the summer of 1840 a column was sent out to rebuild Miliana. It consisted of a Legion battalion, a French infantry battalion, and five guns, numbering altogether about 1,200 men. Bazaine had rejoined the Legion and was a company commander in the force. The men had scarcely finished raising the stone and mud walls of Miliana when a strong element of Abd-el-Kader's *Smala* struck once more. Repulsed, the Arabs settled down to besiege the fort on its sunbaked hilltop. The French and Legionnaires had been told that they would be relieved at some time late in the year, but they did not know when. Food grew short, but worse was the lack of medical supplies when fever and dysentery racked them.

The Arabs attacked each night, and the time came when less than 100 men could crawl from their blankets to defend the walls. Men went mad and some who deserted were captured by the Arabs and tortured. As weeks crept by, the death rate from fever and amoebic dysentery rose to ten and fifteen a day. When all available burial space within Miliana had been used, bodies were burned so that the Arabs would not realize the weakened state of the garrison.

At last a Legionnaire volunteered to try to slip through the Arab lines and summon help. He was an Italian who had spent his spare time learning Arabic. Wearing native dress and carrying a coded message from the commandant, he dropped over the wall one night and disappeared. Days passed, and the dying garrison was convinced the Legionnaire had been captured and killed. The days grew into weeks and the men in Miliana resigned themselves to death. And then, five weeks after the Legionnaire had disappeared into the darkness, there was a stealthy tap at the gate. Three knocks and then one; three, and then one. It was a Legion signal. Sentries cautiously opened the heavy gate a couple of inches and made out their comrade. Slipping in, he said that help was on the way.

It came a fortnight later, a long red and blue column winding over

49

the hills. Men too spent to cheer found themselves weeping. Of the 1,200 who had rebuilt Miliana, nearly 900 were dead.

General Nicolas Changarnier led the relief column, and beside him rode a young colonel named MacMahon. As the exhausted remnants of the Miliana garrison stiffened to attention and the relief column paraded into the fort with rolling drums, Bazaine's eyes lighted at sight of MacMahon. They were good friends, but the years were to do strange things to their friendship.

Colonel Marie Edmé Patrice de MacMahon was a great favorite with the Legion. In temperament he was more Irish than French. Descendant of an Irish family that had fled to France in the age of the Stuarts, he was a tall, handsome, forthright man, who would sooner lead a charge than plan a battle. His career embraced many ironies. A staunch monarchist, he became the President of the French Republic. A poor administrator, he became a marshal of France. Wise and honorable in his personal life, he was suspicious of intellectual pursuits and made it a practice to strike from the promotion lists the name of any officer who had written an article or a book. Bugeaud sized him up shrewdly when he said of him, "I believe him to be an excellent officer, very soldierly, very firm; but I do not think he has the intellectual grasp necessary for governing Europeans and Arabs."

In the fall of 1844, MacMahon led two Legion battalions in a French expedition against M'Chounech, a stronghold perched like an eagle's nest on a peak of the Atlas Mountains. The Kabyles who had fortified the mountain village considered it unconquerable, and it must, indeed, have appeared so to the expedition which tried to invest it.

The only approach to M'Chounech was across a sandy plain where troops were sitting ducks for the artillery on the peak above. At first the French tried to dislodge the Kabyles from their fortified village by artillery. When that failed and ammunition began to run low, a frontal infantry assault was made across the plain. Beaten back by a hail of musket and artillery fire, the French infantry and the Legion battalions regrouped and advanced once more. Again they were hurled back with heavy losses.

Then, as happened so often, it was decided that a third and final attempt would be spearheaded by the Foreign Legion. Wearing their baggy red pants, long blue coats and kepis, MacMahon's Legionnaires advanced at a swinging lope. Under the withering Kabyle fire they clawed their way up the slope to a breach which French artillery had made in the walls of M'Chounech. MacMahon and Major Espinasse were in advance of their men, shouting the words that Saint-Arnaud had made famous at Constantine: *"A moi, la Légion!"*

A force of about 500 Kabyles counterattacked into the breach and were beaten back with fire and bayonet. A bullet spun Espinasse around, but he did not fall and continued to pace among his men and encourage them. A second bullet struck him as the Kabyles counterattacked again, but still he did not fall. Before French reinforcements clambered up the slopes, the Legion withstood twenty counterattacks by the fanatical Kabyles. On the last, Espinasse finally fell with a bullet through his stomach. In the melee Kabyle hands clutched for him, but a dozen Legionnaires lunged more quickly and snatched away their mortally wounded officer. M'Chounech was taken.

Brave leadership did not, however, mean that Legionnaires always were led with military wisdom. There was, for example, military folly at the Oasis of Zaatcha and at a village called Seriana.

The year was 1849, and there was a widespread illusion in France that Algeria finally had been conquered—an illusion held by many Frenchmen for more than a century. After Abd-el-Kader surrendered in 1847, some French newspapers reported that peace at last had come to Algeria. With their fondness for treating conquered enemies gallantly, and even royally, the French transported Abd-el-Kader and his harem to France where they were ensconced in the lovely Château of Amboise, overlooking the Loire River. Abd-el-Kader's later years were passed in writing works of philosophy and he died in bed in Damascus at the age of seventy-five, wearing the decoration of the French Legion of Honor and surrounded by five young wives, who were said to be beautiful.

Meantime, the French and their Foreign Legionnaires had learned that the departure of Abd-el-Kader in no sense meant peace in Algeria. A score of chieftains aspired to his role. One of the most ambitious and ruthless was the Sheik Bou-Zian who ruled over the Oasis of Zaatcha, a green paradise flowering in a hellish desert south of Biskra. (It was at Zaatcha, nearly a century later, that Hollywood movie makers chose to film some of their romances about the Foreign Legion.)

In the heart of his great oasis of palms and fig and apricot trees Bou-Zian fortified a small city with high towers and crenelated walls, surrounded by a wide moat. Its outworks, a complicated system of ditches, deadfalls, and communications trenches, were almost as formidable as the fortress itself. Within his oasis Bou-Zian gathered an army of 6,000 well-armed tribesmen and then calmly announced that he never would submit to French rule.

It was, of course, an intolerable situation to the colonial government. It also was a nasty job to seize Zaatcha. So the task was assigned to the Foreign Legion. Major Gaillard de Saint Germain was ordered to take Zaatcha with a battalion of 500 men. Presumably a general as wise as Bugeaud would have seen the folly in such an attempt, but Bugeaud had recently died in Paris.

Saint Germain, having received his orders and being a brave and dutiful soldier, proceeded to try to execute them. He led his battalion south from Biskra on a long and exhausting march until they finally glimpsed Zaatcha shimmering like an enchanting mirage in the heat glare of the July sun.

Apparently Saint Germain spent little time in reconnaissance. He flung his battalion into the oasis like a needle into a haystack. Sweating and cursing, the Legionnaires hacked and stumbled through the outworks under the lethal fire of sharpshooters. Surprisingly, many reached the walls of Zaatcha. There, flaming artillery and muskets drove them back again and again, shredding their strength until the moat was red with their blood.

Under cover of darkness the survivors crept away, defeated, carrying their wounded with them. Only a remnant of the battalion staggered back to Biskra. Saint Germain survived—only to fall victim to another military folly.

The defeat of the Legion at Zaatcha enhanced Bou-Zian's reputation and gave him a breathing spell in which to organize the resistance of neighboring tribes. Soon most of southeastern Algeria was in revolt. Down from the fastnesses of the Atlas came a loyal lieutenant of Abd-el-Kader's, a chieftain named Sidi Abd-el-Afidt, gathering the fierce tribesmen of Aurès and Zab-Chergui as he advanced. When he reached the village of Seriana he had an army of 4,000 men.

Saint Germain followed orders again. He marched against Seriana with 300 Legionnaires on September 17, 1849, and died from a bullet in the head while leading his men toward the walled village. The Legion unit was wiped out.

Now the French decided that at all costs Zaatcha must be taken and Bou-Zian destroyed. Late in September an expedition of 4,000 men, mostly Legionnaires, marched against it under the command of General Herbillon, who told his troops, "Abandon any thought of ever returning unless you take Zaatcha!"

The siege began October 4. It was one of the most savage battles in North Africa, fought under the most trying conditions at the end of a long and uncertain supply line. The Legionnaires were constantly on the verge of running out of ammunition and food, while their foul water supply doubled them up with dysentery. But slowly, methodically, they pressed through the outworks of the oasis to the walls of Bou-Zian's city.

The cold nights of the desert were even more harrowing to the besiegers than the fighting during the blazing days. For at night parties of the defenders slunk out to steal arms and capture sentries. In the morning the comrades of a captive would see him bound and stripped naked on a high tower of the fortress beyond the range of their rifles. Arab women, like shrieking furies, swarmed upon a captive with knives, emasculating him and sometimes literally skinning him alive. One day, after subjecting a young sergeant to prolonged torture, they turned dogs loose on him and let them devour him while he still was conscious.

It was not surprising that the Legionnaires showed little mercy to the inhabitants of Zaatcha. Once the walls were breached, the tribesmen and their women fought them from house to house and room to room while priests on the towers screamed encouragement down at them. A company of 100 Legionnaires assaulted a tower and was driven back with 13 killed and 40, including the captain, seriously wounded. Nevertheless, they regrouped and attacked again.

At last, fifty-six days after the siege began, Zaatcha was taken. Bou-Zian, his son, and his chief priest were decapitated and their dripping heads exhibited on pikes as a warning to all who refused to submit to French rule.

6

Dubious

Friends in High Places

WHEN WORD REACHED Sidi-bel-Abbès in May, 1854, that the Legion
would embark to wage war against the Russians, not every Legionnaire was pleased. Some who had survived the vicissitudes of life in
Algeria had come to think of it as home.

In moments of peace North Africa can work a certain charm on a
European exile. Its immemorial sights and sounds and smells, which
at first may repel a foreigner, begin to beguile him in time. Those
glimpses through white horseshoe arches, the turbaned men gos-
siping in the shade of fig trees, the minarets against a dusty blue sky,
the horizon that is a perpetual olive green—such scenes cannot be
found in the cold mists of Scandinavia or the sooty din of the Saar.
In North Africa, too, there are strange, delightful sounds: the distant
throbbing of a lonely drum, the murmur of the market places, the
rattle of storks tapping their great beaks on rooftop tiles. And when
camels begin to smell pleasantly familiar, a Westerner knows that
the East truly has entered into him.

These things came to mean a great deal, often unconsciously, to men who had survived as Legionnaires in Algeria. There were other, more tangible, things, too, such as Sidi-bel-Abbès, which had become the home of the Legion. There Legionnaires had dug, planted, built; now a thriving village was growing outside the white walls of Legion headquarters.

When the message arrived from Paris, it was rushed to Bazaine. He was Colonel Bazaine now, grown much heavier since the hell of Miliana. If it was good news to him that he was to lead the 1st Regiment of the Legion into the war against the Russians, he did not show it. His heavy features bore a perpetually impassive expression and his thick-lidded eyes seemed to stare through one. He was forty-three then, and if he had done rather well to be a colonel at that age, there were others, with better connections and more dash, who had risen higher.

MacMahon was a general, as were other former Legion officers, François Canrobert and Aimable Pélissier. Most surprising of all, the unstable Saint-Arnaud, who had shouted that egotistical phrase at Constantine, now was Marshal of France and the commander of the French forces in the joint expedition with the British against the Russians.

In 1848, Louis Philippe had been tipped from the throne and fled to England disguised as "Mr. Smith." By luck and shrewd management Louis Napoleon, the nephew of the great Napoleon Bonaparte, had secured for himself the office of President in the new French Republic, which lasted less than four years. Then, in a careful *coup d'etat,* of which Saint-Arnaud had been one of the chief executioners, the President had had himself declared Napoleon III, ruler of France "by the grace of God and the will of the people." Now the Republic had become the Second Empire and Saint-Arnaud had risen to a marshaldom on the wings of the Napoleonic eagles.

So complex was the character of Napoleon III that almost anything said of him may be proven true—or false. He was an emperor with democratic leanings, an autocrat who sought the approval of the mob. Though he considered himself a military genius, he could

56

not read a military map accurately. Though his passionate love affairs with numerous women were the talk of Europe, he was a loving and indulgent husband to the beautiful Empress Eugénie. He was venturesome, ostentatious, sentimental, but he was not a fool. He was one of the first gamblers with modern power politics, and he lost eventually only to a better gambler—Bismarck.

There is blundering in all wars, but it is difficult to find in history such massive blundering as characterized what became known as the Crimean War. When Alfred Lord Tennyson wrote of that war's foolish charge of the British Light Brigade that "Some one had blundered," he might have better written that nearly everyone had. Pierre Bosquet, the French General, phrased it more courteously: "It is magnificent, but it is not war."

The British suffered from too much experience gained too long ago in the past. The French suffered from too much experience gained too recently in Algeria. Afterward everyone said that no one really had wanted the war. But no one tried very hard to prevent it and no one seemed to know how to win it once it had begun.

It must have come as a great surprise to any thoughtful Legionnaires to learn that they had become allies of the Infidel, the same Turkish Ottoman Empire whose crumbling North African outworks they had seized. Certainly it came as a surprise to Nicholas I, Czar of the Russians, to learn that his apparent friends, England and France, had declared war on him. He died less than a year later —of shocked surprise, Disraeli once said.

A religious squabble among Christians was the pretext that led to the war: Roman Catholic and Greek Orthodox monks in Jerusalem began quarreling over custody of Holy Places. As a devout member of the Greek Orthodox faith, Nicholas decided to intervene. Yet he was out for bigger game than the role of ecclesiastical protector afforded. He wished to expand his own empire at the expense of the Ottoman Empire, which he called "the sick man." Though it sprawled from the Adriatic to the Persian Gulf and from the Black Sea to the deserts of Africa, its government was weak, corrupt, and apparently friendless. Nicholas ventured boldly: a Russian fleet wiped out the Turkish navy at Sinope in the Black Sea while Russian armies crossed the Danube into the Turkish Balkan frontier provinces.

Although England had no love for the Ottoman Turks, its more vociferous leaders saw the Czar as posing a threat to the route to India. Fear of Russia was fanned into public ardor for war against it. Queen Victoria, in some astonishment, told Leopold I, the King of the Belgians, that the idea of war was "popular beyond belief."

France's involvement against Russia as the ally of her ancient enemy, England, was even more surprising. The French had less love for the Turks than did the English, and Russia in no sense threatened them. But Napoleon III wanted England for an ally, and there is nothing like a war at the side of a powerful ally to make a new and insecure emperor feel more secure.

Wars are fought at many levels, of course. At the level of Legion enlisted men one could scarcely glimpse the big picture of it. In the Legion's barracks a source of greater consternation than who was allied with whom was the fact that Colonel Bazaine was taking his bride to war with him. She was darkly beautiful, Spanish, coquettish, and twenty years younger than Bazaine. Her name was Soledad, and it was said by men who had been stationed at Tlemcen in western Algeria that she'd been a wonder with the castanets there. While no one at barracks level knew much else about her, there was a bit more to the story.

Bazaine had met Soledad when he lodged at her mother's boardinghouse while on duty at Tlemcen. She had been seventeen then, an age that did not prevent him from falling in love with her. She had been most willing to marry him. But when he sought official permission to marry, as then was necessary in the French Army, his request had been turned down by his superior and old friend MacMahon. When MacMahon bluntly told Bazaine that Soledad was not the girl for him and would do his career no good, he spoke as his friend. But a lover recognizes no friend who fails to agree with him. Bazaine and MacMahon had an angry scene. In light of the events of later years one might wonder whether Bazaine ever forgave Mac-

Mahon. The marriage was postponed for six years while Bazaine defrayed the cost of Soledad's further education in France. There she acquired more ladylike accomplishments than playing the castanets. Among them was skill on the piano.

Thus it came about that bemused Legionnaires found themselves carefully lowering Soledad's piano into the hold of a ship in Oran when the Legion sailed for the Dardanelles that June. If Bazaine remembered the detested Madame Bernelle sailing with the Legion to Spain, he presumably did not speak of her.

On June 21, 1854, the Legion landed on the shores of the Dardanelles at a filthy town called Gallipoli. They were a part of a heterogeneous army of French, British, and Turks that overflowed the twisting, filth-strewn streets and alleys of the town. Here the romantic East was less alluring than in the Casbah of Algiers. The price of wine was beyond the meager resources of most Legionnaires and the women looked like bundles of dirty bedclothes. Nevertheless, drunkenness quickly became the chief problem, followed by an alarming rise in the rate of syphilis.

After lingering briefly at Gallipoli the Legion sailed to Varna on the Black Sea coast of present-day Bulgaria. There the armies were grouping while it was decided what to do next. Actually the purpose of the war already had been achieved. With something like chagrin the Russians had retreated across the Danube. The Turks pursued and trounced them soundly. Thus the Turkish Empire had been saved.

It is easier to start a war than to end it, however. In London and Paris public enthusiasm for war was rising feverishly. But there had not yet been a pitched battle, let alone a victory, in which the sons of England and France had been engaged.

When the Legion arrived at Varna, it found an epidemic of cholera. Within a few weeks nearly 200 Legionnaires were dead. It was the most virulent cholera the Legion had yet experienced. A man in the best of health could be stricken suddenly with vomiting, diarrhea, fever, and within four hours his body would turn blue and he would be dead. Others lingered in agony for days. The epidemic swept all of southern Europe and the Balkans during that hot, dry summer. In the armies at Varna it created panic that led to widespread pilfering and drunkenness.

The hospital in Varna was a charnel house, infested with huge gray rats that scampered among the sick. Men tried to hide symptoms of illness in order to avoid going there. One moonlit August night a correspondent for *The Times* of London counted fifty carts assembled to carry the dead from the hospital.

Meantime the British Cabinet had decided what to do about this baffling war of no battles. On a map it was discovered that the Russion fortress and naval base of Sebastopol was located on a huge Black Sea peninsula called the Crimea. Why not pinch off its narrow neck and take the Crimea and Sebastopol? Albert, the Prince Consort of Victoria, logically pointed out that "the first difficulty is the absence of all information as to the Crimea itself." But Napoleon III in Paris liked the idea; members of his court even consulted the ghost of his uncle, the great Bonaparte, by means of ouija boards and found the omens favorable. It proved impossible to pinch off the neck of the Crimea, however, for the simple reason that its shores were shoal water which prohibited landings.

But an expedition to the Crimea there would be. After tiresome bickering and dissension a great fleet bearing about 35,000 French, Legion, and Turkish soldiers and about 24,000 English sailed from Varna on September 7, 1854, bound for the Crimea. It was the largest expedition that ever had set out for war overseas.

Saint-Arnaud's capacity to lead a large army in the field never had been tested. And his mercurial temperament was not helped by the fact he was seriously ill. His English counterpart was Lord Raglan, a conscientious officer sixty-six years old, who had passed the previous forty years of his military service at a desk. Although he had lost his right arm at Waterloo, he never had commanded so much as a battalion in the field. He was reserved, hard-working, as brave as Saint-Arnaud, and, since he had been the protégé and military secretary of the great Duke of Wellington, it was felt that he should know the business of leading an army. Despite his unfortunate lapse of calling

60

his Russian enemy "the French," he was tolerant of his allies. But he did not, at heart, want to co-operate with the French—even as they, at heart, found co-operation with the English difficult. Furthermore, Raglan was poorly served by his divisional generals, all but one of whom approached seventy and were, as Lord Wolseley had said of Wellington's generals, "mostly duffers."

Although they conducted themselves like gentlemen, Saint-Arnaud and Raglan rarely agreed or even seem to have understood each other. Each labored under inept and sometimes foolish directives from his home government. Napoleon III was especially impatient with the somnolence of affairs on the shores of the Black Sea and his friends had to restrain him from coming out to take command in person.

The Legion regiment under Bazaine was placed in the French 1st Division commanded by Canrobert, who had been the commander of a Legion regiment in 1849. Canrobert was a popular officer, a theatrical-acting little man with a high, domed forehead, waxed mustache and piercing eyes. When Napoleon III learned that Saint-Arnaud was seriously ill, he decided that Canrobert was the man to succeed him in time. Though brave and dutiful, Canrobert was not suited to high command. He himself wrote that "A commander-in-chief must not be sensitive on the battlefield. An officer who is tender-hearted in every-day life must become indifferent to the point of hardness in battle." But Canrobert never did manage to be so.

Five days after leaving Varna the fleet dropped anchor off Eupatoria, a Crimean town about thirty miles north of Sebastopol. Officers went ashore with a written order to the Russian mayor of the town to surrender. After gravely fumigating and reading the document, the mayor replied with a straight face that the armies could land at Eupatoria but must remain under quarantine there for several days.

The Legion battalions took up perimeter positions about four miles beyond Eupatoria. There one battalion had its first glimpse of the enemy on a hillside: a troop of Cossacks mounted on shaggy ponies, wearing bulky sheepskin coats and caps and armed with heavy sabers and fifteen-foot lances. Their officer, on the other hand, was elegantly dressed and rode a black charger. The Legionnaires, even the many Russians serving among them, were not impressed.

The Czar's Army was overrated in western Europe. It was poorly led, its officer system corrupt; the regiment belonged to the colonel instead of the colonel to the regiment. Its infantry was armed with smooth-bore muskets and maneuvered in massive trancelike formations. The efficiency of its artillery was hampered by the threat of execution that hung over the heads of any who lost their guns. The individual Russian soldier, however, was capable of great courage and stamina. Like his counterpart in the British and French armies, he deserved wiser leadership and care than had been granted him.

Lord Raglan was a gentleman; it was, indeed, his chief fault as a soldier. After the armies landed in the Crimea he forbade plundering. The French command at least paid lip service to his wishes: in general orders it said that whatever was taken must be paid for in cash or barter. The orders gave rise to a story passed down from the Crimea through generations of Legionnaires.

The day after the landing at Eupatoria, a Legion column swung inland on a foraging expedition. Coming upon a prosperous Tartar village, the Legionnaires thought they had entered the Promised Land. Remember, an officer said, everything must be purchased. But first, someone else said, we must decide what we want to purchase. They went about the business methodically. Some assembled carts, horses, and a few camels in the village street while others drove in all the cattle and sheep from the surrounding fields. Then they went from house to house, collecting poultry, cheese, grain, fruit, and vegetables. After they had carefully loaded the carts and camels with everything available, an officer summoned the village head man. Ripping a button off his tunic, the officer handed it to him and enunciated the French equivalent of "It's a deal." The laden caravan crept back to the lines where astonished soldiers demanded how they had come by such bountiful supplies. Every Legionnaire gave the same answer: "By barter!"

Not all of the foraging expeditions were as successful. One English cavalry foray led by the Earl of Cardigan, a martinet who earned his soldiers' sobriquet of being "the military maniac," returned virtually empty-handed. A disgusted trooper named Arthur Godfrey called it "the most absurd expedition it has ever been my ill luck to be engaged in."

Saint-Arnaud, who grew sicker daily, begged Raglan to get a move on toward Sebastopol. But a week passed before the armies marched south. They were woefully lacking in transport, maps, and accurate information on the strength and locations of their Russian enemies. The idea of reconnaissance seems not to have occurred to them. They marched compactly. Raglan led his army on the left and Saint-Arnaud ambled at the head of his men between the English and the fleet which kept pace with them at sea. Behind the French tagged the Turkish Commander, Omar Pasha, the most experienced officer on the expedition, at the head of a motley column of fierce-looking Turks.

They marched for a day through beautiful rolling country where fern and lavender grew in profusion. But it was a dry country, ominously quiet, deserted by all except lance-bearing mounted Cossacks, who constantly flitted on the horizon as they watched the advancing host. To those Legionnaires who were in good health it was a leisurely stroll. But soldiers who had been trained less strenuously suffered terribly from thirst and heat. More alarming was the fact that men continued to fall from the ranks with cholera.

Nightfall found them on the northern banks of the shallow Alma River, seventeen miles above Sebastopol. And in the gray light of the next morning, September 20, they gazed across the river at an army of 40,000 Russians which Prince Mentschikoff had deployed on commanding heights. The Legion moved quickly into its position as the spearhead of the 1st French Division under Canrobert. Then it waited—and it waited as the sun burned hotter in a bright blue sky. The English camp on the left appeared in confusion; those chaps were late as usual, the Legionnaires grumbled.

It was the Legion's first experience in a battle on such a grand scale. The men in the ranks never did have an eagle's-eye view of it. Indeed, when the survivors of the Crimea returned to Sidi-bel-Abbès, they were still wondering aloud just what had happened at the Alma. Military historians might have enlightened them.

The preceding night Saint-Arnaud, eyes glittering with fever, had offered his battle plan to Raglan. He proposed that the French army attack on the right and roll up the Russians while the English attacked in the center and on the left; caught in a pincers, the Russians would have to withdraw. The more loquacious Saint-Arnaud became, the more taciturn grew Lord Raglan. When Saint-Arnaud left, he apparently believed they were in agreement. As the next morning wore on, however, it became evident that no co-ordinated plan existed. Each army would fight in its own fashion.

The fashion of the English still was that of Waterloo: to hit head on, to close with the foe and never yield. Tactics that English troops had learned in India were considered bad form at Whitehall; indeed, Indian service made an officer vaguely suspect to the elderly headquarters types who directed the British Army. The French Army, on the other hand, had been forged in Algeria where what counted was the quick march, the swift assault, and where, unfortunately, there had developed the tacitly understood motto *"débrouillez-vous"*—"muddle through." Saint-Arnaud's plan at the Alma sounded logical enough, but it was based on insufficient reconnaissance of the fighting terrain; it was a gambler's long shot. Raglan's plan was little better; it was simply to get his boys across the river and fling them at the Russian positions in the fond hope that they'd drive the enemy away.

The allied armies arrayed on a curving front five miles inland from the sea presented an impressive sight that morning. On the left the British divisions deployed far back from the river and then advanced in long continuous lines toward the distant Russian redoubts. On the right the French advanced in columns. The morning sun gleamed on lances and the burnished headpieces of dragoons, on the scarlet *chéchias* and short blue jackets of Zouaves, the epaulettes of the Legionnaires, the red burnooses of Spahis. Big drum majors stepped along under fluttering tricolor plumes and the bearded, white-aproned Pioneers wore towering bearskin hats. It was magnificent, but there was one trouble with it: the movement of each army was unco-ordinated with that of the other.

Raglan's orders to his division commanders were brief and vague; soon he trotted off and found an exposed vantage site from which to enjoy the pageantry. The fact that Saint-Arnaud was a dying man is the only excuse for his rattled actions. For everything suddenly seemed uncertain to him. Bosquet's division forded the Alma un-opposed and began clambering up the hills until Bosquet decided he lacked sufficient artillery to advance farther. Canrobert and Prince Napoleon, the Emperor's nephew who was an excitable man called Plonplon by the Bonaparte family, asked orders of Saint-Arnaud for their divisions. Waving an arm wildly toward the river, Saint-Arnaud delivered a rhetorical inanity: "With men such as you I have no orders to give. I have but to point to the enemy!" So Canrobert led his first division across the river toward the cliffs.

The Legionnaires spearheading the assault under Bazaine finally were satisfied to be going into action. They entered the zone of Russian artillery fire, which spattered their blood among vineyards; they passed on and began scaling the cliffs with relative ease. And then, unaccountably, they were ordered to halt. Behind them the division bunched up under artillery fire. Canrobert had decided, like Bosquet, that he could not advance without more artillery sup-port. The Legionnaires clung there, looking around, puzzled. Can-robert was fighting by a book they had not learned by heart: no matter what the Legion's experience in Algeria, it was a maxim of French infantry tactics that massed troops should not advance across open ground without artillery support.

Prince Napoleon was not fighting by any book at all. He kept his division on the north side of the river, squatting there under the belching fire of Russian guns until his men howled that they were being massacred and two Zouave regiments took off on their own across the river. Saint-Arnaud chose this odd moment to add chaos to confusion by throwing in his reserves, one brigade after Bosquet and another in support of Canrobert.

Canrobert, strolling with Bazaine among the Legionnaires under the lip of the plateau, gazed enviously upriver where it appeared to him that the British lines were advancing against the Russian center "as though they were in Hyde Park." Years later as he watched Queen Victoria dancing the complicated steps of a quadrille with precision at a Court ball in Paris, he exclaimed, "The British fight as Victoria dances!"

Canrobert failed to see through the eddying smoke that matters were not proceeding with such precise efficiency on the British sector upriver. The divisions seesawed in on a narrowing front. Their individual units were not better led than those of the French; they were not braver men. But their goal, the Russian redoubts, was more obvious and they were employing the conventional military methods of the time to achieve it. British troops always had died well on fire-raked slopes, and the British at the Alma were no exception.

Prince Mentschikoff blissfully believed that his left flank was unassailable. When informed that the French were assailing it, he became almost hysterical. He ordered eight battalions to the left, decided to take command there himself, and then thought better of it. The sight of the Russian battalions crossing the front, above the draws where the reserves and Prince Napoleon's men were now hopelessly congested, made Saint-Arnaud even more excited. He sent a stream of messengers to Raglan asking for help. But Raglan felt, quite rightly, that he had enough to contend with on his own front.

Canrobert's division, perched awkwardly on the steep slopes, received the order to retreat. The Legion turned back sullenly. At last, however, Canrobert got his artillery working efficiently and it forced the Russians to withdraw from the heights. Then the Legion climbed the heights again and wiped out a weak rear guard of Russians.

But the battle was decided in the center where the English repulsed the counterattacks of massed gray squares of long-coated Russian infantrymen. In the fierce fighting there, the Russians finally broke and fled. The Allies did not pursue.

In London and Paris the outcome of the battle was hailed as a great victory. But precisely what had happened continued to puzzle Legionnaires accustomed to less confused battles. As an old Legionnaire once remarked, "The Legion never did understand any victory in which it didn't have a winning part."

The Battle of the Alma was but the beginning of confusion. Most military historians believe that the Allies could have taken Sebastopol from its northern approaches quickly and with relative ease. But the French and English high commands let themselves be argued out of an immediate attack by a wizened seventy-two-year-old general of the Royal Engineers. He was Sir John Burgoyne, the illegitimate son of the popular singer, Susan Caulfield, and Lord John Burgoyne, whom the Americans had defeated at Saratoga. Sir John prevailed on the Allies to march *around* Sebastopol and attack it from the south. In the course of this maneuver Prince Mentschikoff, fearing to be trapped in Sebastopol, marched his Army out of the city and across the entire front of the Allied Armies without being molested. Military confusion continued to be the order of the day when, on October 25, the British Light Brigade made its foolish and tragic charge on the Russian guns at the Battle of Balaclava.

After Saint-Arnaud died and Canrobert succeeded to command, he confessed himself appalled at the thought of a frontal assault on the city. So, while the men, women and children of Sebastopol built their defenses higher, the Allies sank into siege trenches around the city.

On November 5, Mentschikoff made a determined effort to relieve the defenders. The bloody, confusing fight which ensued on a nameless ridge was to be remembered as the Battle of Inkerman. The battle, lasting ten hours in fog and drizzle, was fought principally by the British until Bosquet's corps became involved. Leading companies of the Legion, along with Zouave units, were at first overrun by a mass of Russian infantry who charged out of the mist.

Regrouping, they counterattacked with the bayonet while Bosquet in person excitedly urged them on, crying, "Prove yourselves, children of fire!"

The Legionnaires, roaring hoarsely, drove the Russians down into a valley and out of the battle.

"They are panthers!" Bosquet exclaimed. "They are panthers bounding into the bush!"

As the siege lines grew about Sebastopol, Canrobert employed the full strength of the Legion whose losses were offset by frequent replacements from Algeria.

The men suffered terribly in the trenches about the city during the bitterly cold winter. They were not adequately clothed and never had sufficient fuel. Their dugouts were infested with lice and huge rats. Thaws turned the dugouts and trenches into muddy morasses while cholera continued to take a toll.

As always, the Legionnaires proved themselves adept at stealing anything which was not nailed down. From scraps of iron they improvised stoves and did everything possible to make their dugouts habitable. Eventually the English called them "the cabbage column" because of their skill at stealing cabbages.

Reinforcements from Algeria swelled the Legion's ranks and Bazaine was prompted to brigadier general early in 1855. In the stalemate of the trenches around Sebastopol, Bazaine's disciplinary duties became trying, for the Legion was performing as it always had. Magnificent in combat, it became a good deal less than magnificent during enforced idleness. Men began deserting, and one disclosed the locations of French mines to the Russians with disastrous consequences. In an army where nearly everyone drank anything available, the alcoholics among the Legionnaires became especially notorious for concocting vile, blinding potions.

Canrobert, a fastidious man, was shocked during inspection one day to discover that a Legionnaire had sold his shoes to buy brandy and then had blacked his feet in the hope that no one would notice the difference. The incident sent Canrobert into a tirade in which he cried that within the Legion ranks he found thieves, murderers, lunatics, ruined noblemen, and—he concluded breathlessly—a former Prefect of Police in Rome.

Bazaine passed the winter somewhat more pleasantly than his

Legionnaires in the trenches. For his beloved Soledad had crossed the Black Sea to be at his side in the Crimea, bringing her piano with her. Somehow Bazaine contrived to find quarters for her. Their most frequent guest was General Pélissier, a gay and impetuous man of sixty, who succeeded Canrobert as commander of the French forces. In 1845, Pélissier had become the object of public indignation when a force under his command had smothered to death more than 1,000 Arabs who took refuge in the Dahra caves in Algeria and refused to surrender; Bugeaud had maintained, however, that Pélissier had had the right idea and promoted him. Pélissier was a great admirer of Soledad and enjoyed listening to her play the piano. When Bazaine was on night duty in the trenches, Pélissier sometimes invited her to dinner at his quarters. There they laughed and talked and sometimes waltzed to the music of a regimental band. Sometimes Pélissier let Soledad wear his general's cap and sometimes she let him pinch her chin. When that grew boring, Pélissier would place chairs in a row and command his little dog to jump over them, a trick that invariably pleased Soledad.

Life was quite different, of course, in the snow and mud of the trenches which ringed Sebastopol. Raiding and counter-raiding increased as spring came on. The Legion's facility with the bayonet made it a dreaded enemy to the Russians. Although its old muzzle-loading muskets had been replaced by percussion, breech-operated weapons, reloading still was cumbersome and it remained the custom to fire one round and then charge with the bayonet. As in Algeria, the Legion's officers continued to display personal courage in leading their men. In May the 1st Regiment's new commander, Colonel Vienot, was killed while leading a raid. Bazaine was cited more than once for bravery. And though MacMahon was now a divisional general, he still frequently acted like a Foreign Legion officer. When the Russian works were breached, he personally led the way in. Told that he was standing on Russian mines, he replied with a typical MacMahonism: "Here I am and here I'll stay." But someone coaxed him away before the mines were detonated.

Women, like men, find varying roles in war. While Soledad

Bazaine was thumping her piano, the English nurse, Florence Nightingale, was risking her life by toiling day and night, caring for the wounded and trying to improve sanitary conditions in the hospitals.

Finally the defenders of Sebastopol capitulated and the Legion entered the city on September 10, 1855. Pélissier appointed Bazaine commander of the occupying forces, but within a month he found employment for him elsewhere. Putting him at the head of a force of Legionnaires, French and English, Pélissier sent him off to capture the Russian fortress at Kinburn. During Bazaine's absence, Pélissier consoled Soledad with daily visits. He had requisitioned what seemed to be the only coach in the Crimea and had an artillery team hitched to it. In this ancient vehicle he lumbered to Soledad's home each afternoon at three o'clock and lingered there late into the evening. When Bazaine captured Kinburn and returned to Sebastopol quickly, Pélissier did not seem especially pleased.

The Crimean War ended soon afterward. The Legion had lost one of every two men engaged in it. Altogether, the war took nearly 300,000 lives. It had no other conclusive results.

7

"Bonjour, Ma'moiselle"

OLD LEGION HANDS were disgusted. The cause of their annoyance was Napoleon III, whom they called many things, the most printable being "the upstart."

Returning from the Crimea in the late summer of 1856, all units found themselves lumped together as the *Second* Regiment at Sidi-bel-Abbès under Colonel Chabrière. The *First* Regiment was a new unit composed entirely of Swiss whom Napoleon had recruited in France because he admired Swiss fighting prowess. The Swiss Regiment was stationed at Philippeville and commanded by a Colonel Ochenbein, a personal friend of the Emperor's. Ochenbein let it be known that the Emperor had a low opinion of the mixed regiment of veteran foreigners and that it soon might be disbanded. It was no wonder, said the old hands, that enlistments had fallen off and that many men refused to sign up for a new term.

Dedicated Legionnaires—meaning men to whom no better way of life than that of the Legion seemed possible—wondered why French governments always displayed short memories about the deeds of the Legion. Why didn't some of the French generals who

71

had served with it and knew its strong heart speak up for it? Ah, well, a general's memory seemed to be as short as that of a politician.

These dedicated Legionnaires included a great variety of men.

One was Captain Juan Martinez, a Spaniard with a great bladed nose and a shock of graying hair, whose booming laugh disguised a quick temper. As Martinez told the story, he had been a pure-hearted Spanish guerilla fighting for the rights of his people against the might of royal oppressors. But everyone believed that a Spanish guerilla was the polite name for a Spanish bandit, and Martinez displayed a quickness of hand and eye that might have been developed while snatching purses. In any event, he had proved quick in the trench fighting before Sebastopol where he had been a sergeant, gathering a faltering company around him and leading it to victory in the Russian outworks. A commission had been his reward, and now Sergeant Juan was *Captain* Martinez.

Quite a different sort of captain was Jean Danjou, the son of a tradesman in Carcassonne, whose only desire in life was to be a professional soldier. What verse was to a poet or wine to a drunkard, so was military life to Jean Danjou. He was twenty-eight, a straight, prematurely balding man with a flowing mustache and grave dark eyes. Meticulous, fair, cool-headed, he was excellent at paper work. But he was every bit as brave as Martinez. He had proved that at Sebastopol. When a Russian shell tore off his left hand, he had calmly helped a Legionnaire fasten a tourniquet about the stump of his arm and then had led his company ahead. Now he wore a left hand fashioned of wood, which he kept covered with a clean white glove.

Not all dedicated Legionnaires were officers, of course.

There was Corporal Jean Vilain, only twenty years old, a dark and impetuous youth who had joined the Legion because he wanted to lead an adventurous life. He had found adventure in the Crimea, where he had won the Legion of Honor.

Different from Vilain, yet equally dedicated, was Corporal Clement Maudet, twenty-seven, who also had been decorated in the Crimea. Quiet, reflective, handsome, Maudet, as a journalist, had vehemently opposed Napoleon's rise to power in 1848. He had joined the Legion in order to avoid jail as a political prisoner. Now, on foreign soil, he served the man he detested.

There were many such men. There was a private named Sobieski, a Pole of great dignity, who kept much to himself as if he bore a dark secret. Another who acted as if he kept a secret was an Austrian private named Wildermann; an intelligent, first-rate soldier, he refused for some reason the opportunity to become a noncommissioned officer.

At times it seemed that the dedicated Legionnaires were waiting for something, as if they had a rendezvous with destiny. Certainly each exhibited a marked difference of manner from the mere time-servers.

Martinez predicted that the doldrums would pass, that there would be another good campaign which would snap the Legion back. Meanwhile they drilled and mended roads. They sang a lot, and they drank a lot.

Wilhelm, the aging German bandmaster, wrote a new Legion march after they returned from the Crimea. It had a fine, stirring quality, but Wilhelm was uncertain what to call it and he never had been much good at lyrics for the songs and marches he composed. Various Legionnaires tried their hand at lyrics for Wilhelm's new march and finally, by popular acclaim, it was called *"Le Boudin"* in honor of the blood sausage they were rationed on lucky days. There were many songs and marches more popular with Legionnaires at the time, and no one would have believed that *"Le Boudin"* would win enduring fame as the official song of the Legion.

The rolls for 1857 show that the Germans had become the largest national group—which may have helped account for so much singing. Close behind them came the Belgians, Italians, Russians, Poles, and Spaniards. Other nationalities included Greeks, Dutch, Portuguese, Austrians, Hungarians, Serbs, and Turks. And there was a lone Chinese who sometimes curled his pigtail in his kepi and sometimes let it hang down his back.

73

In the spring of 1857 Martinez's prediction of another good campaign came true.

By this time the French and their Legionnaires had conquered all of northern Algeria except the massif of Greater Kabylia. In order to become the master of this mountainous terrain the French assembled a force of about 35,000 men that spring and split it into four divisions. The Swiss Regiment advanced on the Kabylia area with the division moving from the north. Two battalions of the veteran Legion composed the advance guard of the division converging from the west under the command of MacMahon. Guerillas harassed the veteran Legionnaires nearly every step of the way as they pressed into the Kabylia stronghold.

Before the strongly held craggy ridge of Ischeriden, MacMahon opened up his artillery and sent two French line regiments charging up the steep hill. When heavy Kabyle fire stopped the French infantry and sent it scrambling pell-mell back down the slope, Mac-Mahon studied the ridge through his field glasses for a long time. To the left of the position from which the French infantry had been repulsed, at a higher point on the ridge, he made out another Kabyle encampment.

Summoning Major Paul Mangin, who commanded the Legion battalions, MacMahon ordered him to seize the higher Kabyle encampment and then swing down the ridge and take the position where the French had failed. It appeared to be a suicidal mission and MacMahon's tactics could not be called those of a military genius.

But, as Mangin said later, a soldier should not expect to lead a long and happy life. Forming his battalions in extended order, Mangin mounted his horse at the head of them and said gravely, *"Marchons!"*

Behind him the Legionnaires advanced slowly and calmly, their blue overcoats swaying rhythmically in the glare of burning sun. To the watching French it was madness, and not the least of it was the fact that men wore their overcoats in such blazing heat. But each Legionnaire was issued only one overcoat, and if he left it someplace it would be stolen, causing him untold discomfort if he lived until the cold of night settled in. So they marched along in their overcoats, and when they came within range of the Kabyles on the ridge, the full power of muskets and ancient fieldpieces was brought to bear on them. The slope seemed to shake under the hail of fire, but Mangin rode on and the Legion walked behind him without firing a shot.

When the ridge became too steep for his horse to climb higher, Mangin dismounted and clambered ahead on foot. The Legionnaires climbed behind him, silently and still not firing, until they reached the crest. There, with bayonets swinging, they fell upon the Kabyle encampment. The Kabyles fled.

Reforming the battalions in extended order again and commanding them to continue to hold their fire, Mangin led them down the ridge toward the lower Kabyle stronghold. The Kabyles, unnerved at seeing their position outflanked so easily, fired wildly at them and then surrendered or fled. It had taken the Legion precisely thirty minutes to seize the ridge of Ischeriden at a cost of only one officer and eight men killed and three officers and eighty-seven men wounded.

Afterward a Kabyle chieftain discussed the battle with Mac-Mahon.

"It was the movement of the Long Capotes (the overcoated Legionnaires) that made us quit," he said excitedly. "Without them you never would have taken our positions and we would have descended on you and given you the *coup de grâce*. But when we saw the Legionnaires turn our fortifications without firing a shot, we ran away. Tell me, General, who is this veritable devil who rode on horseback ahead of the others? I shot at him twice myself. We all saw it. We saw the bullets hit the ground around his horse. But he kept on advancing. Tell me his name so that I can treasure it!"

The seizure of the Ischeriden broke the core of resistance in Kabylia. Several senior French officers who watched the Legion's action were deeply impressed and vowed that the regiment of mixed foreigners never should be disbanded.

The veteran Legionnaires were pleased, of course. And their delight was enhanced when they learned, after the campaign had

75

ended, that the Swiss Regiment, which was the darling of Napoleon III, had not played any important role in it. Not long afterward the Swiss were set to work building roads.

In May, 1859, Napoleon III summoned every available Legionnaire to war against Austria. They numbered less than 2,200 men when they landed at Genoa that month. It was the lowest effective fighting force in the history of the Legion. It reflected a decline in the capacity of the French Army, a decline of which the French people and the Army itself still were unaware.

There were several reasons for the waning quality and capacity of the Army. For one thing, it looked to the past rather than the future and still believed itself as invincible as it had been under Napoleon Bonaparte. For another, it was the victim of parsimonious military budgets and poor or mediocre leadership. A fault of its leaders was that all had been trained in Algeria where reckless courage and "muddle through" was substituted for careful strategy and logistics. War as it was fought in Algeria simply was not a proper training for war as it was fought in Europe.

Although Napoleon III seems to have shared his people's desire for peace and their ignorance of the true state of the Army, he was not averse to making war. Above all, he wished France to have allies, and he believed that a united Italy would be a strong ally.

At the time southern Italy was a mixture of Papal and city states, grand duchies, and the Kingdom of the Two Sicilies. Lombardy and the Veneto were Austrian while the provinces of Savoy and Piedmont were part of the Kingdom of Sardinia whose ruler was King Victor Emanuel II. Napoleon concluded a secret alliance with Victor Emanuel, who then purposefully provoked Austria. When the Austrian Emperor, Francis Joseph, sent an ultimatum to Victor Emanuel in April, 1859, Napoleon ignored the advice of his ministers and announced his support of the Italians. This time he would lead the armies in the field himself. It was one of the biggest risks of his gambler's career.

When the Legionnaires came ashore in Genoa, the 2nd Regiment of veterans commanded by Colonel Chabrière numbered about 1,500 while the 1st Regiment, the Swiss, was less than 600 strong. The men were armed with the new Chassepot rifle and bore a new flag which cited their battle honors, but their morale was low. Many Austrians among them were reluctant to fight their countrymen and Italian Legionnaires did not feel they were fighting for a great Italian cause. To most it was just another war conceived by "the upstart."

The Legionnaires were placed in the division of General Charles Espinasse, a former Legion officer, which was a part of the 2nd Corps commanded by MacMahon. They were not surprised to find themselves on the point of the 2nd Corps as it slogged along muddy roads in pouring rain. As in the Crimea, the French command lacked adequate maps and the troops plunged ahead almost blindly. All anyone knew was that MacMahon's Corps was to make a wide flanking sweep and attack the town of Magenta from the north while two other corps attacked simultaneously from the south and west.

Early on the morning of June 4 the Corps moved out of the town of Turbigo toward Magenta, eleven miles to the southeast. The Legion regiments under Chabrière were on the extreme left wing of the advance, which was on a broad front through a country of vineyards and trees. The Legionnaires met little opposition until they came to the hamlet of Marcollo, where the Austrians were dug in strongly. Under the hail of Austrian fire the veterans shrank back. Chabrière, waving his sword, rallied them angrily. What ailed them? Why didn't they act like Legionnaires?

Chabrière plunged toward Marcollo ahead of them. Moments later he fell dead with a musket ball through the head. A couple of Legionnaires snatched up his body, but the momentum had left the assault. Men paused uncertainly and began falling back.

Suddenly Martinez, who had been promoted to major, sprang up ahead of them.

"Mes camarades!" His voice rose above the clatter of Austrian small-arms fire. And then a wolfish grin spread over his face as he called the names of old veterans.

A bullet twanged through his right sleeve and he raised his arm with a mocking expression. Bowing to the hole in his sleeve, he cried, *"Bonjour, Ma'moiselle!"*

Someone laughed and Martinez walked ahead toward Marcollo as bullets whined about him and raised dust around his feet. Bowing and moving with the grace of a matador, Martinez kept shouting, *"Bonjour, Ma'moiselle!"*

He did not pause in his slow advance into the hamlet. The Legionnaires did not pause either as they followed him, some laughing and others trying to imitate him in the hail of fire by bowing and shouting, *"Bonjour, Ma'moiselle!"*

And then, quite suddenly, they lunged upon the entrenched Austrians with bayonets.

Marcollo was cleared quickly, but Magenta still was two miles distant. From vineyard walls and farmhouse windows the white-coated Austrians fought them most of the way. Martinez did not exhort the Legionnaires. He simply walked down the road and they followed, clearing out nests of the enemy efficiently while they swapped bets on whether Martinez would make it alive to Magenta. What bullet had the name of Martinez on it? Which Ma'moiselle would silence his infectious laugh?

Combat was not a game. Everyone knew that. Then how did Martinez manage to make it seem so? Yet, speaking of bullets and speaking of women, both had much in common.

The Legionnaires came to Magenta and dashed up a street toward the railroad station. The color bearer—was it Schmitt or Leshefka?—let himself be carried away with enthusiasm. He was too far forward when the sheet of Austrian musket fire burst from the station. As he fell, his hands clawed to drive the staff into the ground. Seeing the standard, a couple of Austrians dashed out of the station to capture it. But a dozen Legionnaires beat them to it and the Austrians fell with mortal bayonet wounds.

They had recovered the flag, but how would they take the cursed railroad station? Someone, perhaps Martinez, remembered that they were not fighting this war alone. A request was sent to the French on their right, who soon set up an enfilading fire, and under its cover the Legion took the station.

They crossed the tracks and fought from house to house, from street to street. Around nine o'clock in the evening the last Austrians were driven from the town.

A couple of hours later Napoleon III rode up in a state of alarm. His grand plan had gone awry; the three corps had failed to co-ordinate properly. But MacMahon's Corps had saved the day by bulling ahead alone in the style of Algerian fighting. In relief and gratitude the Emperor made MacMahon a marshal of France on the spot. And then, as an afterthought, he also named him Duke of Magenta.

But another incident of the battle made a greater impression on many veteran Legionnaires. Private Sobieski had been killed in the street fighting and a comrade felt free to disclose his secret. He had been the last descendant of King Sobieski of Poland, who had saved Vienna from the Turks, and now he was dead in a small Italian town from an Austrian bullet.

What determined a man's fate? Was it chance alone? There was Legionnaire Sobieski, dead. And there, on the dusty road to Milan, rode former Legionnaire Bazaine, a grandly caparisoned general now—and blessed if he hadn't brought his Soledad to war with him again. Such matters were food for thought, sufficient to nourish a man through many a lonely night in the desert—if he lived to see Algeria again.

If a Legionnaire was of a reflective turn of mind, he might also ponder the suddenness of events in war. Time crept, sometimes seemed to stand still. And suddenly . . . ! No better words described war. And suddenly many were dead. And suddenly MacMahon was a marshal of France and the Duke of Magenta. And suddenly Martinez, whose raffish face surely was that of a brigand, was *Colonel* Martinez, commander of the 2nd Regiment. And suddenly the 1st Regiment of Swiss, which had aroused such jealousy in Algeria, was left behind in Milan to recruit because it was too depleted to go on.

So the regiment of veteran foreigners, reduced to less than 1,300

79

after Magenta, marched on east across the plains of Lombardy. They still were in the van. Far to their left they sometimes caught the glint of sun on the snows of the Bergamo Alps. No one knew precisely where they were going; they were simply chasing Austrians. Ahead lay Lake Garda, Verona, Padua. The women of Padua were said to be something special, but they had heard the same said about the women of many other places, and it always turned out that women were much the same the world around.

On the night of June 23 they bivouacked beside a stream. Martinez was restless. He said he could *feel* Austrians close ahead of them. Danjou studied a map intently by firelight. It showed that they were close to a village called Solferino in a fold of hills. Martinez turned them out early, almost as early as for a desert march. They were under way again shortly after three o'clock on the morning of June 24. And suddenly, in the gray light of dawn, they crashed head on into the main body of the Austrian Army.

The Legionnaires knew their job. They recoiled from the first blast of Austrian fire, then formed in squares on high ground and waited while a messenger dashed back on Martinez's horse to give the alarm. The Zouaves came up fast this time, fanning out to left and right of the Legion. The whole army was coming up fast and forming in line.

In the growing light the Legionnaires found themselves facing directly on Solferino, a town strung along a single street. The hills about it swarmed with Austrians. The din of battle rose slowly as the wings of French and Italian partisans curled forward. At last the Legion was ordered to advance and take a hill called the Spy of Italy, which flanked the town. It was an easy mission; the Austrians defended it halfheartedly and then retreated. Now the Legionnaires looked directly down into Solferino, which lay beyond a stone-walled cemetery.

Orders came again: Advance into Solferino by way of the cemetery. As the Legionnaires swung down the hill and came within musket range of it, they were met with a withering blast of fire. The Austrians had converted the high walls into a veritable fortress.

To the surprise of some Legionnaires, Martinez did not urge them on to try to take the cemetery. Instead, he pulled them back out of musket range and they waited while he studied the fighting on the surrounding hills. The battle ebbed and flowed fiercely there, and still Martinez waited.

Veterans understood why he was waiting and blessed him. The cemetery was not yet worth the price of the taking. The Austrians dug in there could easily be reinforced, while the Legion had no reinforcements; if the Legionnaires managed to take it, they could readily be driven out by artillery fire. Martinez was worthy of his rank, for he understood the economy of battle and was no spendthrift of his men's lives.

While they waited, someone exclaimed and all gazed around at an incredible sight. To the rear of the French lines a huge balloon with a basket slung below it rose on trailing ropes. Two men in the basket were studying the Austrian formations through binoculars. It was the first time in history that an observation balloon had been employed in battle.

What the observers saw was apparent to the Legionnaires by noon. The battle was deadlocked. Neither side could make further headway without reinforcements, which each lacked. An hour later a cloud of dust rose in the west and the Legionnaires heard faint cheering. The tide of battle had been turned; the Emperor had arrived with reinforcements.

In midafternoon, as the Austrians on the hills began to recoil, Martinez again was ordered to attack the cemetery, which now was the key defense of the town. The Legion sprang forward at the double, clearing the wall and then fighting on among the graves. In the swirling melee among the stone crosses Martinez observed the cool courage Danjou displayed. He also observed that Corporals Vilain and Maudet conducted themselves like good officers in leading their comrades. At last they took the cemetery and loped into Solferino on the heels of the retreating Austrians.

When they counted up their dead, they found Legionnaire Wildermann among them. Not long afterward his secret was learned. He had been one of seventeen Austrian generals involved in a revolt against Russia in 1849 and the Russians had condemned him to death. Now, ten years later, he was dead of a fellow countryman's bullet.

The aftermath of the Battle of Solferino was like the aftermath of many battles throughout history. It had been hard fought and aroused bitter hatreds, especially between the Austrians and the Italians. The screaming of dying men mingled with the screaming of wounded horses. In the humid evening the stench of putrefying flesh rose from the hills. Everywhere wounded men moaned for water. Some, among both victors and vanquished, plundered the dead and the wounded. Some of the wounded were slain. The medical facilities of both the Allies and the Austrians were utterly incapable of coping with the carnage of the battle in which the Allies lost about 17,000 men and the Austrians about 22,000.

Yet the horrors of the battle and its aftermath were to have far-reaching consequences because of the impression it made on three men.

One was Napoleon III, who was more humane than his more famous uncle. It was true that he had begun to realize he was leading France into a trap in Italy and must extricate his forces quickly because the Prussians were arming on the undefended eastern French frontier. But it also was true that he was sickened and horrified at Solferino by the suffering and cruelty caused by war.

Another who was equally shocked by the scenes at Solferino was Austrian Emperor Francis Joseph. As a result, he met Napoleon gladly a few days later and they concluded terms of peace. Napoleon's Italian allies were outraged, feeling that they had been betrayed. As a result of the negotiations, France gained Nice and Savoy.

There were even more significant consequences, however, because a sensitive Swiss businessman named Henri Dunant happened to visit the battlefield. Horrified and angered, Dunant wrote a pamphlet describing what he saw. His pamphlet stirred other humane persons, and from their joint efforts there grew the International Red Cross.

8

To the

Halls of Montezuma

THROUGHOUT THE LONG VOYAGE the Legionnaires had beguiled themselves with tales about the fabulous land of Mexico. It was, they told one another, an exotic country, where everyone would find rich booty. The women all were beautiful and willing. There was bountiful food and drink everywhere.

Now they were in Mexico, and what did they find?

A country so poverty-stricken that surely it would make an Arab wince. Stinking jungle swamplands, where swarming mosquitoes could eat a man alive. Billets in tumbled-down, vermin-infested old convents. A people who seldom spoke, but simply stared at foreigners as hated enemies. There was yellow fever and typhus, too, with its frightening black vomito. And there was an impossible drink called *pulque*.

The Legionnaires were in Mexico as a result of an idea that had obsessed Napoleon III and the Empress Eugénie. Lord Palmerston,

British Prime Minister, had said that foolish ideas multiplied like rabbits in the mind of Napoleon. Although the Emperor might have said the same of the Prime Minister, Napoleon's folly did appear great in his Mexican venture.

In January, 1861, an incorruptible Indian leader named Juarez assumed power in Mexico City, determined to free his country of outside intervention and clerical domination. He sent home the Spanish Minister and the Papal Nuncio and suspended payments on all foreign loans. The result was inevitable once the United States was torn by Civil War. France, Britain and Spain intervened in Mexico with a "punitive expedition" that had the improbable mission of collecting old debts from an impoverished nation. Spain and Britain soon withdrew, leaving France alone. On May 5, 1862, the *juaristas* checked a French Army at the gates of Puebla and turned it back. As a result, that dangerous form of pride known as military prestige was at stake; the humiliation of defeat must be avenged. Another army was shipped to Mexico while the Emperor and his Empress began to caress the thought of a Mexican empire in the image of their own.

Of course it was a grab, as power politics is always concerned with the grab. Only a few years previously the United States had grabbed almost half of Mexico's territory in a war that was called "punitive." The Empress Eugénie, a devout Roman Catholic, viewed the proposed effort as holy—and romantic. When the Emperor grew uncertain about the project, she gave him certainty in a way that only she ever could. Naturally an empire needs an emperor, and a Mexican emperor needed the blessing of the European great powers and the Pope. A candidate was sought and found.

He was Archduke Maximilian, younger brother of the Austrian Emperor, Francis Joseph. He was royal, Catholic, handsome, ambitious, and not very bright. His wife, the attractive and mettlesome Charlotte, daughter of King Leopold I of the Belgians, was delighted at the prospect of becoming an empress in an exotic land. The great powers and the Pope approved the candidate. Maximilian asked for a plebiscite to assure that the Mexicans wished him to be

84

their emperor. What he received and accepted was a stacked deck of votes: a junta of arch-conservatives urged him and Charlotte to come to Mexico City and become their Emperor and Empress.

As soon as France became involved in Mexico, Legionnaires began to yearn to be sent there. There was peace in Algeria; the Legion's days were occupied by the monotony of patrolling and building roads.

The monotony was too much for Colonel Martinez. He resigned his commission and disappeared. It was rumored that he went to South America and involved himself in one revolution after another, but no one ever was certain what became of him.

Enlistments increased and the Legion's rolls began to grow again after the war in Italy. But there was a mood of restlessness in both officers and men, a vague fear that they were in the stagnation of enduring peace. When the Legion was not included in the French expedition to Mexico, restless junior officers acted over the head of their commander and petitioned the Emperor to send the Legion there. Among the petitioners were Captain Danjou and Second Lieutenants Vilain and Maudet, both of whom had been commissioned from the ranks after Solferino.

The petitioners did not know that the Emperor planned to send the Legion anyway. Neither did they know that he was toying with the idea of giving Maximilian the Foreign Legion outright, as Louis Philippe had given it to the Cristinist Government in Spain.

On March 31, 1863, two battalions of the Legion under the command of Colonel Jeanningros landed at Veracruz. They were to be followed by a third battalion. Altogether about 4,000 men, representing the total strength of the Legion, were shipped to Mexico. Less than half of them ever returned to Algeria.

They came ashore in high spirits, believing that they were launched on their greatest adventure and would immediately be sent into combat in the remote interior. Their old friend, Bazaine, had a division somewhere upcountry in the army commanded by General Élie Forey. By that time the French had established a corridor from Veracruz to Mexico City, 260 miles distant, but the conquest of the vast country barely had begun and it would be some time before Maximilian and Charlotte arrived. Positively, the Legionnaires assured one another, Bazaine would send for them.

But to their disgust and rage, Bazaine was powerless to call on them. Their fate was in the hands of Forey, a martinet who knew little and cared less about the Legion. Forey, like Napoleon Bonaparte, whom he wished to emulate, assigned his mercenary troops to low, unhealthful areas and kept the French regiments in more salubrious climates. To the Legion, Forey gave the dull, irksome task of guarding the road from Veracruz through the fever swamps and up into the plains. They were to be treated no better than other ordinary mercenary units the French had scraped together, such as an Egyptian Legion whose members wore red fezes and prayed to Mecca.

Colonel Jeanningros dispersed his companies at posts along the section of the "fever road" they were to guard. Within a few days of their landing their ranks were decimated by sickness and morale was at ebb. The despondent men hung up their caps and took to wearing straw sombreros as a gesture of protest at their lot, but their change of headgear did not last long.

At the lonely posts beside the road the Legionnaires listened avidly to the accounts of travelers coming down from Mexico City. They described it as a surpassingly lovely land of purple mountains, wide uplands, and luxuriant flowers, once one left the fever swamps and approached the Cerro Gordo, a mountain pass where the road wound along the edges of breath-taking precipices. There was an indolence in the air, a subtle invitation to drowse, as if time had ceased to matter. Far beyond Puebla one crossed through a lofty pass in the Rio Frio Mountains, 11,000 feet above the sea, and looked down on a broad valley of sparkling lakes and shining fields, where Montezuma's ancient capital stood in imposing splendor.

It was the route of Mexico's conquerors, pioneered by Cortez, who had burned his ships on the beach at Veracruz and given his men the alternative: Conquer or die! In 1847, an American Army commanded by General Winfield Scott had marched and fought along the same route in another conquest of Mexico.

The Legionnaires in the fever swamps listened and pondered, they ailed and pined for the distant high country.

This was their state of mind and body and spirit on April 29, when it fell the turn of the 3rd Company of the 1st Battalion to convoy a caravan bound from Veracruz to Puebla. The caravan, composed of 60 carts and 150 mules, bore a quantity of munitions and three million francs in gold bullion to pay the French Army.

The 3rd Company normally had a complement of 112 men and 3 officers. But 50 men and all 3 officers were ill with fever and unable to stand formation. Colonel Jeanningros asked for officer volunteers to take the place of those who were ill. Captain Danjou, then serving as battalion adjutant major, stepped forward. He was followed by Vilain, the battalion pay officer, and Maudet of the 1st Company. Jeanningros offered Danjou additional men, but Danjou replied that 62 Legionnaires were adequate for such a task and he did not need more.

Jeanningros hesitated. The caravan was one of the most valuable which had left Veracruz in a long time and the Mexicans, with their excellent intelligence system, undoubtedly knew about it. And yet, thought Jeanningros, there was no more reliable and competent officer in the Legion than Danjou. Jeanningros shrugged and turned away.

In the early morning hours of April 30, the 3rd Company moved out of the village of Chiquihuite to scout the road for the caravan which was to follow two hours later. There was nothing exceptional about the 3rd. Its men and noncommissioned officers were composed of the Legion's familiar international mixture. Before joining the Legion they had been students, weavers, bookbinders, blacksmiths; among them were a former saddler, a couple of sailors, a wood gilder, several waiters, two tilemakers, a draper. As far as is known, no former general, no prince or nobleman served in the ranks of the 3rd. They were ordinary men who, for one or another personal reason, had joined the Foreign Legion.

87

Danjou grouped them behind Maudet and Vilain in two extended files about one hundred yards on either side of the road. He himself marched in the road with two pack mules which bore the rations and extra ammunition. Shortly before 7 A.M. they passed through the destroyed hamlet of Cameron. Because Danjou was an excellent officer, he was observant; in Cameron he noted that the only building still standing was a deserted farmhouse surrounded by a broken wall and a few tumbled-down outbuildings. About a mile farther along the road, in a rolling country of tall grass and thick clumps of brush, Danjou halted the company for breakfast. The men had not eaten since the preceding evening and they were hungry and thirsty.

Fires had just been lighted to boil coffee when a sentry whistled shrilly and cried, "To arms!" As the men sprang up, the mules bolted away with the rations and additional ammunition. Into view from both left and right rode lines of armed horsemen, who flushed out and curved around the forming Legionnaires. Danjou instantly estimated their numbers in the hundreds and realized his exposed men would be quickly overwhelmed. Their only chance was to fall back to Cameron and make a stand in the deserted farmhouse.

The Mexican Juarist cavalry totaled about 800 men, well armed with American rifles, and behind them came 1,200 militiamen on foot. They were guerillas led by Colonel Milan, the commander of the Juarist irregular forces in the district, who had been informed of the gold shipment. Milan erred in attacking the Legionnaires rather than letting them pass and sweeping up the caravan which was a couple of miles to the rear. Presumably, however, the company looked weak to him and he had not heard of the fighting capabilities of Legionnaires.

This was the sort of action in which they had been well rehearsed. Danjou formed them into an extended rectangular formation and moved them back slowly through the thickest undergrowth where the cavalry could not charge them. Despite his care in extricating them, 16 men became separated and were captured.

Panting and sweating, the remaining 46 Legionnaires and the 3 officers loped into the courtyard of the farmhouse at Cameron. To

88

their dismay, musket fire immediately rained on them from the upper story, wounding a few men. Militiamen had beaten them to the house. Danjou organized an attack on the house, but it had scarcely begun when Milan's cavalrymen swooped down on the walls of the yard. Caught between two fires, the Legionnaires turned back to the walls.

In one corner of the yard they found an area where fire from the house windows could not reach them. Reinforcing the broken wall and a tumbled-down shed in the corner with straw and logs, they repulsed another charge by the cavalry.

About nine o'clock Colonel Milan rode forward with a white flag and called in Spanish, "I ask you to surrender! You're surrounded by two thousand soldiers. If you surrender now, you will be treated fairly."

"We'll die before we surrender!" Danjou called back.

The maneuvering cavalry raised great clouds of dust over the courtyard of Camerone. To the Legionnaires the heat seemed nearly as bad as the Mexican rifle and musket fire. As the sun burned through the eddying dust, their parched lips in grimed, sweating faces formed but one word: water. Two men who tried to creep to a well on the farther side of the house were shot. One lay in an angle of the wall, writhing from his wound and shrieking with pain. A comrade who tried to crawl to his aid was shot dead from the house.

Danjou paced calmly behind the wall, his lips cracked from heat and thirst. "Hold your fire," he repeated in French. "Make every shot count. You"—he spoke the name of a Legionnaire—"do you swear to die before you surrender?"

"*Oui, mon capitaine.*"

"*Bien!*"

"You." He spoke to another. "Before you were a Legionnaire you were an Italian, eh? Is it true the French die better than the Italians?"

"*Non, mon capitaine.*"

"We shall see," said Danjou. "We shall see that we are nothing now but Legionnaires and Legionnaires die better than any men in the world." He raised his wooden hand. "They come again. *Aux murailles, mes enfants!"*

The Mexicans came in short rushes, firing wildly and then falling back. A wounded horse began screaming somewhere, the chilling sound rising above the cries of wounded Mexicans and Legionnaires.

"Well done," Danjou said as he continued to pace behind the wall. "We'll be relieved in time. Mark my words." He waved his wooden hand toward the east. "Aid will come."

They were almost the last words he spoke. Moments later there was a slapping sound and Danjou pitched face down, dead from the bullet of a sniper who had clambered to the roof of the farmhouse. Two Legionnaires, whirling, fired at the sniper and he plunged from the roof.

"Mes enfants!" Vilain, who outranked Maudet by only a day or two, stepped across the body of Captain Danjou. "I command you now. We may die, but we never will surrender."

In the stifling heat and choking dust the Mexicans rushed the walls again and again and strengthened their position in the farmhouse. Around two o'clock in the afternoon Vilain was killed and Maudet took command.

"Mes enfants!" he said hoarsely. "It is the same. Death before surrender!"

Soon afterward Milan rode forward under a white flag again and asked them to surrender.

Before Maudet could shout his refusal, a Legionnaire bawled an obscene answer that seems to be universally understood by men of all tongues.

By five o'clock only Maudet and 12 enlisted men still were standing. Others lay in the grotesque postures where death had struck them, with flies swarming on their bodies, while the wounded moaned piteously for water. Again Milan called on them to surrender, and again they refused.

The Mexicans attacked more furiously than ever, fighting their way into the courtyard through a breach in the wall. Standing alone in the breach, severely wounded, yet thrusting and lunging his bayoneted rifle, was Corporal Berg, a Jew who had lost his lieutenant's commission in the French Army after he quarreled with a superior officer. When he fell at last, the retreating Mexicans dragged him away.

Now it was six o'clock in the evening and only 5 men still were standing with Maudet. They were Corporal Maine, a thirty-two-year-old Frenchman; and Privates Katau, a Pole; Wenzel, a German; Constantin, an Austrian; and Leonhart, a Swiss. They had stripped the cartridge cases of the dead and wounded and only one round apiece was left them. Their Minié rifles were so hot from firing that the barrels burned their hands.

"Load," said Maudet. "At my command, fire. Then follow me through the breach. We'll end this with our bayonets."

They reloaded their rifles and Maudet licked his lips.

"Fire!"

As the sound of their fire died away, Maudet led them through the breach with bayonets fixed. He was on the point of the flying V as they raced into a dense mass of Mexican militiamen. So great was the force of their drive that they almost passed through the Mexican formation before they were overwhelmed and lost from sight by the sheer weight of the Mexicans who swarmed upon them.

Milan, galloping up on his horse, beat back his men with his sword as they flung themselves on the Legionnaires who were down, wounded, and disarmed.

Rarely did the Legion ever engage with as gallant an adversary as Milan, who thought the courage of the defenders at Camerone magnificent. Indeed, he became so enraptured with the fight at the farmhouse that he seems to have forgotten about the gold bullion he had set out to capture. In any event, when the caravan heard the sounds of firing ahead in the morning, it turned back and avoided capture. The Legionnaires paid with their lives for the French gold, which was saved.

All of the 6 Legionnaires who joined in the last charge were severely wounded. Milan had them placed on litters and carried to a Mexican hospital fifty miles distant. Of the 6, only Corporal Maine and Private Katau survived their wounds. Another who survived was Corporal Berg. Several of the 16 wounded men whom the Mexicans took captive in the courtyard after the last charge also lived. Despite the fact the Mexicans lost nearly 300 dead and as many wounded at Camerone, they treated their Legionnaire prisoners well and later exchanged them on a one-for-one basis.

At dawn the day after the battle Jeanningros marched into Camerone with a strong relief force and found it a smoking ruin. In the rubble he searched vainly for Danjou's body. It had disappeared. But, pushing aside a stone, Jeanningros found Danjou's wooden hand, stripped of its white glove and blood-stained. He felt, he said later, a sense of reverence, as if he had touched something holy. Throughout the long campaign in Mexico he carried Danjou's hand among his personal effects and took it back to Sidi-bel-Abbès with him. There it became a relic increasingly revered by Legionnaires with the passage of the years.

It would be pleasant to report that after Camerone the French command was so impressed by the Legion's fighting qualities as to transfer it out of the fever country. But there is little poetic justice and rarely a happy ending to mankind's trials by arms. More than a year passed and more than 1,200 Legionnaires were lost to fever, combat, and desertion before the Legion was transferred to the highlands north and west of Puebla.

Meantime Corporals Maine and Berg were commissioned second lieutenants soon after they were exchanged. Maine rose to a captaincy and had a distinguished career. Berg was not so lucky. He quarreled with a fellow officer again and was challenged to a duel. One account relates that the officer who challenged Berg was his old comrade, Maine, but the report appears spurious. In any event, one day at dawn Berg stepped onto a dueling ground where he was shot and killed.

The Legion's transfer to a better climate occurred after Bazaine succeeded Forey as commander in chief of the French forces in

Mexico. Bazaine never forgot the capabilities of the Legion. Because he released them from the swamps the Legionnaires took to calling him "that blue and red doll."

Employing the tactics he had learned under Bugeaud in Algeria, Bazaine, within months, brought at least the semblance of pacification to Mexico. It was arduous, ruthless work. It earned him the gratitude of Napoleon III—and the undying hatred of the majority of Mexicans. Bazaine was not a humanitarian philosopher; he was a soldier, trained in the hard world of the Legion and accustomed to following orders unquestioningly. While Juarez fought for democratic ideals, Bazaine fought for Napoleon III and his dupe Maximilian.

Although Bazaine had come a long way for a sergeant of the Foreign Legion, he still rankled with ambition. Sometimes it must have seemed that everyone but him had become a marshal of France —Saint-Arnaud, Canrobert, Bosquet, Forey, MacMahon, Pélissier. Pélissier with his carriage in the Crimea and his little dog that jumped over chairs! The Emperor had even settled a dukedom and a stipend of 100,000 francs a year on him. Sometimes Bazaine's only consolation was the thought that Soledad soon would join him in Mexico. Though her health had become delicate, they would live together here happily. And then came tragic news: Soledad was dead.

Eventually Bazaine must have heard the story that was gossiped in the salons and cafés of Paris. Yes, Soledad always had been coquettish, but the world didn't understand that surely she meant no harm. According to the cruel story, she had smiled at a man who had a jealous wife in the Comédie Française. She had written the man a foolish letter, which his wife had found. Angrily the jealous woman had mailed the letter to Bazaine and then told Soledad what she had done. Soledad, frantic, rushed to the Emperor. Who understood an indiscretion better than Napoleon III? Gallantly he ordered the mail for Mexico City halted. But it was too late; the ship had sailed, bearing the damning letter. Soledad went home and died by her own hand.

But the gossips said that Bazaine never saw the letter Soledad had written. In Bazaine's office in Mexico City there worked a lean, taciturn former Legion captain named Willette, who heard and saw all and kept his own counsel. Bazaine trusted Willette above all men. Willette burned the letter. It was no wonder everybody called him "the Padre." Several days later Willette told Bazaine that Soledad had died after a long illness. Then for weeks Bazaine locked himself within a silent grief.

In May, 1864, Maximilian and Charlotte finally landed in Veracruz. The slowness and vacillation that characterized the young would-be emperor had delayed their departure from Europe. A Legion company stood at attention in a pass beyond Puebla and watched the splendid caravan which bore them to Mexico City. The Legionnaires saw them: young, attractive, smiling happily upon an empire that did not, in fact, exist. Maximilian was talking animatedly and Charlotte gesticulating with her little hands. There was a pathos about their charm, an officer observed, as if he visualized the tragic ends to which their young lives were hastening. They entered Mexico City on June 10, riding over carpets of flowers to wild acclaim, and it never was clear to them why the mass of Mexican people did not want them to stay as benign rulers.

By that time the Legion, on Bazaine's orders, had been transferred to southern Mexico. Through jungles and among volcanic wastelands of splintered lava it pursued elements of the phantom army of the phantom leader Porfirio Diaz. It did more marching than fighting, more seeking than finding. Although it always had been exclusively an infantry organization, it proved adaptable to the conditions of the campaign. A unit of mounted Legionnaires was created for scouting. And when six small mountain guns somehow came into the Legion's possession, an artillery battery was formed.

In 1865 the Legion was transferred to northern Mexico and its battalions dispersed to press Juarez's guerillas toward the border. Bazaine's tactics seemed to be successful. Long forced marches and quick hard fights captured most of the Juarist strongholds.

After a march of three hundred miles the Legion's 2nd Battalion occupied Monterey, close to the border of the United States. It met no opposition; indeed, Monterey went *en fête* when the Legion marched in. There, for almost the only time during their adventures in Mexico, the Legionnaires found what they had anticipated when they sailed for the Western hemisphere. The wine was copious and good, the women lovely and complacent, the song uncontained.

The 2nd Battalion was no more religious than any other Legion unit. Precisely why the Battalion decided to attend Mass in Monterey is not clear, but apparently it was because the Spanish bishop announced that Legionnaires were forbidden to enter the Cathedral. Finding the Cathedral doors closed and barred to them, the Legionnaires threatened to blow them off the hinges. Attendants opened the doors and the Legionnaires filed in respectfully and bareheaded. Then they discovered that the priests had disappeared.

As the men and officers muttered to themselves, a private asked permission to speak to the commanding officer, Major Brian. Before becoming a Legionnaire, the man told Brian, he had been a Roman Catholic bishop. Absinthe had been his undoing, he confessed, but he had not been unfrocked; he had withdrawn from the church voluntarily and still was a priest. "Then celebrate the Mass," Brian ordered him. Donning vestments over his uniform, the man celebrated it with a moving dignity. Although the Legionnaires found it hard to believe he actually had been a bishop, they found it equally hard to believe that such an obviously devout man could tell a lie in church.

For a brief period life was so pleasant for the Legion in northern Mexico that many men wanted to stay. Desertions increased as they tried to slip across the border into the United States, but few appear to have gotten away safely. Nearly all were taken by Juarists or nomad Indians or perished in the vast wastelands of the Southwest.

One story has persisted, however. It is of dubious authenticity, the kind of story with which generations of Legionnaires have enjoyed frightening themselves when they talk about "the long arm" of the Legion that pursues a deserter to his grave.

One day in 1865 a young Swiss Legionnaire who spoke some English slipped away from his company and crossed the Rio Grande into the United States. Captured by Indians, he eventually escaped from them and reached a white settlement. Then he wandered east as far as St. Louis where he found employment with a railroad. Intelligent and industrious, he advanced rapidly with the line—always taking care to keep his identity a secret. Even when he fell in love and married a young American woman, he did not tell her that he had deserted the Foreign Legion in Mexico.

Twenty-four years after he deserted he was a happy, prosperous American citizen, the father of two daughters and a vice-president of the railroad line. He had, indeed, almost forgotten that he ever had been a Legionnaire. And then, in 1889, his wife and daughters begged him to take them to the Paris Exposition. Though reluctant to set foot in France, he was indulgent of his family and was certain no one could possibly guess that this bearded, prosperous American businessman ever had been a member of the Legion. He took his family to Paris. At the Exposition they were standing beside the Ferris wheel—in all its versions the story is specific about the Ferris wheel—when someone exclaimed behind him, "Legionnaire——!" He whirled, his heart pounding in fright, and recognized a graying man who had been an officer of his Legion company. Panic-stricken, the man pushed his family into seats on the Ferris wheel and leaped in beside them just before it began turning. When the man stepped to earth again, two gendarmes seized him. Under intense questioning by Legion officers, he finally broke down and confessed he had been Legionnaire——. His pleas for forgiveness were refused. Neither the United States Ambassador nor anyone else could help him. He was taken back to Algeria in irons and sent to the Legion penal battalion. His American family and friends never heard of him again.

Legionnaires tell the story with a straight face. And then the dramatists among them glance uneasily over a shoulder. . . .

Although Bazaine employed his Legionnaires and French troops effectively in "pacifying" northern Mexico, circumstances beyond their military control forced them to withdraw. Once the Civil War had ended, the United States Government was able to do more than lodge diplomatic protests at the grab by Maximilian and Napoleon.

It recognized Juarez as the rightful ruler of Mexico and sent General Philip Sheridan and a strong American force into the Southwest. Bazaine began withdrawing his troops southward, wishing at all costs to avoid a brush with American forces. Both Maximilian in Mexico City and Napoleon in Paris realized that their venture now threatened to lead to war with the United States.

In the general French withdrawal the 2nd Legion Battalion moved from Monterey to Parras, where it paid a costly price for its worship of the tradition of Camerone. In Parras, Major Brian learned from a Mexican informant that a small band of Juarists was quartered at Santa Isabella a few miles distant. Bazaine had given strict orders for a general withdrawal southward and specified that no unit was to venture alone into Juarist territory. But Brian believed he had a splendid opportunity to avenge the Legion's defeat at Camerone. He disobeyed orders.

Shortly after midnight on February 28, 1866, Brian led a Legion force of 7 officers and 188 men out of Parras toward Santa Isabella. But the information given him had been a bait. In the darkness of early morning he led his men into a trap set by the Juarists. Rifle and musket fire suddenly shattered the stillness in a narrow defile. Within five minutes Brian and 80 Legionnaires had been killed. Captain Moulinier took command and the Legionnaires tried to drive the Juarists from their ambush. But the counterattacks were of no avail. Except for one man who managed to escape and tell of the disaster, the entire Legion force was killed or captured.

Meantime Napoleon, harassed by European problems, realized that the Mexican venture was doomed to failure. In January, 1866, he informed Maximilian that he was going to withdraw his forces. Charlotte rushed back to Paris, where she pleaded and raged in vain for further aid. The strain became too much for her. She went insane and was taken to a château in Belgium where she remained for sixty years until death released her from madness.

In Mexico City, Maximilian was beside himself. Grief for his beloved Charlotte was mingled with rage at Napoleon and fear that he would be the laughingstock of Europe if he returned there. Yet the French withdrawal into the closing corridor between Mexico City and Veracruz went on slowly, inexorably. Bazaine begged the wretched man to leave with the army. Once Maximilian started to leave and then turned back, saying he could not bear to quit the country.

Although Bazaine realized that the military and diplomatic position of the French in Mexico had become untenable, he himself was of two minds about leaving. He would go, of course, because his Emperor had commanded him. He had at last been made a marshal of France and new responsibilities and honors awaited him when he returned home. On the other hand, his heart had brought him a hostage in Mexico.

For his experience long ago in Tlemcen had been repeated. At the age of fifty-four he had fallen in love with a girl seventeen years old. Her name was Pepita Peña. Like Soledad, she had a dark beauty, large eyes—and no money. This time there was no MacMahon to argue with him. Bazaine married Pepita, and Maximilian gave them the Buenavista Palace as a wedding gift.

Pepita did not want to leave Mexico, but she must, for a wife of Marshal Bazaine would have but a brief, unhappy life once the French forces left. Now the good life at Buenavista was drawing to a close and they had to go.

Slowly the evacuation continued. Maximilian had one last chance to leave. He hesitated—and then decided to stay. Bazaine, his young wife, and the last Legion battalion sailed from Veracruz March 12, 1867. Three months later Maximilian died before a firing squad.

9

End

of an Era

THE SECOND EMPIRE OF Napoleon III was dying in what nearly everyone took to be its moment of greatest triumph.

Ironically, its downfall began because Napoleon had erroneously believed that a unified Germany would contribute to the peace and stability of Europe. He encouraged the efforts of Prince Otto Leopold von Bismarck—and then the Prussian turned on him. Bismarck provoked Napoleon into declaring a war which the Emperor believed he could win. But the Chancellor was convinced Napoleon could not win it.

Only from the perspective of later years did the French understand why Bismarck was right. France's weakness lay in its army and in widespread public resistance to universal military training. The French people, desiring peace, relied too heavily on military leaders who had grown old and tired.

On July 19, 1870, Napoleon declared war on Germany. Before

many weeks had passed the weakness of France became apparent to astute critics.

The Foreign Legion was held in reserve in Algeria during the opening phases of the Franco-Prussian War. It had been forbidden to fight in metropolitan France since its founding, and there was a fear that German Legionnaires would not be loyal to the French.

French mobilization proceeded confusedly as reservists wandered about the country looking for their regiments. Some reservists in Alsace had to travel across France and the Mediterranean to obtain their equipment in Algiers before returning to Alsace to find their units. Enlisted men were not the only ones confused. A French general wired the War Office in Paris: "Arrived at Belfort. Cannot find my brigade. Cannot find my divisional commander. Do not know where my regiments are. What shall I do?"

Despite the confusion, the Army by August 1 had 270,000 men in Alsace and Lorraine on the eastern frontier. The Emperor, although suffering from a severe kidney ailment of many years that made it painful for him to sit a horse, took the field in person, leaving Eugénie as Regent in Paris. Although English and American public sentiment was largely with the Germans, nearly everyone believed in the myth of the French Army's invincibility and expected it to be victorious within a few weeks. First reports were, indeed, of French victories, and the Second Empire appeared on the verge of its greatest triumph.

But then the truth came filtering back from the front and the French people were thrown into increasing dismay. Their army's effort was unco-ordinated; each corps commander acted as if he were fighting the war by himself. Although the German divisions were far from highly efficient, they pressed their advantages. They out-flanked MacMahon at Wörth and soon had Alsace in their grip. A few days later Napoleon appointed Bazaine commander in chief with absolute powers over the French Army.

Later it was the verdict of French national opinion that Bazaine acted foolishly, even disloyally. A torrent of abuse was heaped upon him by an emotional people. Almost invariably a military defeat de-

mands a military scapegoat, and Bazaine became the scapegoat of
the Franco-Prussian War. In the opinion of some historians, however, he did not merit it.

After MacMahon's defeat at the Battle of Wörth, military wisdom
decreed the moving of the French armies closer to Paris. But Napoleon feared that such a withdrawal would result in the downfall
of his government. In bidding farewell to Bazaine near Metz, the
Emperor told him to withdraw east to Verdun—but no farther—
when he was able. In Bazaine's opinion his position would have been
no stronger at Verdun than at Metz. And in the fighting about Metz
he began to have grave doubts as to the capacity and morale of his
forces.

Among the charges leveled against him later was that, in the
battles around Metz, by pausing to direct the fire of a battery and
exposing himself so needlessly that he was almost captured by German cavalry, he acted like a regimental commander rather than the
commander of an army. Perhaps the charges were true. Yet Bazaine
simply was leading as he—and every other general officer in the army
—had been taught to lead in Algeria. The image of Colonel Conrad
rallying the Legion in Spain with cap aloft on a cane still was the
ideal. Bazaine's opponents maintain that when he fastened on
Metz, he was displaying inertia and an unwillingness to share the
responsibilities of the campaign with MacMahon. His proponents
say, on the other hand, that he had found his army incapable of the
offensive and felt his only hope was the defensive. "I thought," he
said later, "that if I gained time for the Army of Châlons to form,
it might be strong enough to come to our relief." Again, he was
thinking and acting as he had been trained to do in the Foreign
Legion. When too weak for the offensive, did one not hold out behind the walls and wait to be relieved? Had it not happened at
Miliana thirty years before?

MacMahon had been in the relief column that marched to
Miliana. And it was MacMahon who led the Army of Châlons, 120,-
000 strong, toward Metz. With MacMahon rode the Emperor, suf-

fering agonizing pain from kidney stones, his cheeks carefully rouged to hide his deadly pallor from the troops.

It was a forlorn hope, the last desperate act of inevitable tragedy. The French had fought as courageously as the Germans, but bravery was not enough. They had been outmaneuvered, outgunned, their command riven by jealousies and ineptitude. Now, while one German army drew a noose around Bazaine at Metz, another army advanced toward Paris on a fifty-mile front. Skirting the advancing German host by a northern route, MacMahon's army advanced uncertainly toward the relief of Metz.

When, by sheer chance, the Germans learned of MacMahon's move, they wheeled and began encircling him at the little fortress of Sedan. There, on September 1, the Second Empire crashed to defeat—not gloriously, except for one magnificent French cavalry charge, but with bickering and tears. MacMahon fell early in the day, wounded by shell fragments, and perhaps he was glad to be temporarily discharged from a command that had become intolerable to him. The general who succeeded him tried to organize a retreat, but he was relieved by another who bore secret orders from the War Council in Paris, countermanding any orders for withdrawal. The Emperor, knowing at last that all was lost, sought honorable death upon the field. Bewildered, racked with pain, he found his suicidal thrusts toward the German lines thwarted by aides intent on saving his life. At the very end of his career he was reduced to tears and pain and grief. His last command as Emperor was to raise the white flag over Sedan, and then he surrendered his army and himself. The Second Empire had fallen and the Third Republic was about to rise.

In Paris the Empress Eugénie escaped an angry mob thanks to the aid of her American dentist, who got her safely to Deauville. There he put her aboard the yacht of aged Sir John Burgoyne, the same Sir John who had counseled the Allies so foolishly at Sebastopol. After the Germans released Napoleon, he joined Eugénie in England, where they lived quietly for two years until his death. Later Eugénie built herself a villa at Cap Martin on the French Riviera and lived to see Sedan avenged by the Treaty of Versailles. She died in Madrid on July 11, 1920, in her ninety-fifth year, while visiting her favorite goddaughter, the Queen of Spain.

The German victory at Sedan did not mean the end of the war, however. While the Germans besieged Paris, Bazaine continued to hold out at Metz, where the presence of his army immobilized a Prussian force of 200,000. Although the Empire had fallen, Bazaine gave the Third Republic time to step into the breach and continue to fight in the ruins. Although a war had been lost, the self-respect of the French had been saved.

One of Eugénie's last official acts as Regent had been to authorize the formation of a Legion battalion of foreigners. This battalion, which had nothing to do with the Foreign Legion in Algeria, joined the Third Republic's newly forming Army of the Loire as the German tide washed around Paris and invested the city. The situation of the Third Republic in Tours was desperate. Every available man was enlisted, and on October 13 two battalions of the Foreign Legion finally were summoned from Sidi-bel-Abbès.

It was a tatterdemalion Army of the Loire which the veteran Legionnaires joined. Transplanted sailors marched at the side of Catholic volunteers with the emblem of the Sacred Heart upon their sleeves; old pensioners and semi-invalids were grouped under officers whose only military experience had been in quartermaster supply. The German high command scoffed contemptuously at them as a rabble.

And then the incredible happened. On November 9 the Army of the Loire attacked a German concentration at the village of Coulmiers, three miles from Orléans. The Legion battalions were in the van of the attack, German Legionnaires shouting mockingly at their fellow countrymen and then falling savagely upon them with the bayonet. At Coulmiers this so-called rabble did what the professional army had failed to do in Alsace and Lorraine: it hurled the Germans back. The Germans' confidence melted into near panic as they realized that the Army of the Loire might force them to raise the siege of Paris.

But the ironies of the war had not yet run their course. Bazaine, finally believing his position hopeless, surrendered Metz. His action freed the forces of Prince Frederick Charles and they hurried west. If Bazaine had held out one day longer at Metz, said Prince Frederick Charles, the Germans would have been forced to raise the siege of Paris.

It was a time of heartbreak and misery for the French people. Outclassed and outnumbered, the Army of the Loire was pressed back in heavy rains and sleet across the great plains of the Beauce. On December 4, north of Orléans, the Legion battalions finally turned and drove the Germans from the village of Cercottes with bayonets. Their action halted the German pursuit only briefly. A few days later the Legion battalions turned once more at the village of Chevilly and checked the German advance. In these two actions the Legion lost 210 men. But the Army of the Loire continued to retreat. Though the French cause was hopeless, the war had not yet ended.

The Legion and what remained of the Army of the Loire swung east with a vague hope of cutting German communications and possibly relieving Belfort, where the French still held out. An effort was made to transport the men east by railroad, but in the bitter winter cold the trains broke down and many froze to death in the cars. Starving, freezing, clad in rags, the survivors left the trains and tramped on east. Some came within sound of the guns of Belfort, but could not break through the German lines. At Besançon, near the Swiss border, the Legion lost its last battle of the war against the Germans. The surviving Legionnaires clung on in the vicinity while 80,000 broken French troops poured over the border into Switzerland in search of refuge.

It was the end at last. Paris, bombarded and facing starvation, was powerless. On January 26, 1871, the Third Republic accepted the armistice terms handed down by Bismarck and the Germans entered Paris. But a stranger and even more bloody battle awaited the remnants of the Legion before it returned to Algeria.

In the formation of the Third Republic, strong political sentiments divided Paris from the provinces. The peasant districts, disliking the fact that the Republic was prolonging the war, returned a majority of monarchist deputies to the Assembly, while Paris elected extreme Republicans and wished to fight on. Adolphe Thiers, who was selected as Premier, believed that the disarming and crushing of the National Guard of Paris was essential to the restoration of order. An effort to capture its artillery was fumbled, two generals were shot, and the Government fled from Paris to Versailles. On March 26 the people of Paris elected a revolutionary and socialist municipal council which took the name of "the Commune." While the German army of occupation looked on indifferently, Paris moved toward civil war against the Government of Thiers.

The workers of Paris, tough craftsmen and tradesmen who did not mind spilling their own blood or anyone else's, could raise 40,000 combatants in their National Guard. The forces of the Thiers Government were weak and had little stomach for fighting their way into Paris. The Foreign Legion battalions, which had proved to be absolutely loyal and the toughest fighters in the Army of the Loire, were hastily summoned to Versailles from Besançon. At the same time Thiers begged Bismarck to release veterans of the regular army who were prisoners of war in order that they could help crush the rebellious Commune.

On April 2 the Army of Versailles, spearheaded by the Foreign Legion, attacked and seized the suburb of Courbevoie. Acting under the orders of Thiers, the troops killed the prisoners they took in retaliation for the shooting of the two generals who had tried to seize the National Guard artillery. Civil war had begun.

The Commune began seizing hostages; the Archbishop of Paris and numbers of priests, nuns, and policemen were herded into jail. Meanwhile the Army of Versailles started bombarding the walls of the city without noticeable enthusiasm. MacMahon, who had survived a hundred crises simply by remaining a predictably blunt and straightforward soldier rather than by ever acting brilliantly, commanded the army. For once in his long career he was hesitant, however. It was one thing to defy the Kabyles at M'Chounech, the mines at Sebastopol, and the Germans at Sedan; it was quite another to defy the people of Paris. The teeming, twisting streets of the capital made him uneasy.

On Sunday evening, May 16, agents of Thiers opened some of the gates of the city and the Army of Versailles poured in. It is possible that if the forces had pushed ahead swiftly they could have occupied most of Paris by morning without much difficulty. But MacMahon and his staff were afraid of ambushes and their troops advanced slowly.

The Legion battalions came through Neuilly in the warm spring evening, swinging up the long avenue that leads to the Place de l'Etoile. Pausing there around the Arc de Triomphe, they gazed down the Champs toward the heart of Paris, where they heard the tap of drums and the murmur of preparations under the horse-chestnut trees. The men of the Commune had decided they could not resist effectively west of the Rue Royale and the Boulevard Saint-Michel; the heart of their resistance lay to the east of this line.

Dawn found the Legionnaires moving along deserted streets to the north of the Champs, rifles cracking at occasional snipers on rooftops. Behind them artillery was warming up, lobbing shells into concentrations of *communards*. Fires began to blaze in the heart of Paris, and by the time the Legionnaires reached the Rue Royale, they faced a wall of smoke and flames. Fire flickered on the dome of the Palais Royal, and minutes later it crashed in. The Ministry of Finance went up in flames, the records of decades rising in blackened sheets of paper which scattered over the city. Brigades of fire fighters who hurried behind the troops of Versailles arrived in time to save the Louvre.

The *communards* claimed that the shells of MacMahon's artillery started the blazes, but many of their own members were setting fires with a desperate and fanatic determination to destroy Paris. Before the end of the day the fighting had become as savage as any the Legion had experienced in Algeria. The people of Paris and the Army of Versailles became as blood-mad as Kabyles and Arabs. No quarter was asked or given on either side of the street barricades. Wounded soldiers and wounded shopkeepers were shot by their foes. Prisoners were lined against walls and fell in windrows before squads

106

of executioners. Women danced obscenely around the bodies of fallen soldiers in the smoke-filled streets.

Columns of the Army of Versailles groped out like two hands to seize the throat of Paris. The Legion was on the left, fighting ferociously across street barricades toward the hill of Montmartre. When at last it was taken, the entire right flank of Commune resistance was exposed. Coming down off Montmartre, the Legion attacked the Gare du Nord and drove the *communards* from railway cars and finally out of the station.

Raoul Rigault, the most fanatic and ruthless leader of the Commune, determined to hold out on the Isle of the City, the island in the Seine that had been the cradle of Paris. There he set fire to Nôtre Dame and the Palace of Justice, but his forces were driven out and both fires extinguished before much damage had been done. Rigault's house was surrounded. As he came out to surrender, he fell in a fusillade of rifle shots, crying, "Long live the Commune!" Then the infamous *pétroleuses,* wild, drunken women who had danced around the bodies of enemies of the Commune, stripped Rigault's body and pranced about it obscenely.

Yet Paris demanded still more blood. The Archbishop and other clerical hostages were brought down to the courtyard of La Roquette by the *communards* and lined against the wall while a mob screamed at them hysterically. A priest asked the Archbishop whether they would die as martyrs. Yes, the Archbishop replied calmly, because they would be killed as representatives of the Church rather than as individuals. After the first blast of rifle fire only the Archbishop was standing. On the next round he fell dead.

Resistance hardened in north and east Paris, where the Legion moved ahead slowly with veteran units of Zouaves. During the brief pauses in the crackle of rifle fire there sometimes rose from the billets of the occupying German troops the notes of accordions playing waltzes. The music did not soothe the nerves of the fighters. French soldiers and Legionnaires killed as mercilessly as the *communards* had slain their hostages. Occupied areas were searched carefully; any man found in National Guard uniform or wearing army boots or even bearing discolored marks on his right shoulder which might have been caused by a rifle butt was condemned to death without evidence by summary court-martial. Anyone who even looked like a leading *communard* was shot on the spot. At least one unfortunate tourist, a Dutchman, died in this manner. In some streets of east Paris the gutters literally ran with blood and the stench of putrefying flesh was stronger than the fragrance of spring lilacs.

One of the Legion's fiercest fights occurred among the warehouses and slaughterhouses of the Villette barge basin. There robust dockers and carriers fought from building to building to the last man. The Legionnaires pressed on east after mopping up the Villette and struck another hard pocket of resistance among the wooded glades of the public park of the Buttes-Chaumont. A couple of days later die-hard adherents of the Commune fought their last battle behind the walls and stones of the Père Lachaise Cemetery.

During the "Bloody Week" of the Commune at least 20,000 and possibly as many as 36,000 Parisians were slain in the streets of the city. Even the Reign of Terror during the Revolution had not equaled the casualties of the frightful days in 1871. The Army of Versailles lost less than 1,000 men. Once the Commune had been wiped out, Thiers moved out his troops quickly and left Paris to the German army of occupation. Two weeks later the Legion was sent back to Algeria.

The convulsion that racked France after its defeat by the Germans had a final spasm in the trial of Bazaine. After the fall of Metz, hysterical Frenchmen, seeking someone to blame for their defeat, decided that he was the culprit. He was vilified as having betrayed everyone—the Emperor, MacMahon, the Republic, the troops of his command—for a huge German bribe. The falsity of the charges is evident from the fact that he spent the rest of his life in poverty. But few cared to use reason in the mood of hysteria.

After Bazaine was released from a German prison he and his spirited wife, Pepita, and their three young children, settled in Switzerland near Geneva. There he pressed Thiers to let him re-enter

France and vindicate himself before a court of inquiry. Permission finally was granted in September, 1871. Bazaine took his family to Paris and vainly sought an army command in order to support them while the campaign of vilification mounted against him. Now he was blamed for everything, even the defeat of MacMahon at Sedan.

When formal charges were brought against him, he insisted on putting himself under house arrest in Versailles while Pepita lived in a nearby convent. Over the course of several months a massive document was prepared against him. Meanwhile MacMahon became the President of the Republic. Though he might have been expected to look tolerantly upon the plight of a brother officer, his Minister of War finally decreed that Bazaine should be tried by court-martial for premature capitulation of a fortress and surrender in the field.

Bazaine was sixty-two years old when he came to trial, but the strain under which he had been living made him look much older. During most of his seven weeks' trial his lined face was like an expressionless mask. Sometimes, however, the virulence of the prosecutor made him cover his eyes and often, at the end of a day of testimony, court attendants found that his feet had ripped the carpeting around his chair. On December 10, 1873, the prosecution and the defense made their concluding speeches and the court asked Bazaine if he had anything to add.

Rising, he said slowly and distinctly, "I wear two words: *Honneur et Patrie*. They have guided me through all my military life. I have never failed them either at Metz or elsewhere in the forty-two years I have loyally served France. I swear it here before Christ." Then court attendants led him away.

The verdict of the court was guilty. The expected sentence was death. Bazaine said calmly that he was ready. Pepita rushed to MacMahon's residence, stormed her way into his presence, and demanded to know if he intended to let her husband die. MacMahon replied that he did not. Although his ministers favored banishment from France for life, MacMahon insisted that his old comrade be sentenced to life imprisonment. At the last moment he was prevailed on to reduce the prison sentence to twenty years—the equivalent of life imprisonment to Bazaine, who would be sixty-three in a few weeks. At the last moment MacMahon decided that Bazaine need not undergo the degradation of being publicly stripped of his military rank and honors.

Bazaine was taken to the little citadel of Ile Ste. Marguerite, which lies off the Mediterranean coast midway between Cannes and Cap d'Antibes. There, in a prison built by Richelieu where the Man in the Iron Mask had been incarcerated for several years, Bazaine had two rooms on the battlements. The faithful Willette was still with him. Pepita came, too, bringing the children and trying to make a home on the lonely rock.

The view was lovely, but Bazaine was not the sort of man who could find solace in a view. He was a soldier, not a philosopher; he wanted involvement with life rather than contemplation of it. As his restlessness increased, he and Willette began reopening an old passage through the battlements. The jailer courteously admired the tomato garden they were cultivating, but they spent more time removing broken rocks from the battlements than in tending their tomato plants.

Pepita, who was only twenty-six, grew restless too. Taking the children, she went to Paris and managed to obtain another interview with MacMahon. Recalling the days when he and Bazaine had served together in the Legion, she beseeched the President of the Third Republic to release ex-Marshal Bazaine from prison. But MacMahon adamantly refused. Bazaine had told her that he would refuse. So now there was no recourse but to follow her husband's proposed escape plot.

Accompanied by a venturesome young Mexican cousin, Pepita took the children to Belgium and left them in a convent there. Then the young couple, disguised as a Castilian duke and duchess, went to Genoa and rented a yacht with the announced purpose of taking a pleasure cruise along the Riviera. Before sailing from Genoa, Pepita sent a cryptic message to the intermediary in Monte Carlo whom Bazaine had selected. He was a former Legionnaire, Captain Doineau, whom Bazaine had befriended years previously in Algeria when Doineau had been accused of murder. Time had not improved Doineau's fortunes; he was now a bored employee of the gas works in Monte Carlo. Hearing that Bazaine was a prisoner on Ile Ste. Marguerite, he had come out to visit him—and entered happily into the plot by agreeing to inform him of the time when Pepita and her cousin would help him escape.

The night of August 9, 1874, was cloudy. Bazaine, a prisoner of less than eight months, discussed astronomy with his jailer at dinner that evening. Then he retired early to his apartment, for Doineau had informed him the attempt would be made at dusk. Soon, through the murk of evening, a small steam yacht slowly approached the island and hove to. Willette, watching from the battlements, saw a small boat lowered and a couple cast off from the yacht. All was ready, he murmured to Bazaine. Did the Marshal still wish to go through with it?

Bazaine did not hesitate. Though he always had been courageous, he was undertaking his most hazardous adventure at the age of sixty-three. More than 300 feet of precipitous cliffs separated the battlements from the sea and Bazaine must entrust his heavy weight to a tenuous cord of luggage straps which Willette had sewed together. The two crept through the passage they had cleared in the battlements. Bazaine lashed one end of the line about his chest and Willette secured the other end to an iron bar. They shook hands silently and then Bazaine swung out into darkness. They never saw each other again.

Willette paid out the line slowly while Bazaine's feet groped for rests on the cliff. He lost his footing, swung out dizzily. Pepita glimpsed him dimly from the rowboat below and cried out in alarm. But Willette continued to pay out the line slowly from the battlements above and soon Bazaine found a foothold again. Moments after reaching the rocky shore, he was in the boat with Pepita and her cousin, who rowed quickly to the yacht.

By the time the jailer discovered the next morning that he was gone, Bazaine was stepping safely ashore in Italy with Pepita.

Bazaine's escape was the most sensational news story of the time.

The press roared angrily and politicians protested. Willette and Doineau were brought to trial and served a few months in prison. Then both disappeared, leaving no trace as to their whereabouts.

For many months, however, the world knew precisely where Bazaine was. First he and Pepita visited the Empress Eugénie and her son, the would-be Napoleon IV, who were spending a season in Switzerland. The Former Empress greeted him warmly; both she and Napoleon III, to the day of his death, had felt that Bazaine had done everything possible to save the Empire at Metz. Next Bazaine and Pepita went to Belgium to collect their children; then they were in Germany; and then in England. Above all, Bazaine sought vindication of his military record. Since the sword had failed him, he took up the pen, writing to anyone who would listen to him—and some who would not.

Midsummer of 1875 found him in Madrid, almost penniless, eking out a subsistence for his family from heaven knows what resources. The Spanish sun warmed him, as it always had, and he felt at home. He labored at a book which set forth the truth about his conduct as he honestly saw it, dedicating it to Queen Isabella II for whom he had fought with the Legion in Spain long ago.

The book was not a success. Nothing succeeded. Pepita did not like Spain and returned to Mexico. But Bazaine never could return there. He lingered in Madrid, a lonely man walking the side streets, living with his memories. Not all of them were bitter. On January 6, 1888, he wrote a friend in Paris about an officer who had testified against him at his court-martial: "The past is dead, as the Arabs say, and all is forgotten. Give him a sincere handshake from me in token of my friendship."

In the following September, when he was seventy-seven, he was found dead in the scantly furnished room where he lived alone. His sons and a few acquaintances followed his body to the foreign cemetery.

His former Legion comrade, MacMahon, outlived him by five years and was accorded one of the most magnificent funerals ever held in Paris.

10

Sahara

THE FIERCEST AND MOST POWERFUL ENEMY the Foreign Legion ever helped to vanquish was a phenomenon of nature. It was the Sahara, immense, mysterious, and awesome.

Many decades passed before the French and their Foreign Legionnaires began to try to penetrate the mysteries of the desert which stretches like a vast inland sea from the Atlas to the palmyra trees of Black Africa and from the Atlantic to the Nile. While the French proceeded with their conquest of coastal Algeria, the desert waited. It affected men according to their diverse natures, beckoning some and repelling others, arousing curiosity or fear, but rarely creating indifference in the minds of those beguiled by Africa.

The Legion first glimpsed the true Sahara in 1844. That spring a battalion struck south from Constantine through the wild Jebel Aures Mountains. Its mission was the familiar one of subduing warring tribes. But the Legionnaires appear to have been carried away by the grandeur of the country as they hauled themselves up towering cliffs of sandstone and forded rushing wadis and plunged through green valleys. They went on farther than was essential to their mission.

One day, as their column wound through a twisting gorge, the advance guard halted. As the men began to shout excitedly, those behind them pressed forward and saw that the gorge had opened. Before them stretched a limitless panorama of blazing tawny sand and rock; they seemed to be gazing into the heart of the continent which still was unknown. Lyric words did not come readily to Legionnaires, but music did. A man raised his trumpet to his lips and from it blasted sweet high notes. Another trumpeter joined him, and then the drummers began to beat the long roll. Soon the battalion musicians, grouping together, were sending the tune of a marching song into the Sahara.

For they had come to the place which today is called El Kantara, the Mouth of the Sahara. The French painter Eugène Fromentin has described it as "a sudden passage from one season to the next. The curtain lifts over the gate of El Kantara and at once you are face to face with the Orient. On the one side, toward the north, the mountainside is black, or the color of rain; on the south side it is the color of good weather."

The next day the Legionnaires turned back reluctantly.

While the Sahara waited, the work of knitting the bonds of colonial empire continued to the north.

The downfall of Napoleon III was a signal to Arab chieftains in Algeria to foment a general uprising against the French. Savage warfare flared across the plains and mountains in 1871 and 1872. The Legionnaires, who had scarcely recovered from the bloody battles of the Paris street barricades, were thrown into equally fierce struggles against rebellious Arabs.

Among those coming to Algeria with the Legion was a volunteer who claimed to be an American named Robert LeFort. Actually he was the Duke of Chartres, a grandson of King Louis Philippe. Exiled from France and living in England, he had answered the last desperate call of the Empress Eugénie for volunteers and had enlisted before the fall of his hereditary enemy Napoleon III. A brave and capable soldier, the Duke of Chartres was content to fight as a sergeant in the service of the country which had banished his family.

From his service as a Legionnaire on the Algerian frontier the Duke developed a lifelong enthusiasm for the Foreign Legion. His recollections, passed on to his grandson many years later, give vivid portraits of Legion life in those years.

The Duke, like so many members of crownless European royalty, seems to have been of a romantic turn of mind. Certainly he instilled in his grandson, Prince Aage of Denmark, an impression of a Foreign Legion that was a veritable citadel of romance. Bronzed men, brave and true, princes and commoners together, all good fellows longing for battle. And always, in the Duke's imagination, came the call of the Sahara beyond the mountains.

It cannot have been precisely so, however. Certain facts about what was called "the Great Arab Uprising" belie some of the Duke's memories. It was a dirty war, marked by extreme cruelties on both sides. The French stamped out the rebellion ruthlessly. Troops poured from France to Algeria, and the German victors who occupied Paris were glad to speed them on their way, for they preferred to see French energy expended outside of Europe. Within a few months French regulars and Legionnaires received the submission of tribe after tribe, while those who would not surrender were chased over the borders into Tunisia to the east and Morocco to the west.

Then the French Government began to concentrate its energies on colonizing Algeria as it had not in the preceding forty years. Hundreds of thousands of acres of land seized from the Arabs in punishment for their rebellion were offered cheap to French colonizers. A growing wave of colonists came from Alsace and Lorraine, which France had lost under the German peace terms. Colonists from other countries followed.

As uneasy peace settled on the north, columns of Legionnaires and regulars began to grope out into the fringes of the Sahara. Their purposes were vague, their accomplishments nebulous. Sometimes a mission was "punitive," against a pillaging tribe of the Ouled Sidi Cheikh or the Shamba. Sometimes a column was assigned the duty

115

of guarding engineers who were making a halfhearted survey of some areas of the country. Sometimes it appears that a unit went out prompted by little more than the curiosity of its commanding officer about the nature of the Sahara.

The ancient Greeks and Romans knew far more about the Sahara than did Europeans in the mid-nineteenth century. Thus when the German explorer Heinrich Barth set out on his great trans-African journey in 1850, he took with him a copy of Herodotus, the Greek historian of the fifth century B.C., as his only reliable reference work.

The Legionnaires on the northern reaches of the Sahara knew little or nothing about the white explorers who had suffered and perished in its wastes. They had heard fragmentarily of the great trading empire which the Arabs had created, but they understood little of its scope.

This far-flung empire, a loose confederation of princes, sheiks, and merchants, at times more powerful than the greatest banking houses of Europe, sprawled from Genoa and Venice to the Bight of Benim, from Morocco to Madagascar and the islands of the Indian Ocean. It fattened on insatiable human appetites: on Black Africa's appetite for salt; on Zanzibar's for slaves; on Algeria's for skins; on Europe's for gold, ivory, bright feathers, spices, rare scents, and woods. The heart and crossroads of the empire was the Sahara with its tenuous camel trails.

One could trace the trading operation by beginning with almost anything marketable in Africa, but salt was the best clue now that the West Coast ports had been closed to slaving. At Taudeni, midway between Morocco and the beginning of the forests, and at Bilma, midway between Lake Chad and the Libyan Fezzan, were Africa's greatest salt pans. In these places salt was cut from the desert in huge glistening blocks and shipped by camel along trails which wound north, south, east and west. One of the most important trails of the vast network was the six weeks' journey from Taudeni to Timbuktu on the fringe of Black Africa. Twice a year, in March and September, a huge caravan of 10,000 to 12,000 camels, called the *azalai,* laden with salt, muskets, and cheap cottons, left Taudeni for Timbuktu. It returned four or five months later, bearing gold, ivory, and feathers for Europe, and manacled columns of black slaves for the East. The trails forked out from Taudeni and Bilma in the seemingly endless trading process. The caravans which trudged to the ports of Algeria and Morocco returned with Birmingham muskets, bright bolts of Lyons cottons, cheap Dresden beads. The profits were as enormous as the hazards. Fortunes rose and fell in this trading empire as quickly as on the stock exchanges of the Western world. Alliances were formed and dissolved in murder and tribal wars.

Less by planning than instinct the vast fluctuating confederation cloaked its operations behind the veil of the Prophet. As Christianity accompanied Western commerce, so did the traders of the East take with them the precepts of Mohammed. To Western eyes it was a cruel and fanatic religion that would not brook even mild inquiry. In its effort to maintain its way of life, it bade its followers destroy the Christian dogs. By sadistic torture or swift murder the Arabs wiped out many of the first Western explorers of the Sahara. Although they acted in the name of their religion, they were often intent on preventing Westerners from learning the secrets of Eastern trade.

It took decades of involvement with the desert before the Foreign Legion began to understand its history, its economy, its uncertain laws of survival. The first Legion columns which probed into the Sahara felt, according to some of their members, like men who had come to another planet.

They found, first of all, heat such as they did not believe they possibly could survive. It strikes one suddenly, like a blow on the head, pricking the eyes like fire, making every movement a torture. A man thinks he cannot live until that moment when the sun goes down. Yet when it sinks in its mauve haze, he may find within a few minutes that his teeth are chattering. The temperature may drop 20 to 30 degrees in ten minutes and usually the temperature at midnight is about 80 degrees lower than that at noon. A Legionnaire who had suffered through a day of torturing heat and left a can of water outside the warmth of his tent found the next morning, to his astonishment, that a skim of ice had formed on it.

One of the first Legion companies to venture into a rocky area of the Sahara sprang to arms in alarm at sundown one evening. From all sides of its bivouac came a sharp crackling, like a salvo of hundreds of rifles. The Legionnaires searched the growing dusk in vain for sign of an enemy. What they had encountered was a phenomenon of rocky areas of the Sahara: a sudden change of temperature makes stones split and crack and the noise reverberates in the silence like rifle fire.

The Legion's early encounters with the desert resulted in experiments with its uniform. In the hellish heat of the days it seemed absurd for a man to wear a long, heavy coat. When some cast off their coats, however, they soon found that they were exhausted on the march more quickly than men who wore their long capotes. They discovered what the desert Arabs had learned centuries previously: if a man dressed too lightly, the wind dried his sweat and the salt of his body was evaporated quickly, weakening him. So the Legion retained its long coat, though a Legionnaire took pains to obtain an outsize that fitted him almost as loosely as an Arab's cloak. The white neckcloth was attached to the cap to protect a man's neck from the beating sun. White duck trousers, such as the old Legion had worn in Spain, replaced the baggy red woolens—and white quickly became a dirty gray. Units in the desert also adopted the Arab *shech,* a muslin wrap to cover the face in sandstorms.

Besides heat and cold, an arch enemy was wind—the hot blast of the simoon that parches and withers life, cracking lips and blistering the skin with stinging sand. A Sahara sandstorm was a more terrifying experience than an attack by Arabs. Thousands of Legionnaires have endured such storms and hundreds have perished in them. The experience of Alfred Perrott-White, an Englishman who served in the Legion in this century, is like that of countless others. Describing his first encounter with a sandstorm on a desert-training march of forty miles, in which he served as an advance scout, Perrott-White said:

About three o'clock I noticed a change in the weather. The air had become heavy, without a breath of wind. The sky lost its blueness and had a coppery tinge along the horizon. The heat waves made it difficult to see my companions, and the mirages were numerous. . . .

At four o'clock I guessed that we were about six miles from our objective, provided the adjutant's compass was in good order. I was not sure about that. Most of the Legion compasses I had worked with could not be called reliable.

Suddenly I realized the weather had changed for the worse. A wind had sprung up accompanied by a peculiar moaning sound that made me feel uneasy. It was a shock when I looked across to my left and found I could no longer see the adjutant; the haze was too thick.

I paused for a moment to get my bearings and decide what to do. I could still see the sun, now blood red in the thickening blur of the wind-blown sand. Should I carry on to the oasis, the general direction of which I knew, or should I work across and link up with the adjutant?

I never did make up my mind. In an incredibly short time the wind rose to a shrieking fury, so strong that I could not stand upright against it. It became dark as night while the almost solid, wind-driven sand lashed at my face. It was now too late to do anything except lie flat on the ground and cover my head over with my *shech*. The heat was almost overpowering and I felt that if I did not drink I would die, but it was impossible to drink just then. Exposing my face to the driving sand would have skinned me in an instant. Every few minutes I had to raise up a little to heave the sand off of my body to avoid being buried. . . .

Seven hours passed before I felt the wind pressure letting up, and the storm ceased as suddenly as it started. It had been dark for some time, and soon I could see the stars shining through the settling dust haze. I looked at my watch. Midnight.

By good fortune Perrott-White found the fellow Legionnaire who had been serving as an advance scout with him and the adjutant. He was buried in sand up to his waist and could not move until Perrott-White dug him out. Together they managed to make their way to the oasis. Not all of the thirty-eight Legionnaires following them were as fortunate; two were trapped by the blowing sands and tribesmen caught them. All that their searching fellow Legionnaires found were two naked bodies, emasculated and horribly disfigured.

Generation after generation of Legionnaires learned with surprise that the Sahara is not totally sand. In fact, only about one-seventh of its three million square miles is composed of shifting, rippling dunes. The major part of it is a weird jumble of flinty plains and jagged, boulder-strewn mountains and hills.

Many years passed before Legionnaires penetrated to the heart of the Sahara, to the Tanezruft and the Hoggar.

The Tanezruft is a level, gravel-strewn plain 250 miles wide, where not a blade of grass grows. Today it is crossed by the great North-South Road along which truck convoys highball in the night. But in years past a man had to cross it by camel—and a camel could make the journey only after it had been specially fattened and only if it could endure a fast of seven or eight days.

The journal of a young Legion officer, Lieutenant Cortier, who crossed the Tanezruft in 1905, reflects the despairing numbness that overwhelms one in the unending monotony of the desert.

"My first encounter with the Tanezruft left me full of wonderment," wrote Cortier. "Here at last was a place where one could think, gather one's thoughts, analyze them, where indeed one had nothing else to do but look inward."

Gradually, however, depression settled on him. His words expressed the mood of innumerable Legionnaires who lived in the solitude of the Sahara when he wrote:

"Once again the day's route unrolled itself before you, sad, immensely sad, on the eternal lustreless ground and under the gray sky. The hours lengthened and dragged on desperately slowly while the mind wandered off, reliving old memories, thinking over and over again thoughts already mulled a thousand times, clutching at all memories of the past and all the hopes of the future. Little by little, the emptiness of earth and sky created an emptiness in the mind as one went on through this dreadful solitude, broken, heavy of heart and with unseeing eyes."

To the east of the Tanezruft lies an even more terrifying area of the Sahara, the Hoggar, which Legionnaires reached eventually. It is a mass of writhing mountains and tortuous gorges about 300 miles long and 200 miles broad where live the fiercest warriors of the Sahara and one of the strangest people on earth, the Tuareg.

One enters the Hoggar by an intestine-winding path between sheer walls of basaltic rock. According to the time of day, the mountains leap high above the traveler in the colors of fire or of smoke. Orange, yellow, and red by morning light, they turn violet and mauve toward sundown. Over the course of thousands of years the keening winds of the Sahara have shaped the peaks of sandstone and basalt into flawed towers and minarets, into a torment of broken hands and twisted arms, as if recording some eons-old agony of the earth.

When Legionnaires encountered the Tuareg of the Hoggar, they came face to face with the most savage, the most diabolically clever fighters they ever faced in Africa.

As the Legion came to know the Sahara, it learned to cope with the torments of heat, cold, wind, solitude, and fanatic tribesmen. And it became obvious that the secret of survival in that vast wasteland, the giver of life, the matter that determined the trade routes and the source of the precarious tribal way of life was water.

The desert rats, those Legionnaires who for some reason preferred duty in the Sahara to any other place, usually accepted the Arabs' belief that a huge and mysterious subterranean lake is the source of the desert's water supply. Few, if any, geologists agree with them. But the desert rats, who learned to live and think like Arabs, asked questions that are difficult to answer.

Why is it that most Saharan water holes contain catfish? How does it happen that the easiest thing to find in the desert is the fossil of a fish? And why, when rare rainfall sends flash floods hurtling down the dry wadis, should they abound with a species of small tropical fish which disappear as mysteriously as they appear? Where do they come from and where do they go? And, say now, would the roots of the tamarisk bush be 100 feet long if they were not reaching for the mysterious underground lake?

In discussion of such myth and lore Legion desert rats have been known to while away days and nights.

But there is no myth about the fact that water does rise to the surface of the Sahara in hundreds of places. Water creates the oases, and the oases sustain life and determine the course of the camel routes. Trade and war, life and death, all were centered for centuries on the oases of the Sahara.

There are hundreds, perhaps thousands, of oases, some with palms two centuries old. They vary from a few trees about a damp hole to the two million palms which thrive around the artesian wells of the great Tuggart region. The palm sustains the life of the Saharan nomad. From it he obtains his principal food, dried dates; its fibers furnish his ropes, his fats, much of his clothing. His wives even obtain their cosmetics from powdered date stones.

The Legionnaires found that nearly every oasis was a center of tribal life, whether a few tents or a white-walled village. In each a wanderer of the desert was made welcome, provided he came as a Mohammedan and a friend. There he exchanged gossip and rumor, and normally found peace, refreshment, and prayer.

But there was little peace in the oases of the northern and central Sahara in the spring of 1881. Tribes took up arms against the French again in a widespread rebellion. At the time it was believed they rose because French troops were busy with the occupation of Tunisia. More recent evidence indicates, however, that the rebellion had another motivation.

The growing French overseas empire finally had come into conflict with that loose and nameless confederation which was the great African trading empire. One searches in vain today for evidence that Paris realized the extent of that powerful trading empire. What the Parisian bankers and government officials saw was the opportunity of "bringing 100 million black customers within reach of French trade influence." Thus the Chief Engineer of the Ministry of Public

Works, Duponchel, phrased it in his report recommending the construction of a railway across the Sahara to link Oran with Black Africa. But the Eastern trading combine had an acute intelligence system; word of the plans flashed to Genoa and Venice and on to the seat of the empire's power in Tripoli, as Libya then was called.

It appears now that powerful elements of the trading empire, alarmed by the prospect of economic competition, made a concerted effort to halt further French expansion into the Sahara. Gunrunners in their pay smuggled improved models of rifles and large stores of ammunition from Europe into North Africa. Agents in their pay fanned out along the camel trails, inciting tribal chieftains and supplying them with arms.

Ironically, the expansionist ambitions of the French were thwarted, at least for a time, by a people who were themselves enemies of the trading empire—the Tuareg of the Hoggar. It was the Tuareg, riding out of their wild mountain citadel, who harried the great trading caravans between Taudeni and Timbuktu and exacted tribute from tribes hundreds of miles distant. No stranger who entered the Hoggar ever had returned.

Although they numbered no more than 40,000 or 50,000 people, they made up in ferocity for what they lacked in numbers. A Targui (singular for Tuareg) warrior stood more than six feet tall and bore a shield of dried gazelle skin, which was almost his own height. He wore a high white turban, a wide blue flowing cloak, and his lean features were covered with a blue veil to the lids of his dark, piercing eyes. A sword, a dagger, a musket or rifle, and a seven-foot spear, so light that it quivered in the wind, were his arms. His habits among his own people were civil, though marked by extreme sexual curiosity and exhibitionism. But when he plotted against an enemy, he employed poison and a diabolical imagination. And when he fought, he was unmatched for savagery.

Old hands in Algeria were aghast at the proposal for a trans-Saharan railroad so casually put forth by the Government of Charles de Freycinet in Paris, which had sufficient troubles in metropolitan France without taking on more in North Africa. They were even

123

more aghast at the choice of the man who was to lead an expedition in quest of the best route. He was Lieutenant Colonel Paul Flatters, who was fifty-one years old; a taciturn, melancholy man, he bore the reputation of being naïve and displaying poor judgment.

Flatters decided to lead his expedition south to Timbuktu by way of the Hoggar, despite a warning letter he had received from the ruler, or Amenokal, of the Taureg, a man named Ahitagel whom no European ever had seen. In his message Ahitagel wrote Flatters:

"We have received your letter. We have read it and understood it. You ask us to open the road to the South for you. We will not open it. . . . Try the other roads, the one that goes from Ghat to the Sudan and the other from the Tuat. They are better. We have neither cities nor villages. We have only the wadis and the tents. . . ."

The force which left Ouargla on December 4, 1880, under Flatters consisted of 300 camels, 10 French, 47 native Algerian *tirailleur* troops armed with Le Gras rifles, and 32 caravaneers. Nearly all of the *tirailleurs* and caravaneers were Shamba, a small, tough people who still are the most durable travelers of the Sahara. It was said that if a Shambi ever became lost in the desert, he simply covered his head with his cloak, turned around three times, and then invariably set off in the right direction.

Among the French most experienced in the life of the desert was Sergeant Jacques Pobeguin of the Foreign Legion, who was on detached service with the expedition. A lean, tough Breton who had taught himself Arabic, Pobeguin was skeptical about the purpose of the expedition and Flatters' capacity to lead it. As the long caravan entered regions never before seen by a European, Pobeguin's skepticism grew.

On February 13, 1881, as the expedition coiled across the vast, flinty Plain of Amadror, the figures of men riding camels loped out of the mirage ahead. They were thirty Tuareg warriors and they were armed to the teeth. But they made the sign of peace and their leader, a chieftain named Attici, rode forward with another letter from his uncle, Ahitagel. It was a strange message, addressed to "Sheik Flatters," warning of dangers ahead yet concluding, "But take this road. If something happens to you, you will know it."

Four of the Tuareg band remained to guide the expedition on its way, while the others rode off. Slowly the expedition wound on, now strung out and then bunched in a reptilelike crawl across the wasteland toward the Hoggar. Pobeguin was uneasy; his Legion training made him deeply concerned over Flatters' refusal to put out forward and flank scouts. Pobeguin had made a close friend of a *tirailleur* private named El Madani. A bandy-legged little Shambi with the nose of a hawk and the mottled skin of a leopard, El Madani had excellent military sense and worried, as Pobeguin did, over Flatters' naïve lack of precautions.

On the afternoon of the fifteenth they entered the blue and gray shadows of the Hoggar. As the tall basaltic peaks towered above them, it seemed that everyone except Flatters had a sense of alarm or depression. The next morning one of the Tuareg guides reminded Flatters that his water reserves were low and told him there was a well about two hours' distant. He pointed into the mountains of the Hoggar.

Flatters hesitated only briefly. Then he issued his orders. He and four of the French would go ahead with the guides. All the camels of the caravan, carrying only empty waterskins, would follow them. They would be closely supported by Sergeant Dennery and fifteen *tirailleurs*. El Madani and five men would post themselves midway between the base camp and the water hole to maintain communications. Incredulously El Madani saw that Flatters did not protest when one of the guides left his party and disappeared into the mountains in another direction.

It happened quickly. Dennery saw it from the lip of the valley where Flatters, the four Frenchmen, and several camelmen led the beasts to the well. Suddenly there came the long lugubrious beat of *tobols*, the Tuareg war drums, and the guides took to their heels. At almost the same instant a wave of blue-clad Tuareg, bent low in their camel saddles, charged hell-for-leather from the opposite end of the valley. Dennery and his men plunged down the hill, but the en-

125

counter was over before they could come within rifle range. Swords flashed and the heads of Flatters and the other Frenchmen rolled beside the well. In the melee the camels of the expedition panicked, kicking their heels, raising a cloud of dust. Through the dust rode a blue wave of Tuareg with spears leveled. Within minutes Dennery, too, was dead and his men scattered.

As soon as El Madani heard the *tobols* and the crackle of rifle fire, he sent a messenger back to the base camp and dashed forward with the other men. From the lip of the valley where Dennery had stood, El Madani saw what had happened and knew instantly that the camels were the only thing they could hope to salvage. But the brutes had gone wild and all El Madani's knowledge of how to handle them was of no avail. They were rounded up by the Tuareg, who greeted such captured wealth with ecstatic cries.

El Madani deployed the survivors and they retreated toward the base camp in good order. Wounded, hysterical camelmen stumbled among the *tirailleurs,* shrieking of the scenes they had witnessed. The Tuareg had sliced open the back of one of their friends and clamped a great iron ring into his shoulder blade and then dragged him away by it. Over the head of another captive the Tuareg had forced a wet leather skin which the sun would shrink, causing him slowly to suffocate.

Lieutenant Dianous and twenty *tirailleurs,* rushing from the base camp, reached El Madani and the survivors early in the afternoon. Dianous realized that the situation was crucial. They were 750 miles deep into the Sahara; without camels their plight was hopeless. With thirty-three men, Dianous marched into the mountains in search of the animals.

In a narrow defile the column ran into murderous rifle fire. Dianous tried every tactic he had been taught: infiltration, flanking movements, a headlong charge. All were in vain against the Tuareg. Despairing, the survivors retreated to the base camp.

Now the expedition numbered five Frenchmen, fifty-one *tirailleurs* and camelmen combined—and not one camel. Dianous was its leader. The other surviving French were Pobeguin; Santin, a civil engineer; Flatters' servant, Brame; and the cook, Marjolet. Dianous invited his fellow Frenchmen into his tent that evening and asked their opinions on what should be done. He also invited El Madani; even though he was a Shambi and only a private of *tirailleurs,* he had fought wisely and heroically that day.

They argued long and heatedly. Pobeguin, talking like a belligerent Legionnaire, wanted to go back into the Hoggar and fight for the camels. Santin, a man who abhorred violence, wanted to return to Ouargla as quickly as possible. Brame and Marjolet were incoherent with fright. Dianous appeared uncertain what to do. At last he asked El Madani's opinion.

El Madani was embarrassed. He was accustomed to accepting orders instead of proposing them. He spoke slowly, hesitantly. Like his friend Sergeant Pobeguin he understood that they could not travel far in the desert without camels. But, in his humble opinion, they simply did not have the strength to wrest their camels back from the Tuareg. True, some of the men were wounded. True, not even a healthy man could hope to cross the desert on foot. But, if Allah pleased, there was nothing they could do but try.

At dawn the next morning, February 17, they turned back north. Each man carried a rifle, ammunition, a blanket, extra sandals, and as much water, rice, and dried meat as he could manage. They were beginning the most ghastly retreat ever undertaken in the Sahara.

Dianous was a better soldier than Flatters: he put scouts ahead and on the flanks of his column. On the third day a flanking scout rushed back to him, gasping, "The *rezzou!* The Tuareg are following us!"

Dianous followed the scout to a rocky spur and what he saw made him catch his breath. Not far out on the Amadror Plain ambled a long camel column of blue-coated Tuareg. Dianous counted 200 of them, riding at ease parallel to the French column, their spears and rifles glinting in the sun. Their design was apparent. The Tuareg would keep pace with the retreating men, stalking them to the last moment of exhaustion. All the choices lay with the mobile Tuareg; they could spring their trap when and as they pleased. The French column had no choice but to march on into oblivion.

So the Tuareg added fear to the agonies of heat and thirst and hunger and exhaustion and bleeding, pus-suppurating feet. El Madani observed that Dianous seemed to resign himself to death from the moment he glimpsed the shadowing, blue-veiled Tuareg. But Pobeguin did not. Pobeguin gave the column heart and spirit. He ranged along the column, smiling and sometimes croaking a bit of a strange Foreign Legion tune. He kept a sharp eye on the water supplies and fixed the times when a man could swallow a few drops of precious water, as it was done in the Legion.

"You," Pobeguin would growl good-naturedly to a stumbling *tirailleur*. "Is is true, as I've heard, that a *tirailleur* can only march on his backside aboard a camel? A *tirailleur* is no match for a Legionnaire. To a Legionnaire this is just a little stroll."

Again, Pobeguin would say to a lagging Shambi camelman, "There's never been a Shambi in the Foreign Legion, but if you keep up the pace, I promise I'll enlist you and a dozen Shamba in the First Regiment of Strangers."

El Madani secretly admired Pobeguin and wished that he could emulate him. But he had no way with words. He could only express himself with deeds—and he did have a way with camels. On the day he glimpsed a camel to the west, in the opposite direction from the shadowing Tuareg host, El Madani thought his senses had left him. He halted and covered his face with his cloak and turned around three times, but when he opened his eyes the camel still was there. He asked Dianous' permission to leave the column, promising to return that evening.

He did return, leading not one but four camels. They had run wild from some previous caravan and were nearly as hungry as El Madani. He tamed them with a few handfuls of his precious supply of rice and led them back to the bivouac with bits of rope he carried in his pack. Men who had thought they were too tired to stir, leaped to their feet, shouting praise of El Madani. Eeee, long live El Madani, the tamer of camels!

Surely the Prophet himself in all his wisdom never had faced a more vexing problem than this: whether to kill a camel and eat him, or keep a camel and let him bear your burden through the heat of the following day. The French, with their talent for compromise, resolved the problem. Two stringy, bony camels were killed and eaten; two stringy, bony camels were preserved for a few days to carry Santin and Marjolet, who could not walk another step.

For five days they stumbled through a hellish rocky country covered by a film of volcanic ash which stuck in the throat. And on March 1, El Madani spoke to Dianous. In ten or eleven days, he said measuredly, they would reach the wells of Amguid. There was their only hope of water, rest, and perhaps food. But they would have to fight for it. For surely the Tuareg would attack them as they approached the oasis.

On March 4, one of the scouts stalked and killed a small wild ass. Belcacem, the butcher of the expedition, who somehow had retrieved Colonel Flatters' huge sword and wore it slung over his shoulders, cut up the animal into fifty-six portions and the men wolfed down the stringy meat ravenously. The next day their only food was a small cactuslike plant which the Shamba called edible.

By the morning of March 8, El Madani estimated they were about twenty-five miles south of Amguid. But he knew that not all of them could last it out. They were at the end of their strength, stumbling on weakly, leaving a trail of blood behind them from their broken feet. And then came the dreaded cry: "The Tuareg!" Weak though they were, they leaped to Dianous' command and formed a skirmish square.

Three men on camels streaked over a dune toward them and halted just beyond rifle range. Dianous ordered El Madani to question them. The riders told him they were not Tuareg but tribesmen from the Great Erg who pitied them. El Madani did not believe them when they said they would return the next morning with food and then rode away.

During the night the column crept on to a small water hole which a scout had found in a dry wadi bed. In the dawn of the following morning they saw that the Tuareg had drawn closer in the east. They sat on their camels in a long line, watching, waiting for something, motionless silhouettes against the rising sun. A trick of some sort was in the making, said El Madani. And then, while the Tuareg watched and waited, the three riders who had approached the column the day previously, raced toward them from the west. Without pausing, they tossed three bundles toward the column and then wheeled and loped away. It was a trick, said El Madani. Why did the watching Tuareg not try to stop them?

But few paid any attention to his warning. The bundles were greasy dried dates, and the men fell upon them hungrily, stuffing them into their mouths. The Frenchmen, who were boiling water from the wadi hole, dropped their share of the dates into the pot. El Madani begged them not to eat the dates, but they scoffed at him and began popping the cooked dates into their mouths.

Suddenly Belcacem, the butcher, uttered a piercing scream and sprang to his feet, his mouth frothing, his eyes wild. As El Madani rushed to him, other men began to scream and writhe. They clawed at their faces, their mouths foaming, and began to eat sand. Dianous seemed to spring six feet into the air and crashed down into the fire. Leaping to his feet again, he seized his rifle and fired it wildly. Then he raced straight toward the watching Tuareg. El Madani raced after him, tackled him, and pinned him down.

As he held Dianous, he glanced around in despair at the camp where it seemed that nearly everyone had gone mad. They had, indeed, been tricked. The Tuareg had stuffed their gifts of dates with *falezlez,* the poison they distilled from henbane. Though not necessarily fatal, *falezlez* sent one into hours-long madness. The scene at the camp now was one of frenzy. Some men fought frantically with one another while others lay moaning and writhing on the sand. The few Shamba who had followed El Madani's example and refused to eat the dates tried to separate the fighters and hold them down. Now surely was the moment when the Tuareg would attack. But they did not; they sat motionlessly on their camels and watched.

The long day waned into a night of agony and terror. In the first few minutes when the poison began to take effect, six men had dashed off into the desert and disappeared, among them the expedition's *mokkadem*, or holy man. By nightfall thirty-one still were seriously ill. Some kept trying to creep away into the desert to die; others had to be physically restrained from killing themselves. El Madani and other Shamba dashed here and there, caring for them. El Madani personally staked the five Frenchmen to the ground so that they would not harm themselves. He knew the remedy for *falezlez:* four or five days of complete rest in the shade and plenty of water. But the remedy was, of course, impossible there by the nearly dry water hole in the wadi.

Dianous and Pobeguin began to recover more rapidly than their fellow countrymen. Toward midnight Dianous asked El Madani weakly if he thought they could move on yet.

El Madani replied with two words: "We must."

So, in the first light of dawn, the column lurched forward, men retching and moaning and bent double with excruciating pain, but creeping on nevertheless toward the gorge and oasis wells of Amguid. Two hours later Santin toppled over, dead. They buried him in a shallow grave and staggered on, muttering unintelligibly, laughing insanely, until night closed on them.

The next morning they went on without a drop of water. Around seven o'clock they crept to the crest of a rise and halted. Ahead of them they saw the Amguid Gorge, where sweet cold water bubbled among the palms. But between them and the oasis the 200 blue warriors of the Tuareg were mounted in a silent, watchful line.

Dianous, his head sunken wearily, his eyes half closed, croaked his commands: a strong center, an extended wing to left and right in open order, and then forward. Pobeguin commanded the left wing, El Madani the right. They inched forward slowly, cautiously, like barefoot men creeping over broken glass. Then, just short of rifle range of the waiting Tuareg, Dianous' command came down the wings: Halt! Pobeguin and El Madani looked around in surprise. But then they saw the situation as Dianous did. Attack was hopeless. Against 200 fit, well-armed and mounted warriors they numbered only 49. Indeed, they were less than 49 in effectiveness. Even now Marjolet the cook and Brame the servant swayed giddily, eyes dilated, while Belcacem laughed and talked insanely to himself. If they attacked, the blue Tuareg line would curl around them and crush them.

They sank to the sand and waited. And the Tuareg waited as the sun blazed higher in the sky. An hour, two hours passed while they stared dazedly at the Tuareg and the Tuareg stared back inscrutably above their blue veils. To El Madani's surprise, the Tuareg nerve broke first. It was as sudden, as unexpected as the snapping of a coiled spring. From the center of the Tuareg line about 50 mounted warriors charged forward at breakneck speed.

Dianous did not need to give the command to fire. Coolly, deliberately, the experienced *tirailleurs,* kneeling and prone, brought their Le Gras rifles to bear on the charging warriors. The sound, the feel of their rifles seemed to bring them back from the edge of madness. Their sharpshooting broke the charge and the Tuareg camels, snuffling in fright, wheeled and skittered away, dragging wounded riders and leaving dead on the sands.

El Madani observed that Pobeguin on the opposite wing was employing old Foreign Legion tactics and coaxing the enemy to try to infiltrate his line by spreading his men and offering inviting gaps. Small groups of Tuareg were coaxed into the gaps—and quickly slain.

About three o'clock the Tuareg broke off and withdrew closer to the gorge. El Madani counted 34 Tuareg dead between the lines. Then his gaze was drawn to the farther wall of the gorge, where the Tuareg were leading forward the *mokkadem* and 5 other prisoners who had raced into the desert after eating the poisoned dates. A cry of rage rose from the Shamba as the Tuareg decapitated their holy man with a huge flashing sword and shoved his body into the gorge.

Dianous, incredulous, forgot himself and rose to his feet. Instantly there was the crack of a Targui sharpshooter's rifle, and Dianous fell dead. It was too much for Marjolet and Brame. Staggering to their feet, sobbing convulsively, they stumbled toward the Tuareg line. The Tuareg let them come close before they shot and killed them.

Meantime the execution of the prisoners continued slowly across the gorge. One by one each man was led forward and made to shout his name before the great sword flashed and his decapitated body plunged into the gorge. Powerless to aid them, the Shamba raged and cursed and prayed. El Madani crawled among them, begging them to remain calm and patient while they begged him to let them attack. But an attack was precisely what the Tuareg were trying to goad them into, El Madani told them. Be calm and trust in Allah. El Madani met Pobeguin near the body of Dianous and gripped his shoulder in a dark hand.

"Pobeguin, my friend, now you are the leader. What do you counsel?"

Pobeguin's lids were nearly closed on his bloodshot eyes. He was the only Frenchman left. Besides El Madani only thirty-one men still were alive. None of them had eaten a mouthful in two days. More than a day had passed since they swallowed the last drop of water. It was an end such as every Legionnaire might expect. It was Camerone again, without even the bargain of life in exchange for surrender.

There seemed no alternative to Pobeguin except a last charge in the tradition of the Foreign Legion with each man saving one bullet for himself. But El Madani shook his head slowly. There was another way, he said, a hopeless way, but at least one the Tuareg did not anticipate. They would turn their backs on the cool, bubbling waters of Amguid. They would hasten away from the wells, as if they did not exist. They would go *around* the Amguid and walk on home.

Pobeguin looked at El Madani aghast. How could men nearly mad with thirst turn their backs on water?

"This way." El Madani put a small pebble in his mouth and handed one to Pobeguin. "Let us drink our own spit and march around Amguid."

They pulled out silently soon after darkness fell, with El Madani leading them and Pobeguin bringing up the rear to urge on stragglers. El Madani struck a fast pace, going due west by the guidance of the stars. He knew that they must think as the Tuareg did. And Pobeguin agreed with him that an idea must have become fixed in the minds of the Tuareg: it was that the waters of Amguid had become fixed in the minds of the Shamba. They would expect the Shamba to try to infiltrate the gorge from another direction. Thus the Tuareg would circle round their trap and so, in turn, be trapped by it while the Shamba marched far away.

Of course not all, perhaps none, of them would survive. El Madani and Pobeguin agreed on that, too. But some *might* survive this way, while none possibly could live if they fell into the trap of the sparkling waters of Amguid.

Dawn found them far to the west, their trail lost on a flinty plain where not even the sharp-eyed Tuareg could trace it. Some said they could not go on. Then do not, Pobeguin told them; stay here and die. . . . All went on, north now, after a few hours of rest. El Madani set the direction and Pobeguin the marching pace. It was the Legion pace of five kilometers an hour with five minutes of rest each hour.

Some were totally mad now, and the madmen seemed to have more energy than the sane. Belcacem, mad as a hyena, pranced around the column, grinning and rubbing his hands while Colonel Flatters' huge sword clattered on his back. The cunning looks he cast stragglers, the way he licked his lips and fingered the sword, frightened them and spurred them on.

Another night passed, and on the morning of the next day El Madani believed he smelled the freshness of water. It was only a mudhole with a little parched grass about it, but they fell upon it as if it were the wells of Amguid. Clawing aside the mud, they sucked up the brackish water in great greedy gulps and then ate dried grass.

They went on, except for one madman who turned west and disappeared into a mirage. No one had the strength to pursue him. They saved their strength for hunting lizards which they ate raw. Belcacem was an outcast now; no one would speak to him, but he did not seem to care as he chuckled over some dark, amusing secret. Sometimes Pobeguin fingered his rifle as he stared at Belcacem broodingly.

Early one morning El Madani awakened with a start. The stars had been darkened and the air was oppressively warm. A strange moaning rose in the south and soon he felt stinging sand.

The sandstorm lasted throughout the day and into that night. Those who struggled out of their holes the following morning, found that three men were dead. The rest went on.

Pobeguin began to stumble and complained of dizziness. El Madani supported him as he tottered along at the head of the column. Toward sundown they found the skeleton of a camel; grinding the bones between stones, they ate the powder.

The next night they found another brackish water hole and drank their fill. Too exhausted to put out sentries, they slept the entire night. In the early light of dawn Pobeguin felt someone nudging him with a foot. Opening his eyes, he saw Belcacem grinning down at him, bent nearly double by the burden of something on his back.

"Take your share," Belcacem croaked. "I killed a big wild sheep last night."

Raising himself on an elbow, Pobeguin blinked at Colonel Flatters' sword dripping with blood in Belcacem's hand and saw that the burden on Belcacem's back was the decapitated body of a Shambi. Uttering a strangled cry, Pobeguin turned his head and retched.

"Belcacem!" The voice was El Madani's. "Belcacem!" El Madani had sat up a few yards distant, his rifle raised.

As Belcacem turned, El Madani shot him through the head.

They went on, but Pobeguin could not go far that day. Toward nightfall he fell into a coma and then became delirious. In his delirium he muttered of Brittany, of Sidi-bel-Abbès and the Legion, of water and wine and girls and song and the Tuareg and Colonel Flatters. About six o'clock in the morning he died and they covered over his body with sand.

They went on, stumbling through a yellow land that offered neither food nor water, chewing on their belts and sucking at stones. Now El Madani knew that each night one or another exhausted man would die in his sleep. He came to a decision that defied the laws of the Prophet. But when he announced it, all agreed it was sensible. At least they would not break the law against murder. He who died in the night would serve to break the fast of the others and give them strength to go on.

On the morning of March 19, 1881, the captain commanding the garrison at Ouargla was summoned by the sergeant of the guard.

Before the gate of the little fort twelve emaciated Shamba, barefoot and clad in tatters, were drawn up at attention. One stepped forward, saluted, and spoke.

"Sir, Private El Madani reporting. We are all that remain of the caravan led by Lieutenant Colonel Flatters."

El Madani was promoted to Private First Class.

11

The Fort
in the Desert

DRIFTING SANDS HAVE OBLITERATED all trace of Blockhouse Seven. Yet
it stood for decades on the camel trail which wound north from
Gadames, threading the wastes of the Grand Erg Oriental and pass-
ing on into the dark ridges of the Chott Melrir. Sometimes it was
called Fort Bel Zebla after the small oasis of a few score palms which
lay a couple of miles to the south of it.

The oasis was not visible from Blockhouse Seven. All that one
standing behind its white parapets could see in every direction was
the glare of sun on rocks and rolling sand dunes. Even the camel trail
which passed close to its walls was not clearly defined until one
emerged from the fort.

There was nothing exceptional about Blockhouse Seven. It was
typical of scores of other small fortresses which the Foreign Legion
built in Algeria and Morocco and the Southern Territories. In construction it was as standard issue as the blue capotes handed out to

Legionnaires. It had no special adornments and as few comforts as the cell of a Trappist monk. Yet to Legionnaires it served for months on end as a home, a detested haven, the whole wide world compressed within the infinity of time and the Sahara. Blockhouse Seven on the Grand Erg Oriental Trail can serve—as could dozens of identical small forts on other trails and roads—to tell the story of a phase in the life of the Legion.

Like everything man-made, Blockhouse Seven was built for a purpose. It came into being as a result of the troubles of 1881 and 1882 when the tribes rose again. The Legion, in its full strength of four battalions, was sent into the lower Atlas and upper Sahara to try to calm its enemy of many years, the peoples of the Ouled Sidi Cheikh tribes.

The campaign had the familiar, exhausting pattern of blundering among hills and deserts, of seeking and not finding, of constant tension and sudden surprises. Someone at Army Headquarters in Algiers decided that the camel caravans coming up the Grand Erg Oriental Trail from Bilma deep in the Sahara needed greater protection against the depredations of the Ouled Sidi Cheikh. Someone else assigned a portion of the task to the Legion. And someone else looked at a map and said blockhouses should be built somewhere around here—and here—and here.

As the sands have obliterated Blockhouse Seven, time has buried the names of the men associated with its building. Presumably, however, the Legion followed its customary procedure.. The task was assigned to a single company with a full complement of 112 enlisted men and noncoms and 3 officers. At Sidi-bel-Abbès the personnel section made sure that the officers had had desert experience and that one of them, though not necessarily the captain, had at least rudimentary knowledge of engineering.

At the time the Legion was entering a phase which found a decreased number of French officers below the rank of major. There were more Russians, Poles, and Austrians holding commissions than in preceding years, while the number of German officers and enlisted men was declining. By 1885, in fact, the German element among

138

enlisted men fell to the lowest in the history of the Legion—only 12 per cent of all those enlisted.

Long before the age of highly developed military specialization, the Legion developed a facility for placing men where their skills were the most useful. It always managed to have a strong complement of competent masons in a company assigned the mission of building a fort. Besides representing a medley of many nations, the Legionnaires who marched along the camel track toward the Oasis Bel Zebla included a careful mixture of seasoned desert rats and recruits who had just finished their basic training. Behind them rolled mule-drawn carts carrying provisions for at least six months.

That was the length of their assignment in the desert—if they were lucky and were relieved on time. But it was not unusual for a company to remain eight or nine months or even a year in the desert. The supplies they took with them promised a diet as unvarying in its monotony as the long days and nights: flour, lard, salt, sugar, coffee, rice, macaroni, hardtack, dried beans, peas, and beef, besides barley for the mules. Rarely did the casks hold enough to supply each man with his cup of wine a day for longer than two or three months.

There were two basic requirements in the location of Blockhouse Seven, as in all Legion forts. It must be built on the highest possible ground and close to a supply of fresh water. It could not be built in the small Oasis of Bel Zebla, which lay in a low wadi and was the home of a nomad clan of the Ouled Sidi Cheikh. The tribesmen would fight for the water rights to their own well and the oasis was placed off limits to Legionnaires.

Near the camel track a couple of miles north of the oasis the Legionnaires found and cleared an old water hole. Though the water was brackish, men experienced in the ways of the desert assured themselves that the supply would remain ample to furnish a gallon a day for each member of the garrison.

On high ground above the water hole the officers outlined the site of the proposed fort. Its dimensions already had come to be regulation size in the Legion and would continue so for several decades.

Built in a square, it consisted of walls 100 yards long, 3 yards high and 1 yard thick. At each corner of the square was a projecting tower 15 feet high. There was a single entrance of just sufficient width for a cart to enter; its gate, of heavy oak, was almost the only thing of wood in the fort and its timbers had been painstakingly transported hundreds of miles by mule. A stone firing platform ran all the way around the fort behind the parapets which were crenelated at intervals for firing points. Considering the size of the garrisons, which often numbered only a half company of fifty or sixty men, the forts built by the Legion were surprisingly large.

The men lived in tents while they built the walls. Not until the walls were completed did they begin constructing permanent barracks, storehouses, a cookhouse, and a small hospital. These, like the walls and towers, were built entirely of stone and mud, which became as hard as cement in the blazing sun. In the remote desert, at a post such as Blockhouse Seven, each stone-and-mud barracks housed ten to twelve men or three officers. Their earthen floors were sanded freshly each day and, until better days brought collapsible canvas cots by mule, the men spread their blankets on the floor. Sometimes they devised hammocks from bits of canvas and rope. But generally, in the last century when wood was even more rare than water, the barracks of a Legion fort in the desert lacked any furniture.

Mules or other animals belonging to the garrison were kept in stone shelters outside the walls for sanitary reasons. In a protracted siege the animals usually were brought into the fort and slaughtered for meat. Eventually, when barbed wire came into common use, a wire entanglement was strung in a perimeter around the fort.

Recruits who had made the long desert march to Bel Zebla found that their physical trials had only begun. The old desert hands suddenly emerged as all manner of experts; some became masons and straw bosses, others served on the patrols which each day ranged around the site of the fort in a vast sweep of the desert. Recruits were introduced to another hardship of Legion life: the rock quarry. For the basic elements of life had been reduced to rock and sand and water, and it was as essential that a fort be built near the site of a suitable rock quarry as near a source of water. Thanks to the nature of the Sahara, the Legionnaires nearly always were able to open a quarry close to a water hole.

As the temperature soared to 135 and 140 degrees, the men broke rock with sledges and lugged it from the quarry to the lines where masons prepared mud and shaped the walls. The noncoms drove the men hard at the heavy, exhausting work. For most of them the routine was like life in a penal unit.

Reveille was at five o'clock. Breakfast consisted of coffee and hardtack or dry bread. By six o'clock everyone was at work and toiled until eleven o'clock when dinner was served. A typical menu was greasy soup, macaroni, beans, bread and coffee. Some Legionnaires who served in remote posts in years past have maintained they went for months on end without being given a sweet. In the hottest seasons the men were given a rest break until two o'clock and then they resumed work until six. At their evening meal they usually were served soup, rice, bread, coffee and a cup of wine when it was available. Then a man's time was his own until bed check at nine o'clock.

Every other night a man must stand guard duty, two hours on and two off, without interrupting his daytime schedule. He was not allowed to wander outside the perimeter of the fort except when on a work detail or patrol. One afternoon a week the routine was interrupted in order that the men could do their laundry and bathe. Laundry and bath water was as strictly rationed as drinking water. The Legion did not issue soap; in place of it, a Legionnaire had to learn to use sand and stones as did the desert nomads. The scarcity of water in most desert posts probably gave rise to the canard that Legionnaires do not bathe. Whenever water was plentiful they were— and are today—as clean as any soldiers in the world. In more recent times cleanliness has become an obsession of most officers and many men in the ranks.

But during the building of a fort such as Blockhouse Seven it was difficult for a man to stay clean. It was difficult for him to care about anything in the searing heat and fatigue of work. Usually he lacked incentives except to try to survive from one day to the next. His pay, which was less than ten cents a day at the time, was meaningless in the desert because he rarely had any means of spending and enjoying it.

The walls of Blockhouse Seven were completed in a remarkably short time, less than four weeks. Then the Legionnaires turned to the task of building barracks, storage houses and a hospital which had not a single convenience except a straddle trench latrine behind it. By the time two months had passed the fort was habitable and as comfortable as it could be made until someday—or some month or year—a supply train brought a little something extra besides the customary fodder for men and beasts.

A commander knew that in times of peace it was easier to build a fort than to garrison it. The time passed more quickly during the work of building. Although it was exhausting work, it at least offered the builders a purpose and the chance to see tangible results grow from their labors. After the fort was completed, Legionnaires who had hated the toil found themselves regretting its end. For now the days stretched ahead emptily. Guard duty was a matter of standing in burning heat or the chill of night and gazing vacantly into space, one's rifle locked to his wrist by a three-foot chain so that no pillaging Arab could steal it. Patrol meant floundering around in the desert, looking for things that seemed not to exist.

In the monotony the commander of a remote fort set tasks for his men. Everyone knew that they were meaningless, but at least they helped to pass the time. A full field inspection and dress parade was one of the most irksome. Another was to tear down a perfectly sturdy section of a wall and then rebuild it.

The tedium was as difficult for the officers as for the men. In some respects it was even harder on the officers who lived unto themselves and had little direct association with their men except in combat and on patrol. Three officers—sometimes only two—living together and eating every monotonous meal together often got on one another's nerves. The officers were as various in character and background as the enlisted men. One young graduate of St. Cyr, who had enjoyed the advantages of growing up in a wealthy family, found himself serving under a Sicilian soldier of fortune, a brutal man of no refinements, who enjoyed holding his young lieutenant up to ridicule. The lieutenant endured it stoically until the tour of duty ended, but he admitted later that one thing almost made him crack: he could not bear the slurping sound his captain made when drinking soup. Another captain, who became obsessed with the paranoidal idea that his lieutenants wished to murder him, always placed his cocked revolver on the table beside his plate at mealtime.

A doctor never was stationed at Blockhouse Seven. Always among the men or officers there was someone who could set a broken arm or leg or was willing to probe for a bullet in a wounded man. A sick man either died or recovered with the aid of—or in spite of—the medicines given him. Despite the heat and the diet at desert posts, the health of their garrisons appears generally to have been superior to that of garrisons near the malarial swamps of the north. One disease that occasionally afflicted some men was scurvy. In time it was overcome, after the Legion added bottled lemon or lime juice to its rations.

Until comparatively recent times the Legion offered its men nothing in the way of leisure activities. In the early days of Blockhouse Seven it is doubtful if the fort contained a single book. Undoubtedly both men and officers had a few decks of greasy cards, though gambling never was widespread in the Legion because very few men had enough money to play cards for stakes. When wood became available, some Italian Legionnaires probably carved and sanded a set of bowls with which to play *boccie* on the parade ground after supper.

Outside of the fantasies of romantic fiction there is no record—not even a tall legend—of a lovely woman or women appearing at a post such as Blockhouse Seven and throwing its lonely garrison into a turmoil. If such a woman had appeared, it would have been

143

better for her if the commander had turned her back into the desert. And then it would have been better for him if he had locked himself in the guardhouse.

Sex, when it existed overtly at a desert post, took a depraved form or at least required a heartier sexual appetite than one normally finds in so-called civilized men. Occasionally a wandering Arab whoremaster would camp near Blockhouse Seven and offer his grimy child prostitutes, little girls eleven or twelve years old, for hire. Or, in periods of prolonged peace, a Greek or Cypriote—those boldest of the East's inveterate whoremasters—would wheel a couple of his most shopworn articles by donkey cart down the camel trails. The women, aging, ugly, and usually diseased, had reached the nadir of their trade.

Legionnaires in the remote desert seldom met the prostitutes whom they claimed to be the most beautiful and best in the world— teen-age girls from the Oulad-Naïl tribe of Constantine. These Kabyle girls had a century-old tradition of serving as prostitutes throughout North Africa. Some even followed the Legion to Indochina, Madagascar, and Europe. After they had earned enough money for a dowry, they returned to their villages in Constantine, married local boys, and had the reputation of becoming perfect wives and mothers.

Occasionally a sutler, who had no traffic in women, penetrated into the desert with his cart of wines, sweets, and trinkets. Many of the sutlers were venturesome Jews who had discovered, to their surprise, that the Arabs tolerated them as they never would tolerate Christians. In time nearly every Legion unit in northern Algeria and Morocco had a favorite sutler who followed it from place to place and became a kind of unofficial Legionnaire.

In the Sahara and the Atlas some Legionnaires, bereft of women for months, practiced homosexualism. Many published reminiscences discuss this fact. In his study of Legion life, *The White Kepi,* former Legionnaire Walter Kanitz maintains that homosexual practice is widespread. Officers, when questioned on the subject, deny that there is a larger proportion of sexual perverts in the Legion than in any other military body.

It is easy to see the Legion makes an ideal breeding ground for abnormal sex behavior [says Kanitz]. The environment of a Legionnaire, the circumstances surrounding him, are such that a normal man's resistance to homosexual activity is easily broken down. The fact that for years he has to live in close proximity to scores of men of low moral standards only facilitates and speeds up the process.

Once the Legion gets hold of a man's mind the effect on him is disastrous; individuality very seldom survives in the ranks. The Legion is a steamroller which, in a giant levelling-out process, presses every individual thought out of its victim's mind. After ten years of service a man has lost his individuality entirely. . . .

The severe discipline to which he is subjected, the adverse climate, deadly monotony, vicious influence and above all, alcohol, tend to undermine the Legionnaire's mental faculties, to transform him slowly into a dull robot with the intelligence and mentality of an adolescent if not a child. His moral standards weaken gradually. Homosexuality grows on him in easy stages as his system adapts itself to his environment in the Legion.

On the other hand, former Legionnaire Anthony Delmayne claims that, while homosexualism was practiced, there were few true homosexuals in the Legion and the vast majority of its men were heterosexual when they had the opportunity. "Our attitude to sex was not exactly positive or creative," he said. "We regarded desire as a nuisance that had to be removed, and whether with a man or a woman the sexual act was more for relief than pleasure."

It was at isolated posts like Blockhouse Seven that Legionnaires conceived their idea of a collective drunk—a custom still observed today in the Legion. When men were issued their ration of wine, they pooled it and chose a volunteer who could drink all of it he wished while standing before them and entertaining them. Some-

145

times the entertainer was witty; at other times he was a pathetic spectacle.

Whatever his personal inclinations, a Legionnaire on desert duty was confronted by perpetual boredom and constantly stood on the threshold of emotional depression.

A renowned Legion commander, Colonel Georges de Villebois-Mareuil, who was killed while fighting the British as a general of volunteers in the Boer War, learned much about the character of Legionnaires when he served at desert posts like Blockhouse Seven. He once said:

There are strange contrasts of good and evil in this mixed body of men. Some are potential heroes; others may be irreclaimably corrupt. Yet from this peculiar combination are engendered an iron energy, a passion for adventure, self-reliance, resourcefulness and a supreme contempt for death which together constitute the basis of splendid military valor.

The Legionnaire lives in a dream. What sort of dream? He would find it hard to explain that even to himself. But it is to his obsession by that dream that he attributes his misfortunes. He calls his dream *le cafard*. If he is asked the reason for some outbreak, he will give no other reply. It is always *le cafard*.

That word stands for a great deal. It is not surprising that hazy memories of the past that may have been in sharp contrast with his present circumstances should sometimes overcome his better judgment. His life is an abnormal one, and by the same token he does not willingly accept the present as it is in its monotony and commonplace routine. His instinct is to dramatize everything, to weave legends around his affairs. He atones for the dullness of the conditions that surround him by indulging his imagination—so much so that in the end he comes to believe in his own fancies.

It is this that makes it difficult to investigate a Legionnaire's past career —not that he displays reserve on the subject; to the contrary, unless he has some special reason for dissimulation, he likes to boast about it and paint it in the highest colors.

Above all, he enjoys asserting himself as a character out of the ordinary, which indeed he is. For the Legionnaire is an outlaw who has fallen out of the ranks of orderly society, where he was ill at ease. He has a natural taste for risks. He wants to live his life. It is the only personal property left to him, and he stakes it boldly. If need be, he even sacrifices it altogether, with a spirit worthy of the highest military traditions.

A literal translation of the French *cafard* means "bug." It has no precise meaning in medical science and is Legion slang. When it is said that a man has *le cafard,* it means, in slang, that he has been bugged or gone bugs. In effect, the term covers any abnormal emotional or mental behavior. Legionnaires take it most seriously. According to their interpretation, the word covers everything from extreme mental illness, such as dangerous paranoia or schizophrenia, through the effects of alcoholism to a mild state of depression in which a man wants to be let alone. It is erroneous to try to assign a single reason to all cases of *cafard,* as Legionnaires are inclined to do, by blaming behavior on a man's past life or the discipline of the Legion or the rigors of a monotonous life in the desert. When Legionnaires ran amok and killed their comrades, it was said they had *le cafard.* The same explanation was offered for most of the Legion's numerous suicides—and for the old hand who merely growled morosely at his sergeant one day.

Although the word can mean many things and at the same time has no precise meaning, it entered the vocabulary of Legionnaires soon after they reached the true desert in the latter part of the last century. *Cafard* described the behavior of some men assigned to lonely posts for long periods. And so, before the advent of psychology and psychiatry, the cause of *cafard* was traced to life in a fort like Blockhouse Seven.

Erwin Carlé, who tried to retain the equilibrium of his analytical mind through long assignments in desert forts, discussed the subject thoroughly. He described more vividly than any veteran of the desert the nature of garrison life in Blockhouse Seven at times:

The *cafard* of the Foreign Legion, a near relative to tropical madness, is a collective name for all the inconceivable stupidities, excesses and crimes which tormented nerves can commit. The English language has no word for this condition. In *cafard* murder hides, and suicide and mutiny; it means self-mutilation and planless flight out into the desert; it is the height of madness and the depth of despair.

I myself lived in a state of continual irritation. The least trifle put me in such a rage that I can hardly credit it today. My vexation, my irritability, my brooding was the madness of the Legion. No Legionnaire escapes from it.

Crowded together like horses in a bad stable, the men became dangerous. They fought over the quarter of a liter of the Legion wine that was apportioned to us every day, and watched with ridiculous suspicion that the next man did not get more than he did; one quarreled over a piece of bread; one took one's neighbor for a thief who wanted to steal a bit of black wax for leather polishing. If one man got more work to do than his neighbor, he cried murder and roared out about protection and favoritism and vicious preference.

This was the atmosphere in which the Legion's whims were developed. It was really strange how many of the Legionnaires had a screw loose, often only harmless peculiarities, but which could increase to madness.

All idiocy in the Legion is called *cafard*. A Legionnaire is gloomy, sitting sullenly on his bed for hours, speaking to no one. If you ask him what is the matter, he will answer with gross insult. He sits thinking all the time and does the queerest things. He has the *cafard*.

His madness may turn into a senseless explosion or fit of fury; men suffering from *cafard* will run a bayonet through their comrade's body, without any reason, without any outward cause. Sometimes they rush out into the desert, sometimes they tear every piece of their outfit into rags, just to vex themselves and others thoroughly.

The *cafard* is at its worst in the hot season when the sun burns down relentlessly from the cloudless, deep blue sky, with the strange greenish coloring peculiar to the horizon. Then the barracks yard of the Foreign Legion lies deserted. It is so hot that stones on the yellow, clayey ground seem to move in the glimmering, overheated air. Then in the infernal heat the *cafard* has often been the cause of great disaster. . . .

Whole numbers of soldiers are affected by it in the same way. The Legionnaires of half a company would put their heads together, planning some act of desperation. One time it would be mutiny "en masse," at another time desertion in a body. This madness is well known wher-

148

ever a company of Legionnaires is stationed. In some kind of form it is always present. It is the cause of the horrible tattooing, of drinking and brawling; it is the reason for that peculiar longing for continual change, that restlessness typical of the Foreign Legion.

The Legionnaires themselves are not aware what influence *cafard* has on them. When an old Legionnaire says grumpily *"j'ai le cafard,"* he is just telling his neighbors to keep clear of him, that he has a bad fit of the blues, that it is advisable for his comrades to leave him alone. He has no idea that a hidden power, like madness, is making him act in such a manner, he only believes himself to be in bad humor. But the bad humor rises and increases, often driving him to murder—more often to suicide.

The Legionnaire cannot foresee the effects of *cafard*. The typical *"cafard* demoniacs," the old grumpy fellows who do their duty like machines and at other times hardly speak at all, are instinctively feared, as if their comrades knew that at any moment the least trifle could lead to an outbreak of the dormant madness.

Many Legionnaires never suffered from such a mood on desert duty, however. Some sought assignment to it, especially after the *Compagnies Sahariennes* were formed. To such men service in the desert fulfilled a personal psychological need. It meant complete freedom from complexities of society that had overwhelmed them. In the desert they found life reduced to its bare essentials and thus they felt better able to cope with it.

Legionnaires have left testimony of joy as well as grief in the desert. Virtually all recall how much they liked to sing. Night and day they raised their voices in songs of their native countries or the wild, throbbing songs which Legionnaires themselves created.

In his diary of his life in the Legion, Major Zinovi Pechkoff frequently mentions the singing of the Legionnaires. "Forty kilometers today! The wind was very strong. The men marched singing all the time—every one in his mother tongue. The dust covered us, and it was difficult to advance."

Perhaps the words of Prince Aage are appropriate: "Music is a perfect drug for the soldier. It chases away reason which would render sacrifice difficult or impossible. It abolishes fear."

Many men kept *le cafard* at bay by occupying themselves with handicrafts. Legionnaires became first-rate carvers of wood and shapers of metals wherever the opportunity afforded. Wherever they possibly could, they tried to make the desert and bleak mountains bloom with flowers and trees and vegetable gardens. Later, after the Legion entered Morocco, it created a miracle in an arid area of rock and scrub at Le Krieder. Channeling the waters of a warm-water spring there into a swimming pool and an irrigation system, the Legionnaires developed a large and productive farm. The food it supplied, prepared by excellent Legion chefs, led the post at Le Krieder to be known as "Maxim's in Morocco."

At another remote Moroccan post Pechkoff noted in his dairy how his men became absorbed in gardening:

We have planted a vegetable garden near the post, and although the men are skeptical about planting in June, it has come out wonderfully. One of my gardeners is a Swiss, who knows how to do the planting. Another man was very ingenious in capturing a stream flowing not far away and making a complete system of irrigation. At daybreak, when the gates of the post are thrown open, the two men, the gardener and the irrigator, go out and water the garden. In the evening, after the day's work is done and the evening meal eaten, there remain about two or three hours of leisure before the men go to bed, and there is always a procession of them going out to see the garden. One sees groups of Legionnaires of different nationalities stopping at one corner or another of it, discussing the plants, and talking about gardens and plants in their own countries.

There is such a tender expression on the faces of men who watch a growing plant—something that comes out of the earth, something that is brought forth by the will and energy of men, something that is created. The transmutation of matter. . . . The creation of new forms. . . . What mystery!

12

"We Have Fought
a Thousand Years"

WHETHER LEGIONNAIRES ACTED MADLY or sanely did not especially worry Colonel François de Negrier. The important thing to his mind was that they be tough, well trained and eager to fight. If they also wished to die, it was perfectly agreeable with Negrier—provided they died in the cause of the French overseas empire, which he heartily espoused.

Negrier was a forthright, intelligent, energetic man, who was destined for moderately high command in the French Army. Before he assumed command of the Legion in July, 1881, he had commanded a battalion of *Chasseurs d'Afrique* and had not had any experience with Legionnaires.

He took to them at once because they professed to be devils who wanted to fight. And they took to him because he led them out of the doldrums in the Algerian fighting of 1881 and 1882. If he had not assumed command of the Legion when he did and led it ener-

151

getically, it might have deteriorated into a labor unit and faded out of existence.

Negrier's first innovation was to form a Legion mounted company such as never had been seen before in Africa. It consisted of 100 men and 50 mules which were used solely for transport. Although Negrier admired the Legion's marching capability, he wished to extend it. In the mounted companies which he formed, two Legionnaires alternated in riding a mule and marching beside it for one hour. Such a company could cover almost fifty miles a day on a forced march.

In April, 1882, a Legion mounted company and two regular companies were convoying a party of surveyors near the Moroccan border south of Gerryville when it was attacked by an Arab force of 1,800 horsemen and 6,000 on foot. The Legionnaires were descending into a desolate valley called the Chott Tigri about six o'clock in the morning when they ran into a sudden, blinding sandstorm. Almost simultaneously the Arabs attacked.

In the swirling sandstorm the surprised Legionnaires were separated into three groups. About five hundred yards behind the mounted company was the largest group while a smaller party was separated farther to the rear. Each formed in a square and repulsed the Arab attacks. Gradually the center section worked its way to higher and more easily defensible ground. But the mounted company was pinned down on low ground and could not move.

Within minutes after the sandstorm cleared, the two officers of the mounted company were dead. An aging sergeant took command and ordered all the mules slain and their bodies piled in a circle. The Legionnaires, crouching behind the barricade of dead mules, held off the swarm of Arabs for seven hours. Their will was hardened by the fates of a few comrades whom the Arabs had captured in the first scramble. Well beyond rifle range and within clear view of the raging Legionnaires, the Arabs pegged their captives to the ground, emasculated them, and then decapitated them.

Eventually the mounted company and the small rear guard managed to link up with the main body. Forming in a large square with their wounded inside it, the Legionnaires withdrew slowly, harassed through the night and another day by attacks of mounted Arabs.

At the beginning of the attack a couple of friendly tribesmen who had been accompanying the column escaped in the sandstorm and rode as fast as they could to Negrier at Gerryville. Within minutes after he received the word, Negrier was marching at the head of a relief column. In one of the most grueling forced marches in the annals of the Legion, he led his column all night and all the next day. The men marched more than fifty miles before they came within sight of the slowly retreating units. When the Arabs saw the relief force, they broke off and fled.

There were reciprocal feelings between Negrier and the Legionnaires during the two years in which he served as their commander. The men did not forget that, as one of them expressed it, Negrier "would march through the gates of hell to come to our aid." And he, for his part, never forgot the fighting heart of the Legion.

He knew that an important element in its morale was its love of military pomp and ceremonial. For several years before he assumed command of the Legion, its commanders had done little to maintain its pride. Negrier ordered more parades, more spit and polish. It was he who made the seven-flamed grenade the official badge of the Legion. The origin of the badge is obscure. The grenade itself had for many years been the emblem of all elite units in the French Army, but the significance of the seven flames the Legion added to it is not certain today.

When Negrier was promoted in September, 1883, and left the Legion to lead a brigade in Indochina, many Legionnaires felt they had lost a personal friend. But he had not forgotten the Legion. He asked for, and obtained, a battalion of volunteers from its rank and file. Another battalion of volunteers followed it to the Far East two months later.

Thus there was established the Legion rule of volunteering for duty in Indochina, a rule that was not abolished until the desperate days following World War II. There was nothing unusual about a special battalion being formed to serve a specific purpose. Almost from the first days of its founding the Legion had created special columns or task forces, which were dissolved after they had accomplished their purpose. Indeed, it would be hopelessly confusing to try to trace the table of organization of the Legion. At times it reminds one of an amoeba, expanding and contracting and breaking and rejoining. The number of its regiments grew with the years, but the size of the regiments varied. Companies were detached for special duties and the forces of a single battalion might be so widely spread that it was impossible to maintain its records with much accuracy. It is for this reason, as well as because of Legion policy, that it is difficult to determine casualties precisely.

The first Legionnaires to set foot in Indochina landed at Haiphong in November, 1883. As was usual when they landed on a strange shore, they knew little about the causes that had led them there. Negrier simply had asked for them and there they were. It was an appealing land at first sight, a place of huge Buddhist temples and bright noisy bazaars. The women were small, smiling, exquisitely formed creatures. The air was languorous and sweet with the music of temple bells. And the French promised the Legionnaires extra rations of wine and a daily ration of rum, too. What more could they want?

But first appearances could be deceiving. In time the Legion would learn that Indochinese rulers and many of their people never would be reconciled to French domination. For centuries they had fought against oppression by one or another foreign power. Not for seventy years would Legionnaires take seriously a saying of Vietnamese nationalists: "We have fought a thousand years. And we will fight another thousand if need be."

French traders and missionaries had been in the area called Cochin China since early in the century. In 1858, when Napoleon III was rustling the silks of empire, a French expedition was sent to Cochin China to punish the Vietnamese for their treatment of Roman Catholic missionaries. The French seized half the area and when the ruler of Viet Nam, Tu Duc, tried to get it back, they gobbled up the other half. In 1883 the French resorted to force

154

again, moving this time against Annam and Tonkin with the hope of opening the road to trade with China.

Winds of imperialism were blowing over Asia and Africa from the West. Jules Ferry, the Premier of France when troops moved against Annam and Tonkin, has been characterized as "the first French statesman whose foreign policy was dominated by concern for colonial expansion." He believed that France would decline to a third- or fourth-rate power unless it industrialized at home and had protected markets abroad for the export of manufactured goods and capital. Negrier was a disciple and instrument of Ferry's theories of imperial colonialism.

Negrier quickly summoned the Legion battalion upcountry to Hanoi, where it formed part of a force of about 5,000 French marines and soldiers. Tu Duc had rallied the Tonkinese and asked aid of the Empress of China to repel the French invasion. Then he had died at a time inconvenient to his cause. The Viet Nam resistance deteriorated into large bands of Tonkinese and Chinese, who generally failed to co-ordinate effectively; some were merely bandits. The French called them the Black Flags because of the predominant color of their banners.

On December 16, 1883, the French force under Negrier marched from Hanoi against a fortress called Son-Tay, thirty miles to the northwest, with the Legion battalion serving as the advance guard. It was jungle country, where visibility usually was limited to a few yards, a terrain unlike any the Legionnaires ever had encountered. The Black Flags took full advantage of it by springing ambush after ambush on them. But the Legion adapted itself quickly to jungle tactics in which the squad became the vital unit with one man covering another.

Reaching Son-Tay, the Legionnaires swept through the outworks of the fort. A sergeant, inspired by tales of past glory, indulged in heroics. Seizing the flag from the standard-bearer, he scrambled up a parapet and shouted, *"A moi, la Légion!"* The words still worked their magic. Legionnaires scrambled after him and all leaped down into a mass of astonished Tonkinese six times their numbers. As the

Legion bayonets flashed among them, the Tonkinese decided to fight another day. They scampered out the rear gates of the fort while the Legionnaires opened the main gate to the French. As the French Marines marched in, they cheered the Legionnaires, who were vastly pleased. "We felt," one said later, "that we had proved the wisdom of those who had brought us to the East."

There seemed no end to the proving. As ever, guerillas were a thorn to conquering heroes.

The second battalion of Legion volunteers from Algeria joined the first at Son-Tay. Both formed the spearhead which fought through ambushes and chopped a path through jungle swamps for the French column which moved against the stronghold of Bac-Ninh. There it was again principally a Legion battle. Bac-Ninh was taken on March 12, 1884—and almost at once came the annoying news that the Black Flags had reoccupied Son-Tay.

Negrier decided that the country would have to be occupied by garrisons and heavily patrolled in a pattern similar to that in Algeria. He sent the 1st Battalion north to take and hold the ancient Viet Nam bastion of Tuyen-Quang on the Claire River. Aided by field guns, the Legionnaires accomplished their mission without great difficulty on June 1.

In August the Black Flags began pouring south in greater strength, beefed up with three detachments of Chinese regulars. In September they began investing Tuyen-Quang, which then was garrisoned by the 1st and 2nd Companies of the 1st Battalion. By early January, 1885, the investment was complete; 390 Legionnaires faced an army of approximately 20,000.

Although the French and other Legion units were too busy elsewhere to relieve Tuyen-Quang, the Legionnaires there were not especially worried. They had plenty of food and ammunition. They were in a fort of traditional Chinese design: square, built of brick, with a double line of walls. It stood on a height, commanding the densely wooded south bank of the Claire, and its walls appeared thick enough to withstand anything the Black Flags' ancient field-pieces could throw at them.

On January 26 an outer blockhouse about 250 yards from the main citadel was overwhelmed by a suicidal Chinese attack such as the Legion never had met before. The Chinese swarmed upon the blockhouse in a dense mass, advancing with utter indifference to their casualties, clambering over their dead and wounded until the Legionnaires abandoned the outpost.

Gradually the Chinese sapped closer and exploded mines which breached the walls at two points. The detonation of the second mine hurled a half-dozen Legionnaires into the path of the advancing infantry, but comrades rushed out and rescued all of them. The Chinese swarmed through the breaches with bloodcurdling screams into a hail of bullets. After hand-to-hand fighting, the Chinese recoiled. But they refused to give up.

A few days later the fort was rocked by a series of roaring explosions. Dazed Legionnaires, groping in the smoke, counted three, four, five wide breaks in the walls. And through each breach dashed screaming Chinese. The Legionnaires were pressed back by overwhelming numbers, but before long the Chinese began to recoil from lunging Legion bayonets. Counterattacking in one breach after another, the Legionnaires finally drove the horde outside the broken walls. The Chinese maintained pressure, however, giving the Legion no chance to repair the walls.

Now the Legionnaires tried a sortie, hoping that it would demoralize the Chinese. They captured two standards and retired inside their broken fort. But their action had the opposite effect from that they desired. Enraged at the loss of their flags, the Chinese hurled themselves into the breaches with renewed fury.

Word of the crucial state of affairs at Tuyen-Quang finally reached Negrier and he marched to its relief with a strong column of Legionnaires and regulars. On March 2 the column ran into elements of the Chinese force south of Tuyen-Quang; the Chinese, finally realizing they were outmatched, withdrew that night. About half of the Legion defenders of the fort had been killed or wounded in the series of battles.

That month a third Legion battalion arrived in Indochina from

Algeria and a fourth landed on Formosa. France was formally at war with China now, and the mission of the 4th Battalion was to subdue Chinese forces which were preying on French shipping from the island.

The moment the Legionnaires hit their assigned beachhead on Formosa they were enveloped by heavy Chinese fire. They fought their way off the beach and broke and scattered the Chinese in the surrounding hills. On March 17 the French and Chinese agreed to an armistice. Under the Treaty of Tsiensin, which followed the armistice, China recognized a French protectorate over Annam and Tonkin.

Several Chinese war lords and the Viet Nam nationalists refused to recognize the Treaty, however. The Black Flags continued to harass the French with guerilla warfare. At last Negrier grouped several Legion units into a special task force which marched against the Black Flag stronghold of Lang-Son near the Chinese border. A powerful Black Flag force ambushed the column as it moved in extended order through heavily wooded country. Negrier was seriously wounded in the first attack and had to give up command. Recovering from the initial shock, the Legionnaires struggled out of the trap and fought a fierce retreat against well-managed Black Flag assaults. Thanks to the Legionnaires' coolness and experience in rearguard actions, the orderly retreat never became a rout.

Various authorities offer various dates as marking the end of hostilities in Indochina. To many Legionnaires who continued to patrol the hills and jungles it must have seemed, however, that hostilities never ceased totally. But organized resistance to the French did gradually die away and by the late 1890's the Legion had settled into garrison life and was engaged in building roads and railroads.

Yet the East has many subtle ways of conquering its would-be conquerors. One is by disease.

The Indochina malaria, typhus, and an amoebic dysentery worse than any encountered in North Africa cut a wider swath in the ranks of the Legion than did the bullets of the Black Flags.

An English Legionnaire, George Mannington, who served in

Indochina during that period, recalled that in the oppressive heat of July "half of the detachment's effective was laid up with fever, which takes a most virulent form. Its commencement, like ordinary malaria, is generally announced by shivering fits, during which the sufferer experiences a sensation of extreme cold. The hands and feet are numbed and glacial; the teeth chatter continually. This is succeeded at the end of an hour or more by a feeling of burning heat; perspiration ceases, the sufferer's temperature rises to over a hundred; he is the victim of terrible pains in the head, and is often delirious. At Cho-Trang this condition was usually complicated by hematuric symptoms (bloody discharges). There was no doctor in the fort and it was the lieutenant who examined the sick men and served out the medicines provided by the authorities. It was noticeable that the first among my comrades to fall victims to sickness were the younger members of the detachment; hard drinkers were longer in resisting the attacks of the fever fiend but once the illness got a hold upon them, the results were generally fatal."

Although the French made remarkable contributions to the health of Indochina, advancing the study of tropical diseases, building hospitals, and dispensing medicines, their program of hygienic education seemed to be of little benefit to the health of Legionnaires assigned there. The wards of Legion hospitals in Algeria were constantly filled by veterans of Indochina who returned suffering from the diseases of the East.

Dread of disease was the reason many Legionnaires refused assignment to Indochina during the years when they had a choice. In an effort to overcome their reluctance, the French offered inducements that it was difficult for some Legionnaires to resist.

Undoubtedly the greatest inducement was women. For another subtle way in which the East conquers its would-be conquerors is by offering its women. The majority of Legionnaires seem to have found the small, childlike, passive women of Indochina irresistible. The French command allowed any Legionnaire in Indochina to take a local woman as his common-law wife and live with her. Men accustomed to the infrequent, crude, cash-and-carry coupling of the

159

North African bordellos welcomed the opportunity of normal sex life. Many Vietnamese girls and women and their parents, living at a level of bare subsistence, in turn welcomed life with a foreign stranger. It was the old story of the invader: impoverished though he might be personally, he appeared to be a man of wealth and power to the people of a poor, vanquished country. Many a man who had deserted a wife in Europe to join the Legion, and had decided he hated all women, found himself charmed by an Eastern woman who served him as a slave and worshiped him as a god. Often a Legionnaire in Indochina began callously a relationship with a *congai,* as a common-law wife was called—and then found himself falling in love with her. Often a tough fighter who had rejected love and family along with country and God found himself turning into a benign paterfamilias with the woman he loved and the children she bore him.

And that was the supreme irony, the way the East stretched a would-be conqueror on the rack. For, with extremely rare exceptions, a Legionnaire could not or would not marry a Vietnamese woman he loved and take her back West with him. He could not or would not remain in the East; he must return to the West, his fleeting sense of happiness curdled into regret and a sense of loneliness from which surely he never would recover.

It was a veteran of Indochina, certainly a Legionnaire who could not forget the woman he had loved there, who wrote a poem for the Legion magazine, *Képi Blanc,* that began:

> Be not content to sleep with a Congai.
> Her designs are black
> Her breasts are yellow
> With black nipples.
> Touch not the cursed things,
> For if she gives them to you
> You are lost. . . .

Legion veterans of Indochina generally agreed that its pleasures were fleeting, that the things they blessed at first turned into curses.

One was alcohol, which many loved. As Mannington pointed out, those who indulged heavily in it found their health undermined.

Indochina offered a drunkard a more copious supply of alcohol than he ever could afford in North Africa. It was offered both by the conquerors and the conquered. In order to encourage Legionnaires to volunteer for duty in the Far East the French released the tight purse strings with which they usually bound the Legion and bade it supply its men with larger rations of wine than they received in North Africa. In addition Legionnaires were given a special ration of rum. If this was not enough to satisfy an alcoholic, he could buy for a song the wine of the country, "choum-choum," as the Legionnaires called it, an almost-pure-alcohol liquor distilled from rice.

Eventually the French administration had a substantial interest in spreading the use of both alcohol and opium because it held a monopoly on them and profited directly from their sale. Each village was assigned a quota of alcohol which it must consume. There is on record, for example, an order of a French prefect who announced that his canton must consume 800 liters a month and that "The villages which have consumed much will be recompensed, and the villages which have consumed or sold little will be punished."

Although the smoking of opium was a criminal offense in France, it was one of the financial supports of the French administration in Indochina. The same was true of British, Portuguese, and Spanish administrations in the Far East and of the independent government of Siam. The stock reply of administrators to European critics of the monopoly was that the opium habit had become so deeply ingrained in Eastern peoples that it could not be eradicated and had better be "controlled" for Western profit. Although the administrators exaggerated the extent of the habit in their cynical argument, opium did have a hold on many Indochinese.

Mannington saw its effects in a strange drama which unfolded before a platoon of Legionnaires. Guided by Tonkinese, Mannington's platoon entered the jungle to capture a rebel leader named Linh-Nghi. The guides led them to Linh-Nghi's thatch-roofed house which was screened by green blinds of split bamboo. Through the blinds the Legionnaires peered in at Linh-Nghi, wearing cream-colored silk and lying on a wooden couch beside a beautiful woman in a green sarong. Beside them was a little silver box and a small lamp burning in the sunlight. As the Legionnaires watched, the woman languidly filled an opium pipe and gave it to Linh-Nghi.

The Tonkinese guide, a man named Tho, told them to let him finish his pipe. As Linh-Nghi smoked it, eyes half closed in his emaciated face, he stared out at the Legionnaires indifferently while the woman smiled in her drugged dream. When Linh-Nghi had finished his pipe, Tho told him, "You must surrender and come with us." Indifferently Linh-Nghi replied that he preferred to die where he was.

But the Legionnaires dragged him to his feet, bound his arms, and hustled him along the trail back to the bivouac. Behind them Mannington heard the woman running, panting for breath and beginning to sob as the elation of her opium dream passed.

At their bivouac the Legionnaires manacled Linh-Nghi to the ground under the porch of a native house and his woman insisted on being similarly manacled beside him. Except for the manacles, both were treated humanely and were well fed. Through the native informers the Legionnaires interrogated Linh-Nghi endlessly about the strength and location of his supporters. Though both he and his woman were half crazed for want of opium, he refused to disclose anything.

"Speak," the Legionnaires told him, "and you shall have opium, the very best." But Linh-Nghi, writhing and moaning beside the suffering woman, refused to speak. Their agony moved the Legionnaires, and perhaps they would have given the two relief before long.

But relief came to Linh-Nghi in a stranger way.

One of his followers who wished to succeed him convinced another rebel leader named De-Nam that Linh-Nghi had betrayed him. The next morning a Legion guard at the edge of the bivouac found a basket containing the heads of Linh-Nghi's parents.

Later in the day when Mannington passed his lieutenant's quarters, he saw Linh-Nghi crouched on his heels in front of the officer and carefully shaping exact clay models of the fortified positions held by De-Nam.

As the Legionnaires marched off to take De-Nam, they saw the smoke of opium pipes eddying from the hut where Linh-Nghi and his woman lay at ease.

Legionnaires always were the first to admit that they were a breed of men who sought self-forgetfulness and even oblivion. Inevitably some men with such psychological drives turned to opium, which was almost as available as alcohol in Indochina. Although dope addiction never was a problem of the Legion in North Africa, it destroyed a few Legionnaires in the Far East.

It represented one of the ironic and immemorial perils of military conquest. Invariably some of the conquerors were overwhelmed by the fruits of their conquest. In the aftermath of every victory some Legionnaires uncovered the seeds of self-defeat.

13

The War

Against Women

THERE WERE TWO POSSIBLE VIEWS of the African Kingdom of Dahomey. One was the view of King Behazin, absolute ruler of the Dahomians. The other was the viewpoint of the rest of the world.

Behazin was pleased with the state of affairs in his kingdom, which extended in a width of about 100 miles up from the Slave Coast on the Atlantic's Bight of Benin some 350 miles into the interior. He had 100 wives and more concubines than he could count. His slaves ran into the thousands and his army was unique in the history of the world. In his small inland capital city of Abomey he drank trader's rum from goblets made of dried skulls and his court was cobbled with the bones of his enemies.

Europeans, who led more prosaic lives than Behazin, felt that the situation in Dahomey was intolerable. They did not care that Behazin simply was living in the manner in which he had been raised. For, in addition to land, wealth, and power, he had inherited the centuries-old customs of his country. These were of two kinds: the "grand customs," held on the death of a Dahomian king; and the "minor customs," held twice a year.

Behazin always insisted that the grand customs, pageants of great splendor, were motivated by piety rather than bloodthirstiness. After all, you couldn't send the spirit of a king into the hereafter alone and unattended. With his spirit must go the spirits of slaves, wives, warriors, and others who would serve him.

The funeral of a king began with dancing and speechmaking in which his subjects whipped themselves into a frenzy of loyalty to his memory. Then the human sacrifices, many of whom were said to be most eager to fulfill the role, were placed in wicker cages and lifted to a high platform where a crocodile, a cat, and a hawk also were caged. When the loyal Dahomians had become sufficiently frenzied, warriors tossed the cages down to the mob which tore them open and killed the humans and animals inside them. If one can believe the accounts of early European adventurers, there was some variety in the grand customs. The body of at least one king reportedly lay in a canoe which had been placed in a tank of hides, and he was not considered properly launched into the hereafter until his canoe floated in the blood of those sacrificed. On one thing nearly all accounts agree: the dismembered bodies of the sacrificed were roasted on coals and eaten smoking hot.

The day's ceremonies were followed by *zan nyanyana*, or "evil night," when the new king, accompanied by his wives and prime ministers, issued from the palace. After personally cutting off a few heads, the new king sprinkled the victims' blood on the grave of the dead king and his ancestors. But the ritual still had not ended. Throughout the day and night the wives of the dead king had been tearing their clothing to shreds and whipping themselves into paroxysms of grief in their harem. At last, toward dawn of the next day, the hysterical women ran wild in the harem, smashing everything within reach, stabbing eunuchs who attended them, and finally falling on one another with tooth and nail and knife. When the new king felt that the wives of the old king had committed enough murder, he went to the harem and restored order.

For a week after the grand customs things were rather quiet around the royal court of Dahomey.

Compared to the grand customs, in which hundreds were slaughtered, the minor customs held twice a year were mild. Sometimes less than a hundred humans were sacrificed during the semiannual rites. And, as Behazin liked to point out, no truly valuable bodies were wasted in these ceremonies. Only enemies of the state and those so aged or infirm that the slave traders would not buy them gave up their lives to nourish the souls and bodies of those loyal to the state.

Before the slaving trade was outlawed, and even for many years afterward, slave ships from Britain, France, Spain, Portugal, the United States, Denmark, and Holland conducted a highly profitable business with agents of the kings of Dahomey. By late in the nineteenth century the contest for colonial empire in Africa had narrowed principally to France and Britain. In their vast and complex bickering and dickering, the two powers finally agreed that France should establish a protectorate over the Dahomian coast and France announced it would give King Behazin an annual pension amounting to about $4,000 a year.

Behazin did not react graciously to the arrangements in which no one had consulted him. He sent expeditions beyond his borders and killed and enslaved some Christian Africans. With a cry of moral outrage the French assembled a force of 4,000 men to end once and for all the rule of the kings of Dahomey. A special *bataillon de marche* of the Foreign Legion, numbering 800 men, was formed under Colonel Faurex to serve as the spearhead of the expedition.

The Legionnaires who sailed from Oran late in July, 1892, had become accustomed to hearing wild tales about the places to which they were sent. They were willing enough to believe that they were headed for a rough time in Dahomey. But they could not believe the report that the strongest fighting arm of King Behazin's army was a force composed exclusively of women.

Yet it was true. Classical authorities disagree on whether a nation of ancient Greek women warriors called Amazons was legendary or actually once existed. But it was a fact that for at least two centuries the kings of Dahomey had employed an army of women warriors so fierce that all enemies were terrified of them. No force comparable to the Amazon army of Dahomey can be found in the history of the world.

As best its beginnings can be reconstructed, the Amazon army appears to have started as a gesture of feminine protest by the wives of an ancient king of Dahomey. They numbered at least 700 and possibly more than 1,000—which is a large number of wives even for the most virile of men. Not surprisingly, their lives were largely celibate in the huge harem where they were closely guarded by eunuchs. Young, restless, and having little to do except quarrel among themselves, they begged the king to let them go out on hunting expeditions. He must have been willing enough, if only to keep them quiet, but he refused to let them go tramping through the bush for game with men. They were, after all, *his* wives. Finally he agreed that they could go hunting in bands composed exclusively of their own members and unaccompanied by men. They proved to be superb hunters, fleet, crafty, strong, all their feminine wiles directed against the game of bush and savanna.

Taking great delight in stalking and killing animals, they naturally began to think it would be even greater sport to stalk and kill men. They begged the king to take them on war expeditions, and he consented. At first they served as bands of undisciplined irregulars. But as their prowess grew, they became disciplined warriors. When they captured strong and willing females, they enlisted them into their ranks and their numbers increased rapidly.

Some of the kings of Dahomey appear to have married all members of their Amazon army. When the size of the army increased to about 10,000, however, marriage to all of the warriors presented problems to even the most maritally ambitious of kings. Apparently there was, for a time, a tradition of celibacy among the Amazons, but it did not last long. As the Amazons increased in strength and fighting skill, the male elements of the Dahomian army declined. When it came to war, there was a widespread inclination among the men to let the women wage it.

And they waged it surpassingly well. They were divided into units of about 400 Amazons, commanded by female officers who wore white headdress to denote their rank. Each unit had its own flag, ceremonial umbrella, and a detachment of drums. The pick of the Amazons was assigned to the king's guard and allotted the best firearms available. Those who lacked muskets or rifles were armed with swords, spears, machetes, and bows and arrows. From time to time a king hired a European or American soldier of fortune to improve the training of his Amazons. At all times, except in battle, they were kept segregated from the male warriors and were as strictly disciplined as Foreign Legionnaires.

The Amazon uniform consisted simply of a loose, widely slit skirt belted at the waist. Veteran Amazons wore human bones or skulls dangling from their belts as badges of active service. Members of the king's bodyguard wore coquettish red caps on their shaved heads. A cartridge belt slung over a bare shoulder, a water gourd on one hip, and a haversack on the other completed their uniform.

Each fall the King invited Europeans and Americans from the coast up to his capital at Abomey to observe the annual "maneuvers" of his Amazons. These delegations, often composed largely of seedy and gin-soaked derelicts of the fever coast, brought back titillating descriptions of the leggy Amazons marching along with beautiful bare breasts swinging in cadence, or tearing off their skirts as they hurled themselves over thorn barriers. Even more titillating, declared the old Africa hands, were the erotic dances the naked Amazons performed with sticks and masks when preparing for a raid. Long residence on the coast had made some of these gentlemen color-blind and impervious to such imperfections of feminine beauty as filed teeth and shaved heads.

If the Amazons were to be admired as women, they were even more admirable as fighters. They were tireless marchers and had developed highly successful infiltration tactics. The chief purpose of

168

their raids became to capture slaves for the insatiable marts of Dahomey. They flitted through the bush, surrounded a village in the night, and swooped upon its inhabitants at dawn. Although their numbers had declined by 1892, they were as skilled fighters as ever.

But the Legionnaires sailing from Oran did not believe a word of it.

They passed through the Pillars of Hercules and rolled south in the green Atlantic, past the high peak of Teneriffe floating like a feather in the sky. Beyond the belt of storms and calms, they rounded Cape Palmas and sailed east along a coast marked by three interminable lines of surf, beach, and jungle. On August 23 their ship dropped anchor and the next day the Legionnaires rode through the crashing surf in outrigger canoes, which were skillfully handled by sweating, good-natured Fon. On the beach they pitched their tents near a small village called Cotonou and found themselves in a different Africa than Legionnaires had yet seen.

Beyond the beaches stretched black lagoons and vast mangrove swamps, and beyond the swamps rolled dense, steaming jungle. In the humid heat the din of billions of insects was almost deafening to men accustomed to the silence of the desert. After nightfall the din rose awesomely, the roaring of crocodiles mingling with the howling of monkeys, while mice shrieked and owls moaned.

General Alfred Dodds, a mulatto who had been born in Senegal, commanded the expedition. He had timed the landing to coincide with the short dry season of the coast which ended around September 15. Already the dry winds of the harmattan were dying and the lagoon mists rose more thickly each night. Each evening, too, mountainous cream and orange clouds piled higher in the sky, while lightning flashed among their cones. When the great cloud mountains fell upon one another torrential rains would explode along the coast.

Dodds worked quickly and efficiently, assembling an army of 5,000 African porters. On the last day of August the long column of guides, porters, Legionnaires, *tirailleurs* and a few French troops wound out of Cotonou. African scouts led the way, followed closely

169

by the Legion battalion. Dodds knew that the Legion would make the best possible advance and retreat guard; that was why he had requested it. Behind the Legionnaires stretched the snakelike column. Behind them, too, garrison forces and porters peeled off the formation every couple of days as Dodds developed his long and difficult supply line.

They were headed for King Behazin's capital of Abomey, a march of 150 miles by the only feasible route. It was slow, tortuous work through swamps which sucked a man up to his waist before comrades could pull him out. Mosquitoes, snakes, and fever were their most dreaded enemies at first. And soon ahead of them they heard the hollow thrumming of Behazin's signal drums. As the bush telegraph continued its messages by day and night, they knew that they were being watched carefully, but they did not know when they would be attacked. There was simply no way that Dodds could learn anything about the strength and displacement of Behazin's army. He could only take every possible precaution. Each night the force dug trenches and bivouacked in a square. Each dawn the men waited tensely for an attack until the sun was well up.

The attack came, finally, at dawn on September 18 near a village called Dogba when the strength of the column had been reduced to well under 2,000 by illness and garrison and supply duties. At one moment the bush surrounding the trenched square was the silent domain of the insects. And the next moment there was a salvo of musket and rifle fire like the explosion of a powder keg.

From the ground in front of the Legion's trenches rose screaming, bare-breasted women. As they charged, the morning sun shining on their oiled bodies, the Legionnaires blinked and shuddered. They had not been told a lie about the Amazons of Dahomey after all. Yet they felt paralyzed at sight of the onrushing horde. Legionnaires who hated women and Legionnaires who loved them found themselves fumbling with the trigger guards of their rifles. Their officers roared at them to fire and they got off a ragged volley. But the Amazons charged on through the smoke. Some Legionnaires who loved a fight above everything in the world suddenly had no stomach for

170

war. Some scrambled back out of the trench, wanting only to flee from the Amazons, as if they might be avenging wives. As their line bent, Colonel Faurex dashed among them, rallying them. Suddenly he fell, mortally wounded. The sight of Faurex down partially restored the Legionnaires to their senses.

They crashed into the Amazons with their bayonets. But they lacked anger, even though Faurex had fallen, and the bayonet work was sickening. Although the Amazons swung swords and machetes and hurled spears with the supple, strongly muscled arms of men, their firm dark-nippled breasts rose before the eyes of the Legionnaires. To some it seemed that the Amazons were offering them their breasts, not tauntingly and not with hatred, but with a kind of innocence. Some men who lunged their bayonets into the dark torsos of the Amazons scarcely had the strength to draw them out. And the women wounded and dying did not cry out; they endured the pain silently and stoically, gazing up at the Legionnaires with a kind of mild reproach in their dark eyes.

Somehow the Legionnaires beat back the attack. On the opposite side of the square the *tirailleurs* and French were throwing back a weaker assault by the men of Behazin's army. Then the Amazons, regrouping silently, charged once more. The Legionnaires resumed their sickening work and repulsed them. Still the women re-formed and charged again and again for two hours. And then, exhausted at last, they lifted up their wounded and walked away into the bush.

Outside their perimeter the Legionnaires and French counted 825 dead, the majority of them Amazons. Some Legionnaires, though drenched with sweat, found themselves shivering as they paced among the bodies of their enemies. One, who kept a diary, remarked that he could not stop shaking as he gazed down at the mild and peaceful expression of the Amazon dead.

The Legionnaires marched on gravely, eager now to get the war over with. Perhaps they were too eager, for on October 4 they walked straight into an Amazon ambush near the village of Porguessa. Again the cursed, fierce, lovely women seemed to hypnotize

171

them at first. Again they had to use their dirty bayonets on the creatures. Again they repulsed them.

A sense of guilt hung heavily over the Legionnaires as they slogged on north in the van of the column. The officers tried rhetoric on them. These Amazons were not really women, they said; they were brutal savages, black fiends, hellish furies, who wanted only to kill. But the arguments of the officers sounded hollow even to themselves. For they also had been among the Amazons with the bayonet; they had seen how stoically the women endured excruciating wounds and the looks of mild reproach they cast their executioners.

On October 5 the Dahomian Army hung along the flanks of the column, but did not attack it. At dawn the next day, however, the Dahomians attacked in force. A Legionnaire howled that the Amazons were attacking *them* again. Why didn't those women attack the *tirailleurs* for a change? Why did they always attack *them?* Keep them out of bayonet reach, someone shouted. The Legionnaires accepted the advice as the best idea of the campaign. They loaded and fired more frantically than they ever had in their lives. When the Dahomians finally withdrew, the nearest Amazon dead were thirty yards from the Legion lines.

On October 9 and again on October 10 bands of Amazons, swinging swords and machetes, sprang out of the bush upon the point of the Legion advance guard. On each surprise occasion the Legionnaires fired at them wildly and then ran pell-mell toward the rear. Roaring curses, officers raced after them. Each time the Legionnaires rallied and drove the women off with heavy fire, as if they had forgotten how to use their favorite weapon, the bayonet.

An officer harangued them on the evils of the Dahomians, crying that they were cannibals, murderers, torturers, mortal enemies. The men did not seem impressed by his lecture. They were more impressed by the suggestion of one among them who said that the Amazons were not really Dahomians, they were just brave *women*.

Although the Legionnaires had repulsed every attack and performed admirably as the advance guard, their state of mind finally was brought to the attention of General Dodds. Assembling them, and taking care not to mention Amazons, he tried another tack. The Legionnaires, he said, were the finest soldiers in the world and it was the greatest privilege of his military career to command them.

But Dodds could not make them hate Amazons or enjoy working them over with the bayonet. He did have a reason for trying to brace them, however. He had learned that the enemy had taken up a strong position at Koto, a village which covered the approach to Abomey. The next morning, October 14, the expedition would advance in a three-sided square on Koto. And the Legion, that finest body of soldiers in the world, would form the front side of the square.

Leading the assault of a French column was nothing new to the Legion. But leading it against *women* was quite another matter. They growled and cursed among themselves, telling one another it was the dirtiest war into which they ever had been sent. Officers and noncoms pontificated in the way of officers and noncoms since the beginning of wars, talking about their pride as a unit, their great fighting tradition, and all that cant.

They formed up on the front of the hollow square the next morning and advanced toward Koto in a sweating, muttering double line. They moved slowly through a parklike land of kapok and acacia trees, dressing their lines and glowering at their officers. Soon they heard the rumble of drums, and a few minutes later they came into a clearing and saw before them the thorn *boma* and thatched roofs of Koto.

Behind them the two little field guns of the expedition belched and trembled. Then they were going forward at the double, rifle butts slapping against thighs. Halt and fire! Fix bayonets! Forward! The ragged fire from the *boma* did not thin their lines. They crashed onto the barrier of sharp thorns, clawing and ripping their way through it. And there, waiting for them on the other side, were the cursed Amazons.

One hurled her spear at a Legionnaire, who ducked it. Then she came at him with her machete. As she swung it at his head, he parried the blow with his rifle and the machete clattered from her hand. As she swooped down to snatch it from the ground, he stepped on it. The back of her neck was exposed. One sharp downward drive of his rifle butt, in the dirty fashion of combat infighting, would snap her neck. But he could not bring himself to do it. Almost gently he pressed the butt against her neck, holding her head to the ground. And then, suddenly inspired, he shouted, *"Abandonnez-vous!"*

Probably they were the first words of French the Amazon ever had heard. She writhed, twisting over on her back, but the rifle butt still held her to the ground. Panting from exertion, she gazed up at him calmly, awaiting death.

"Mère de dieu!" the Legionnaire howled. *"Abandonnez-vous!"* He twirled his rifle and the point of its bayonet touched her throat. *"Comprenez?"*

Her hands fluttered in a strange gesture and then lay flat upon the ground. Slowly he withdrew the bayonet point and stepped back, but she merely gazed up at him inscrutably, making no move to rise.

Other Legionnaires who saw what had happened yelled with delight. These cursed women would surrender when fairly outmatched! Their cries rang out in the dusty melee within the *boma:* *"Abandonnez! . . . Abandonnez-vous!"* One Legionnaire with blood trickling from a machete wound in an arm simply tackled an Amazon round the legs, bore her to earth, disarmed her, and sat on her, laughing and gripping his bleeding arm.

Not all of them would surrender. Some died. Others retreated through Koto, fighting a valiant rear-guard action. But when the Legionnaires had cleared the village, they found that they had a score of Amazon prisoners.

The disarmed women sat in a circle, heads lowered, while Legionnaires crowded around them, staring curiously and muttering to one another. These Amazons were not beauties by the standards of the Louvre. For one thing, their skin was the wrong color; some had flat noses and all had shaved heads and filed teeth. But in strength and proportion of body most were magnificent, and even in exhaustion and defeat they sat with a surprising grace. Perhaps the grace that came from courage and fighting was the thing that made them attractive, thought at least one Legionnaire. It did not matter that they smelled of sweat and palm oil, that they were dusty and caked with the dried blood of wounds. These matters, in some strange way, merely accentuated their grace. They were Godless, but nevertheless creatures of God; they were killers, but from the necessity of their profession rather than the urge of their hearts. By heaven, they were not unlike Foreign Legionnaires!

Well, someone said, best give them some water. A dozen canteens were thrust forward, but the Amazons merely looked at the canteens warily. Then one Legionnaire crouched beside a woman, drank from his canteen, and handed it to her. She raised it to her lips, drank thirstily, and then passed it to the woman beside her.

Well, another said, best patch up their wounds. Legionnaires went among them with first-aid kits. At first the women shrank from the sting of iodine, but when the men bandaged their wounds, they began to smile. Gesturing animatedly to their beautiful white bandages, they chattered among themselves.

Someone fetched a Fon porter who spoke the pidgin English of the coast and a Legionnaire who spoke English was told to serve as translator. But what would they ask or tell the Amazons?

Tell them, someone said, to throw away those obscene skulls and bones they wear at their waists. Yes, all agreed, that was a good beginning.

As the Fon addressed the Amazons, however, they began to frown and shake their heads. One who wore the white headdress of an officer replied sharply and at length. The Fon turned to the Legionnaire who spoke English.

"Them sabby you big soldiers. You no sabby them big soldiers. Them tell you true mouth [the truth]. It be them country fash [the custom of their country] wear 'em bones. Them bones o' der enemy, took true an' hard by fight. Them say you wear 'em pants you took true an' hard by fight. Them say you no like if'n big man taken 'way you pants. 'Cause 'tain't fash for big soldiers lose der honor."

When the English-speaking Legionnaire had translated to the

175

others, they agreed without argument that the Amazons should keep their honorable trophy bones.

Ask them, someone said, if they know what's going to happen to them now?

After the Fon spoke, the Amazons murmured among themselves for some time. Finally the woman officer replied briefly.

"Them t'ink mebbe all you ——— all dem much." The Fon rolled his eyes. "Den you kill 'em. Them no like dat."

Some of the Legionnaires laughed and others frowned and finally a sergeant said no, they certainly were not going to do that; they were men of honor. He glowered around at his comrades fiercely. Well, God damn it, they were when it came to Amazons. . . . Well now, just ask them what they thought should be done with them.

The reply came quickly. "Them say you give 'em back them guns an' them go 'way. Tomorrow them meet you other side o' Koto an' have big good fight together."

No, no, *no!* That was impossible. They were prisoners of war and —well, a prisoner was a prisoner. Was there anything the Amazons wanted?

This time the women talked long and animatedly among themselves before replying.

"Them no like go to pokey [jail]. Them sabby them slaves now. But them wanna be you slaves. Them like big white soldiers better 'n big white rogue mans or big black rogue mans. Them fight 'longsides you. Them no fight they own people, but them go far 'way wid you. Them give you dash [a gift]. Them give you them. Them march wid you an' carry you burden on dem heads. Them fight 'longsides you. Them cook for you. Them sleep wid you an' ——— you. But them no wash for you. You git other slaves to do dat."

The Amazon officer spoke rapidly again and the Fon shook his head doubtfully, and translated:

"Them wants one big woman soldier to one big mans soldier. Them gits other big woman soldiers for odder big mans soldiers. Them an' you be wife an' husband. Just one wife, one husband. Now them wants pick 'em husbands."

Nearly all of the Legionnaires began to talk at once and some of the Amazons started getting to their feet. At last the sergeant who had mentioned that they were honorable men asserted his authority and shouted them into silence. He wanted several things made clear, and the Legionnaire who spoke English addressed the Fon in pidgin.

"You tell 'em women we like 'em an' they all right. But when we want woman we pick her. She no pick us. There one big trouble. We Foreign Legionnaire no can marry women in war. You tell 'em we like women of peace. War no good anyway. But war specially no good for women. You tell 'em be peaceful and we take care of them and for them not to get any more crazy notions."

How ably the Fon translated their thoughts to the Amazons the Legionnaires had no way of knowing. They only knew that the women acted passively and made no effort to escape. While the column rested beyond Koto and awaited reinforcements from down country, the Legionnaires found, in fact, that they did not need to guard their Amazon prisoners. They fed them and tended their wounds, and when they marched on toward Abomey, the women helped them carry their gear.

One day late in October the women asked permission to bathe in a forest pool. Stripping themselves, they sported in the shallow water. Laughing, they gestured to the Legionnaires to join them. Some Legionnaires went and watched them while others turned their backs. Those who watched them always insisted that they were among the loveliest women on earth.

It seemed, indeed, that some of those who went and watched the Amazons bathing saw many things differently after that. They said, for instance, that the Dahomians were not really cruel, despite all the tales told about the savage customs of the kings of Dahomey; after all, they did not torture their victims as had the so-called highly civilized Romans and the so-called Christians of the Spanish Inquisition. Some of those who went to the Amazons seemed to become possessed by many strange ideas. They said a black African was not necessarily inferior to a white European. He simply had adjusted to the climate and conditions of his country. When he did foolish things, it was because he was the victim of a foolish religion. In basic matters he acted wisely. For example, the fact that black Africans never had employed the wheel did not mean that their mental capacity was inferior to whites; it simply meant that in the dense bush where they lived the wheel was an ineffective instrument for helping them to carry their burdens.

The Legionnaires who said such things were not in haste to leave Black Africa. But the others scarcely could wait to go, and to their relief the campaign was completed quickly.

On November 6 the Legion entered Abomey. King Behazin had set fire to the city and fled. But his royal palace still was standing. To the surprise of the Legionnaires it was not the grand building they had been led to expect. It consisted only of a number of huts built of mud and straw in various sizes and surrounded by a thorn *boma.* As the stories had recounted, it was true that the throne room was cobbled with human skulls and a few skulls which had been sawed into drinking cups lay in a corner. But the king, his wives and concubines, his ministers, priests, and warriors all had gone, leaving only a scene of squalid meanness and no sense of grandeur.

Two days later a Legion patrol captured Behazin in a village to the north. He was as unprepossessing as his palace: a stubby, stout man who seemed totally indifferent to his fate. Wearing a loin cloth and puffing on a large pipe, he walked back to his deserted capital with the patrol. The French, as usual, were kind to vanquished royalty. They increased the amount of the pension they had at first conferred on Behazin and sent him with three of his wives into exile, first to Martinique and then to Algiers where he died fourteen years later after eating too heavily of a goat's-meat stew.

The original force of 800 Legionnaires had received about 250 reinforcements from Algeria before the short campaign ended. Of these 1,050 men, only 450 returned alive to Sidi-bel-Abbès. The majority of those who died were victims of fever.

As they sailed north, they speculated over what had become of the Amazons. Once there had been too many of them. And now there were none. When General Dodds had ordered the release of all prisoners, the Legion's captured Amazons had left reluctantly. But they went like good soldiers because the Legionnaires, some of them perhaps with reluctance, had commanded them to go.

The Amazons never were heard of again as fighters, not even as hunters. As women, however, some of them may have made good wives.

14

Of Men and
Mules and Empire

THERE WAS AN OLD LEGION SAYING that a Foreign Legionnaire is a
friend of the mule because, like it, he is stubborn, can carry heavy
burdens long distances with little food or water, combines the qualities of an ass and a horse, and is forbidden by the powers on high to
sire offspring.

Although exaggerated, like most sayings, it was true that the mule
became a fast friend of the Foreign Legion. The Spahis might ride
their fleet horses and the mounted units of *tirailleurs* might canter
about on their camels; the Legionnaires walked, and behind them
or beside them walked their mules. The mule lay back its ears, uttered a whistling groan, and slowly but doggedly it got there. It
supplied the Legion's remote posts; it carried the Legion's wounded
out of battle; and, when necessary, it sacrificed its carcass to provide
a Legionnaire with food or a slight cover from which to fight off
attacking tribesmen.

Neither mules nor Legionnaires ever were noted for possessing affectionate natures. Yet between many of them there grew a kind of mutual respect, a concern for the other's welfare. Legionnaires fed their mules before they fed themselves. Mules, for their part, developed a perceptive sense of imminent danger; when they halted and refused to go on, Legionnaires knew that an ambush was in the offing. A Legionnaire often cursed his friend the mule and slugged it with anything at hand, and the mule often kicked its friend the Legionnaire. But there is only one recorded instance of downright indecency between friends. Legionnaire Jean Martin once saw a moronic, perverted Legionnaire trying to commit sodomy with a mule; enraged, the mule kicked him over a wall and knocked him unconscious.

When Colonel Negrier formed his first Legion "mounted company" of two men to one mule, he passed up the horse as deficient in durability and calmness. He contemplated the camel briefly and then passed that up, too. Legionnaires, like all Europeans, were inept in handling camels. Though the camel performs feats of endurance, it is a stupid and savage beast, the males becoming almost unmanageable in the rutting season. Negrier settled on the mule as ideally suited to the missions of the Foreign Legion.

Considering the nature of the beast, it probably is appropriate that the mule shared some absurd as well as some heroic adventures with Legionnaires during the building of the French overseas empire. For the Legion, while ever mindful of the heroic tradition of Camerone, had plenty of experience in the Quixotic aspects of war.

Not every goal in military conquest is readily discernible. Sometimes a soldier can find great truth in Ralph Waldo Emerson's warning: "Beware of your goals lest you achieve them." Sometimes soldiers exert elephantine effort to catch a gnat.

Shortly after the Legion battalion sailed to fight the Amazons of Dahomey in 1892, a notice appeared on Legion bulletin boards in Algeria, asking for volunteers who were under twenty-five and exceptionally fit to undertake adventurous service in West Africa. Four officers and 120 men were quickly selected from the volunteers and a few weeks later, in September, they found themselves ascending the Senegal River in West Africa on a river boat. When the boat reached the town of Kayes at the head of navigation, the Legionnaires filed ashore into a dismaying situation: tethered in lines awaiting them were nearly 200 mules.

Colonel Archinard, who was responsible for pacifying thousands of square miles of the interior of West Africa, addressed the Legionnaires flatteringly. He said he had asked for them because they were the best men to seek out and destroy armed bands of slave raiders who were operating from the Sudan to the Ivory Coast. Furthermore, they would ride the mules as *mounted* troops at the head of Senegalese infantrymen.

A few days later they rode off into the interior and nearly a year passed before they were seen in Kayes again. For months it was rumored that they had disappeared, and Legion headquarters at Sidi-bel-Abbès finally wrote them off as a lost company.

Actually they were engaged in an exciting but pointless adventure. Lacking supplies, they lived off the country. Lacking solid intelligence about their enemy, they followed rumors. At Bamako the Legion officers decided to split their men into two forces. One rode north and east along the Niger River, searching for a notorious slaver called the Sultan Ahmadan. The other force swung south, seeking a slaver called Ali Kari.

The northward-ranging Legionnaires rode into a land of rolling yellow steppes scattered with mimosa and gum trees. At night their bivouacs echoed to the roar of lions and cries of hyenas. By day their mules picked a way through the haunts of more dangerous enemies: crocodiles, huge boas and pythons, hooded cobras, great centipedes, and deadly scorpions.

Ahmadan—if in fact he existed—avoided battle. Occasionally a small band of slavers fired on the Legionnaires and then fled. But they went on, like insatiable tourists, through the Upper Volta and even into the lower Sudan.

Meanwhile the southern force was being equally frustrated in its search for Ali Kari. It entered the great rain forests and passed into

French Guinea. Hearing another rumor, the mule-mounted Legionnaires swerved, lost themselves among the Nimba Mountains for a time and blundered into Liberia before they turned north again. If Ali Kari ever was in their vicinity they did not find him.

The Senegalese infantry had long since ceased following them and the French authorities had abandoned hope of seeing them again when they rejoined at Bamako six or seven months later. As best their officers could estimate, the two forces had ridden their mules a total of nearly ten thousand miles, had crossed and recrossed twelve major rivers, and fought fourteen engagements. They did not claim, however, that they had stamped out slavery in West Africa.

Orders soon reached them to return to Kayes, and there further orders sent them back to Algeria. No record exists as to how many men and mules survived. The Legion appears to have wished to forget that wild-goose chase.

As the survivors rode back to Kayes, they came upon two disgruntled companies of Legionnaires who had been sent from Algeria early in 1893. The unhappy men had believed they were volunteering for a great adventure only to find that they had the prosaic assignment of helping to build a railroad from Kayes to Bafoulabé. The officer in charge of the railroad construction was Major Joseph Jacques Joffre, who was to become the commander in chief of the French armies in World War I.

In December, 1893, the Legionnaires on the railroad-building detail were elated when Joffre was ordered to cease construction immediately and lead a force of Legionnaires and Senegalese at all possible speed to Timbuktu six hundred miles distant.

Timbuktu! The Legionnaires rolled their eyes and slapped one another on the back as they climbed on their mules and rode off with Joffre. Only four Europeans had visited the fabulous city near the Niger and lived to describe it. Timbuktu was the source of the gold, bright feathers, scents, and rare woods which the long camel trains bore north across the Sahara. Its women were said to be most desirable on earth, one traveler reporting that "Many men had died caressing the memory of their images . . . the women carried in their

183

blood and bones the gratitude of men . . . they had bathed in love for centuries."

The French had been trying to reach Timbuktu from one direction or another for decades. Now word had come that seven French marines and a dozen Senegalese, acting against orders, had deserted their gunboat on the Niger and "captured" the city. Other boats in the river flotilla had been destroyed or turned back by a horde of tribesmen. Now a force commanded by Colonel T. P. E. Bonnier was marching to their aid. And Joffre and his Legionnaires had been ordered to march also.

Joffre was a big, taciturn, heavily paunched man. His admirers called him a tower of strength, while his detractors insisted that he was slow thinking and lacking in feeling. In any case, he had the combination of stamina and courage that the English used to call "bottom." When a runner brought word that Tuareg tribesmen had destroyed Bonnier and most of his force near Timbuktu, Joffre did not turn back his small column of men and mules. They plodded on through a country infested with lions, crocodiles, poisonous reptiles, and fierce tribes. Though Joffre usually was slow to compliment troops, he later praised the Legionnaires for their "courage, abnegation and good comradership" as they clawed their way through the brush and swampland of the Niger basin.

Whatever their abnegation on the march, there was no question but what the Legionnaires looked forward to a life of ease and pleasure in Timbuktu. Anticipation made them drive themselves and their mules hard. Thus, as they clambered over a sandy rise on the morning of February 12, 1894, and Joffre said there lay Timbuktu ahead, the Legionnaires insisted among themselves that he must be mistaken.

For the fabled city of the myth was in reality almost a ghost town. Once its wealth had been great, but persistent warfare had reduced it to a shrunken ruin of a city stung by the wind-blown desert sands, without trees or birds, forever struggling to obtain enough firewood and water. If its women once had been beautiful, disease and poverty had brought them ugliness. Legionnaires who had expected to stuff their pockets with gold and enjoy the favors of lovely women found themselves hauling wood and water. And soon Joffre, the indefatigable engineer, had them hard at work repairing buildings and repaving streets. They were glad to be ordered back to Algeria a few months later.

There the Legion found that the empire builders of France still had an insatiable appetite for new colonies. For several years the island of Madagascar in the Indian Ocean, fourth largest in the world and bigger than metropolitan France, had been resting in their gunsights. When the Government of Queen Ranavalona III refused to accept a French protectorate over Madagascar on the reasonable grounds that it had no enemies except France, the French Government decided it was time for another colonial war.

The Malagasy peoples of Madagascar were largely peaceful agriculturalists. They did not, indeed, learn to become fierce fighters until they had lived under civilizing French influence for several years. But in 1895, when France decided to invade the island, its military leaders believed for some reason that they faced savage opposition. The ruling tribe, the Hovas of the central plateau, maintained their capital at the inland city of Tananarive. The feasible approach to it was from the east coast port of Tamatave, slightly more than 100 miles distant. But General Duchesne, the leader of the French expedition, feared the Hovas would resist so strongly along the route that he chose to land his expeditionary force of 8,000 men at the northwest coastal port of Majunga, about 350 miles from Tananarive by narrow trails which wound through jungles and over saw-toothed mountain ranges. Since surprise was out of the question and there had been no reconnaissance of the Hova defenses, his decision was curious. In terms of American geography, it was comparable to an invader deciding to attack Washington, D.C., by way of Boston rather than Norfolk because he believed he would meet greater resistance on the road from Norfolk.

A Legion battalion of 800 men and 200 mules landed at Majunga on April 23, 1895 and was assigned the familiar role of advance guard for the expedition. A few days after starting inland, the Legionnaires found that even their mules could not keep their footing on the tortuous trails and they had to leave them behind. They hacked their way through dense jungles, plagued by insects and heat and choking red dust which rose in clouds from their tramping feet. When they emerged on a ridge a couple of weeks later, a few Hovas fired wildly at them and fled.

By mid-June the column was so weakened by fever and a shortage of food that it had to halt until the trails back to Majunga were widened so that mules could bring up supplies. Three months later the staggering men still were 125 miles from Tananarive and in a desperate plight. Deciding on one last great effort, Duchesne selected about 3,500 of his fittest French and colonial troops, placed 350 Legionnaires at their head, and told them they must march to Tananarive or die. Legionnaires called it the March or Croak Column as they pressed ahead followed by the other troops and 3,000 mules which had been shipped to Majunga from France. In a steep mountain pass where the Hovas might have checked the force, they merely fired a few shots and ran again.

On September 28 the column came within sight of Tananarive. The small city spilled down a steep hillside from the Palace, an architectural monstrosity of wood and four brick towers which a Scotsman had constructed for Queen Ranavalona. Her aged Prime Minister had been running about with an umbrella for several days trying to organize resistance. Duchesne, for some reason, still believed that the Hovas might resist valiantly. He ordered an elaborate, cautious enveloping movement of the town. But before anyone was hurt, a white sheet was hung out a window of the Palace in surrender. The Hova army simply evaporated, leaving the French without a single military prisoner.

Queen Ranavalona III was sent into exile, first to Réunion Island in the Indian Ocean and then to Algiers, where she died in 1917. The French had added another huge territory to their growing overseas empire. The cost in lives lost in combat was slight—7 Frenchmen and 5 Legionnaires. But hundreds had been lost to fever; in the Legion battalion alone 221 died of malaria.

186

Three weeks after it entered Tananarive the remnant of the Legion battalion was ordered home to Sidi-bel-Abbés. If the Legionnaires did not feel exactly like conquering heroes as they returned to Majunga along the tracks they had climbed, they had a certain sense of luxury. For they rode on their mules.

15

Cheap

and Dirty?

ENLISTED MEN WHO DID NOT accept the mystique of the Foreign Legion usually led miserable lives. To them the Legion was a cheap and dirty outfit. All of them wanted to escape from it, but few succeeded.

In this century numerous books have been published by men who served in the Legion and hated it. All stress the brutality and degradation of Legion life. Most felt that its methods of disciplining its men were outrageous. The most devastating criticism of these chroniclers was that men who fought and died without complaint did so only after they had been literally beaten to their knees and "brainwashed" of any desire to live longer.

Here, for example, is former Legionnaire Ernst F. Loehndorff, a German, discussing the subject.

After several months at a Legion fort in the desert, when both men and officers began to feel like caged beasts,

. . . comrade Pieter de Gries, a blackhaired Walloon with a Dutch name, neglected to salute the captain, whom he had nicknamed "Machine-gun," as he crossed the yard. As a punishment he must now count one by one the contents of a big sack of dates. The Walloon looked at the commandant when he heard the command, his eyes glared, and it looked as though he was going to attack his tormentor. Then he grunted: "No!"

He is now locked up in the hottest of the cells, with chains on his hands and feet, while Machine-gun has already been walking up and down the yard for hours, stopping frequently in front of the cell and waiting to hear whether Pieter is going to whine or yell with rage or despair like his fellow-sufferers in the other holes. Gries, however, is a tough lad, and he keeps quiet. He is silent during the night as well.

It is now midday again, a blazing heat streams down from the burning sky, pressing one to the earth and making one feel like a dried-up wash-rag. The Walloon is taken outside the fort, stripped and buried naked in sand up to his neck. His eyes had a mocking look at first, but became bloodshot, and after about half an hour an appalling shriek comes from his vivid lips. And while we stupefied Legionnaires stand glaring at him, he yells for mercy without ceasing. He is willing to count ten sacks of dates, a hundred even, if only somebody will take him out of the terrible blazing heat that is burning and stifling him!

The night is over. And the Walloon's spirit is broken. He now belongs to the Legionnaires who execute every command, be it ever so crazy, submissively and idiotically, with the greatest hurry.

One has Loehndorff's word of this incident, as one has the word of many other Legionnaires about equally brutal acts. Inevitably the Legion had sadists among its officers and noncoms, as military bodies have had since the beginning of time. But the inference made by some ex-Legionnaires that such acts were a universal custom in the Legion of the past must be rejected in the light of the Legion's accomplishments in battle. A beating never gave heart to man or beast. And men of heart—not submissive automatons—win battles.

There must, too, have been one other consideration that commissioned and noncommissioned officers of combat units always have had to bear in mind: a bullet in the back of an officer's head in battle

189

can be an enlisted man's response to ill treatment. There are reports of such incidents in the Legion. But they are totally outweighed by incident after incident in which enlisted men have risked their lives to save a wounded officer or even simply to retrieve his dead body.

Critics have said that the Legion flogged its men. Late into the nineteenth century flogging was a common form of punishment in many of the world's armies and navies. When the French Army outlawed it in 1893, so did the Legion. Undoubtedly it occurred illegally on occasion and definitely the whip was used in the Legion's punishment battalion at Colomb-Béchar. But the report that flogging was a commonplace form of Legion punishment until comparatively recent times simply is not true. Kanitz, who served in the Legion at the beginning of World War II, says that he never saw an instance of it, though old Legion hands told him that it used to be practiced. Ex-Legionnaire "Tiger" O'Reilly claims to have witnessed a flogging in the mid-twenties, but in the view of at least one reader the Tiger's tale lashes about so wildly that it fails to strike anything with much accuracy.

For many years too much authority was vested in the noncoms, and some became little Caesars. Some misused their authority. Some honestly believed that brutality was the only means of disciplining certain men. The most effective check on some of them was the fact that the role of a Legion noncommissioned officer is more fluid than that in most national armies. There is great competition for his grade and corporals and sergeants frequently are broken back to private. Although the broken man normally is posted to another unit, he usually meets in time some of the men who have served under him. If he has been brutal, he is in for trouble. One man broken from sergeant walked into the mess hall at his new post and saw a man he had mistreated; the man rose from a table with a knife in his hand and sliced open the stomach of his former tormentor.

Nevertheless it is true that in years past noncommissioned officers improvised a great variety of punishment in an effort to maintain discipline.

Perrott-White, who had been a first-rate British soldier before he joined the Legion prior to World War II, saw an old Legionnaire strung upside down between two posts with his head just off the ground for seven hours. Sometimes, he says, a man would be forced to lie for a week under a tent on a floor consisting of sharp stones and would receive only bread and water twice a day. In another punishment he describes, a man was spread-eagled to a tree or a wagon wheel in the blazing sun and occasionally doused with water.

Perrott-White found some justification for these punishments, saying, "when dealing with some of the types of men we had in the Legion, such brutality may have been necessary, for they did not respond to any other treatment. A little brutality at the right time might possibly contribute to saving their lives in the future."

Still another punishment, described by Carlé and other Legionnaires, was the "silo." It was a funnel-shaped hole in the ground, broad at the top and narrowing to a point at the bottom. A man could neither stand nor lie down in it, but must half crouch in his own excrement through the heat of the day and the cold of night.

Early in this century General Negrier, making a surprise inspection of the barracks at Saida, found a row of fifteen silos, all occupied by prisoners. Angrily he ordered the men released, the holes filled up, and an end to that form of punishment in the Legion.

Even more brutal was the *crapaudine* treatment. *Crapaud* means toad in French, and a man subjected to the punishment found himself in the shape of a toad, lying on his belly, his wrists and ankles lashed tightly behind his back. The torture of having circulation cut off sometimes drove men insane. The *crapaudine* was used freely as a field punishment in the French Army before a man named Jacques Londres exposed various forms of cruelty in the Army's disciplinary measures. Officially it was stopped in 1920, but it persisted for many years afterward in the Legion's penal battalion.

A Legionnaire may be condemned to death by a court-martial board for any of three offenses: treason, desertion in the face of the enemy, and premeditated murder. In years past, cases of treason or desertion in battle rarely were brought to the attention of a formal court of inquiry. Legionnaires fighting on the colonial frontiers devised their own crude justice, as rough as that of the vigilantes of the American frontier. If a man turned cowardly in battle or divulged information to the enemy, everyone knew he no longer could be trusted. In a small fighting force where the safety of all depended on basic trust in everyone, such a man was a liability who must be removed. A drumhead court of officers convicted him on the spot and he was shot at once.

Rarely has the death penalty been pronounced by official Legion court-martial. A board seldom has been able or willing to establish premeditation in murder because a murderer usually has been drunk at the time he committed his act. His punishment commonly was sentence to two or three years in the prison battalion at Colomb-Béchar—which sometimes was tantamount to the death sentence.

Though not a capital offense, a second attempt at desertion in time of peace is almost as heinous a crime as murder in the eyes of the Legion hierarchy. A first attempt, provided the Legionnaire did not take his rifle with him, usually was punished with sixty days in the garrison guardhouse. A few officers even expected nearly every man to try to break away once and treated it rather tolerantly, as if it were a mild case of juvenile delinquency. Brief absences without leave, commonly because a man was drunk or had found a willing woman, used to be so commonplace that a system known as the *cinq-vingt-trois* was devised to determine the difference between desertion and a binge. Under the *cinq-vingt-trois,* a man could be absent from his post for five days and twenty-three hours without being considered a deserter. But one hour longer and he was in for it. If a Legionnaire tried to desert a second time and was caught, he was sentenced to Colomb-Béchar, sometimes for an indefinite term.

The rigid official view of the Legion was expressed by Colonel Fernand Maire, who commanded a regiment in Morocco and believed with all his heart in the Legion mystique.

"Before the Legion existed, weren't there enough disinherited men with unhappy love lives, men beaten down by adverse fate?" demanded Colonel Maire. "Before the Legion's birth haven't men known the pangs of hunger and the torture of disillusion?

"Passions are liable to burn the heart. Hunger ruins the stomach and consequently morale. The Legion restitutes hearts and stomachs to men who believe they have lost them. One asks oneself, therefore, why a few dirty weaklings, deliberately, in reward for the good things they have received, take advantage in turning their backs on the very institution which has supplied them?"

His was the viewpoint of most high-ranking officers and those Frenchmen in government who helped formulate the official policies of the Legion. Enlisted men who would not accept the mystique and believed they were the cheap pawns of the French Government were infuriated by such a patronizing attitude. To them it was like saying that slavery was a good institution because it improved the lot of the one enslaved.

Yet Colonel Maire meant every word that he said. The men had made a bargain, and those who did not want to live up to it were "dirty weaklings." He was a ruthless disciplinarian. When a battalion under his command was near the border of Spanish Morocco in the 1920's, 106 men deserted in a body. Only 20 were captured and the rest got safely over the border.

Calling in the friendly Arab chieftains of the area, Maire told them in front of the assembled battalion: "For every deserter you bring back to me, twenty francs for you. If you bring me his head—one hundred francs!"

No one else tried to desert while the battalion was in that region and the deserters who had been captured were sent to Colomb-Béchar, far down in the blazing Algerian desert.

The correctional battalion, as it was called, lived in tents at Colomb-Béchar. The men were guarded by trigger-happy Arabs and directed by tough sergeants who carried whips. When a prisoner arrived there in irons, his shoes were taken from him and he was paraded before his fellows. They were sun-blackened, red-eyed, stony-faced men with shaven skulls and skin stretched tightly over their bones. After a new prisoner's head had been shaved, he was issued a pair of dungarees, the only article of clothing he would wear during his imprisonment. Invariably the dungarees were in filthy condition and a sergeant told the prisoner he had forty-eight hours to scrub them as white as milk—without soap. If the dungarees were not in a satisfactory condition within that time, the man received no food until they were.

One of the jobs of the penal battalion was making bricks. The men worked in teams of five, two digging clay, one mixing it with straw, and two molding bricks and placing them in the sun to dry. Each team had to produce one thousand bricks a day; if it failed, its members received no food. Prisoners were not allowed any rest periods during working hours. In the blistering heat, which usually rose to 120 and 130 degrees, bareheaded and barebacked prisoners often fainted and were put back to work after they had been revived.

An Englishman, Adolphe Cooper, who served time at Colomb-Béchar nearly forty years ago, after a second unsuccessful attempt to desert the Legion, says he suffered cruel discipline not long after his arrival. It was the customary discipline of the penal battalion where there was no court-martial for any offense except murder. Guards had the right to shoot to kill, and a desperate prisoner sometimes provoked them to murder him as his only way of escape from an intolerable life.

One day Cooper, craving tobacco, leaned down to pick up a cigarette butt which a sergeant had dropped. Instantly the sergeant's whip lashed his bare back. Cooper instinctively balled a fist to hit him. Though a fellow prisoner stopped him, Cooper was sentenced to fifteen days in "prison."

At the time there were no cells at Colomb-Béchar; instead, a man received the *tombre*. Cooper was ordered to build his own prison by digging a hole the size of a grave—and then lie in it. A bit of canvas was put over him, but his head was left exposed to the blast of sun. On the first day he received some bread and a couple of pints of water. But the next day he received neither bread nor water as he lay there in the torment of heat and his own excrement.

"The third day I was starving and parched with thirst," Cooper recalled. "A man told me he would get me something really nice to eat so that I thought he was taking my part and was really going to do me a good turn. He brought me a mess tin of soup; I could see the grease on top and pieces of meat floating in it; it looked good and I sat up in my 'grave' and seized it ravenously while he smiled benignly. I took a great gulp and nearly choked; it was pure brine, so salted that I could hardly swallow it, but I was too hungry not to eat it all. Then began the torment of an intolerable thirst. I begged the sentry for some water. The man came and said that the pipes had burst and I should have to wait."

That night Cooper, nearly insane with thirst, staggered up from his "grave" and struck a guard. Whirling, the sentry knocked him out with a blow of his rifle butt. When he regained consciousness, he found that he was being given the *crapaudine* torture. Although some men did not survive the agony of that treatment, Cooper lived to write a book about his experiences in the Legion.

He was, in fact, surprisingly forgiving of the treatment he received in the penal battalion. After he had endured his punishment, he was brought before the commandant, a Captain Solomon.

"He really talked to me as a father might to a son," said Cooper. "The whole change in my later service came from that conversation with him."

Had Cooper been brought to his knees and "brainwashed" into thinking he had been punished justly? If so, he reformed his conduct only temporarily, for later in his Legion service he was in and out of more hot water than most picaresque heroes of literature. He seems to have been a man who could not carry hatred in his heart for a long time, a man who, after his enlistment had ended, left the Legion honorably with the feeling it was a fine military organization in which individuals sometimes acted with poor judgment.

Relatively few Legionnaires ever saw Colomb-Béchar. It appears that even fewer managed to escape from the Legion, though reports on the subject are confusing. The Legion's official position on the subject is silence. Once, however, in an unguarded moment, someone reported that about 2,000 Legionnaires had deserted during the fighting in Indochina after World War II. Some made their way safely home to Europe through China and Russia and some settled behind the Iron Curtain. Many also deserted during the struggle for Algerian independence, when the rebels offered them many inducements, including passage on "the Sicilian express," as small chartered fishing boats plying between Sicily and the Algerian coast were called.

But in earlier days in Algeria escape was extremely difficult. Arab goums, the French-appointed North African *gendarmerie,* were the most effective means of repressing desertions. A goum was given a modest reward for any deserter he turned over to the authorities. But any Legionnaire considering desertion thought twice about the hazards he ran with the goums, for the clothes on his back were worth more than the French reward. How often did a goum shoot a deserter in the back, strip him, and bury his body in a lonely grave?

Michael Alexander, who wrote an amusing account of his successful attempt to rescue a friend from the Legion, offers an apt explanation of why Englishmen—and Americans—usually detest the life of a Legionnaire.

"An Englishman is not as a rule a good linguist; he arrives in the Legion and probably doesn't understand a word anyone is saying. He has no friends and may well never meet a fellow countryman, for there are comparatively few in the Legion. Meanwhile he watches his colleagues palling up with one another and forming national cliques. He begins to feel himself an outcast and all the time some German non-commissioned officer is bawling orders at him. Moreover his life is desperately dull. If he joined up for excitement, romance, action—what does he find himself doing? Mending roads!"

It would appear that the cause for attempted desertion has been boredom far more often than ill treatment. There are numerous instances of men who had tried to desert during the monotony of garrison life and then became enthusiastic Legionnaires when their boredom was alleviated by combat.

There is not a known instance of a man's family or friends buying him out of the Foreign Legion. There are some instances of the Legion releasing as an undesirable character a man who had not the slightest chance of ever becoming even a passable Legionnaire. Great political pressure sometimes has been brought on the Legion to release a man, but almost invariably the Legion has resisted.

One exception involved the case of Legionnaire Bennett J. Doty of Biloxi, Mississippi, who deserted the Legion when it was fighting the Druses in Syria in 1927. He was captured quickly and somehow the news of his escape was reported in American newspapers. His family immediately announced that he was "shell-shocked." Then his mother remembered that his great-grandfather had saved the life of a Frenchman while defending him in a murder trial in Biloxi and had, as a result, been honored by King Louis Philippe, the founder of the Legion. Journalists, huffing and puffing for a dramatic story, reported that Doty was going to be executed, which was as unlikely as that President Calvin Coolidge would vote the Democratic ticket. Someone said that the "historic incident" involving the Biloxi murder trial should be used to "obtain clemency" for Doty—if the poor chap still was alive. Senators orated, urging that his execution be stayed "at least to permit the youth to return to his mother, who is ill in Biloxi." The State Department contacted its ambassador in France. Although the Foreign Legion did not quail before the combination of Louis Philippe, ancient Biloxi murder trial, ailing mother, United States senators and State Department, it was mortally embarrassed by so much publicity.

Doty was released from captivity and began a triumphal tour home from Syria by way of Sidi-bel-Abbès, Marseilles, and Paris. Few determined deserters ever were as lucky as he. Most ended up at Colomb-Béchar.

16

Appointment
in Morocco

FEW PROFESSIONALS AT ARMS, whether privates or high-ranking officers, ever viewed the Foreign Legion with indifference. It was,
usually, a matter of love or hate.

One of the most fascinating and intelligent French soldiers of his
age, upon first acquaintance with Legionnaires, took an instinctive
liking to them that was to last throughout his long lifetime. The
feeling was mutual; Legionnaires somehow always felt that they
were better men and soldiers when in the company of Louis Hubert
Lyautey.

Few men seemed less destined for a military career than Lyautey.
When he was two years old he fell out a window and, as a result,
spent his childhood in a plaster cast; not until he was ten was he able
to walk. Nevertheless, he graduated from St. Cyr and the Staff Col-
lege with high honors and took to military life with an energy that
may have been compensatory for his invalid childhood. Despite his

energy and intelligence, Lyautey was only a captain at the age of forty when, in 1894, the chief of the French Army's General Staff, General de Boisdeffre, called him on the carpet for having created a scandal.

In 1891 *La Revue des Deux Mondes* had published an anonymous article, "Concerning the Social Role of the Officer in Universal Military Service," that had shocked the upper echelons of the Army. The author called on officers to become the educators of the men entrusted to their charge. "The legal obligation to do military service is matched by the corresponding moral obligation to ensure that it shall produce the most salutary consequences from the social point of view," he wrote. Otherwise, the Army would offer nothing to the millions of men who passed through its ranks except "a weakened moral sense, a disdain for a simple, laborious life, and on the physical plane habits of intemperance and a vitiated blood."

It did not matter that the article eventually would have a profound influence on French military thought. Initially it was greeted as heresy and the anonymous author was termed a revolutionary. When Lyautey freely admitted to Boisdeffre that he was the author of the article, the Chief of Staff told him that his military career was finished. Lyautey was a royalist and a devout Roman Catholic—both anathema to the anticlerical civilian leaders of the Third Republic. Lyautey, said Boisdeffre, should either resign or betake himself to the backwash of Indochina. Captain Lyautey chose Indochina.

Soon after his arrival in Haiphong he visited the Legion's hospital and raged about conditions there, sounding like the unhappiest Legionnaire recruit. "In a ruined house," he wrote home angrily, "men are crowded together on camp beds like convicts, just a rug over each, no light, no air. What a tonic before the Legionnaire plunges into the jungle!"

Lyautey urged that a sum the equivalent of about $1,000 be raised in France to provide a new hospital for the Legion. "Can't the women of France send out some money for a new infirmary rather than the absurd luxury of cigars and liqueurs for the Legion?"

Lyautey was not assigned to the Legion. He appeared in Indochina as "an intelligence officer," that area of vague military duties to which the armies of the world used to assign officers who seemed to be out of step with the established order of affairs.

But his capabilities were instantly recognized by another extraordinary officer, Joseph Simon Gallieni. Then a colonel commanding the second military division of Tonkin, the lantern-jawed, energetic Gallieni put Lyautey in command of a company of French regulars and sent him into the jungle in pursuit of rebels.

On a height near a place called Hoang-Man, Lyautey and his company were surrounded by a strong Chinese force. When they were unable to break out after repeated efforts, Lyautey sent off carrier pigeons with messages asking specifically for the aid of the Foreign Legion. Half a company of fifty men commanded by Captain Bérenger marched to his relief. Looking down from the height, Lyautey saw the Legionnaires smash into the Chinese. He fought his way down the hill to link up with them, "a Calvary inch by inch," and had to abandon his own dead behind him. But he observed that the Legionnaires did not abandon their dead. When Bérenger fell, mortally wounded, Lyautey saw half a dozen Legionnaires spring forward to lift up his body. When they joined forces and fought out of the trap, he watched "the splendid brave wounded come slowly in." Nineteen Legionnaires besides Bérenger were killed and Lieutenant Pauvrehomme was among the wounded.

On February 12, 1896, Lyautey led a force of Legionnaires and Tonkinese allies against a contingent of Chinese who were holding out "on a sugar loaf with holes in it like a Gruyère cheese." With Lyautey in the lead, the Legionnaires dragged themselves toward the peak of "the devil rock," which echoed with rifle fire and the war cries of the defiant Chinese. At last they drove the Chinese off the summit which was crowned with a luxuriant growth of wild roses. The bugler sounded "To the Colors" and the Legionnaires came in slowly. Lyautey was moved almost to tears, he said, when the smiling Legionnaires "spontaneously gathered roses and brought them to me."

Campaigning with Lyautey, remarked a Legionnaire, was like being one of a group of happy children on an outing with a benign father. This handsome man with the heavy brows and flowing dark mustache seemed to be interested in absolutely everything under the sun; he had a novelist's eye for significant human detail and a statesmanlike view of the relative importance of his mission. The essay he had published in Paris about an officer's moral duty to educate his men was not just a polemic; as his columns floundered through the jungles of Indochina, he practiced what he preached by exchanging thoughts and information with everyone from the bugler to the second in command. He had no disciplinary problems. Even the most reluctant Legionnaires could not bear to offend "Father Lyautey." On one thing he did insist: a man must keep up with the column, for if he did not march, he assuredly would die. The stern looks he cast stragglers made exhausted men stumble on hurriedly, as if they sought his forgiveness. He allowed himself only one luxury and bowed to the Legionnaires' wish to carry him across rivers and streams on their shoulders. As his pen confided wryly to the page of a notebook, a commander did not keep his men dry by getting wet himself.

It was natural that Lyautey and the equally inveterate scribbler Gallieni should become fast friends. And it was natural that the Legion liked Gallieni almost as much as it did Lyautey. Both undoubtedly were the most intellectual officers with whom the Legion had yet come into contact. Both saw men as individuals and recognized the worth of abstract as well as practical ideas. They did not give offense because it did not occur to them to be offended.

The first systematic studies of the best means of pacifying an occupied area are to be found in the writings of Gallieni and Lyautey. They understood that an enemy's political structure could not be separated from his military organization and that both penetrated all levels of the population. Thus, in their opinion, the complex work of pacification should rest with a reasonable and intelligent army of occupation which vested all powers in regional commanders. Gallieni's "Instructions," written in Madagascar and dated May 22, 1898, remained the charter of the French Colonial Army until World War I:

"We must bear in mind that in colonial conflicts, which are, unfortunately, often forced on us by the unruliness of the population, we must never destroy except in the last extremity and, even when this is unavoidable, bring ruin only in order to build better. . . . Every time that warlike incidents oblige one of our colonial officers to proceed against a village or occupied center, he must never lose sight of the fact that his first responsibility, once the submission of the inhabitants has been assured, is to reconstruct the village, to set up a market in it and build a school."

This was a far cry from Bugeaud's concept of scorched-earth "pacification." To the men of the Foreign Legion the ideas of Gallieni and Lyautey were translated into terms of military employment over the course of many years.

In 1896, Gallieni was appointed Resident General and then Governor General of Madagascar. One of his first acts was to request the services of a Legion battalion whose members were veterans of Indochina. A battalion was formed promptly at Sidi-bel-Abbès and sent out to him. Eventually two others followed. For ten years the scattered Legion units on Madagascar were employed in carrying out the "Instructions" which Gallieni outlined as the wisest means of pacifying a territory. The Legionnaires did little fighting but a great deal of patrolling and even more construction of roads and buildings. Under Gallieni's direction the political supremacy of the Hova was destroyed and the autonomy of other tribes developed. He improved the economy of the huge island and was conciliatory toward economic interests other than those of the French. He was not responsible for the introduction of French customs to which the Malagasy did not take kindly.

Early in his administration he summoned Lyautey from Indochina and the two worked together closely. There was a marked change in Lyautey's career. His extraordinary talents for administration could not be ignored, even by the bureaucrats whom he detested. A couple of years before Gallieni left Madagascar in 1905 to assume command of an army corps in metropolitan France, Colonel Lyautey was transferred to eastern Algeria. His tact and shrewdness in handling affairs on the troubled Moroccan border soon led to his promotion. In time the career of General Lyautey became inextricably joined with the fortunes of France in Morocco. And, inevitably, the lot of the Legion was tied up with both.

French businessmen, army officers, and politicians who believed in the "civilizing mission" of overseas empire had long felt that France had an appointment in Morocco. Its Sultan, a weak and foolish man, exercised virtually no control over large areas of the mountainous interior inhabited by warring tribes. Morocco, said the French empire builders, should be made safe for Europeans and for capital investments. In complex diplomatic negotiations the great powers of Europe haggled among themselves for many years over the subject; each wanted all or at least a slice of the Moroccan pie, but coalitions among them prevented anyone from wielding the knife. The French at least had a legitimate complaint about the depredations of Moroccan tribes which sortied across the border into Algeria and the custom of dissident Algerian tribesmen of finding temporary sanctuary in Morocco.

The Legion had firsthand experience with the problems of the border. In August, 1903, as a Legion mounted company was escorting a caravan near the Oasis of Taghit about fifty miles from Colomb-Béchar, it was struck by a mounted band of more than 2,000 Moroccan tribesmen. Forming in its traditional square, the company fought off repeated attacks for more than eight hours. Before the Moroccans gave up, the company commander, the second in command and 39 Legionnaires were dead and 57 were wounded.

Lyautey arrived from Madagascar in the following October and was given command of the troublesome area. He set up headquarters at Ain Sefra, the city of nomads at the mouth of the desert. Wherever he inspected units of the Legion, he asked, "Have any of you men served with me before?" Always men stepped forward, replying, "Yes, sir, I was with you at . . . I saw you in . . . I was in your escort to . . ." Although power never corrupted Lyautey, he grew more feudal in manner as he aged. He lived grandly at Ain Sefra, dining off silver with flowers on the table while Legionnaires with exceptionally fine voices sang sad German songs for him and his guests.

But comfort did not soften him. He set up systematic patrols and stripped his columns to bare essentials so that they could move faster. He was frequently in the field with Legion and French units, sharing their long marches, the monotonous fare of *kessara*—rice and grease —and whatever water was available. Wherever he was, Lyautey always carefully explained the mission of the day to the men under him. Meanwhile, the French awaited an excuse to invade Morocco.

An excuse came in March, 1907, when a French physician was murdered in far-off Marrakech. A French force led by a mounted company of the Legion struck across the border and occupied the Moroccan town of Oujda without opposition. In the following August a riot in the Atlantic coast port of Casablanca provided France with a further excuse for intervening in Morocco. A Legion battalion of 600 men was landed at Casablanca with French units. When tribes in the area began resisting, the Legion force was increased to regimental strength and soon a force of 7,000 was deploying across the Plain of Shawiya.

The French press was represented in the expedition by what seemed to be a battalion of war correspondents, each with his personal ideas of how the battle of Morocco should be fought and won. At first the gentlemen of the press looked askance upon the Legionnaires, who were displaying their customary raffish wartime manners. They appeared to be in fear of imminent starvation, wrote one correspondent, for they stuffed the huge pockets of their coats with the products of the country—live poultry, piglets, small kids. Bent nearly double under their great packs, they stumbled along like gypsies, even piling firewood on top of all their other belongings. But at a place called Mediouna, where the correspondents first saw the Legionnaires under fire, they began to respect them. For the Legion proved imperturbable under heavy fire, maintaining its formations, halting to return the fire when ordered, responding precisely to the commands of its officers. When Legionnaires complained to some correspondents that they were not receiving extra combat pay like the French soldiers, the newspaper men obliged with stories about the unfair treatment. As a result, the Government eventually raised the combat pay of Legionnaires in Morocco.

From the Plain of Shawiya forces ranged into the foothills, attacking or attacked for week after week. In February, 1908, a horde of Moroccans swarmed upon a French and Legion task force in a gorge of the Mellah River. Two companies of Legionnaires, kneeling behind their wall of fixed bayonets in the front of the square were charged by 2,000 horsemen, each of whom had one or two footmen clinging to his stirrups. The square shook, but did not break as the Legionnaires drove back the tribesmen again and again. The battle ended at nightfall when both sides collapsed from exhaustion within rifle range of each other.

Meanwhile, fighting broke out on the eastern borders of Morocco. It would seem that the mere names of the places where the Legion fought would cover the face of a large monument to their numerous dead in the campaign. In the east, Lyautey commended them for their conduct in a pass known as Taforalt. At a deserted village called Menabha a Legion infantry company and a detachment of a mounted company lost 120 men, more than half their total numbers, in a surprise dawn assault; only a wild bayonet charge reminiscent of Camerone saved the remainder. There were almost as many casualties at the Oasis of Beni Ouzien. And when a company of 75 men was besieged at the frontier post of Bou Denib by a force nearly 20,000 strong, it held out for a day and a half before it was relieved by a Legion battalion. There were dozens of similar battles and skirmishes in both eastern and western Morocco.

It usually is forgotten, of course, that a soldier involved in a so-called skirmish cannot distinguish it from the Battle of Waterloo, for the size of a conflict has no relationship to the value a man places on his life. Legionnaires and French soldiers enduring months of hardship, marching, and combat in Morocco might have been astonished to learn that their efforts had become muted in the European press. They were merely involved in "the pacification of unruly elements" and the life blood they expended rarely was worth a paragraph.

But the French command had a plan; it was only awaiting an "incident" to put it into execution. The plan envisaged by Lyautey was a corridor across Morocco from the Algerian border through Taza and the inland capital of Fez to Casablanca and Rabat on the Atlantic coast. In anticipation of it, forces were built up in both the east and the west. The necessary incident, whether actual or faked, finally came in April, 1911, when Europeans in Fez reported that they were besieged and sent out an appeal for aid.

An expedition of 35,000 men landed at Port Lyautey, the harbor which the French had developed north of Rabat, and marched east toward Fez. Meanwhile, another strong force began to penetrate Morocco from the east. There were Legion battalions in both expeditions and they were to engage in much bloody fighting before the plan had been completed.

The newspapers warmed to the subject of war in Morocco again, for it had taken on an honorable tone: the relief of European Christians surrounded by ferocious heathens in the remote city of Fez. But an action typical of the Legion's role in the bloody Moroccan war was not worth a paragraph in the press.

On May 15, 1911, while the French force probed westward into Morocco from the Algerian border, two Legion platoons of the 6th Battalion were ordered to peel off and scout a village called d'Alouana. As the Legionnaires entered a bowl in the hills, they were suddenly struck from all sides by heavy rifle fire. Pinned to the earth in a circle, they fought off continual attacks. Gradually the circle shrank smaller and smaller as wounded men crawled toward its center. The dead were dragged in and their bodies served as a slight cover for those who still lived and kept firing.

Five hours later, when two companies of Legionnaires came in search of the missing platoons, they found only six men still alive. On the bodies of a corporal and a private were found the rifle bolts of the other dead men. The two had collected them in order to render the rifles useless if they fell into Moroccan hands.

Resistance was so fierce in eastern Morocco that the French gave up their effort there temporarily and concentrated on pressing the corridor from the west. The Legion units were kept busy building and manning blockhouses and skirmishing against tribesmen until an all-out offensive was begun in May, 1914.

Then forces totaling more than 40,000 men under Lyautey struck at Taza from both east and west. There were Legion units with both forces. Fighting against fanatical Moroccan resistance, the two armies finally linked up and completely opened the corridor across the country in mid-June.

Six weeks later Lyautey received orders to halt all offensive activities in Morocco. France was mobilizing for war against Germany.

17

"A Rendezvous
with Death"

IF A VETERAN LEGIONNAIRE had heard anyone say that the century between the downfall of Napoleon and the outbreak of World War I had been an era of relative peace, he would have laughed. Yet many were saying that in 1914, especially in America.

To many idealistic young Americans in 1914 it seemed a long time since there had been a cause worth dying for. Now the war between France and Germany offered, to their minds, a clear-cut case of right versus wrong. They saw it in the caricature of a popular political cartoon of the day: France, an innocent and virginal maiden, threatened with rape by a German beast. Knowing nothing about the agonies of war, they were eager to enlist in one that offered them the role of brave crusaders.

A similar feeling swept young men in all areas of the world. They knew something of the spirit of the French people as expressed in their art and literature, though they knew practically nothing about

French arms and politics. From every continent and most of the islands of the seas they hastened to enlist with the French. And then they discovered an awkward situation. There was a law on the books that said he who fights in the Army of France must be a citizen. But for many a legal technicality in France there is another legal technicality that circumvents it. These enthusiastic young men were welcome to join the Foreign Legion for the duration of the war with Germany.

Mobilization for the war found the veteran Foreign Legion in a predicament. More than two-thirds of its members and nearly all of its noncommissioned officers in North Africa were Germans or Austrians. The French high command, feeling that they were not to be trusted to fight for France against their countrymen, ordered them kept on duty in Algeria and Morocco. A few hundred German and Austrian Legionnaires who spoke too vociferously against the French were jailed for a time, but most Germans and Austrians served loyally throughout the war. Within a couple of weeks, in fact, some were sent to France to help train the growing numbers of foreigners who were enlisting for the duration.

Altogether 44,150 foreigners served in the Foreign Legion in France during the course of the war. The records of the French Ministry of Defense list them as coming from 101 countries. Italy led the list with 6,463 volunteers. Thousands came from Switzerland, Russia, Belgium, Spain, and Greece. Almost 1,100 were listed as American citizens, though some of these turned out to be French who had disguised their nationality for one reason or another. Panama, Paraguay, Hong Kong, Gibraltar—each was represented by one man.

The numbers fluctuated with the fortunes of war, as did the units of the Legion. After November, 1915, however, all units on the Western Front were fused into a single regiment—the *Régiment de Marche de la Légion Etrangère*. Known as the R.M.L.E., it served throughout the remainder of the war in the Moroccan Division, which also included Zouaves and Algerian *tirailleurs*.

The first wave of volunteers surprised the French. A training camp with a cadre of veteran Legionnaires hurriedly shipped from Sidi-bel-Abbès was set up at Rouen and then was moved to Toulouse when Rouen was threatened by the German advance.

The first Americans to join, numbering seventy-odd, had a great variety of backgrounds. There was the aristocratic Edgar J. Bouligny of New Orleans, a descendant of General Dominique de Bouligny who had commanded Napoleon Bonaparte's troops in Louisiana. And there was Herman Chatkoff, a Brooklyn Jew who had been washing cars in a Paris garage. Kiffin and Paul Rockwell of Atlanta, descendants of French Huguenots, became pals of Bert Hall, whose most recent venture had been driving a Paris taxi without being able to speak French. John J. Casey of San Francisco and James Stewart Collins of New York, artists studying in Paris, came in with Alan Seeger, a Harvard graduate who was gaining a reputation as a poet.

Edmond Genêt, descendant of the French Minister to the United States during the French Revolution, deserted the United States Navy to enlist. Other Americans left wives, families, jobs—all impelled by the motive Seeger expressed: "It is for glory alone that I engaged." René Phélizot of Philadelphia, a renowned African big-game hunter, signed up behind Harry C. Collins of Boston, a sailor who had jumped ship. Others included a professor of philosophy, and a barber, two lawyers and a pharmacist, a professor of Oriental languages at Columbia, and a boxer, several engineers, a drygoods salesman, four Harvard men, a Yale man, and two tough Paris apaches, who spoke not a word of English but had papers that proved they were American citizens.

In the training camp at Rouen and then at Toulouse these Americans milled around with other foreigners whose backgrounds were as various. There was Rif Baer, an Egyptian, and a brown-skinned little man from Ceylon whose name was so unpronounceable that the Americans dubbed him "Gunga Din." All were impressed by the bearing of a Persian prince named Karaman Khan Nazare-Aga. And all were fascinated when one day twelve Cossacks in native dress appeared.

No one knew how they made their way to France, for the Cossacks spoke not a word of French or Russian or any language that anyone in the camp of numerous tongues could understand. After a few days the Cossacks grew morose and refused to turn out for formation. Then they went on a hunger strike in their barracks while officers and men pleaded with them to explain what was wrong. Finally a Russian enlisted who understood their dialect and he explained the trouble. The Cossacks had left the Crimea to join the Foreign Legion Cavalry and now to their horror they found themselves in the infantry. Sadly the French told them that the Legion had no cavalry and released them from service.

The veteran Legionnaires from North Africa looked on all the duration volunteers dourly and vowed they never in their lives would make passable soldiers. Chatkoff maintained he already was a professional soldier. When a Legion sergeant grimly asked where he had served, Chatkoff replied gravely, "Five years in the Salvation Army." When Seeger, who claimed to have served in the Mexican Army, was dressed down for his awkwardness at drill and his corporal said that even the Mexican Army couldn't be that clumsy, Seeger said, "But I was a guerilla fighter."

The commander of Seeger's squad in Battalion C was Corporal Weidemann, a tough old German Legionnaire with sixteen years of service, who was typical of the Legion cadre. Nearly every morning he began with the same speech to his awkward squad, "You have good will, but you never will make good soldiers. The Germans will win the war, but I've given my word to France and will keep it."

Tough though he was, Weidemann had moments of surprising tenderness when he fretted over the blisters on his men's feet.

After the sketchiest training, Battalion C, in which most of the first American volunteers were serving, left Toulouse on September 30, 1914, for a quiet sector of the front in Champagne about thirty-five miles southeast of Rheims. On October 21 the Battalion toiled up through the vineyards from Hautvillers to Verzy. Colonel Passard, an old Legionnaire, rode behind them, rounding up stragglers.

When he came on Carstairs and William Thaw, recently of Yale, lying down and resting their feet, Passard demanded, "What are you doing there?"

In his best undergraduate French, Thaw explained that they were tired.

Passard, drawing his revolver, roared, *"Marchez!"*

And they marched.

After they entered the trenches, the new Legionnaires began to learn that war is—among other things—monotonous. Weeks grew into months and they did not find any glory in the dreary routine of the trenches.

In a dispatch dated December 14, 1914, to the New York *Sun,* Seeger vividly described a way of life that was to become familiar to millions of soldiers in World War I:

The typical trench dugout resembles catacombs more than anything else. A long gallery is cut in the ground with pick and shovel. Its dimensions are about those of the cages which Louis XI devised for those of his prisoners whom he wished especially to torture; that is, the height is not great enough to permit a man to stand up and the breadth does not allow him to stretch out. Down the length of one curving wall the soldiers sit huddled, pressed close, elbow to elbow. They are smoking, eating morsels of dry bread, or staring blankly at the wall in front of them. Their legs are wrapped in blankets, their heads in mufflers.

Slung or piled about them, filling every inch of extra space, are rifles, sacks, cartridges, belts and other equipment. A villainous draft sweeps by. Tobacco smoke and steaming breath show how swiftly it drives through. The floors are covered with straw, in which vermin breed. The straw is always caked with mud left by boots which come in loaded down and go out clean. To get new straw we sometimes make a patrol in the night to the outskirts of a ruined village in front of our lines and take what we need from a deserted stable. It is our most exciting diversion just now.

The roof of the dugout is built by laying long logs across the top of the excavation; felling trees for these coverings occupies a large part of our rest intervals. On the completeness with which these beams are covered with earth depends the comfort and safety of the trench. Wicker screens are often made and laid across the logs, sods are fitted over the screen so as to make a tight covering, and then loose earth is thrown back on top. This is an effective protection against all but the heaviest shells. If the roof is badly made, out of branches, for instance, the rain drips through and makes life even more miserable inside.

Where the lines run close together the soldiers sleep in simple trenches and fire through small holes in the wall of the combined trench and dugout. Generally there is room to build the trenches out in front of the dugout or alongside. There is a section of a company of infantry for each trench, and between the trenches are deep communication ditches.

A squad has stayed behind in the woods to bring us the day's provisions. Before daylight it arrives and the distribution takes place. Great loaves of bread are handed down the line; each man takes his ration of half a loaf. There is one box of sardines for each two men. A cup of coffee, a small piece of cheese, a bar of chocolate must last us all day, until darkness permits another squad to leave the trench to go down after the evening soup. . . .

By a system of reliefs by alternating battalions the disposition of our time is as follows: Six days in the first line trenches, six days repose in our village headquarters ten kilometers back; then six days' reserve in the woods; six days again in the village, and so the routine recommences. Thus we have three distinct kinds of existence. . . .

The smell of wicker screens and the branches in the dirt on top of the trench reminds me of Christmas odors in American homes decorated with green things for the holidays. Then the smell of powder from the shrapnel kills the holiday reminder. . . .

We shall go on waiting as patiently as we can for the day when we shall be ordered to advance against the shell and steel of the invisible enemy. It will be a happy day for all of us, for uncomfortable inaction has more terrors than shell and steel. . . .

The Legionnaires in the trenches naturally had only the myopic view of war that always has been the lot of the ordinary soldier. Actually the war of maneuver on the Western Front had ground to a deadlock by the end of 1914. Both sides had fumbled golden opportunities and had time and again been saved from disaster only by the confusion of their enemies.

213

In the decade previous to the outbreak of war new leadership had come to the high command of the French Army. It came from the veterans of the colonial empire, in men such as Gallieni and Joffre, and its military philosophy was that of the offensive. Gallieni, ready for retirement, was offered the role of commander in chief but refused it and recommended Joffre in his place. Lyautey was the one empire builder who could not be tempted to the Western Front; except for a brief period in 1917, when he served as Minister of War, he remained in Morocco struggling to maintain and even to expand French rule.

Both the French and the Germans had plans for the offensive in the war for which each had long been preparing. The German plan was better than the French, which was based on a faulty estimate of German strength. But the Germans diluted their design for a vast scythe sweep with their right wing through Belgium and down upon Paris, and then they bungled it with their left wing, which did not withdraw according to plan. Gallieni was the first to see the opportunity as the German right curled short of Paris on the Marne in the opening days of September, 1914. He finally prevailed on Joffre to smite the Germans there. Though the French were victorious, Joffre was slow to make up his mind and faulted by failing to strike the Germans on flank, as Gallieni had urged. Perhaps Gallieni would have made a better commander in chief, though nothing is more fruitless than the guessing game of choosing replacements for men who have filled historic roles. If Gallieni was a military genius, Joffre did not choose to recognize it by placing him in an important command. On the other hand, when Gallieni became Minister of War, he defended Joffre against numerous critics.

To the Legionnaires who were training and marching into the trenches such matters seemed remote and unimportant—if they knew about them at all. Yet the fates of soldiers in the ranks inevitably are affected by the characters and plans of their leaders. Because the leaders of both sides failed in their plans to lead their armies to a quick victory in World War I, millions of men were doomed to die in the long and bloody warfare of the trenches.

As the war sank into deadlock on the Western Front, Gallieni and Winston Churchill, then first lord of the British Admiralty, were among those who strenuously urged that the problem in the West could best be resolved in the East. Both were deeply versed in military history. They knew that "the longest way round is often the shortest way there" and that warfare had long proved it wiser to try to overcome problems of terrain than to attack frontally an enemy who is firmly posted and prepared. Lord Kitchener described the situation succinctly on January 2, 1915, when he wrote: "The German lines in France may be looked upon as a fortress that cannot be carried by assault and also that cannot be completely invested, with the result that the lines may be held by an investing force while operations proceed elsewhere."

Gallieni urged that if a powerful army were landed at Salonika in Greece, it would convince Greece to join the Allies; it would seize Istanbul from the Turks, giving Russian shipping an outlet from the Black Sea, and then it would advance up the Danube with the co-operation of the Romanians against the Austro-Hungarian Empire. But the Western Front commanders, wedded to their hope of an early breakthrough, viewed the plan recommended by Gallieni and Churchill as harebrained military infidelity. What developed was an effort by a minor force in the Dardanelles against well-fortified and superior Turkish numbers. Four British divisions and one French division comprised the landing forces; with the French division went a Foreign Legion battalion of 600 veterans from North Africa.

The effort had the almost invariable result of military compromise: failure. Slowness and uncertainty further spoiled the chances of success. The British landed at Gallipoli while the French division made a diversionary attack at Kum Kale on the Asiatic shore. There, after helping to establish a beachhead, the Legion battalion was cut off in a small valley fronting on the sea. But it managed to hold out until relieved. On June 20, 1915, the Legionnaires again hurled themselves at the Turkish containing lines. In the battle every commissioned officer was killed and a sergeant major finally pulled back all that remained of the battalion, less than 100 men.

Brought up to strength again by Legion veterans from North Africa, the battalion joined a token Allied force sent to aid Serbia. Again it was a matter of too little and too late. As the Bulgarians pushed south, the Legionnaires fought a rear-guard action throughout the long route of the Serbian retreat. After Serbia fell, the remnants of the Legion battalion retreated into Greece where they remained until August, 1916, when Romania joined the Allies.

Once more the battalion was brought up to full strength by North African veterans and marched north to join the Serbs, who had risen again. In the Serbian drive against the Bulgarians the Legionnaires were the only infantry to keep pace with the Serbian cavalry in the advance guard. Inevitably the pace and constant fighting took a toll; when the Legionnaires marched into Monastir with the cavalry, the battalion had lost 200 men.

After Monastir the story of this unit, known as the 1st Battalion of a paper regiment, grows dim. Few replacements trickled through to it and its numbers were wasted away by fighting and disease. Finally, at the end of 1917, it was recalled. But there is no record of how many men returned to Sidi-bel-Abbès. Strangest of all, a small group of about platoon strength stayed on in the Serbian mountains until after the Armistice. Apparently these men were presumed dead. Ciphers lost in the records, they possibly never received an order to return. It cannot be learned today what they did or why they stayed together in Serbia. But one day after the war had ended, military bookkeepers in Sidi-bel-Abbès were startled by an inquiry from the lost platoon in Serbia as to when it might expect to be paid and return to Algeria.

In September, 1915, the French ruled that all Americans in the Legion on the Western Front could join a regular French regiment if they wished. The following month Seeger wrote his mother that "Most of the other Americans have taken advantage of [the new rule]. There is much to be said for their decision, but I have remained true to the Legion where I am content and have good comrades. I have pride particularly in the Moroccan division, whereof we are the first brigade. Those who march with the Zouaves and the

Algerian *tirailleurs* are sure to be where there is honor. We are *troupes d'attaque* now, and so will assist at all the big coups, but be spared the monotony of inactive guard in the trenches, such as we passed last winter."

Like every good soldier, Seeger desired action. Apparently he was not yet content with the action he had seen, though all the Legion units on the front had been heavily engaged.

In November, 1914, Lieutenant Giuseppe Garibaldi, a grandson of the famed Italian liberationist fighter, had brought a large number of Italian followers into France to fight the Germans. A regiment composed largely of Italians was created on the rolls of the Legion and was known popularly as the "Garibaldi Brigade." Five members of the Garibaldi family fought in it.

This hastily assembled regiment—the 4th—was thrown into action promptly. On Christmas night, 1914, it moved against German positions in the heavily wooded and ravined Argonne near Bolante. It was war such as the Italians never had visualized. Carefully placed and concealed German machine guns caught them in an enfilading fire and within minutes 4 officers and 44 men had been killed and more than 170 wounded. Two days later the Italian Legionnaires attacked again and were repulsed with even heavier losses. In January, 1915, the Germans began to increase their pressure in the Argonne. A French unit holding an important ravine panicked and the Italians were rushed into the gap. They checked the Germans, but could not recover the ground which the French had lost. By the time Italy joined the Allies in May, 1915, the Garibaldi Brigade had lost 429 killed and more than twice as many wounded. The French released the survivors in order that they could join the Italian Army.

That month Joffre launched a new offensive in Artois where he hoped to capture the commanding height of Vimy Ridge and thrust into the German transportation network on the plain of Douai. The 1st Legion Regiment, sent north to join one of the nine front-line assault divisions, was placed in the corps commanded by General Henri Philippe Pétain.

Before daybreak on May 9 the Legionnaires formed up at a farm

217

known as Berthonval. For four hours the French artillery smashed at the draws and ridges in front of the lines, and then came the order to the 1st Battalion to take off. Its destination was a section of the ridge called Hill 140. The Legionnaires advanced through open country plowed so heavily by the French bombardment that it seemed there could not be a German left alive. Suddenly, however, there came the rattle of machine-gun fire from emplacements which the Germans had reoccupied as soon as the French barrage lifted. Men fell in windrows, but others struggled on for three hundred yards before they were pinned hopelessly to the churned earth.

The 2nd Battalion moved to support the 1st at the double, but was pinned down in the same manner. The 3rd Battalion dashed forward at an angle and managed to seize a German strong point on the flank. The dazed men of the 1st and 2nd Battalions, getting to their feet and scrambling on, overran a few outlying posts. But then heavy German artillery fire was zeroed on them and they had to release their tenuous hold and dig in farther back. The next morning they were relieved. Of 4,000 officers and men of the 1st Regiment who had started the attack, only about 1,800 were able to walk back numbly to Berthonval.

On June 15 the battle burst out again. Three times the Legionnaires swarmed out of their trenches before Berthonval, and three times they were beaten to earth by what seemed solid sheets of machine-gun fire.

The same thing was happening all up and down the flanks of Vimy Ridge. The German lines were like a wall of steel. A gain of about two miles cost the French 100,000 lives while the Germans paid a price of only 75,000 lives for their defense. In the previous great battles of the war the losses had been about equal. But following the horrible carnage in Artois the French General Staff decided that a breakthrough could be achieved and exploited only after the Germans were so worn down that they had no reinforcements. In effect this made naked attrition the sole aim of the General Staff.

Joffre would not give up the offensive. Sometimes it seemed that he threw his divisions like snowballs at the ironclad German positions. It happened again in Artois in September when the 2nd Legion Regiment, in which Seeger served, was assigned the objective of a farm known as Navarin. Regimental strength was so depleted that only 1,600 men rose from their trenches on signal and swarmed into withering machine-gun fire. Numerous officers and men lunged ahead, trying to rally others behind them in the established tradition of the Legion. A trumpeter rose from the ground and played a few notes of *"Le Boudin"* in an effort to inspire the men—and then he fell dead. But bravery and all the old battle virtues of the Legion were mere suicide in the face of chattering machine guns. On the Western Front of World War I warfare had become more deadly than ever before in history. The 2nd did not reach Navarin. Less than 800 Legionnaires were able to stagger off the field.

This was the kind of warfare in which Seeger and countless other young men of numerous nationalities sought "glory." Several among the first group of Americans who enlisted in the Legion transferred to the international air squadron which became known as the Lafayette Escadrille. Although it has been called "the air force of the Foreign Legion," it was in no way connected with the Legion organization. Genêt made the transfer and was the first American to be killed in air action in the war; in a letter to Genêt's family, United States Secretary of the Navy Josephus Daniels cleared him of the charge of having deserted the Navy and commended his heroism. Another who transferred out of the Legion with Genêt was Zinovi Pechkoff, who had been living in America and was the foster son of the Russian writer Maxim Gorki. Pechkoff was to become one of the most decorated aces of the war—and later would return to the Legion as an outstanding officer in North Africa.

Those, like Seeger, who remained with the Legion on the Western Front had their greatest trials before them. Heavy casualties and fewer volunteers resulted in the decision of November, 1915, to combine all Legion forces in France into one regiment and place it in the Moroccan Division.

In June, 1916, the French and British began planning a huge offensive on the Somme with the intent of relieving German pressure on embattled Verdun. The Moroccan Division, with its Legion component, was moved into a front-line position in that sector.

On June 24 the French and British guns began to roar north and south of the Somme Canal. Hour after hour the guns thundered and shells crashed, leveling German trenches, splintering woodlands, smashing villages. The German artillery replied, and to men huddled in dugouts on both sides it seemed that the earth never would cease its trembling. Day after day the bombardment continued. On July 1 about 100,000 of the half million waiting French and British troops moved out across no man's land at various points. But the Legion still waited, and to men like Seeger the waiting was far worse than going over the top.

In the early morning darkness of July 4 the French artillery supporting the Moroccan Division rose to drumfire crescendo while the men in the trenches poised themselves tensely. The Legion scorned the shrill whistles and stagy megaphones with which the French and British ordered their men to the attack. Its signal instrument always had been the trumpet—never the bugle (even to this day), although its instrumentalists were called buglers. In the hot and dusty dawn of July 4, as the French barrage lifted and rolled away like fading thunder, the trumpets raised their sharp demand to charge. To a man like Seeger they must have sounded like the trumpets of Lancelot and Tristram. But they also were the trumpets of doomsday. For, as he clambered out of his trench with the leading battalion, deafened Germans ran up the steps of their deep dugouts and manned their machine guns. How well the Legionnaires knew the sound of those guns, a little slower than their own and seeming to have a slight stammer in their burst of fire. Before the leading Legion battalion had gone a hundred yards it was struck by the stuttering fire of a dozen machine guns. Within less than a minute it had lost all of its commissioned officers and one-third of its men.

Seeger was well versed in the literature of courage, which offers helpful suggestions on how to get through that necessary business at the very end of life. Its eloquent writers, few of whom have been shot at and none of whom ever has sent back a final report from beyond the grave, advocate a certain grace, as if death were a ballet performance. But there was no grace in a place like the Somme. There was only the terrified whistling of your breath through your teeth, the taste of dust as you lay prone, wanting to claw your way into the earth beneath the chatter-chatter of the guns. At the very end of life, then, there was the frantic wish to prolong it. All the heroes were dead or pinned in the dust or writhing in the agony of ripped bowels and flooding blood. The leading battalion could not stir.

But a second Legion battalion was coming out, moving off at an angle toward the dubious cover of slight hollows. Rushing, weaving, throwing themselves prone, and then running again when the guns seemed to turn their chatter in another direction, the Legionnaires pressed along the flank of their sector. Their goal, remote as Valhalla to all of them, was a splintered hamlet called Belloy-en-Santerre. Hurling grenades and then following their fragmentation with lunging bayonets, they knocked out a machine-gun squad. And then they destroyed another, and another.

In the battalion which had been pinned down, men stirred. Seeger must have gone through one of those swift personal inventories. He was alive, he was not wounded, and if frightened, no one but he need ever know it. The discretionary element in valor must finally have dawned on him. Though a glorious charge at the enemy had become absurd, he could crawl forward. Others were crawling, too —forward. Some may have been making an interesting personal discovery that the cheerleaders of war had neglected to mention: You crawled forward not because you were courageous, but because you were ashamed to crawl toward the rear. Instincts beyond the mere wish to survive were returning to them; habits of training were taking hold. Corporals could serve as captains; the co-operation of a squad was as essential and as delicately balanced as the co-operation of nations. Covering one another, assigning themselves German positions to be taken, they crawled on. They captured a machine gun. And then they burst on a German dugout with grenades, bayonets, and flailing trench clubs. If their actions were those of Neolithic savages, they did not think about it till later. They could think only about killing Germans and trying to stay alive themselves.

When the remnants of both battalions rolled together on the outskirts of the charred and blasted Belloy-en-Santerre, the Legionnaires felt a kind of stunned surprise. They had penetrated the thick German steel wall, though not very deeply. Seeger's company now was commanded by a corporal and as best anyone could make out it was down to a strength of nineteen or twenty men. They could use a fresh third battalion to take Belloy-en-Santerre. But the order of battle willed otherwise. *They* were to take the hamlet and *then* the third reserve battalion was to leapfrog through it. A captain of the second battalion tried to organize the attack into the ruins, but many Legionnaires scarcely heard whatever orders filtered down. They simply went ahead, from broken wall to wall, from ruined house to house, driving out Germans with grenades and bayonets.

As Private Alan Seeger moved around a corner of a ruined house, he came within the sights of a German sniper. He fell, wounded, and cried to his comrades to go on. They were too busy fighting to help him. When they had driven the Germans from the village, several came back to aid Seeger. He was dead.

Belloy-en-Santerre was taken, but the third battalion could not get more than thirty yards beyond it. A decorous curtain has been drawn on the number of Legion dead at the Somme.

But, positively, Alan Seeger was dead. Some of his friends felt that a great poetic talent had been destroyed before it had been fully born. How the war might have affected him had he survived it, no one can say. Perhaps, however, he did not expect to survive it. For he had written at least a few lines of verse that nearly every combat soldier understood:

> I have a rendezvous with Death
> At some disputed barricade,
> When Spring comes back with rustling shade
> And apple-blossoms fill the air—

I have a rendezvous with Death
When Spring brings back blue days and fair. . . .

And I to my pledged word am true,
I shall not fail that rendezvous.

Death was the order of nearly every day for some Legionnaires as the months crept by. The casualties of the French, Germans and British on the Western Front had passed the two-million mark when the French determined to crack the German line between Soissons and Rheims in April, 1917. The objective of the Legion in the battle was the village of Auberville.

Days of bombardment had battered the valley of the Sippe into a muddy marsh by the time the Legionnaires swarmed into it with the Moroccan Division and the French. For six days and nights the battle swayed forward and backward in fighting that seemed more than human mind and flesh could endure. It followed a pattern of horror that by this time had become fixed on the Western Front.

The attacker's artillery smashed the enemy's forward trenches for days while shrapnel swept the communication lines to hold back reinforcements. On the day of attack the fire reached a furious crescendo, then lifted from the front-line trenches and concentrated on the defender's communications. At that moment the attacker's infantry clambered out of their trenches and moved toward the shambles where stunned defenders groped in the fog of smoke.

In the defender's rear, artillerymen frantically slammed shells into guns, loosing a barrage onto the no man's land the attackers must cross. Usually the barrage came too late to catch the first wave of attacking infantry, who knew they must be quick. Hurling grenades, swinging knives and steel-bound clubs which were more efficient than rifles, the attackers almost invariably took the shambles of the first defensive trench. Meanwhile the defender's artillery had checked the attacker's second wave of infantry. Cut off from infantry support and not sufficiently strong to attack the second defensive line, the attackers shored up the trench they had taken while the defenders brought their artillery to bear on it.

Now the attackers became the defenders as those defending the second line counterattacked. The pattern started all over again with the roles of the opposing forces reversed. By nightfall the battle line often was exactly where it had been at dawn. Nothing had been decided—except that thousands of men had died grappling for a bit of torn land the size of a few suburban lots.

In the six days and nights of fighting around Auberville the Legion advanced a little more than a mile at an unmentioned cost in lives and with an expenditure of 50,000 hand grenades.

"Imagine, if you can," said a survivor of the battle, "what it is like to rake water."

The following month a new officer arrived from Morocco to take command of the Legion regiment. He was Colonel Paul Rollet, a veteran of twenty-two battles in North Africa. A slight, peppery, bearded man with piercing blue eyes, Rollet had an elfin sense of humor and the fighting heart of a lion. He was to become the most beloved officer in the history of the Legion. None ever matched him for understanding—not Bazaine or Negrier, not Lyautey or Gallieni. He was a soldier's soldier, who refused greater advancements in order to stay in command of the Legion until his death in 1940.

On Bastille Day in 1917, Rollet led a Legion detachment through the streets of Paris in a large military review, and afterward President Poincaré of France pinned the *Médaille Militaire* to the Legion's banner. It was its sixth decoration and made the Foreign Legion the most decorated unit in the French Army.

The Legionnaires, like all fighting men in the French Army, were little aware at first of a changing military philosophy in the French high command. As casualties mounted appallingly in the war of attrition on the Western Front, the apostles of the offensive gave way to the apostles of the defensive. Gallieni died in 1916, following an operation that was to fit him for active field service. Joffre's star was in eclipse. Pétain, more thrifty of human lives, became chief of the general staff and "military adviser" to the Government following his magnificent months-long defense of Verdun. He had taken no part in the development of the overseas empire; at the outbreak of war when he had been on the verge of retirement, he never had traveled outside metropolitan France.

The great German offensive of 1918 found the Legion flanking British forces on the Somme Front. In the draws of an area called Hangard Wood, a Legion battalion collided with a mass of Germans. Within minutes all officers of the battalion were killed or wounded; a corporal assumed command of one company, a private took command of another. Two other battalions rushed up at all speed, and for five hours there was a swirling hand-to-hand struggle in the wooded draws. The Legion lost 850 men, but it held the road to Amiens against the mighty German effort. Afterward the French pinned still another decoration on its banner.

Before the battalions had recovered from Hangard Wood, Soissons fell to the Germans on May 29 and Paris was threatened. Trucks rushed the Legionnaires to the scene of the breakthrough. They were learning that the defensive could be almost as costly as the offensive, for nearly 400 men were killed or wounded in the bitter fighting; by the time the German offensive died away in mid-June the regiment had lost more than 1,400 men.

Rollet had been roaring for replacements, and they finally came to him early in July, from North Africa and from Russians who somehow had made their way from the collapsed Eastern Front where the new revolutionary Bolshevik Government had made peace with Germany.

Brought up to strength again, the Legion battalions were committed to battle on the Plateau of Dommiers in mid-July. They attained their objective but lost 800 men.

The final phase of the war in 1918 was the most grueling that the Legion had yet faced. Late in August the Moroccan Division was placed in the Third French Army commanded by General Charles Mangin, who sought to smash the Germans' Hindenburg Line and occupy the Coucy and St. Gobain Forests to which the Germans clung frantically. Mangin hurled his divisions forward hard. To every appeal of regimental commanders that their troops were exhausted and could go no farther, Mangin replied that they *must*.

The Legion moved forward on September 2, struggling through a jungle of shattered timberland toward its first objective, the village of Terny-Sorny. German machine-gun nests and blockhouses which contested every foot of the way had to be subdued one by one in day and night fighting with grenade, bayonet and trench club. Worse than lack of sleep was hunger, for the Legionnaires outdistanced their supply runners. On September 4, Major Maire's battalion stormed into Terny-Sorny and captured 500 Germans.

Now the exhausted men hoped for a day or two of rest. But none was given them. They were ordered on immediately to take the heavily defended village of Neuville-sur-Margival. Stumbling on through ravines and woods, they attacked the village the next day and drove the Germans from it. Now, certainly, they would be given a chance to rest. But one of those ubiquitous headquarters messengers appeared with another message: Advance immediately, seize Sorny Ravine. Rollet, red-eyed from exhaustion, chewed his underlip as he read it.

They went on, across the Laffaux Plateau, so tired that they scarcely heard the shriek of shells above their heads, flushing Germans from nests and blockhouses. While it was still broad daylight, Maire's battalion managed a wide flanking infiltration movement that brought the Legionnaires to the lip of the heavily defended ravine. They plunged feet first upon their startled enemies, capturing twice their own numbers and an entire regimental staff. Sorny Ravine had been taken and now they could rest.

But not yet. The supply runners could not find them, but one of those cursed messengers from headquarters was there almost at once. Advance immediately, seize Vauyaillon Tunnel. Rollet snarled when he read it, but he led them on.

The tunnel was a key point in the Hindenburg Line itself. It seemed impossible that an exhausted, depleted regiment could advance more than a few hundred yards farther against the bunkers and machine-gun nests which blocked its approaches. But they went on, methodically reducing one strong point after another in steady day and night fighting. They could not believe it when they reached the entrances to the underground stronghold. They had lost track of time. Each company was down to less than fifty men and some had no officers. But Rollet asked them for one final effort.

Stumbling on, they swarmed into the entrances of the tunnel. Tossing grenades and following them with trench knives and trench clubs, they fought their way against startled Germans into the depths of Vauyaillon. Perhaps only exhausted men who had been living a nightmare for days and nights could have withstood the final underground nightmare of muffled explosions, screams, smoke, and men grappling in semidarkness. The Germans, terrified by the bearded, red-eyed Legionnaires who flung themselves forward as if welcoming death as a rest that had been too long denied them, began shrieking for mercy and holding up their hands. Soon the last pocket of resistance collapsed. The Legion had taken Vauyaillon Tunnel. It had cracked the Hindenburg Line. The day was September 14, 1918, and many men scarcely had slept twelve hours in twelve days. They hung on for several hours until French reinforcements came up to take advantage of the breakthrough.

The remaining Legionnaires found themselves resting dazedly at Saulxures-les-Nancy in Lorraine. No one dared hazard a guess yet as to when the war would end. And then replacements came, this time most of them Frenchmen who had been willing to transfer from their line regiments to serve with the vaunted regiment of foreigners. More decorations had been heaped on the Legion's banner. Pétain had created a special double *fourragère* for the Legion which combined the *Légion d'Honneur* and the *Croix de Guerre*. Now General de Castelnau, a veteran of the Moroccan campaign, had specifically asked for the Legion and the Moroccan Division in the offensive he was planning in Lorraine.

So the worst was yet to come, the Legionnaires thought. But there is no end to the surprises in war. The Moroccan Division was held in reserve in Lorraine for a time and when it finally moved to the front, German resistance melted before it. The Legion had fought its last great battle of the war at Vauyaillon.

Units of the French Army in Lorraine held a victory parade at Château-Salins on November 17, 1918. Paul Rockwell, who had been among the first to enlist in the Legion in 1914 and later had transferred to the French Army, was on hand to witness and describe it.

"The Foreign Legion came across the hill and entered Château-Salins. Colonel Rollet, his breast covered with medals and his sword drawn, rode at the head of the Legionnaires. Behind him came the Legion's band and the Legion's battle flag which was decorated with the Cross of the Legion of Honor and the War Cross with nine palms and three stars, representing twelve citations in the Order of the Day—more citations than ever had been won before by any fighting corps. . . .

"The bemedalled Legionnaires marched by proudly erect, with that look in the eye which only comes from the consciousness of duty well performed. In the ranks were perhaps fifty survivors from 1914, among them the Persian prince, Karaman Khan Nazare-Aga, a volunteer private at the outbreak of the war and now a captain and the 'ace' of the regiment, wearing the rosette of an Officer of the Legion of Honor and the War Cross with ten citations. And more and more nameless heroes, one after the other. . . ."

Of the seventy-odd Americans who had enlisted in the Legion at the outbreak of war and had remained in its ranks, thirty-eight had been killed in action or had died of wounds. All of the others had been wounded from one to four times.

Of the 44,150 foreigners who served in the Foreign Legion in France during the war, nearly 31,000 were killed, wounded or "missing in action," that euphemistic phrase describing a soldier whose grave is unknown.

In the flush of victory the survivors enjoyed the soldier's compensation of medals, banners, and parades, as when Rollet led his most decorated unit under the Arc de Triomphe in Paris. But those who had met a rendezvous with death in the victorious armies were too numerous to be forgotten. The memory of the frightful carnage of the war became deeply imbedded in the consciousness of the French people. At a later date it would rise to affect the destiny of France and the fortunes of its Foreign Legion.

18

The World
of Abd-el-Krim

IN THE PERSPECTIVE OF TIME, most wars appear unnecessary and most victories Pyrrhic. Yet man's will to wage war seems inexhaustible and history involves more lost than victorious causes. Fundamentally the story of the Foreign Legion concerns an inexhaustible will to wage war, numerous Pyrrhic victories, and many causes that eventually were lost.

The holocaust of World War I did not mean an end to war, despite the fond hopes of some who gave their lives in it. Although the lethargy of exhaustion settled on many of the peoples of Europe, fresh energies were seething in other peoples. The war to end war had simply resulted in more effective means of waging it. Improved weapons and improved methods of transportation and communication developed during World War I enabled central authorities to impose their will more easily on dissident minorities. Trotsky was mistaken about the nature of the revolution which he proclaimed would sweep the world; whatever its proletarian disguise in Russia or elsewhere, it was nationalism.

The Foreign Legion continued to reflect, in microcosm, the ferment of Europe and the vicissitudes of colonialism. Soon after the end of World War I, large numbers of Germans and Austrians flocked to the Legion. They included die-hard monarchists, archnationalists, and capable soldiers who wished only to pursue the profession of arms. Almost as numerous were the White Russians, men who had been soldiers in the armies of Wrangel and Deniken and now were homeless, in dire need, and without hope. The French welcomed them to their Foreign Legion, for officials in Paris now saw an important role emerging for the Legion in Morocco. The Legion's table of organization was expanded to four regiments and soon a regiment of cavalry was formed; before long the Legion's strength rose to 25,000 men, most of whom were assigned to Morocco.

At the outbreak of war in Europe, Lyautey had been ordered to ship all his available troops except the Foreign Legion to France, abandon the interior of Morocco, and try to hang on to the coastal cities. He sent two-thirds of his French and Algerian troops to Europe, but far from abandoning the interior, he actually increased the area of French control during World War I despite the efforts of German agents to foment tribal uprisings. This extraordinary feat failed to result in the Government's rewarding Lyautey with the troops he needed in Morocco after the war. For reasons of economy and the demobilization of the French Army he could count on little more than the Legion.

Employing its growing strength shrewdly and exercising his own highly personal brand of diplomacy with Moorish chieftains, Lyautey succeeded in extending the area of French control even farther with relatively little bloodshed. Between 1919 and 1922 the Khenifra area of the Middle Atlas was subdued and the Tache de Taza north of the Taza Corridor was pierced by a line of Legion blockhouses.

Lyautey had a genuine affection for Morocco and the Moors. He

231

wished to preserve the best in their civilization while infusing it with a more modern outlook. Under the terms of the Protectorate Treaty, Morocco had not become a colony but still enjoyed the rights of a sovereign nation, with France acting merely as helper and adviser. Lyautey summarized the principles of his proconsulship in these words: "A protectorate, and not direct administration. Govern with the mandarins, not against them. Do not offend a single tradition, do not change a single habit. Identify the governing class with our own interests."

This was, in effect, benevolent autocracy. It was like the role Britain undertook in India. It made no allowance for the emergence of a middle class with its inevitable upsurge of democracy. Progressive elements in France disapproved of Lyautey as lacking in liberalism, while reactionaries who sought only economic gain in Morocco believed him too liberal. Nearly everyone except his few intimates failed to measure Lyautey accurately.

He was a *grand seigneur,* but he had a genuine humanity. As he had demonstrated in his relationships with Legionnaires, he communicated without condescension with those of simple mind and mean surroundings. But his sincere concern for the well-being of others did not extend to bureaucrats and self-seeking commercial interests. Those he fought as hard as he did the anarchy of savage tribes. He was beguiled by the diplomacy of the East—and proved himself highly adept at it, playing off chief against chief with deft guile and a sure knowledge of mankind's desire for power and prestige. No marshal of France before him ever savored his role more thoroughly. None ever had found a more impressive physical stage than Morocco with its marbled arches and murmuring fountains, its sweet incense and muted stringed music, its purple mountains and dark blue sky.

The Morocco of Lyautey's later years in Fez and Casablanca was, of course, quite different from the Morocco of Legionnaires on the harsh frontier. There it was the familiar story of patrol and garrison, of discomfort and deadly monotony in lonely blockhouses, interrupted by a sortie or skirmish.

The Legionnaires were, as always, the instruments of a French policy that unfolded leisurely. Lyautey wished to extend his nation's influence over Morocco by means of diplomacy rather than warfare. But the Rif War, one of the most incredible of the twentieth century, was in the making. The Rifians were led by a man with no military training, one of whose chief advisers was a deserter from the Foreign Legion. They fought, at first, with century-old muskets, knives, and stones. To stamp out their unholy alliance of terrorism and courage eventually required the efforts of 3 marshals, 40 generals, an improvised air force, and more than 300,000 troops, fighting under the flags of France and Spain.

Muhammad ben Abd-el-Karim el Khattabi was the name of the man who defied the might of France and Spain. He was a Berber of the Rif, that wild mountainous area on the frontier of French and Spanish Morocco, and to Westerners he became known as Abd-el-Krim. Despite his exploits, he was rather unprepossessing in appearance—small, stout, with grave dark eyes.

His father had been a greatly respected Rifian chieftain with uncommonly progressive ideas. Abd-el-Krim went to Fez to study law and then was employed in the Spanish zone teaching officials the Berber language. Strong-willed and quick-tempered, he quarreled with the Spanish General, Silvestre, and was thrown into prison in 1921. A few weeks later he escaped, fled to his native mountains, and began organizing resistance to the Spanish occupation.

He was not merely carrying out a personal vendetta. His success came about because the Rifians, as well as the Moors in general, had a fanatic hatred of the Spanish. In the view of neutral observers at the time, the Rifians' hatred was justified. The Spanish occupation was cruel, corrupt, unjust; worst of all in the eyes of the Rifians, the Spaniards molested Moslem women excessively.

Late in 1921, Abd-el-Krim gathered a few hundred warriors of his own Beni Urriaghel tribe and descended on the advance Spanish post of Anual. Only a score of the Rifians were armed with rifles; the rest carried ancient flintlocks, spears, knives. Abd-el-Krim was motivated by the wish for personal vengeance in attacking Anual;

233

his spies had informed him that Silvestre was visiting the post. But he had no carefully conceived plan of attack. He and his men simply swarmed over the walls of Anual under the cover of darkness and began butchering its Spanish garrison. Silvestre either was slain or committed suicide.

The few survivors who escaped from Anual with tales of atrocities spread panic through the Spanish force of 19,000 men in Morocco. Though Abd-el-Krim lacked any military training, he followed up his victory at Anual quickly and took advantage of the mounting panic among the Spaniards. As he marched toward the sea, gathering a host of tribesmen as his allies, Spaniards deserted post after post in his path. All who opposed him were annihilated. The Rifians reached the walls of Melilla and could have massacred its population of 50,000 Europeans. But Abd-el-Krim wisely turned them back. He knew that such a massacre would bring the wrath of Europe down on his head and he wanted friends rather than enemies. His men, glutted with bloodshed and loaded with loot, followed him back to the mountains.

Around this time a German sergeant who had deserted the Foreign Legion made his way to Abd-el-Krim. His name was Joseph Klems and he came from Düsseldorf. He had fled Germany to avoid military service and after various misadventures had enlisted in the Legion. Promoted to sergeant, he quarreled with and struck a Legion officer in Fez. Broken to private and facing imprisonment, Klems deserted and wandered into the Rif. Captured by tribesmen who started to bury him alive, he was saved by a chief. Besides being a capable soldier, Klems was shrewdly politic; he embraced the Moslem faith, took the name of Hadj Aleman, "German Pilgrim," and married a daughter of the chief who had saved his life. Entering Abd-el-Krim's service, he proved himself of invaluable military aid.

When the American writer, Vincent Sheean, made a hazardous journey to Abd-el-Krim's mountain lair, he talked with Klems, who had taken two more wives and planned to marry a fourth. "By any legal or conventional standard," wrote Sheean, "the Hadj Aleman was, I suppose, a liar, a thief and a murderer; yet I could not help thinking him, on the whole, rather a good man. His influence in Rifian councils was always exercised on the side of mercy and moderation. He did everything he could to prevent the tribesmen from indulging in those excesses which occasionally disgraced them in battle: he was always against torture, mutilation, or any unnecessary form of bloodshed. A large part of his fighting, in fact, was done with his camera and his map-making apparatus. I liked the Hadj for his bold, romantic lies as much as for his kindheartedness and his courage."

Like Abd-el-Kader nearly a century previously, Abd-el-Krim appealed to Europeans and Americans who visualized him as a kind of swarthy Robin Hood. His popularity abroad increased after he captured the notorious bandit chieftain Raisuli, his only competitor among the Moors, who died a captive in his hands. But Abd-el-Krim never did receive anything near the amount of military and financial aid he desired from abroad. Most of his weapons and ammunition he captured from the Spaniards. The Rifians were superb fighters and proved to be mechanically adept at employing modern weapons and material of war. At one time, for example, a fourteen-year-old-boy directed their rather extensive telephone communication system.

Abd-el-Krim and his forces defeated the Spaniards time and again in pitched battles until he was virtual ruler of Spanish Morocco. The Moors there were almost unanimously for him and to the south, in French Morocco, thousands of others prayed that he would drive out all Europeans.

Finally, however, he made the classical blunder of military conquerors: he did not recognize when he had won enough. Encouraged because he had defeated the Spanish, he was ready to turn on the French. France, a first-rate power, was not to be compared with the third-rate power of Spain; it could not brook military defeat at the hands of a "dissident local chieftain." All Lyautey's clever diplomacy among the Moroccan chiefs was to no avail against the military successes of Abd-el-Krim. He had become the champion of almost all the Moors, the symbol and forerunner of a nationalist spirit that had not quite yet been born. At last Lyautey was forced to propose to his Government that France and Spain mount joint operations against Abd-el-Krim.

Late in July, 1925, Marshal Pétain, the Inspector General of the French Army and a hero to his people, arrived in Morocco. The two most distinguished marshals of France put their heads together over how to subdue a Rifian chief, and soon they were joined by the Spanish Marshal Primo de Rivera. A month later the French Government informed Lyautey that Pétain would command the combined operations. Shortly afterward Lyautey submitted his resignation and, in tears, left his beloved Morocco. Friends said he never was content in his French retirement that lasted until his death in 1934.

Pétain launched the large-scale offensive against Abd-el-Krim on September 15, 1925. An observer compared it to employing a steam roller to crush an ant. But it did not seem so to the Foreign Legionnaires. Long before decisions were made at the highest level, they had been fighting the Rifians and allies of Abd-el-Krim.

The Legionnaires fought with special hatred and fear, for never had they faced a more cruel enemy than the Rifians. Almost invariably foreign admirers of Abd-el-Krim glossed over the atrocities committed by his followers. Some claimed that their acts were merely in retaliation for atrocities the Spaniards had committed. The Rifians, as individuals, seemed immune to pain; their army, for instance, had no medical facilities and the wounded either died or recovered without aid. As fanatical Moslems the Rifians had no compunctions about torturing Christians. Furthermore, they had quickly seen that fear of torture had been the chief reason why Spanish troops fled before them. So their torture was calculated, a principal weapon in their war rather than a happenstance of it.

They were in-fighters. Every warrior carried a sharp, curved knife, which it was his delight to use on an an enemy. If possible, even in hand-to-hand fighting, he wished to emasculate his adversary before he killed him. Sometimes the Rifians buried an emasculated prisoner up to his neck and left him bareheaded in the burning sun just beyond the rifle range of his comrades. When this happened to a Legionnaire, one or two sharpshooters usually tried to creep out and put him out of his agony, running the risk of being killed themselves by Rifian sharpshooters.

As invariably was true of Moslem peoples, the Rifian women were even more cruel than the men. When a prisoner fell into women's hands, they customarily stripped him and staked him spread-eagled to the ground. After pulling out his fingernails and toenails, they often roasted the soles of his feet with burning brands. Throughout their fiendish ritual they took pains to revive him each time he fainted. As a climax they castrated him. Sometimes, too, they disembowled him, blinded him, cut off his ears and nose. If he did not die immediately, they poured honey on his wounds to attract ants and flies which swarmed into his still-living body.

To Legionnaires and other front-line fighters in the Rif War, such atrocities were not distant rumors but a fact of combat that might overtake them any day. It was why every Legionnaire usually carried in a pocket a last bullet for himself.

The retaliation of some Legionnaires who found the body of a comrade whom women had tortured is rarely mentioned. Yet every Legionnaire for more than a century knew that atrocity sometimes was repaid in kind, for men who have been brutalized may revert to brutal savagery themselves.

Describing life in the Legion at the turn of the century, Carlé tells of an old Legionnaire who showed him a tobacco pouch "apparently made of fine, soft leather. 'This is made of the breast of an Arab woman,' he said. 'It is a very good pouch. Made it myself. There are only seven in the whole regiment now.'"

Another former Legionnaire recalls a group of veterans searching for a comrade and catching three Moslem women with dripping knives in their hands bending over the body of the tortured and horribly mutilated dead man. Gruesomely he describes the endless screaming of the women as the Legionnaires stripped them, strung them nude by the heels from a beam, and proceeded to carve them up alive in the way they had carved up the Legionnaire.

The Rif, that dirtiest of wars, began for the Legion in 1923, when a detachment escorting a supply convoy was wiped out in a desperate fight near a mountain known as Tichoukt. Dozens of obscure places were the scenes of Legion battles during the next two years.

In April, 1924, Legion and French units went to the aid of friendly tribes whom Abd-el-Krim was attempting to crush. Only after bloody fighting were the Rifians jolted to a halt. A year later Abd-el-Krim launched an all-out offensive with 30,000 warriors who struck the blockhouses of the Taza Corridor with all their might. Of sixty-six blockhouses, the majority garrisoned by Legionnaires, nine were seized and more than thirty had to be evacuated. It was only then that Lyautey admitted that Abd-el-Krim must be crushed by force and that it would take the combined efforts of the French and Spanish governments to accomplish it.

The comparative ease with which the Rifians smashed into the Taza Corridor seemed to surprise even Abd-el-Krim himself. He paused, uncertain what to do next, and thus gave the Legion and French units time to recover and strike back. Slowly the Legionnaires recovered their lost blockhouses one by one.

Abd-el-Krim, apparently prompted by a suggestion from Klems, offered amnesty and passage to Europe from Tangiers to all Legionnaires who would desert and come over to him. There was a steady trickle of deserters, but it never reached the flood proportions that Abd-el-Krim hoped for. Fear of torture prevented large numbers of Legionnaires from deserting a way of life that grew harder every day in Morocco.

Those who did desert were treated fairly, however; they found that the cruelty of the Rifians was not indiscriminate but was directed solely against their military enemies. After spending several weeks working on the road network which Abd-el-Krim was building, they were given some money and sent on to Tangiers.

One deserter was a twenty-year-old Negro named Wesley Williams from Oakland, California. Having heard that a Negro's lot was better in France, he had worked his passage there and listened to the siren song of a Legion recruiter about the romantic life of a Foreign Legionnaire. Williams enlisted and soon found that he had been misled. Pining for California, he deserted when he had a chance and worked on Abd-el-Krim's roads for a while. As he made his way toward Tangiers, he came upon the wandering Sheean who was alone, almost penniless, and seriously ill with malaria. Williams did all that he could for Sheean before going on. Later both were captured by French intelligence agents after they slipped into the international sector of Tangiers. Williams expected to be shot, but Sheean used the one form of persuasion that always seemed to make the Legion quail. He filed stories about Williams's plight to his newspaper syndicate. The Legion, with its customary abhorrence of unfavorable publicity, released Williams a few weeks later and he went home to California.

Few other deserters were lucky enough to escape once the French and Spanish began their combined operations. After building roads for Abd-el-Krim and managing to make the difficult journey to Tangiers, deserters found themselves scooped up like minnows in the huge net of the French intelligence system.

When Pétain launched his grand attack in September, 1925, all four Legion regiments were in the line which struck north. A force of volunteer air fighters, several of whom were Americans, bombed in advance of them. Few Legionnaires ever knew why the bombing was so inaccurate. It was because Paul Painlevé, a pacifist who happened to be both the French Prime Minister and Minister of War that month, would not consent to the use of bombers against the Rifians until the planes' bombsights had been removed.

The war was as unpopular with many of the French people as with the men who fought it. But unpopular or not, it was pursued grimly in hill-to-hill fighting as the fanatic Rifians contested nearly every mile of the way. By April, 1926, Abd-el-Krim realized that his plight was desperate and asked for a conference with the French. His request was brought by a sixty-seven-year-old courier who ran seventy miles between dawn and sunset. The French refused to confer and on May 23 Abd-el-Krim was forced to surrender.

Astride a mule and wearing a brown burnoose, he rode impassively into the French lines. The French denied him the martyrdom of the firing squad. In August he was exiled to Réunion Island in the Indian Ocean and he took with him two wives, five children, and a brother. After World War II, he was granted permission to move to Cairo where he died in 1963 at the age of eighty-one.

Abd-el-Krim's surrender did not bring an end to fighting for Legion units in Morocco. Few of his tribes were willing to surrender without a final battle. Slowly but inexorably they were forced into resentful submission.

In the mopping-up operations a Legion company captured ex-Legionnaire Joseph Klems. Brought to a widely publicized trial, he was condemned to death. Then his sentence was commuted to life imprisonment on Devil's Island. But Klems always had luck when he faced a seemingly hopeless situation. After he had served seven years on Devil's Island, the French finally bowed to repeated demands by the German Government and released him. Klems went home to Germany and an obscure life uninterrupted by newspaper headlines.

The casualties of the Rif War have been estimated at more than 100,000 dead. There is no way of determining them accurately. The French and Spanish governments were reluctant to reveal the true cost of an unpopular expedition and the Rifians, who kept no records, could only quote an Arab proverb: "Who can count the drops of rain that fall, even in an arid country?"

19

The

Beguiling Wound

"The history of a soldier's wound beguiles the pain of it," wrote the author of *Tristram Shandy*. Laurence Sterne, snug in his eighteenth-century English parsonage, might have been describing the mystique of the future Foreign Legion of France.

It cost Alan Seeger his life to discover that there is no glory in war. Thousands of other Legionnaires discovered it without paying as great a price. An arduous life combining that of a combat soldier with that of a day laborer building roads was not likely to appeal to an idealist—unless he believed in the worth of what he was doing.

To an idealist, the Legion said, in effect, "But what you are doing *is* worthwhile. War *is* glorious. Courage in the face of overwhelming odds *is* the greatest virtue a man can possess." And then, as if paraphrasing the words written by Sterne, the Legion added, in effect, "Consider our glorious history. As you ponder it, you will find the pains of the moment charmed away."

241

But the charm of the Legion's history was not quite as effective after World War I. Most Europeans and Americans capable of reflection became a little more knowing about the nature of war after that terrible conflict. They were inclined to question why they were fighting. And the Legion had no patience with the question *why;* it does not to this day. Like every first-class fighting outfit, it takes Tennyson's line without irony and believes "Theirs not to reason why . . ."

Few reflective men ever did blunder into the Legion, however; the ranks of combat platoons always have been marked by an absence of political philosophers. In the 1920's and 1930's, as always, most men who joined the Legion did so of necessity and because they felt they had no other place to go. Once in its ranks, they had to abandon the freedom of making personal choices. There was little use in questioning the rightness of the cause they served. They were too busy trying to stay alive.

It was true in the war against Abd-el-Krim and again in 1933 and 1934 when the Legion helped their French masters ruthlessly stamp down spontaneous and unco-ordinated outbursts of Moroccan nationalism. It was equally true in the warfare which involved Legion units in Syria.

After World War I, France demanded a mandate over the whole of Syria. A United States commission found that the Syrians vehemently rejected such a mandate, but that made no difference to the French empire builders. They obtained the sanction of the League of Nations and went ahead. France was unfortunate in the choice of its first administrators; there were enlightened men in the lower echelons of the administration, but no wise and benign Lyautey at the top. Among the French units sent to Syria in 1922 were a Legion infantry battalion and a mounted company of two men to one mule.

From the outset one of the chief problems of the French was the Jebel Druse, a fanatical mountain sect of fierce fighters, who were as cruel as the Rifians. In May, 1925, the Druse leaders asked the French High Commissioner, General Maurice Sarrail, to hear their grievances. He refused, and the Druses were shocked by the loss of what had been one of the few fundamental human rights in the Middle East for centuries. Then, after a French officer was shot in the Druse capital of Suwayda, Sarrail invited the leaders to confer with him in Damascus. There, on July 17, he treacherously had them arrested and jailed.

The Druses rose as one man. A French force composed largely of Senegalese, Malagasy, and Saharian troops panicked and fled, throwing away their rifles. Sarrail shelled the native quarter of Damascus, and shortly afterward was removed from office. All French forces in Syria, numbering less than 14,000 men, were massed against the Druses.

The Legion infantry battalion and mounted company, totaling 700 men, was attacked on the night of September 16 by a force of 3,000 Druses at the mountain village of Moussiefre. Rifle and machine-gun fire held the Druses at bay, but the next morning they resumed the attack resolutely. They did not break off until the morning of September 18. By that time they had lost 500 killed and the Legionnaires captured another 500, who were too severely wounded to crawl off the field. The Legion lost 47 dead, 83 wounded, and all its mules were killed.

Meanwhile a squadron of the recently formed Legion cavalry regiment was shipped from Algeria and sent to an inland fort called Rachaya. On the evening of November 20, as the squadron of 120 men was watering its horses, a band of nearly 3,000 Druses swept down on the fort. During the desperate night fighting the Druses broke through one wall of Rachaya. At dawn the Legionnaires mounted a savage bayonet charge and recovered most, though not all, of the area the Druses had taken. Carrier pigeons were sent off with messages requesting aid and for three days there was almost incessant fighting in which the Legionnaires, with grenades and bayonets, finally cleared the fort of Druses. On the morning of the fourth day, when the Druses still tightly ringed the fort, the Legionnaires' ammunition was down to fifteen rounds per man and had to be used very sparingly. Each man kept one bullet in a pocket for himself. The commander decided that he would lead a bayonet charge of all the survivors at dusk if a relief column had not appeared by that time. Late in the afternoon, however, a relief force did finally struggle through and the siege was raised. Only 35 Legionnaires survived.

The fighting continued in the pattern of that in Algeria and Morocco for several months and then slowly died away. Eventually the Legion force in Syria was raised in strength and a regiment was stationed there until World War II.

Such fighting in Africa and Asia was, to paraphrase the words of Laurence Sterne, the history of the Legion's wounds for many years. But few Legionnaires beguiled the painfulness of their existence with contemplation of the Legion's record. On occasion, as when the Legion commander at Rachaya was ready to lead a suicidal bayonet charge, the tradition represented by Camerone was a stabilizing and unifying precedent. The only worth of a military tradition is, of course, its effectiveness in the crises of combat. At other times it usually is put away, like clerical vestments awaiting the next religious ceremony.

Certainly the Legion's mystique was lost to the mass of Legionnaires in the monotony of their daily routines. When they tried to forget the pain of their existence they went in search of a soldier's immemorial pleasures: wine, women, and song. Their songs, many of which they created themselves, were by far the best. In most of the remote places where they found themselves the wine and the women were foul.

As the Moroccan campaign progressed, the French wheeled out a mobile force of prostitutes for the relief or pleasure or edification of their troops. It was the *Bordel Mobile de Campagne,* the "Mobile Military Brothel," known as the B.M.C. Describing it in his book on the Legion, Jean Martin says:

As entertainment we had—if one's mind was sufficiently twisted to permit him to participate—the B.M.C. The females following the military columns were generally Mauresques; sometimes a European woman

244

who had reached the last degree of decadence mixed with the crowd of colored whores; every single one was the refuse of Moroccan brothels, old battle horses who, feeling the hour of retreat approach, tried to make a few francs by any possible means.

At Ou-Terbat they numbered ten or twelve, exposed to the fury of 5,000 solid young males, bubbling over with ardor and vitality. . . . But it was during the two or three evenings following the distribution of pay to the Legionnaires when this institution became picturesque in the true sense of the word.

In order to avoid bloody fights it was necessary to reserve one day for each corps: Legion, Spahis, *tirailleurs*. An imposing body of armed guards surrounded the B.M.C. and supervised the adjacent area as well; on pay nights the guards made the clients line up in front of each tent where they patiently awaited their turn as in civilized towns and cities one lines up at a bus stop. The sanitary service overflowing, the personnel was unable to exercise seriously the task of preventing disease.

Many men who could not find solace with such women inevitably sought to forget their surroundings in alcohol. The Legion appears always to have had a fair sprinkling of outright alcoholics who stayed drunk as much of the time as they could afford to and still manage to get by in the performance of their duties. Others were sporadic drunkards who wished to get "blind" instead of enjoying social conviviality. Nearly all Legionnaires, defiant by nature, were proud and boastful of their capacity for drink.

Several years ago a French temperance society, having heard hair-raising tales of Legionnaires' drinking, obtained the permission of the Defense Ministry to put posters in every Legion barracks room. They showed a death's head and bore the inscription:

"ALCOHOL IS DEADLY!"

The Legion removed the posters after it was found that someone in each barracks had printed under the inscription:

"BUT THE LEGIONNAIRE DOES NOT FEAR DEATH!"

For many years the Legionnaires' favorite drink was appropriately called "earthquake." It consisted of raw white Spanish or Moroccan wine heavily laced with Pernod, a potent alcohol similar to absinthe.

A collective Legion drinking bout was known as *"Système D"* and began with a systematic study of the town or area of a city which a company planned to "invade." The area was divided into districts, men were "detailed" to specific bars and cafés, and an elaborate system of "liaison" men between districts was arranged.

On schedule the teams of drinkers entered their assigned cafés and ordered enough to get everyone drunk. When the bill was tendered, the Legionnaires said they were broke. Wise barkeeps shrugged and let them go. The men staggered out in fairly orderly fashion with a well-known Legion accolade: *'A moi, les murs! La terre m'aban-donne!"* ("Walls, come to me! The ground has deserted me!") If a barkeep was foolish enough to call the police, however, the Legion-naires demolished his café. If the police sent for reinforcements, the "liaison" men alerted the entire district with the cry *"A moi, la Légion!"* and Legionnaires poured in to aid their comrades. There have been occasions in Africa and Asia when the police alerted the Legionnaires' rivals, the *tirailleurs* or Zouaves, and it was found ex-pedient for one district to summon the assistance of other districts. But whenever this happened, it was felt that *"Système D"* had not operated with its customary efficiency.

Legionnaires were confined not for being drunk, but for being unable to perform their duties—a fine shade in French and Legion logic.

This fine shade accounts for one of the eccentric customs of Gen-eral Rollet at Sidi-bel-Abbès. Rollet would personally smuggle a drunken Legionnaire back to the barracks past the guard. His pur-pose was to make sure that the man met the standards of duty by being back on time. If the man was still drunk and unfit for duty the next morning, however, Rollet would order him confined for ten days without pay. On more than one occasion, when he learned that such a man was trying to help support a family from his meager pay, Rollet personally sent money to the family and then tried to argue the Legionnaire into paying him back.

Rollet, incidentally, detested wearing a shirt under his high-collared tunic and devised a system of artificial cuffs which he supported by strings passed through the armholes. Once in a while the string broke and he lost his cuffs—usually, it seemed, when he was holding a review or entertaining distinguished guests. A quick-tempered man, Rollet never was known to take out his anger on subordinates innocent of wrongdoing. But he could fume eloquently for days on some matter that irritated him. And nothing ever irritated him more than the factual inaccuracies of the English writer, P. C. Wren, in his romances about the Legion. Rollet was, of course, furious with the American deserter, Doty, who passed through Sidi-bel-Abbès on his triumphal tour home to Mississippi. He called him in to dress him down for being a bad Legionnaire and giving the Legion so much unfavorable publicity instead of quietly going off to serve his term in prison, but Doty shrewdly shifted the subject to P. C. Wren. Rollet spent the rest of the interview ranting at Wren instead of Doty. Yet Rollet was delighted to write a preface to former Legionnaire Jean Martin's book; though critical of some aspects of Legion life, Martin wrote truthfully. The truth was the most important thing to Rollet.

At times Rollet must have felt that he was running a detention home for juvenile delinquents. Yet his fairness and tolerance made him universally liked by his men. Perhaps one with adolescent habits always esteems anyone who takes a tolerant view of him. In any event, tolerance always has been a quality of the best Legion officers. Whenever an officer has diluted sternness with fatherly understanding, Legionnaires have adored him and sometimes been willing to die for him. Whenever he has known his men thoroughly, they have felt that they understood him perfectly.

This was true of a Legion captain at Saida who was told that one of his men was roaring drunk in a café and threatening to kill him. Strapping on his revolver, the captain went to the café and sat down at the table where the man and other Legionnaires were drinking. While the captain sipped a cognac, the drunken Legionnaire stared at him stupefiedly. At last the captain said he was returning to the post and wanted someone to guard him in the darkened streets.

247

Drawing his revolver, he handed it to the Legionnaire who had threatened him and asked the man to follow him at six paces. When they reached the post, the Legionnaire handed him back the revolver.

"Now," said the captain, "you will have eight days in cell for boasting you would kill your captain. And eight days more for not doing it when you had the chance. A Legionnaire should always keep his word. Go report yourself to the sergeant of the guard."

Ever afterward the Legionnaire admired the captain as the most fair and understanding officer he had known.

Understanding also was a characteristic of a major who was marching his battalion back to Fez after especially trying duty in the Rif War. The men had been paid, and the major, knowing their mood of pent-up frustration, realized there would be trouble when they reached Fez. About forty miles from the city the major rode ahead of his column on his motorcycle and returned to the bivouac that evening at the head of a strange caravan of old Ford cars which he had organized in Fez. In the cars rode shopkeepers with winebarrels and sweets and a band of fairly presentable girls whom the major had rounded up in the red-light district. For two days and nights the men of the battalion held a fete at their bivouac. Then they marched on to Fez, hungover and flat broke.

"I had attained my end," the major told Prince Aage later. "Before the next pay day the men had time to reflect and to hope philosophically for the moment when they would be able to conquer the fine tattooed ladies of Mourley Abdallah."

Time always has been the enemy of the Legionnaire. There is too much of it and a man never has enough money to bribe it into beguiling him with its passage. The five-year enlistment term is too much time out of a man's life. That is what Legionnaires say as they sit at café tables, their brown and calloused hands wrapped around glasses of wine.

The usual forms of malingering receive short shrift in the Legion. A man who complained of a chronic aching back would find himself spending a weekend cleaning out a filthy latrine with a toothbrush. Such chores always seemed to cure his back ache.

In years past old Legion hands developed ingenious malingerer's tricks which they would sell to new recruits for a price. For example:

Put a bit of castor-oil bean the size of a pinhead in your eye and bandage the eye overnight. Result—acute conjunctivitis and one month in the hospital.

Soak a pomegranate in milk or coffee overnight and eat the skin in the morning. Result—a case of jaundice guaranteed to fool any doctor. But the trouble is that the symptoms wear off in a very few days.

Smoke tobacco impregnated with quinine and you'll develop a fever. If you cut yourself with a penknife and put a little tartar from your teeth in the wound, you'll develop an abscess good for one month in the hospital. Thread a hair on a needle and draw it through your flesh and you'll develop an abscess good for two months in the hospital. If you can obtain a syringe, a draw blood from your gums and inject it under the skin. The abscess which results should keep you in the hospital for three months.

A simple but more painful trick, good for three to four weeks off duty, is to tie a cork tightly to your heel, put on your boot, and then jump hard on your heel.

Some men have purposely maimed themselves in order to avoid dangerous or difficult duties. But this was considered bad form by professional malingerers who have been called "survivalists"; the idea, they maintained, was to get out of the Legion with a whole skin. The "survivalists" did express admiration, however, for the élan of one man. Tired of going for weeks without meat while on desert duty, he chopped off two of his fingers, tossed them in a cooking pot, and remarked, "Here's some meat for you."

One of the Legion's outstanding malingerers was a Spaniard named Solaud, which can be twisted around to mean "dirty dog" in French. Annoyed that everyone laughed at his name when he enlisted, he picked for his Legion name the only French word he knew: Cochon, meaning pig. To add to his misfortunes, his Spanish name was tattooed on the heel of his right hand and was revealed every time he saluted. Since a Legionnaire had to salute noncom-missioned as well as commissioned officers, Pig the Dirty Dog found himself doing a great deal of saluting and undergoing much ques-tioning about his name wherever he went. Everyone but him was amused. Naturally he hated both noncommissioned and commis-sioned officers and his morale sank to boot level. Twice he sold all of his equipment, a crime almost as heinous as desertion in the thrifty Legion. He spent nine of every ten days in prison, accumulating an incredible amount of "lost time." Indeed he maintained that after six years in the Legion, he had seventeen years left to serve in order to complete his five-year enlistment. Finally someone thought of a solution: Make him a corporal and send him to the remotest desert in command of a camel squad in a Saharienne Company. Corporal Cochon was delighted with his assignment. But a month after his squad had been sent to a far post, the company commander received an aggrieved letter signed by all the squad members: Corporal Cochon had drunk up their year's supply of wine all by himself in two weeks. The commander decided that Cochon was too far re-moved from authority to be punished. During the remainder of his thirsty year in the desert Cochon became one of the strictest disci-plinarians in the Legion, so feared that ever afterward no one called him anything but Corporal.

As Solaud learned, it was important that a Legionnaire under-stand French. One Danish Legionnaire, who does not seem to have been very bright, simply couldn't make head or tail of the language. In the blockhouse where he was serving during the Moroccan cam-paign someone always had to write out the password for him on a slip of paper. When the blockhouse was invested by tribesmen, the Dane did not understand the order that no one was to go out of the fort for water. Being thirsty and seeing others thirsty, he crept out to the water hole with three cans one night. He filled the cans and crept safely through the tribesmen, but he could not remember what to reply when a Legionnaire sentry challenged him. It was too dark to read the password, so he shouted, "Friend!" in Danish. In reply, the sentry shot at him. Suddenly fearing that the tribesmen might capture him and discover the password, the Dane chewed and swallowed his slip of paper. At that moment a couple of sentries came out and slugged him with their rifle butts.

When they dragged him into the fort and discovered who he was, his fellow countryman and company commander, Prince Aage, did everything possible to resuscitate him. He regained consciousness briefly and muttered in Danish, "Funny beggars, these sentries. You go and get water for them and all they do in return is land you one on the head with their rifle butts. If only I could have explained to them. But they didn't understand a word of Danish!"

He died a few hours later and was awarded the *Croix de Guerre* posthumously.

Quite a different sort of Dane was Prince Aage, a fluent linguist who bore the reputation of being one of the bravest and certainly the handsomest officer ever to serve in the Foreign Legion. Like Hamlet, he had not found it easy to be a Prince of Denmark. As a cousin of the King he had nothing to look forward to except the ceremonies of an officer in the Royal Guards in Copenhagen. Romantic and venturesome by nature, he lacked a Graustark, a Mount Everest, a war in which his instincts and energies might have full play. When the bank in which he had invested his money failed, he remembered the stories that his grandfather, the Duke of Chartres, had told him of service in the Foreign Legion. He sent his wife, a beautiful Italian contessa, and their seven-year-old son home to her parents in Italy and joined the Legion as a captain.

Few men ever enjoyed their Legion service so zestfully or described it as vividly as Aage. Of Morocco he exclaimed, "What a country! What a perfect orgy of light and colored harmonies. And its violent and perfumed towns!"

He found an emotionally charged beauty almost every place he went.

"The sand shone strangely in the darkness. Not far away, a few hundred Arab cloaks, stained and red, were stretched out motionless —huge white birds—until suddenly the rising wind lifted them together in a wing-like movement as if the whole desert were gathering to fly away. . . .

"Berkine at this time was nothing but a collection of casbahs, headquarters of the tribe we were to subdue. The Middle Atlas dies there in a stony plateau at the foot of the ramparts of the Great Atlas, whose peaks, covered with eternal snows, tower against the sky like impenetrable medieval fortresses. There in a deep little valley, smothered between the edges of the plateau and the gigantic mass of the Atlas, lies Berkine. The Oued winds between lush pastures and well-cultivated wheat fields, under the dancing shadows of palms."

Except in combat, the lot of Legion officers was, of course, more comfortable than that of the enlisted men. Many of the officers were extremely intelligent men, observant and imaginative, who refused to let time drag emptily.

One of these was Captain Buschenschutz, a German of the 2nd Regiment, who was fond of declaring: "The present has an importance which we must never lose sight of. Each of our fleeting states of mind or even momentary actions is of infinite value, for it represents a whole eternity."

Buschenschutz liked intelligent companionship. And only intelligent fellow officers could play bridge in the way he insisted on playing it. Each of the four players reclined on a couch with a bottle beside him. There was no table; in the center of the room sat an Arab servant. After the dealer had shuffled the cards, the servant distributed them to the players. Each memorized his hand and gave it back to the servant. Then each bid from memory. The servant brought the winning bidder the hand of the "dummy" and he memorized that also before giving it back to the servant. Finally, all hands were played and the score kept purely from memory without the players or the servant touching the cards or a pencil. Afterward, if anyone questioned one of the plays, the servant would turn over the four hands and the players could study them. But Buschenschutz considered it a social *faux pas* if a player raised a question mistakenly.

Music was Buschenschutz's greatest love and he was an accom-

plished violinist. He demanded utter silence and concentration during his recitals. One evening when he was rapturously playing
Schumann's "Kreisleriana," four drunken Legionnaires began brawling and yelling beneath the open windows. Buschenschutz finished
the number with closed eyes, then crept to a window, peered out
carefully and roared, "I *see* you! I'll *punish* you!" The terrified Legionnaires fled.

The next morning Buschenschutz lined up his company and
walked from man to man, staring into the face of each. Then he
picked out four men and ordered them to step forward. All confessed
they were the culprits of the previous evening. When Buschenschutz
asked what musical instruments they played and they admitted to
none, he was horrified. "Then you will *learn!*" he cried. He ordered
them sent to the Legion musicians' school at Sidi-bel-Abbès. Two
years later when he happened to pass through there he found all four
playing trumpets in the Legion band. After listening to them carefully, Buschenschutz admitted that they were four of the best trum-
peters he had heard in some time.

One who enjoyed the rather strenuous intellectual life of Buschenschutz's social gatherings when he had the opportunity was Captain
—later Major—Pechkoff. Aage described him memorably: "Imagine
for an instant a bulldog with the moustaches of a cat, the eyes two
splashes of blazing blue surrounded by thick lashes and crowned
with eyebrows sprawled across the brow by the sweeping brush of a
mad painter. But it was the nose above all that riveted my gaze. An
indescribable nose! Thick and broad and quivering nostrils, his nose
breathed all the human passions: voluptuousness, revenge, bravado,
sensuousness, goodness."

After transferring from the Legion and becoming one of the most
decorated aces of World War I, Pechkoff had lost his right arm in
aerial combat. Discontent with doing anything that kept him away
from the profession of arms for long, Pechkoff applied for a commission in the Legion after the war. The Legion was delighted to have
him; Pechkoff with one arm was better than most men with two.

Legionnaire Adolphe Cooper, who had served his time in Colomb-

253

Béchar, found himself trying to be a good Legionnaire when he came under Pechkoff's command in Morocco. Bullets were merely so many flies to Pechkoff; his fearlessness, fairness, and understanding made his men adore him. When he mounted his horse, he took the reins in his teeth, placed his left hand on the pommel and seemed to flow into the saddle in one lithe movement.

While leading his battalion on horseback against a band of Rifians, Pechkoff's right foot was struck by a bullet which entered at the toe and passed out the heel. Physicians say it is one of the most painful wounds a man can suffer, yet Pechkoff did not cry out or sway in the saddle. His men did not even know he was wounded until they saw blood flowing out of his boot. Even then Pechkoff wanted to ride on. Several Legionnaires had to lift him forcibly from the saddle and carry him off the field.

Pechkoff, lying wounded in the hospital, was as philosophically calm as in combat. He beguiled his pain by reading and writing and listening to music. A skilled violinist whose music he enjoyed was an aging German Legionnaire named Bohlmann. When Pechkoff could hobble about and returned to his battalion, he had Bohlmann transferred to it.

Soon Pechkoff observed that Bohlmann was having great difficulty keeping up with the column on the long marches. Pechkoff offered him a job as a driver, but Bohlmann refused it. He had been an officer in the German Army, he revealed, and as long as he remained a Legionnaire his soldier's pride insisted that he march. A soldier who would play the violin must also march, he said. Reluctantly Pechkoff left him in the ranks.

One day not long afterward Bohlmann fell out of the line of march utterly exhausted. Pechkoff, riding back in search of him, found him dead beside the dusty track. Bohlmann had done a thorough and soldierly job of it, threading a string around the trigger guard of his rifle so that the bullet would enter through the roof of his mouth and he would fall upon his fixed bayonet.

Pechkoff understood.

To Pechkoff there was no such thing as the mystique of the Legion. Rather than mystique, its principles were absolute fact to him. And he made them seem absolute and true to other men.

"We are the pioneers who open a new country," he wrote one evening in the blue shadows of the mountains. "We are the rugged, primitive laborers who do the hardest work. We are the visionaries who see wonderful possibilities in the future. After the Legion, other men will come. These men will be praised. Their names will be known. But it is our men of the Legion who have paved the way with their untiring labor. Every path we have bears the pain of our men. It is they who have opened the way for civilization to come into the heart of this savage country. I like this primitive life. I feel so strong and gay. I feel in communion with my men."

20

A Troubled

Stepchild

THE FOREIGN LEGION implicitly promised its recruits a sanctuary from the political convulsions of Europe by protecting them from the pursuit and revenge of political enemies in their own countries.

This fact helped induce the Legion to believe that it existed in a political vacuum except for loyalty to its paymaster, France. It adopted a parochial viewpoint. For example, veteran Legionnaires seldom referred to wars by their commonly known names; they spoke, rather, of "in Indochina" or "on the Somme" or "at Rachaya," as if a war had no social context or little reality except as it was related to Legion experience.

It was a delusion, as the history of the organization makes abundantly clear. No nation in Europe reflected the political tensions of the Continent more sensitively than France. And no military unit reflected the international political tensions of France more sensitively than the Foreign Legion—which had the role of the expendable stepchild. Its allowance was the first to be reduced in seasons of thriftiness. Its assigned tasks were menial. The opportunity for military glory was offered first to the legitimate sons of France; almost invariably the Legion had to snatch its lion's share under more adverse conditions. It was the advance guard and the rear guard in unpopular campaigns. But none of these things just chanced to happen to the Legion. All were the effects of French involvement in tumultuous international affairs.

World War II shook the Legion out of the delusion that it existed in a political vacuum. Its international character could not remain aloof in that international upheaval. Before the war was over, Legionnaires demonstrated that men *do* fight, after all, for the causes and countries of their hearts.

Upon the outbreak of war the Legion revealed in microcosm the conflicts of Europe and the unpreparedness of France. Even as fine a leader as Rollet, who would die in Paris early in 1940, could do little about it. The world seemed to be changing more swiftly than ever, and the Legion was changing with it. In the late 1930's numerous veterans declined to re-enlist and many excellent officers resigned. Pechkoff, for one, left to reorganize the Army of Peru; Prince Aage died of pneumonia in Fez early in 1940.

For the first time in Legion history a foreign power was infiltrating its ranks with agents and hoping to exploit it. The Nazi regime of Germany, while publicly condemning the Legion, sent scores of men into it with the plan of leading a mutiny against the French when the time was opportune. By 1938, Germans filled 80 per cent of the noncommissioned officer grades and composed more than half of the enlisted strength. Although many were ardent anti-Nazis, the Nazi element was brutal and efficient in its infiltration. The French knew all about it. Many French officers felt they could not trust their noncoms. Mistrust led the high command to decide that the Legion should not be used in France.

When war was declared, hundreds of Legionnaire Nazi sympathizers were disarmed and sent to the desert in work parties. Others suspected of Nazi leanings were sent to join them in the ensuing weeks. Meanwhile between 5,000 and 6,000 anti-Nazis flocked to the Legion to serve for "the duration" and fight Germany. They included large numbers of Jews, Austrians, Hungarians, Poles, Czechs, and Spanish Republicans. Still the French high command felt that units of the Legion would be unreliable if shipped to France. Legion officers, eager to serve in the war, protested to the Government. In the atmosphere of mistrust morale sank steadily.

Morale was not improved by the refusal of the French to supply the Legion with first-rate arms and equipment. Little new came to it except the khaki uniform of the French Army. Its armament still consisted of rifles, light machine guns and personnel mortars and grenades. Its motorized equipment was antiquated. It still had a regiment of cavalry, armed with sabers and carbines, even though the horse had long since demonstrated ineffectiveness in modern warfare. It had no tanks or half-tracks, no artillery except a few outmoded 75's. Although most Legionnaires did not realize it at the time, many regular French units also were ill equipped to oppose the blitzkrieg armored war that Germany would launch. France, still remembering the frightful casualties of World War I and unable to govern itself strongly, had put its faith in a defensive war on the Maginot Line. Officers such as Charles de Gaulle, who had been striving for years to develop a mobile armored army capable of the offensive, were discredited by the defensive-minded General Staff schooled in the military philosophy of Pétain at Verdun.

Large numbers of foreigners living in France meanwhile volunteered to fight against Germany. The Government hesitated before accepting them, but two regiments were formed in October, 1939, and carefully screened cadres of Legion noncommissioned officers were sent to them from North Africa. In November another regiment was formed at Lyons, partially from North African veterans and partially from drafted French reservists. The two elements did not mix well and it was not a happy outfit. The same mood of dissension resulted when yet another regiment was formed in February, 1940, and Legionnaires again were mixed with drafted French reservists who resented serving in the Legion. In May a few regular

Legionnaires were placed in another new regiment of foreigners, composed largely of Polish Jews. Except for the last, these units were stationed in or near the Maginot Line during the period before the German attack that became known as the "Phony War."

Legionnaire Perrott-White served as a sergeant in one of the regiments at an advanced post of the Maginot Line.

"We did not enjoy the comforts of the deep underground fortresses with their good food and nice warm beds," he recalled. "We were under combat conditions, eating cold food and little of it, and sleeping in the deep snow with threadbare blankets. All through that bitter winter of 1939–40 we certainly suffered and if the war was 'phony,' our hardships were real. Coming from the desert of Africa as we did, the bitter cold, the ice and slush, combined with the ever-present body lice, took their toll in illness and disease."

After the German offensive burst upon the French in May, 1940, all of the Legion regiments became involved in the disaster.

The regiment which had been formed of Legionnaires and French draftees in November was in a blocking position between the Meuse and Chiers Rivers when German armor and infantry struck it on May 27. During two weeks of intensive fighting the veteran Legionnaires and the French draftees forgot their differences and became true comrades at arms. By the time of the cease-fire more than 75 per cent of the officers and men had been killed, captured or wounded.

The regiment formed in February of a similar mixture of Legionnaires and draftees never had a chance. On June 6 it was surrounded near Soissons and subjected to a thirty-six-hour artillery bombardment. A breakout was attempted, but less than one-third of the men were able to fight their way free and join in the general retreat of the French forces.

The first regiment of foreigners which had been formed in the previous October was attacked by the Germans in the Ardennes on the night of June 9. It recoiled and veteran Legion noncommissioned officers could not curb the mounting panic of their fleeing men. It was not engaged in battle again.

Despite all that military authorities have said on the subject, it often remains a mystery why some units have a strong morale, while others fail in the pay-off of battle. The other regiment formed at the same time as the one that panicked displayed excellent morale when sent into action near Perrone. Ordered to take a village, it accomplished its mission and then held on there for three days while German armor swirled around it. Not until it had lost half its men did it surrender.

Even more magnificent was the month-old regiment composed largely of Polish Jews who lacked training and were poorly equipped. On June 15, the day after Paris fell, the regiment flung itself against the Germans near Soissons. In the mounting confusion of the French forces someone ordered it to hold a bridge across the Aisne against the Germans. Using rifles and hand grenades against the heavy German armor, the fledgling Legionnaires somehow clung doggedly to the bridge for two days while French forces retreated behind them. Pinched off at last and surrounded, small groups of the untrained men tried to fight their way out. There is no record of any member of the regiment returning to its depot.

Amid the chaos and panic of the collapsing French armies, there were innumerable instances of courage, foolhardiness, and the disappearance of entire units. Some flung themselves savagely at the enemy, while others fled with the terrified civilians who jammed the roads and made orderly military movements impossible.

"Group 97" of the Foreign Legion has been called courageous by the Legion and foolhardy by the French. Composed of drivers of the Legion's only motor transport company, of unhorsed cavalrymen and a few infantrymen who liked the idea of riding instead of marching, it was the only unit formed solely of Legion veterans to fight the German blitzkrieg of 1940 in France. "Group 97" was given some old armored cars and sent to the Somme area in May. Its mission was reconnaissance. On May 18, shortly after the first big breakthrough, the Legionnaires made contact with German armor. Outgunned and outarmored, though not outmaneuvered, the Legionnaires raced their light vehicles about the German heavy tanks rather like boys with peashooters in a herd of elephants. For days on end they fought difficult rear-guard actions as the French retreated. Finally tiring of retreating, the three squadrons wheeled on June 9 and launched a suicidal assault on the heavy German tanks. Within minutes half of the Legion vehicles were knocked out and blazing. But the survivors did not break off and withdraw. Regrouping, they hurled themselves at the German heavy tanks again. There were no Legion survivors.

Only one other unit composed solely of carefully screened veteran Legionnaires was sent to France in the early stages of the war. All of its men had volunteered to aid Finland, and when they sailed from Oran late in 1939 in regimental strength, none realized that they were embarked on perhaps the most fabulous series of adventures experienced by any military unit in World War II. Their outfit was designated the 13th Half-Brigade; some French regiments in years past had been called half-brigades and the Legion had revived usage of the word for some of its improvised organizations. Its commander was Lieutenant Colonel Magrin-Verneret, who was known as Monclar, a hearty, capable soldier with a wry sense of humor.

The 13th trained on skis in France that winter and then was sent to England in April, 1940. There it learned that the German invasion of Norway had resulted in its mission being diverted from Finland to Narvik on the extreme northern Norwegian coast. British naval forces had destroyed several German ships in Narvik Fjord on April 9 and again on April 13. The naval battles were followed by British landings at Namsos and Andalsues on the Norwegian coast. Now, in the third phase of the operation, the Legion was to participate in seizing and holding the Narvik sector against the Germans.

Throughout the the war the 13th tried to recruit new members wherever it went. ("We were like the Salvation Army in that respect," one of its men remarked wryly many years later.) The Legion had, of course, recruited men from 101 nations—and once in Morocco, in a burst of benign paternalism, it had signed up a homeless twelve-year-old boy to prevent him from starving, outfitted him in a specially tailored Legion uniform, and insisted that he draw a soldier's pay. But it remained for the 13th to recruit a woman in England and sign her on as an ambulance driver. She was Miss Susan

Travers, the only woman ever to wear the seven-flamed grenade insignia of the Foreign Legion. She remained with the 13th throughout its long and strange odyssey in the war and even afterward continued as a Legion ambulance driver in Indochina.

Besides one woman, the 13th included some remarkable men. One was Major Amilakvari, a White Russian Georgian prince of great charm and character who had enlisted in 1924 and considered the Legion his home and country. Another was Captain Joseph-Pierre Koenig, a brilliant French soldier who was destined for the highest commands in the Army.

As the 13th was about to sail from Liverpool on April 28, someone discovered that its flag lacked a staff. After hastily rustling about, the British turned up an old cavalry lance which had to serve the purpose. But a staff for the flag in no way improved the depressed spirits of Legionnaires, who felt they were being shipped to an icy backwater of the war.

"It makes me sick," a lieutenant said to Monclar after they sailed.

The Colonel, who had been suffering from hiccoughs for a couple of days, replied gravely and measuredly: "We have to learn to detach ourselves completely from the glamour of glory. *La Légion, c'est le détachment.* What are my orders? To take Narvik. And why Narvik? For the iron ore, for the anchovies, for the Norwegians? I haven't the faintest idea."

The 13th landed at Ballangen on May 7 and marched through the melting snows to Scarnes. When a young English naval lieutenant was assigned to serve as an aide to Monclar, the Colonel tied a white ribbon round his arm to distinguish him, he said, from every other unemotional English boy in His Majesty's Navy.

In the advance on Narvik, where the Legion hoped to surprise the Germans, Monclar happened upon a tanned Legionnaire who was staggering drunk. "What do you mean by advertising your arrival to the world?" Monclar asked him without rancor. "We are camouflaging ourselves and you look as though you were headed for a brothel in Marrakech on the fourteenth of July."

After the first brush with German forces, a severely wounded Legionnaire limped past Monclar. His face was blood-streaked, an arm was in a sling, and one leg was bandaged.

"There are plenty of stretcher-bearers," Monclar told him reproachfully.

For once, however, Monclar did not have the last word. The Legionnaire, looking him straight in the eye, replied, "March or die," and limped on.

The Legionnaires and a Norwegian battalion launched the conclusive assault on Narvik at midnight on May 28. By the next night they had driven out the last Germans.

The Legionnaires expected to linger in Norway indefinitely. But a surprise was in store for them. A few days later they were ordered back to France. On the evening of June 13 they entered the harbor at Brest, and the next day they learned that the Germans had taken Paris.

Monclar set out in search of the nearest French Army headquarters to put his force at its disposal. When he returned that evening looking worn and perplexed, a fellow Legion officer asked him what he thought of the disaster. Monclar turned his head away and murmured, "The French Army has ceased to exist."

But no member of the Half-Brigade could believe that the fight was finished. On June 16 the 13th received orders to move west and defend Brittany with units of the *Chasseurs Alpins* approximately on the line of the Rance River. As it advanced in trucks, however, its puzzled officers began to receive contradictory orders. Finally, when the 13th was told to proceed to a point within the area occupied by the Germans, the officers felt they no longer could trust the French source of their orders.

The next day, while they were eating lunch in a small Breton village, they listened to Marshal Pétain's radio broadcast, announcing the terms of the proposed armistice. Some wept, but Monclar slammed his fist on the table and declared that the last order he had received that he understood was to defend Brittany on the line of the Rance and he would, by God, do it. "I shall advance!"

He had one other gesture of protest that he could make against the soft heads and weak hearts that were leading France down an infamous road behind tottering old Marshal Pétain. The 13th Half-Brigade of the Foreign Legion never would nor could surrender because, by God, he was here and now, officially and unequivocally, changing its designation to the *14th* Half-Brigade.

Whatever its name, the regiment and a battalion of the crack *Chasseurs Alpins* went on, their trucks dispersed over the twisting roads of Brittany. They had a rendezvous the following day at the Rance south of Dinan.

But they did not keep it. For, that night as the Legionnaires and *Chasseurs* bivouacked in small and dispersed groups well off the roads, the darkened hills echoed to the clank and rumble of heavy German tanks. An entire armored division passed through them without being aware of their presence. Monclar himself crouched in the brush and watched a heavy machine-gun company clatter past.

There was no point now in trying to set up a line along the Rance. There was no point in trying to defend anything in France. But the fight against the Germans must go on. This regiment, whatever anyone wished to call it, would fight on *for* France but *with* the British, who had not yet given up this cursed war. The idea seemed to occur to hundreds of Legionnaires simultaneously that night. Monclar never issued an order that fell on more receptive ears. The word fanned out from group to group in the night: Disappear! It was said that Legionnaires were deserters. Well, here was their chance. It also was said that Legionnaires were fighters. Well, here, too, was their chance!

It was difficult, perhaps impossible, but that was the order: Disappear! Make your way alone or by twos and threes across the Channel to England. And who will arrange your transportation? Well, comrade, a Legionnaire is supposed to be ingenious. And where would they rendezvous in England? Monclar and his staff had thought of that, too. Where was a place to which any Englishman could give them directions? London, of course. But *where* in London? Someone thought of the place. Piccadilly Circus in the heart of London.

Comment? Pee-ca-dee-lee *Cirque. Le rondpoint. Comprennez?* You'd better learn English, damn it. Pic-ca-dil-ly Cir-cus. Get it?

They did. They faded away that night in small groups and took to cover as soon as daylight grew. They went north through the hills of Brittany by twos and threes and fours. And soon they began to reach Breton ports—Saint-Malo and Dinard and farther west at Saint-Jacut-de-la-Mer and even beyond at the little basins toward Cap Fréhel where the sea crashes against the red cliffs with the sound of thunder. Regular passenger service to Southampton and Weymouth and Plymouth had been suspended. But silent Breton fishermen wearing wooden clogs still put to sea at sunset in their trawlers. And sometimes they were gone a very long time and returned with remarkably light hauls for men who knew the Channel so well.

A few days previously the French destroyer *Milan* had sailed from Brest with a French officer among its passengers who would affect the course of French history. His name was Charles de Gaulle.

As the days passed, London bobbies in Piccadilly Circus became accustomed to seeing officers of the Foreign Legion standing on a corner day and night. Sometimes a tanned, bearded, raggedly dressed soldier wearing a dirty white cap approached the officer, saluted him, and was greeted with a warm handshake.

Nearly 1,000 Legionnaires and more than 200 *Chasseurs Alpins* made their way across the Channel and were reunited at their encampment in Trentham Park.

When Colonel Monclar learned that the Vichy Government of Marshal Pétain said the 13th Half-Brigade no longer existed, he issued a new order. Henceforth the 14th would resume its original designation and be known as the *13th* Half-Brigade.

Meanwhile the countryside of France, once more looking so peaceful by day, seemed to swarm at night. Thousands of French soldiers who had escaped from captivity or been in hiding from the Germans were trying to reach home or some destination where they hoped to resume the fight. Among them were scores of Legionnaires trudging toward Marseilles.

Legionnaire Perrott-White had a remarkable escape after he was wounded and captured. Accompanied by a Polish Legionnaire, he killed a guard and leaped from a moving prisoner-of-war train near Aachen in Germany. Their trek out of Germany, across Belgium, and halfway across France to Lyons was typical of the nightmare journeys many men were undertaking in those weeks.

"We did not dare approach too near houses and farms," Perrott-White recalled. "The enemy was everywhere. During the first ten days we lived exclusively on carrots and raw potatoes which we stole from the edges of farms and drinking water from roadside ditches. In the daytime we holed up in whatever cover would shield us from view and traveled only at night. It was fortunate that we both knew the general direction we wanted to go, which was the southern coast of France, where we hoped to get on a ship and thus across to Africa or any country we could reach. During the latter part of our trek we managed to get a few comforts from the occupants of isolated farms; but they would not keep us too long. They feared reprisals from the Germans if we were caught."

The Pole lost strength steadily and urged Perrott-White to go on alone. But he refused and they struggled on together. Two months after their escape they learned from a friendly farmer that Lyons was free of German troops and that the French Army was maintaining a garrison there. The Pole died in Perrott-White's arms thirty miles short of their goal and Perrott-White staggered on alone to a French Army post on the outskirts of Lyons. He recuperated there before being shipped back to Sidi-bel-Abbès.

The Legion to which he returned was undergoing the sorest travail in its history, for the German Armistice Commission was putting great pressure on the Vichy Government to disband it. The mass of loyal Legion men and officers found themselves in an insurmountable quandary. Many wanted to join the forces of the Free French which De Gaulle was gathering in England, but they had no means of reaching them. They had to pay lip service to Vichy on whom they depended for survival. And they had to endure the endless cross-examinations and searches of Armistice Commission teams of Germans who invaded every large post. At the same time the Nazi agents in their ranks were creating dissension. Simultaneously, too, the group of 5,000 to 6,000 anti-Nazis who had enlisted for "the duration only" maintained that the war had ended and they should be released.

The viewpoint of these men was expressed by Legionnaire Anthony Delmayne, an Englishman who wanted to fight the Nazis and eventually managed to escape from the Legion.

"Few of us had any wish to fight undernourished natives unable to pay their taxes," he said, "when there were so many Nazis waiting to be killed. Many of us had a considerable stake in the war. There were Jews and other refugees from Germany, Czechs and Poles, Italians and many Spanish Republicans who were naïve enough to think that if fascism was destroyed in Germany, democracy would be restored to their own country too. Rumors that Vichy was going to sell us down the river filled these men with dread, and there were riots, mutinies, fights and suicides in the fort; sometimes there were as many as five or six suicides in a day."

The Legion could not release these men because it had no place to send them. At first the Vichy Government refused to let them into France, though later it relented and accepted some. Legion officers harangued them to sign up for five years as the only way they could be "protected." Some consented and signed for the long term. Others who did not were pressed into work gangs and sent south to the desert where the Vichy Government had decided to extend the railway beyond Colomb-Béchar. Many died in the dire labor of the desert; how many survived and how they eventually managed to escape from North Africa cannot be ascertained.

At the same time the Legion took exceedingly good care of those who were loyal to it. Its recruitment sources in Europe had dried up, and, like a thrifty housewife, it preserved what it had carefully. The chief occupation of many Legion commissioned and noncommissioned officers was outwitting the German Armistice teams. Soon after the fall of France the Nazis began presenting the Legion with lists of "wanted" men. Vichy conceded to the Germans the right to recover deserters from their own forces; though this affronted the

267

principles of the Legion, it served as a precedent for similar agreements made with Russia in 1945 and with the United States and Great Britain in 1948. But the Nazis went beyond the extent of the agreement on their "wanted" lists and included Jews, Poles, Czechs, democratic-minded Germans and others who had been violent anti-Nazis and never had served in the German armed forces.

The German Armistice teams were no match, however, for the century-old intelligence system of the Legion in North Africa. Legion posts always received advance warning of visits by teams and usually were supplied with the "wanted" lists before the Nazis presented them. Men the Germans sought were hastily dispatched to distant posts or sent out on long "training marches" from which they did not return until the Armistice team had departed. The Germans also sought to strip the Legion of its meager, inadequate arms and ammunition. Immediately upon the capitulation of France the Legion had secretly cached away its most valuable arms and its major supplies of ammunition. Now its loyal members played hide and seek with what remained, burying rifles and grenades under the noses of Nazi informers before the arrival of Armistice teams.

Regiments were disbanded as the strength of the Legion dipped below 10,000. The designation of the 4th was changed to the 4th Half-Brigade; it was filled with men whose names were on the Nazis' "wanted" lists and was sent so far into the hinterland of Senegal that Legion headquarters had difficulty in maintaining contact with it.

The lot of the Nazis in the Legion after the fall of France was not the happy one they had anticipated. About 1,000 were released at their own request, but they were not allowed to go home to Germany. Instead, the Germans formed them into a "German Legion" and kept them in North Africa segregated from the Legion proper. Others who remained in the ranks as Germans informers began to have difficult times, as did a sprinkling of Italians who bragged about being Fascist followers of Mussolini.

Delmayne remembers that when a German general of the Armistice Commission visited Sidi-bel-Abbès, two German Legionnaires

268

stepped up to him and declared that they wished to die for the Fatherland. After the general had gone, a sergeant major cried to the guard, "Shove those two swine in the black cell! Take away their bedding. Don't give 'em any more food. They can start dying for the Fatherland right now!"

These long months that crept into years were the most frustrating in the lives of officers and men who hated the Nazis and wished to fight for a free France.

"That period was like a term in prison," recalls a Frenchman who was then an officer in the Legion. "We were without coffee, sugar, milk, tobacco. Worst of all, we were without hope. We had to pay lip service to Vichy because our very existence depended on that government of folly. Some men in the ranks who were no more democratic-minded than many of us held us officers in contempt for not leading them in a revolt. But where were we to go? Were we to march off into the desert and die?"

In London, meanwhile, De Gaulle realized that the Free French must move against the adherents of the Vichy Government in Africa or else wither away as a discredited organization. With the enthusiastic co-operation of Prime Minister Winston Churchill a plan was conceived for seizing the Vichy-controlled West Coast stronghold of Dakar.

The land forces De Gaulle could muster were pathetically small compared to the strength of the British fleet which was to cover them: a battalion of the Legion's 13th Half-Brigade, a company of French recruits, a company of French marines, and a few fragments of volunteers. On August 31, 1940, the Legion battalion sailed from Liverpool with De Gaulle aboard the Dutch liner *Westerland*. After the British fleet arrived off Dakar on September 17, a complicated series of misfortunes resulted in a stalemate. Bombardments were exchanged by the British vessels and Vichy ships and shore batteries, but the land forces were too weak to effect a landing.

Late October found the battalion of the 13th at Douala in the Cameroons under the command of Koenig, whom De Gaulle had promoted to major. De Gaulle personally was flying swiftly about West and Central Africa, organizing resistance to Vichy.

(Efforts to learn why the Free French did not try to enlist the 4th Half-Brigade of the Legion, which had been sent into the interior of Senegal and was composed largely of anti-Vichy men raises an interesting question which cannot be answered conclusively: Was it possible that the Gaullists did not know of the whereabouts and sentiments of this "lost" regiment?)

It was vital to the Free French to seize the port of Libreville in Gabon before the Vichyites in Dakar reinforced it. Already the Vichy General, Têtu, at Libreville had four battalions, some artillery, four new bombers, an armed sloop and a submarine at his disposal. Against this force Koenig led the Legion battalion and a mixed battalion of poorly trained Senegalese and colonials who had been scraped together at Douala. The Free French landed near Libreville and early on the morning of November 9 the Legion battalion ran into heavy fire as it led the advance toward the town. It lost twenty men before the Vichyites suddenly ended their resistance.

With Gabon and the Cameroons securely in Free French hands, the Legion embarked on ships which had brought the remaining strength of the 13th Half-Brigade from England under Monclar. As the regiment sailed south in convoy and rounded the Cape of Good Hope, the Legionnaires speculated on their destination. At Narvik they had been farther north than any unit in the history of the Legion, and now they had come the farthest south.

Their destination was Port Sudan on the Red Sea. *"Le bon Charlie,"* as the Legionnaires called De Gaulle behind his back, had elbowed a way for the Free French into British operations against the Italians in the Sudan and Eritrea. (The Legion was somewhat in awe of De Gaulle but never had for him the affection that it felt for a few field commanders. "It was impossible ever to be familiar with De Gaulle," a Legion officer said later. "You might as well try to be familiar with the Eiffel Tower.")

The British greeted the Legion coldly. They considered the Sudan strictly a British show and cared not at all about the desire of the

Free French to extend their influence over Vichy-held French Somali-land. At first the 13th simply tagged along behind the British column which struck inland to seize Kassala. Then, however, the Legionnaires went into action at Kubkub, and the British began to look at them more respectfully. In the attack on the fortified Italian position at Keren in March the Legionnaires composed the Allied left wing and performed magnificently, sweeping up the Italians like dust before a broom. Thereafter the British became as profuse as they ever could be about the fighting qualities of the Legion.

On March 31, 1941, Monclar led the 13th on Massawa, the capital and redoubt of Eritrea. The Legionnaires stormed through the strongholds of Montecullo and Fort Umberto like a whirlwind and rushed into Massawa on April 7 hot on the heels of a rabble of flee-ing Italians. Making straight for the port, they seized the Admiralty and gave Monclar the honor of receiving the surrender of the com-mander of the Italian Red Sea fleet. In the course of the brief cam-paign the Legion had taken more than 4,000 prisoners in battle and received the surrender of 10,000 more at Massawa while suffering very light casualties itself.

But De Gaulle had an even more trying task in store for the 13th. In May it was decided to occupy Syria before it could be exploited by the enemy. British and Free French forces entered Syria on June 8 from Palestine and Trans-Jordan. As the 13th wound across the hills toward Damascus, it came face to face near Damas with the 6th Foreign Legion Regiment which had been garrisoned in Syria for several years and was under the control of the Vichy Government.

"We faced each other there in the hills for what seemed to be hours," a veteran of the 13th recalls. "Neither side wanted to make the first move. We were brothers. Yet we were strangers. Were we enemies, too? We had been told that the Vichy forces would not put up more than token resistance. But what is a 'token' in war?"

A patrol of the 13th probed toward an outpost of the 6th. As it drew near, neither side wished to fire. At last the outpost members of the 6th turned out and presented arms. But then, as the patrol came on, the men of the outpost took the patrol members prisoners.

"You are the enemy," said the outpost commander, "but first you are Legionnaires."

Soon the battle burst out in all the fury of fratricidal strife. No quarter was given in the attacks and counterattacks. Yet when the 6th took some wounded members of the 13th prisoner and Senegalese troops in the rear began molesting and looting the wounded Legionnaires, men of the 6th dashed back to beat off the Senegalese savagely. Then they hurried forward again and sprayed advancing members of the 13th with machine-gun fire.

Superior arms finally helped turn the day for the 13th and the Legionnaires of Free France passed on into Damascus. In the ensuing weeks there was fierce fighting wherever elements of the 13th met elements of the 6th. When the British and Free French finally gained control over Syria, the 6th was disbanded and its members were given a choice of joining the 13th or being repatriated to Vichy territory. Only two officers and a few noncommissioned officers joined the Free French, but nearly 1,000 men in the ranks passed into the 13th, enabling it to form a third battalion. Both groups soon forgot their fratricidal bloodshed and fought side by side harmoniously throughout the rest of their service.

When Monclar was promoted and assigned to administrative duties in Syria, Colonel Amilakvari assumed command of the 13th. By the great force of his benign personality he did much to heal the differences between the regiment's Free French and Vichy factions and to remind them that they were, foremost, Legionnaires.

Meanwhile Koenig had been sent to Egypt, where he began organizing the first "division" which the Free French could put into the field. As soon as Syria was quiet, the 13th was transferred to Egypt and the Legionnaires formed the core of the new 1st Light Division which General Koenig was forming.

Although the division numbered only 5,500 men and was barely of brigade strength, it took up a front-line position in February, 1942, on the extreme left wing of the British 8th Army in the Libyan desert. It was in the same position in the line at Bir Hakeim when General Erwin Rommel launched his great German-Italian offensive

272

in May. An Italian armored division hurled 100 tanks against the light division on May 27 and lost 40 of them.

Checked in his initial move, Rommel regrouped and struck again, overrunning a British brigade at Got-el-Skarab and driving a breach between the British and the 1st Light Division. Skirmishing quickly jelled into a battle front which found a German and an Italian division surrounding Koenig's 5,500 French and Legionnaires. Now the defensive "box" at Bir Hakeim began to resemble a coffin. Rommel sent Koenig a white-flag spokesman, who asked him to surrender. Koenig replied he had come out to fight, not surrender. Tightening their hold, the Germans shelled the division with 155's and 220's while waves of Stukas dive-bombed it. When Rommel finally sent Koenig a note in his own hand asking him to surrender or be wiped out, Koenig told his artillery to reply for him.

"Hold out for six days longer," the Allied Command ordered Koenig on the evening of June 1. On the evening of June 7 it radioed him, "Hold out for forty-eight hours longer." Rommel's battering of the entire front made the relief of Bir Hakeim impossible. Yet the French and Legionnaires could not hold out much longer. Ammunition was running dangerously low, food was scarce, water was rationed at two quarts per day per man. Finally, on June 10, the Allied Command sent Koenig the coded message: Break out as best you can.

A breakout, that most difficult maneuver, rarely had daunted the Legion in its long history of combat. And it was not disconcerted by the order at Bir Hakeim. Careful reconnaissance had found a mined hole in the surrounding ring of Germans and Italians. Late on the night of June 10, Legionnaire sappers cleared a path through the enemy mine fields and led the way out of the box. Koenig chose to have his own jeep driven by Susan Travers, the English Legionnaire ambulance driver. Moving stealthily in the cold darkness of the desert, the French and Legionnaires slipped away undetected. Dawn found them safely miles away when the Germans and Italians renewed their bombardment of the empty "box."

The free world hailed the daring night maneuver that brought to safety nearly 4,000 men of the 1st Light Division. Yet it had paid a price for its valiant defense of Bir Hakeim. When the Legion's 13th Half-Brigade returned to action it was reduced to a strength of two battalions.

It was on the extreme left of the line again when the British opened their desert offensive in October, 1942. Ordered to clear the escarpment of El Himeimat, the 1st Battalion of Legionnaires was going forward across open ground on October 23 when a German force struck it on the flank. But the 2nd Battalion, moving in reserve, in turn struck the Germans on their flank. In the confused fighting both battalions were pinned down briefly by a German crossfire of machine guns and mortars. Colonel Amilakvari sprang to his feet and rallied his Legionnaires, but minutes later he was killed by a mortar burst. He was the eighty-fourth commander of a Legion unit to die in battle at the head of his men.

While the Free French Legionnaires with the British 8th Army pressed Rommel's army into Tunisia, the Legion garrisons of Morocco and Algeria were awakened from their long somnolence under Vichy.

They were roused rudely by the Americans in the early morning of November 8, 1942, when American forces hit the Moroccan beaches near Casablanca and Port Lyautey. At first many Legionnaires believed they were being attacked by the Germans. Perrott-White, then on duty with a Legion artillery battery near Port Lyautey, expressed the bafflement of soldiers who wished to remain "passive" and yet conduct themselves honorably in the face of an attack by forces to whom they felt friendly. Perrott-White believes that if his pro-Gaullist unit had been notified of the attack in advance, it would not have fired a shot in reply. Yet Gaullist and American intelligence knew how thoroughly German agents had honeycombed North Africa and surprise was essential to the success of the invasion.

In several Legion units there was initial confusion as to what constituted a soldier's honor in yielding passively. Soon, however, the Legion swung wholeheartedly into the Allied cause.

The 4th Half-Brigade was hastily recalled from the depths of

Senegal, reconstituted as the 1st *Régiment Etrangère d'Infanterie de Marche* (R.E.I.M.) and incorporated in the British 1st Army. At the same time the 3rd R.E.I.M. was formed and a unit known as the *Groupe Autonome* was raked together from remnants of Legion cavalry. Skeptical at first of the Legion's loyalty, the Allies did not immediately lavish up-to-date arms on its fighting forces.

The Allies' attitude changed, however, after the 3rd Legion Regiment slammed into the German drive against the Kasserine Pass. The 3rd's aged arms were no match for the German firepower and it soon was surrounded; only the bombing of American planes enabled it to break free. Shortly thereafter the Allies rearmed both the 3rd and the 1st. Both were heavily engaged in western Tunisia while the 13th continued to fight with the British pincer in eastern Tunisia until the Germans finally were driven from North Africa.

Among the prisoners taken were the survivors of the "German Legion" which Rommel had incorporated into his army. Nearly all wished to rejoin the Foreign Legion from which the Nazis had separated them. Although it was forbidden and they were marched off to prison camps, many reapplied to the Legion after the end of the war and were accepted.

Casualties and the sealing off of enlistment sources had brought the strength of the Legion in North Africa to its lowest point in a half century. As a matter of honor it wished to keep in the field its famed 13th Half-Brigade whose strength had dropped below 1,200. But in addition to the 13th it could not support more than one infantry regiment and a cavalry regiment which the Americans equipped with vehicles and arms.

After intensive training in Tunisia, the reinforced and re-equipped 13th sailed in April, 1944, for Italy. There it joined the 5th Army in the painful crawl from hill to hill against dogged German opposition. Its last action in Italy was at Radicorfani, where the Germans were strongly established on a high escarpment. Swarming up the craggy cliffs in small groups, the men of the 13th drove out the Germans with hand grenades.

On August 16, 1944, the 13th landed at Cavalaire on the coast of

Provence, thus returning to French soil after four years of fighting on three continents. It helped seize Toulon and then moved north against heavy opposition which gradually reduced its strength to two battalions again.

The Legion infantry and cavalry regiments landed in southern France in September and were assigned to the heavily defended German front west of the Rhine between Colmar and the Swiss border. A pass near Belfort was the key to the defense, and the 13th was brought from reserve to help take it. On November 22 the Legion units struck with all their might, broke through, and went on to take Belfort.

Six weeks later they fought furiously for the possession of two Rhine bridges, which they finally seized and crossed. In a ferocious counterattack the Germans obliterated one company of the infantry regiment within minutes, but the Legionnaires clung grimly to their gains.

Then they were sent against Colmar. There, in a bitter winter struggle, the 13th fought its last battle of the war. When it finally entered Colmar, only about 700 men still were on their feet. Not until then was the 13th withdrawn into permanent and honorable reserve.

But the Legion infantry regiment pushed on toward Stuttgart which it entered on April 21 after grueling and costly fighting. Still no rest was granted it. With the depleted motorized cavalry regiment, its remnants were sent into the Black Forest and reached the Danube River on April 24. Crossing the Danube, the Legionnaires pressed on into Austria. May 7, 1945, the date of the cease-fire, found the Legionnaires searching out pockets of resistance near Arlberg.

The war in Europe had ended and a freed France was staggering to its feet after debacle, division, and a wrenching salvation. But there was little peace in store for the Foreign Legion.

21

"So That Honor
May Be Saved"

THE WAR IN EUROPE and the great naval, air, and island-hopping operations of the war in the Pacific eclipsed events in Indochina. There French troops and Legionnaires, abandoned by the Vichy Government and shunned by potential allies, fought the first rounds in a long and costly losing battle.

When France fell to the German armies in June, 1940, the French forces in Indochina numbered about 70,000 men, including large numbers of local troops and 5,000 Legionnaires of the 5th Regiment. All were ill-equipped, having obsolete weapons and material with which to protect French interests against the territorial ambitions of Japan and its satellite Thailand.

In September, 1940, Japanese troops entered northern Indochina in order to halt American supplies which then were flowing to General Chiang Kai-shek's Nationalist Chinese forces through Haiphong and the corridor into Yunnan. The French border forts resisted the

277

Japanese move, but were overwhelmed within a couple of days. Soon afterward the Vichy Government signed an agreement permitting the Japanese to station troops in Indochina.

Then began a period of inactivity and frustration for the French and their Legionnaires that lasted more than four years. Nationalist China directed a propaganda campaign at the Legion units, urging men to desert and fight in China, but few Legionnaires were tempted. The long truce ended abruptly on the morning of March 9, 1945, when the Japanese ordered the French and Legion garrisons to lay down their arms and surrender. The Legion units, having anticipated the Japanese move for some time, refused to surrender. Digging up ammunition which they had carefully buried, various units fought through the Japanese and grouped together. Some French units also resisted, but the Japanese quickly overwhelmed them.

Operating according to a preconceived plan, the 5th Regiment, now numbering about 3,300 men, began a fighting retreat toward the Chinese border five hundred miles away. Japanese forces deployed to block them and succeeded in ambushing them several times. But the Legionnaires fought through, making their way along twisting jungle trails, across rivers and through rugged mountains. Fifty-two days after they began their fighting retreat they crossed over the border into the wilds of Yunnan. Still another two hundred miles of marching lay before them until they reached a road which trucks could travel. About 300 Legionnaires died or were lost on the grueling trek. But the reminder, resisting the efforts of the Chinese to incorporate them into the Nationalist Army, rested and waited in Yunnan, like pawns removed from the chessboard of war.

On August 19, 1945, Japanese forces began withdrawing swiftly from Indochina. The defeat of the Japanese and the end of World War II found a vacuum of power in Indochina that was easily exploited by a political party called the Viet-Minh. It was led by Communists, but posed as a democratic nationalist party interested only in ridding its country of French and Japanese imperialists. The well-trained Viet-Minh Communist leaders had little trouble in liquidating small and genuinely democratic groups which bickered among themselves. Under their leaders, Ho Chi Minh and Vo Nguyên Giap, the Viet-Minh formed the independent nation of Vietnam composed of the former states of Tonkin, Annam, and Cochin China.

But the postwar Potsdam Conference of the victorious powers decided that for the time being the northern area of Vietnam should come under the control of the Chinese Nationalists, while Britain should police the southern area. The Chinese Nationalists proved to be slow, corrupt, and inept. It took their foot-slogging forces three months to begin the occupation, giving the Viet-Minh ample time to seize and hide the copious supplies of arms the Japanese had left in their hasty evacuation. Then the Viet-Minh, to their delight, found Chinese who were willing to sell them large amounts of the arms the Nationalists were receiving from the United States. In southern Vietnam the British quickly had enough of trying to maintain order among a fractious people determined on independence. They gladly turned the problem over to France.

A French expeditionary force of less than two divisions landed in northern Vietnam in February, 1946, returning with an air that nothing had changed, that it might as well be 1896 as 1946. Not until the Legion's 5th Regiment in Yunnan learned of the French arrival in February did it start the long return march south. It arrived at Haiphong in April and was shipped back to Sidi-bel-Abbès where it was disbanded.

Sidi-bel-Abbès had become what a Legion officer characterized as "a manpower factory." After the lean war years when its enlistment sources had dried up, the Legion's rolls were fattening again on new resources. As has frequently happened in the history of mercenary units, the Legion began enlisting from the ranks of its recent enemies and within three months after the end of World War II its strength sprang to 26,000.

In its recruitment drive in the French-occupied zone of Germany the Legion accepted a great variety of men. Some were excellent professional soldiers who had lost their homes and families in the war and saw no better future than to continue bearing arms. Others were

279

homeless and destitute displaced persons. A few were minor Nazi functionaries who wished to escape from Germany. Although the United States and Britain protested the Legion's recruiting drive in the French zone, French intelligence officers made sure that known war criminals were barred from the Legion.

In Italy the Legion recruited some former Fascists along with numbers of men who had been uprooted by the war and wanted to start a new life. One Italian who enlisted had been Mussolini's Minister of Education, Bottai. A few French who had been closely associated with the Vichy Government's activities and thought it expedient to disappear for a while enlisted under the pretense of being Belgian or Swiss or Canadian citizens. Principally, however, the new men who flocked to the Legion were victims of the social upheavals caused by the war rather than political fugitives in its aftermath.

It is difficult to estimate the percentage of Germans in the Legion during the immediate postwar years. On the basis of testimony by Legionnaires themselves the official Legion figure of 30 to 35 per cent is too low. On the other hand, German claims that 80 per cent of those enlisted were Germans is too high, for the French mixed their Legion cocktail of nationalities more cautiously than that. Perhaps one-half of the enlisted men, perhaps a shade more, were Germans.

There was, of course, a purpose behind the build-up of Legion strength. It had a mission in Vietnam where the French steadily increased their forces in an effort to restore their former rule. The political figurehead of their regime was Bao Dai, the King of Annam, who was mistrusted by his people and who maintained his throne thanks to French machine guns. There were numerous other factions, but none as significant as the Viet-Minh, which was busily building up supplies of arms, capturing hostages, and training its members in Communist doctrine and guerilla warfare under Chinese and Japanese officers.

In February, 1946, the Legion's 2nd Regiment landed at Saigon and was sent into southern Annam with the mission of restoring French authority. The following month the renowned and reconstituted 13th Half-Brigade arrived in Vietnam and was ordered into the swamps and lowlands of Cochin China on a similar mission. Three months later the newly created 3rd Regiment also went into Cochin China. The 1st Cavalry regiment, equipped with light tanks and armored cars, arrived in January, 1947, and was dispersed for road-convoy duties. The 1st Parachute Battalion, formed and trained in Algeria, reached Vietnam in November, 1948, and, finally, the revived 5th Regiment went into Tonkin in November, 1949. Frequent replacements kept these six Legion formations at full strength and, in time, units of Vietnamese were attached to all of them.

Although the French eventually committed almost 300,000 men to the battle for Vietnam, they never gained absolute control of more than a few relatively small areas. The Viet-Minh, under the guidance of Chinese Communists, wrote a revolutionary chapter in the history of war. It was a war of disguise and terror in which the enemy mingled with the population so effectively that foes often could not be distinguished from friends until they opened fire. Torture was the fate of many prisoners the Communists took; certainly few Europeans could hope to survive the harsh treatment, scant rice, and polluted water of the Communist prison camps. Inevitably some French and Legionnaires indulged in equally harsh retaliatory measures. Yet, contrary to an ill-informed element of opinion in Europe and the United States, the French in general undertook wise and thorough measures and were far more humane than their Viet-Minh enemies.

Typical of the efforts of some Legionnaires was that of Lieutenant Draget, who was in charge of the "intelligence" efforts—the *Bande Noire,* as it was called—in the unit to which English Legionnaire Henry Ainley was assigned.

Draget was a Belgian, who had enlisted in the Legion as a private in 1940, served with the 13th Half-Brigade in its long odyssey from Norway to the end of the war, and then had put in three additional years in Vietnam. In the course of his service he had risen to first lieutenant, amassed ten *Croix de Guerres,* the Military Medal, the

Legion of Honor and several foreign decorations without once being wounded.

At first sight [says Ainley], he was a weedy, palefaced, bespectacled man of middle height and generally a very average specimen. . . . He looked like a little spinster when he led his men out of an evening in battledress and a brush hat pulled down over his ears, spectacles balanced on the end of his nose. He looked even more lamentable when he came back in the morning, soaked, muddy, and worn out, the *Bande Noire* following leading a prisoner or two—the prisoners far fresher than he. His polite and gentle manner of interrogation seemed ludicrous after the performances of [his predecessor] and the prophets reckoned that his day would soon be over. Strangely enough, the sector calmed down surprisingly fast.

In action Draget was calm and merciless; he knew how to maneuver his men and enabled the *Bande Noire* to hit hard without getting touched. He won the respect of his men by his patience, which out-matched that of the Annamites; he would wait days observing a sus-pected region and struck only when he knew the moment to be right. If a native was suspected of liaison with the Viet, he waited until he got the man redhanded and liquidated him on the spot—unlike [his pred-ecessor] who woke up half a province to arrest a man and usually managed to shoot up an entire village before reaching a suspected [hut], by which time the suspect had taken to his heels.

Not far from the spot where Draget's unit was stationed the Viet-Minh had established a stronghold in an impenetrable wasteland of scrub, bamboo thickets, and treacherous marshes. Three years of Le-gion efforts to destroy it had been of no avail when Draget began to study the situation.

One day he asked for three volunteers for a special mission which promised a fifty-fifty chance of safe return. Three Legionnaires stepped forward and Draget explained regretfully that first they must undergo a frightful beating at the hands of the toughest men in the company. Then they were to pretend to desert to the Viet-Minh, learn the routes into its stronghold, and get the information back to Draget.

The three were beaten up and disappeared; all except a few members of the *Bande Noire* believed that they actually had deserted. Ten nights later one of the three crept undetected into the post and told Draget what had happened.

After being beaten up and disappearing, the three had decided it would be wiser if only one made the attempt while the other two went off to Saigon and lay low for a time. They drew lots and the one who returned had been chosen. Going a little distance into the wasteland, he had contacted a Viet patrol, told its leader he was a deserter, and his bloodied and bruised face and body had been sufficiently convincing for him to be taken to the Viet commander. After long questioning and investigation, the Viets had accepted him and trusted him after he led a couple of attacks on Annamites who were friendly to the French.

That night, guided by the volunteer, Draget led a column of the *Bande Noire* into the swamps and destroyed the Viet stronghold at a cost of only sixteen Legionnaire wounded.

As in every war in which the Legion fought, there were all manner of men enlisted for all sorts of reasons. For each Draget there was a reluctant Legionnaire who sometimes deserted. The Viet-Minh leader, Ho Chi Minh, adopted as his son a German deserter from the Legion, who took the name of Ho Chi Long. Many deserters were repatriated to eastern Europe through China and Russia. Some who did not desert, but were captured, found themselves repatriated against their will. Recently there came to light the instance of such a Legionnaire repatriated to East Germany against his will who then escaped through the Iron Curtain by way of Berlin and made his way to France where he rejoined the Legion and completed his enlistment term.

One strange enlistment was that of a Jew named Eliahu Itzkovitz from Chisinau in Romania. With his parents and three brothers Eliahu was thrown into a concentration camp operated by the Romanian Nazi "Iron Guard" during World War II. In the camp his brothers and parents perished at the hands of a Romanian brute named Stanescu, but Eliahu somehow survived and was little more than a breathing skeleton when the Russians released him in 1944. After many vicissitudes Eliahu received Communist permission to migrate to Israel where he was drafted into the Israeli Army and assigned to the paratroops. Throughout his wanderings he never had given up his search for Stanescu, whom he had sworn to kill. One day, by chance, he learned that after the war Stanescu had escaped into the French zone of Germany, enlisted in the Foreign Legion, and volunteered for service in Vietnam. Eliahu immediately decided on his course of action.

Without much difficulty he obtained a transfer from the paratroops to the Israeli Navy. Eventually, when his ship put into Genoa, he deserted and crossed over the border into France where he joined the Legion. In Algeria he applied for duty in Vietnam and was shipped there three months later. Patiently he searched for Stanescu, who had assumed another name, and finally he located him in the 3rd Regiment, which was heavily engaged at the time. The Legion never did object to a man volunteering for duty with an outfit in heavy action, and Eliahu easily arranged a transfer to the 3rd. There, in a brief time, he managed to have himself assigned to Stanescu's company. Eliahu recognized him at once, but Stanescu did not recognize the tough, bronzed, twenty-three-year-old Legionnaire as the skeletal youth of the concentration camp ten years previously.

With the patience that had characterized his hunt for Stanescu over the years, Eliahu waited for the proper moment of execution. For it was, he always insisted, execution rather than murder that he wished to commit. The moment came, at last, on Road 18 between Bac-Ninh and Seven Pagodas.

Eliahu and Stanescu were scouting the brush beside the road when the Viets opened fire about one hundred yards distant. Both men hit the dirt, Stanescu a few yards ahead of Eliahu. They knew they were in no special danger, for their companions on the road would cover their withdrawal.

Eliahu suddenly called out, "Stanescu!"

Stanescu turned around slowly, staring at him.

"You are Stanescu, aren't you?" Eliahu asked him in Romanian.

Stanescu licked his lips. "Yes," he muttered, "but——"

"Stanescu," Eliahu said levelly, "I'm one of the Jews from Chisinau." Then he emptied the clip of his Tommy gun into Stanescu's chest.

As a Legionnaire, Eliahu could not leave the body of a comrade behind, so he dragged Stanescu's body back to the road.

"Tough luck," said a Legionnaire. "He was a Romanian just like you, wasn't he?"

"Yes," Eliahu replied. "Just like me."

Eliahu served out his term and after he had been honorably discharged he presented himself to the Israeli military attaché in Paris and told his story. At first the attaché could not believe it, but a thorough investigation revealed that it was true. Eliahu, at his own request, returned to Israel to stand court-martial for desertion.

After three Israeli Navy judges had deliberated the case, their judgment was read:

"In view of the circumstances of the case, a Court of the State of Israel cannot bring itself to impose a heavy sentence. . . . One year's imprisonment. . . ."

The French in Vietnam sought from the very beginning of their reoccupation a big set piece battle with the Viets. Instead, they found themselves harassed by murderous guerilla warfare. But the Viet General, Vo Nguyên Giap, was only biding his time and carefully training an army that would eventually take the field against the French.

Giap, seeking to drive the French out of northern Tonkin in the summer of 1947, brought all possible forces to bear on the key village of Phu Tong Hoa which was defended by a single Legion company of the 3rd Regiment. On the evening of July 25 the Viets attacked the Legion post in massed waves of men supported by the fire of heavy mortars. By the sheer weight of their numbers they succeeded in capturing three of the four corner bastions. All of the Legion officers were killed in the first assault, but the noncommissioned officers led three counterattacks which swept the Viets from the fort.

285

Dawn revealed that the company had lost half its strength—twenty-three killed and thirty-three wounded.

The commander of the 3rd personally led a relief column to Phu Tong Hoa. When he entered the fort, the Legion guard turned out to greet him in ceremonial dress, as if it were a routine inspection.

After the Chinese Communists drove the Nationalists from the mainland in 1949, they were able to give the Viets greater assistance. The addition of artillery and more expert instructors convinced Giap in September, 1950, that he was ready to drive the French out of Tonkin and back to the Red River. His first move must be the clearing of the Kao Bang ridge. A key to taking the ridge was the fortified village of Dong-Khe, held by two Legion companies of the 3rd Regiment.

Early on the morning of September 16, Giap surrounded Dong-Khe with about 10,000 troops and began shelling it. Waves of infantry attacked while the dawn mists still cloaked the bottom lands. In almost continuous day-long fighting the Legionnaires lost three of their four corner bastions and suffered 40 killed and nearly 100 wounded. After dark they counterattacked and recovered one of the bastions, but then lost it again. Altogether the position changed hands eight times in the night-long fighting before the Viets managed to gain firm possession of it.

Shortly after the second dawn of the battle, the surviving Legionnaires saw that their lot was hopeless. Remembering Camerone, they made a final bayonet charge into the massed Viets. Miraculously, a handful fought their way through and eventually found their way to other Legion units.

Two Legion columns coming to the relief of Dong-Khe were ambushed and suffered heavy losses. Altogether, two complete Legion battalions were written off the rolls in the losing fight to hold Kao Bang ridge. The whole front collapsed under the enormous Viet pressure and Legion units, in their familiar tradition, fought bloody rear-guard actions all the way to the line of the Red River. In this rear-guard fight the 1st Parachute Battalion suffered 90 per cent casualties and was disbanded. It was reformed the following March, however, and another Legion parachute battalion—the 2nd—was sent from Algeria to join it.

Mounting losses and reverses depressed the French and their Legionnaires in Vietnam. Opinion in France was divided over the worth of the effort, and the men in Vietnam began to feel they were "loners," left to fight hopelessly in a lost cause. Anger and frustration became increasingly evident in the conduct of many. Former Legionnaire Adrian Liddell Hart, the son of the noted English military historian, B. H. Liddell Hart, described the mood as a kind of "nihilism."

"Not all men have a strong instinct of survival," he wrote. "In the Legion, indeed, there are disconcerting signs of the reverse—a careless abandon, a suicidal desperation or even a kind of death-urge. This is another reason why it is hard to generalize about the Legion. And these impulses are not only predominant in a minority; in some measure they are inherent in the accepted mystique of the Legion. . . . The inspired pages of *Képi Blanc* were often filled with observations that curiously resembled the nihilism of existentialism of the post-war years—the individual finds himself in a situation where he needs to make this unreasoning gesture of blind courage in the face of his inescapable mortality. In a sense it justifies a courage of despair though the individual Legionnaire may not be the suicidal desperado of popular legend. It is an attitude suited, if not deliberately adapted, to the disillusioned mood of European youth—and to the Indochina War."

Liddell Hart, by his own account, was not a happy Legionnaire—and the Legion seems to have been baffled by him. It never did punish him severely for his infractions of discipline. When he tried to desert in Algeria simply by walking away on one of the main roads, his forthright, naïve act so amused his superiors that they merely begged him not to do it again. He disliked Vietnam, where he asked to be sent, even more than Algeria. At last he and the Legion parted company by mutual consent.

Vietnam was no place for a sensitive young man to be in those days. You never knew when you were going to be shot at. Almost anything you picked up might explode in your hands. The exotic land described by travel writers turned out to be largely composed of heat, rain, swamps, and insects. Saigon actually was just a great tawdry bazaar where everything was bought and sold with the inflated piastre—women, children, opium, booze, military secrets, Cadillacs, chewing gum. Saigon—or its twin ant heap, Cholon—or Hanoi —or Haiphong—usually exhausted the pocketbook of a furloughed Legionnaire before it exhausted his appetite for pleasure.

Then he returned to a post that unfailingly was dismal—a cluster of huts surrounded by barbed wire and walls where bats, lizards, mosquitoes, and an incomparable tropic moon vied for one's attention after dark. The beer was warm, the women not exceptional. You could, through financial arrangements with a broker, find yourself a *congai*, but difficulties could multiply rapidly in that semidomestic situation: her family invariably was hungry and numerous; lovemaking might turn out to be a public spectacle; there usually was trouble getting on and off the post after dark; and, as the Viets drew closer, you began to wonder if you really could trust the girl. It was, perhaps, better to confine one's sexual urges to that cheerful French Army institution, the B.M.C., whose vans of girls were as ubiquitous in Vietnam as they had been in Morocco.

And at the end of all the wishing and seeking and failing to find there was the rattle of small-arms fire, the crump of mortars, and a long sweat-blinding slither through the elephant grass. In such a manner men live and die while empires rise and fall.

The war continued to go against the French. In October, 1952, the Viet-Minh breached the ridge between the Black and the Red rivers and seized another important area of Tonkin. The evolution of Giap's army was extraordinary; it began with untrained roving bands of guerillas, grew into companies, then into battalions and regiments, and finally was organized into divisions of regulars by the spring of 1953. When the monsoon broke, Giap seized the entire valuable opium crop of lower Tonkin and withdrew his divisions north. The ease with which he managed the maneuver upset the French. They had made the *political* decision to defend northern

Laos, which then had to be translated into the terms of *military* action. The command decided Laos could not be defended by a war of movement and that a hedgehog system of fortified camps was the only way to deal with the problem—a decision to which a French Commission of Inquiry later took exception. The area selected for the chief point of resistance was the center of the plain of Dienbienphu in northern Tonkin, where there was an overgrown airstrip.

Despite numerous attempts at explanation, it remains puzzling why the French chose to fight their decisive battle in Vietnam on an "island" in enemy-held territory so far removed from support that reinforcements and supplies had to be flown in from two hundred miles distant. The error was compounded by an intelligence failure that totally underestimated the strength and capabilities of the enemy. Curious, too, was the choice of the field commander, Colonel Christian de Castries, who was promoted to brigadier general after the battle began. A brave and capable armored officer, De Castries was trained in the swift offensive jab and the mobile defensive. Yet he had no armor to speak of at Dienbienphu; it clearly was to be an artillery-supported infantry battle with men fighting doggedly for every foot of the terrain. Since the defense could not be mobile, many infantry officers could not understand the reason for a satellite called Strongpoint Isabelle two and one-half miles south of the perimeter of Dienbienphu; it sapped needed strength from the main position and never was able to aid it.

In November, 1953, the Legion's reconstituted 1st Parachute Battalion dropped and secured the airstrip at Dienbienphu. After the Legionnaires had enlarged it, reinforcements began to pour in. In the next two months five battalions of the Legion's 13th, 2nd, and 3rd Regiments followed. In April, after landings no longer were possible, the Legion's 2nd Parachute Battalion jumped in. Units other than Legionnaires were two T'ai battalions, one Vietnamese paratroop battalion, four French parachute battalions, two battalions of Algerians and one of Moroccan infantry, besides French artillery and a little armor and service personnel. Thus, although Dienbienphu has been called a "Legion battle," the Legionnaires actually constituted about 40 per cent of the fighting forces which reached a total of some 12,000 men.

Two commanding heights detached from the northern perimeter and called Strongpoints Beatrice and Gabrielle were essential to use of the airstrip; if enemy artillery were placed on them, air transport to the garrison would be knocked out. The 1st Battalion of the Legion's 13th Half-Brigade held Beatrice, while an Algerian infantry battalion controlled Gabrielle. Isabelle, detached to the south, was manned by the 3rd Battalion of the Legion's 13th, elements of two other infantry battalions, an artillery group of 105's, and a tank platoon of M-24's.

A series of military surprises was about to unfold for the French. They soon discovered that their control of the air was of dubious advantage. They had counted on air strikes to nullify Giap's artillery, but the battle was fought in the rainy season when wet foliage made napalm ineffective. Furthermore, the Viets were masters of camouflage; a warren of hidden trails supplied the camouflaged artillery, which at the start consisted of a regiment of 105's and 75's, eighty Russian antiaircraft guns, and one hundred 50-caliber antiaircraft machine guns. Finally, the Viet antiaircraft crews proved to be dead shots.

The next surprise to the French was the strength and effectiveness of the Viet ground artillery. As the battle progressed, the Viets received two additional groups of 105's from the Soviets and then a number of multi-tube rocket launchers. In the face of this artillery the defenders could only dig deep under ground.

Yet another surprise was the speed, skill, and tenacity with which the Viet Army of 40,000 dug siege trenches. After it had completely invested Dienbienphu on January 11, it turned inward. Burrowing like frantic moles, the Viets pressed their trenches ever closer despite the heavy patrols the defenders sent against them.

The siege trenches led to the final, overwhelming surprise: the skill and suicidal bravery of the Viet infantryman.

On the morning of March 12 the Viets opened a bombardment on Strongpoint Beatrice and the airstrip that made the earth tremble. A couple of hours later Lieutenant Colonel Gaucher, commander of the Legion's 3rd Battalion of the 13th, was wounded at Beatrice and rushed by jeep into the perimeter. Major Paul Grauwin, chief surgeon at Dienbienphu, described what happened in the underground hospital:

Two grave-faced Legionnaires put down a stretcher in front of me on which lay Colonel Gaucher. His legs and arms were all literally smashed, and his thorax was open; he was dying. "Father, here, quick. . . ."

Father Heinrich had just time to perform the last rites, and Colonel Gaucher breathed his last. . . .

I took a white sheet from a basket and covered up the bleeding remains before me; the two Legionnaires took their commanding officer away to the morgue.

The Viets' crashing bombardment of Beatrice did not let up through the day or the ensuing night or the next day, March 13. And then, toward dusk, the barrage lifted in a sudden stunning silence. Moments later the sweet notes of a Legion trumpet drifted down from the churned and shell-pocked east face of Beatrice. *"Aux armes!"* the trumpet said, and the Legionnaires of the 3rd Battalion tumbled from their dugouts.

Out of the rain forests rolled a green tide of Viet infantrymen, moving shoulder to shoulder, their rifles at the carry, while their bugles keened like bagpipes. Ahead of them the Legion's machine guns raised a staccato chatter above the crump of mortar shells. The fire tore gaps in the advancing green lines, but other ghostlike figures swayed forward to fill them as the Viets came on. Hands clutched at the first barbed wire where the Legion fire stacked the dead and dying in piles five and six deep. The Viet artillery resumed again, blasting the Legionnaires, and over the piles of dead at the barricade swarmed another wave of Viets, wading indifferently into the fire of their own artillery.

By dawn the next day the 3rd Battalion had been wiped out, all of its men killed or wounded, and Beatrice had been lost. Not a

Legion officer survived the holocaust. De Castries, stunned, agreed to a four-hour battlefield truce, which Giap requested, in order that both sides could recover their wounded.

Dr. Grauwin, busily at work in his underground hospital on operations that would continue for fifty-seven days and nights, took the news calmly:

Someone in the main passage announced, "Beatrice has fallen." I paid no attention. Suddenly I became aware that my orderlies were looking at me to see how I took it. "Oh well," I said, "it's a hill just like any other. At Nasan too they captured one hill. It was recaptured the next day."

Hamel, an N.C.O. paratrooper, France's youngest holder of the Military Medal, had now lost his left arm.

Filoche, of the Eighth Assault, was one of the wounded that De Garfort sent me a little while ago. He had lost the lower half of both legs. Before the operation, he was screaming with pain; but now he was quite calm and was smoking. He had just come to. "Bah, what are one's pins? They can be replaced."

Beatrice had fallen and a battalion of the Legion was gone. . . .

Beatrice could not be retaken. De Castries made the attempt, but he lacked the manpower. His perimeter already had eaten up nearly all his reserves. And within twenty-four hours Gabrielle fell, too, the Algerians clawing and fighting for it to the end. Now Giap, mounting his artillery on the commanding heights, could fire directly onto the airstrip and the main position.

On March 16 the artillerymen in Dienbienphu realized that they were hopelessly outnumbered and outgunned. The French command had made a fatal error, they believed, and they had been left out here to die. That night the commander of the French artillery committed suicide.

The last plane, an ambulance transport, landed on the airstrip March 28 to remove twenty-five casualties. Artillery fire destroyed it on the strip, though its flight nurse, Mlle. Geneviève de Galard-Tarraubes, "the heroine of Dienbienphu," was saved. She stayed till the end of the battle, the only woman nurse present, cheerfully working twenty hours a day. Nullification of the airstrip forced a B.M.C. composed of a dozen Oulad-Naïl prostitutes to remain at Dienbienphu; abandoning their profession, they served as nursing aides during the last frenetic days of the defense. A Legionnaire veteran of the battle remembers that they helped the men's morale: "But in a way none of us had expected when they were flown in to us. They stopped being—well, what they were. They became truly *women*. I remember their little brown hands so deft and gentle. Christ, every one of them deserved the Military Medal. But all they ever got was official silence. The French didn't even want to admit they were there. And what became of them in the Death March that followed the surrender God only knows. I hope every one of them became a princess of Vietnam, if they have any princesses in that crazy country now."

Nurse Geneviève captivated the men of Dienbienphu with her courage and good spirits and skill. Dr. Grauwin, in his moving account of the battle, praises her as incomparable.

She had given so much, not only her very presence, which was itself a consolation, but all the pains she had taken, all the thousand and one little sacrifices she had made and had passed off with an unaffected laugh, all the immense weariness which her ceaseless activity cost her, her devotion, which was endless, and all that she had to endure—and then there was the tenderness of a woman which appeared in her lightest gesture.

The Legion made her an honorary Legionnaire, first-class, as it already had Dr. Grauwin, and Geneviève celebrated the Feast of Camerone by visiting the Legion wounded with a few remaining bottles of champagne on April 30 while the Communist artillery continued to blast.

Meanwhile the Communists were strangling Dienbienphu with the oldest noose in war. Digging, ever digging, they wormed their siege trenches more tightly about the shrinking perimeter. They were indifferent to human life—their own or that of their enemies. The symbol of the Red Cross was meaningless to them; they fired at wounded and ambulances as hard as they did at tanks. Thus the job of ambulance driver was one of the most dangerous at Dienbienphu. Two German Legionnaires who volunteered for the job and remained at it until killed were among the most admired of the defenders.

Casualties among the French, colonials and Legionnaires mounted steadily as the April days passed. Supplies and ammunition were parachuted in daily, but it became necessary to conserve carefully. In the hell and chaos of the main perimeter and at Strongpoint Isabelle to the south everyone now was committed to the battle. There were not enough men left on their feet to do more than try to cling to what they held. Slowly the strength of the battalions of the 2nd, the 3rd, and 13th Legion regiments—like those of the other units— was draining away. On April 10, the 2nd Legion Parachute Battalion dropped in, 700 strong. But by the end of the month it numbered only about 250 men while only about 100 of the 1st Parachute Battalion remained on their feet.

The French had no more paratroopers to commit to Dienbienphu. Yet, astonishingly, hundreds of reinforcements started dropping from the skies in darkness. They were men who never had donned a parachute before, but who had volunteered to fight or die at Dienbienphu. Among them were more than 500 Legionnaires, including truck drivers, typists, and almost the entire strength of the mortar companies of the 3rd and 5th Regiments.

Dr. Grauwin was fascinated to observe that of all the untrained men who plunged boldly into the dark perimeter only two suffered broken arms; three, broken legs; and six, minor sprains. As one Legionnaire who had been driving a truck remarked: "What's all the fuss about jumping in a parachute?"

One Legionnaire jumper crashed into the morgue and didn't know where he was until he began fingering the cold faces of the dead. Although his first parachute jump had not troubled him, the morgue so unnerved him that he had to be revived with brandy.

They came down wearing clean uniforms and shining boots and carrying well-oiled Tommy guns, their pockets stuffed with cigarettes, chocolate bars, the most recent newspapers, and—if it survived the landing—a bottle of brandy. Fellow Legionnaires promptly relieved them of these things and offered in return only the remark, "You must be crazy!"

One night a French officer helped a little Vietnamese soldier, who had just made his first jump, disentangle himself from his parachute harness. "What's your unit?" the officer asked him.

The Vietnamese braced to attention. "Me paratrooper."

"Yes, I know, but what battalion?"

"Second."

"Yes, but second what? Second Reserves?"

"No, me no reserve."

"Second Vietnamese?"

The man glared at him, stuck out his chin, and replied, "No, me not Vietnamese reserve. Me Legionnaire."

During occasional lulls in the day and night bombardment the defenders could hear the *k'chuck, k'chuck* of Communist picks and spades as they dug closer. There was a terrifying monotony about their technique: digging, always digging closer in the rain and darkness until suddenly in the eerie glow of flares, they sprang from the earth, firing bangalores onto the defenders' barbed wire and hurling themselves through the gaps. Then there was a melee of hoarsely panting men swinging bayonets and trench knives. It ended with the explosion of a grenade and a scream. The Viets had nibbled a few more yards from Dienbienphu. Perhaps the ground would be recovered tomorrow. But it rarely could be.

With the irony of soldiers, the defenders had chosen to give their sectors lovely-sounding names—Eliane, Dominique, Anne Marie, Huguette, Françoise, Claudine. Yet these amoebalike blobs on the map were the scenes of daily and nightly agony and torment. By late April, Anne Marie had fallen to the Viets and was a wasteland where blue flies swarmed on putrefying flesh in moments of fitful sunlight. Françoise disappeared one day; a Legionnaire stumbled, moaning, from the place where Françoise had been, his lidless eyes mere bloody sockets. And then Claudine went. A

Legionnaire lay on his back in the mud, trying to explain the disappearance, but each time he gasped for breath blood bubbled from a gaping hole in his thorax, and soon he, too, was gone.

One evening Major Liesenfeld, commanding the Legion's 2nd battalion of paratroopers, rubbed his forehead in wonder as he leaned over the bodies of two strapping Legionnaires. They had been lugging in supplies from the airdrop when, within seconds, both toppled in their tracks. They were dead, there was no doubt about it. Yet there was not a scratch on either body. A doctor explained the mystery to Liesenfeld: his men were dead from complete endocrine exhaustion brought on by the constant and extreme physical effort demanded of everyone.

Now it was May. In Paris citizens were muttering about the folly of Dienbienphu. In Geneva the politicians of several countries were gravely seeking a solution to the unpleasantness in Vietnam. Someone in Washington proposed a mammoth American lightning strike from the air to relieve Dienbienphu, but others said it was not feasible "to enlarge the areas of aggression between East and West." Now it was May and the men in Dienbienphu knew that their lot was hopeless.

They always had known it, really. And now they were too tired to jest that they *truly* knew it. They had been led to hope at the beginning of the battle that from the air some *deus ex machina* would be delivered to them which would make defeat impossible. But daily that hope had been further eclipsed by a growing bitterness; they had, after all, merely been sent here to die. And now bitterness had been eclipsed, too; in some by fatigue, in others by a resolve to die honorably. They moved like sleepwalkers through the miasma of the fifty-day battle, which was compounded of constant din, constant stench, constant scenes of horror that finally numbed the senses.

De Castries wore his red forage cap as jauntily as ever as he toured the field outside his command post. But new lines had come to his lean face and sometimes the cigarette drooping perpetually from a corner of his tight lips seemed to tremble slightly. In the first days of May he began one of those hopefully hopeless radio dialogues with General Henri-Eugène Navarre in Hanoi such as always occur at the approach of military disaster. The wish of the man at headquarters and the man on the spot to understand each other sometimes takes a wistful turn.

De Castries filed his situation reports objectively. The garrison had shrunk while fresh reserves kept the strength of the pressing Viets at 40,000 or more. An intelligent schoolboy with a situation map at hand could have seen the approaching defeat. No murmur of complaint passed from De Castries, no wry Gallicisms, no grand gestures with words. His men were dying all about him, but he and they and Navarre and the entire French Army were committed to honor, *honor*. But as the last days waned toward the last hours, the dialogue began to run in effect like this:

Navarre—"You must hold out."

De Castries—"We shall hold out."

Navarre—"You must not surrender."

De Castries—"We shall not surrender."

Under other circumstances General Douglas MacArthur had come closer to the military heart of the matter when he remarked that "There is no substitute for victory."

As blinding rain fell on the morning of May 6, only three French artillery pieces could answer the thunder and roar of nearly 400 Viet guns massed about Dienbienphu. Trenches sagged and crumbled in the rain. The water supply had turned foul and latrines were festering swamps. That morning, with shells whistling overhead, De Castries waded through the mud from his command post to the underground hospital. Two grotesquely twisted bodies, which no one had yet had time to bury, lay near the entrance. When De Castries stepped down the muddy underground stairs, a stench of rotting flesh, feces, urine, and disinfectant assailed him. He went on in dim light, between mud walls, his ears ringing to the sound of sobs, moans, and screams from the wounded who were packed shoulder to shoulder in the muddy dugouts. If he wondered then why he had chosen the profession of soldier, he never did remark on it.

Major Grauwin saluted as De Castries entered the cramped operating room. No one knew how many hundred operations he had performed in the past fifty-five days and nights; no one cared to remark that his hair had turned snow white. Nurse Geneviève tried to brace her exhausted body to attention. De Castries' right hand started involuntarily, as if to pat her shoulder, but then he checked himself and told her that he was awarding her the *Croix de Guerre* and the Legion of Honor.

He went on with Grauwin then, into the terrible heat and mud and blood and stench of the foul holes that had to serve as hospital wards. Water oozed everywhere and the cots on which the wounded lay naked had sunk to their canvas in mud. De Castries spoke to everyone who was conscious, asking how they had been wounded, and giving awards to all. Not until he had spoken to every man did he wearily climb to the surface and walk back to his command post through the rain.

The Communists attacked at dusk that evening. On all sides they rose and rolled forward in waves. Soon the remaining Legionnaires of the 3rd Regiment were cut off; windrows of Communist dead draped the barbed wire, hemming the Legionnaires' machine-gun fire in a wall of flesh. By short wave the Legion commander asked headquarters for permission to try a breakout. Permission was granted, and the Legionnaires, gathering themselves together, lunged forward with bayonets fixed. Then they disappeared as if they had plunged into the sea.

By the dawn of May 7 the perimeter of Dienbienphu had shrunk to a diameter of a few hundred yards. To the south the remnants of the 13th Half-Brigade maintained a steady fire from their shrunken perimeter at Isabelle. Their commander, Colonel André Lalande, was a tough soldier; his men called him *"Barouder,"* the brawler. He had come a long way from St. Cyr, traveling the rough and bloody route of the 13th from Narvik around Africa and back into France in World War II. Now he believed he had reached the end of the road.

During moments of clearing that day he gazed through his glasses at Dienbienphu; it was like sighting a telescope into Hell. A flame of fire ringed it, and within the circle the antlike figures of men scampered briefly before they were swallowed by the churned and steaming earth. Over Dienbienphu and Isabelle, French planes circled slowly like birds that yearned to save their young. The pilots seemed indifferent to ack-ack bursts as they gazed at the troubled earth below.

The last night fell and in the damp darkness the Communist bugles shrilled and wailed through the bursting shells. The Viets pressed on, fighting their way toward headquarters where De Castries had received and sent his final messages. About headquarters the losing fight raged in an area only 1,000 feet wide. French pilots saw it by the ghostly light of flares: bearded Legionnaires; coal-black Senegalese; and tough little Vietnamese with bayonets, knives, and grenades, struggling against the crushing green waves of Communists. Defenders who had lost their weapons snatched up bits of wood and broken iron with which they flailed until they were borne to earth in the crush.

"It was," a pilot said later, "like a ghastly spectacle of wild beasts in a Roman amphitheater."

At 0115 on May 8, Lalande radioed that he was going to attempt a breakout from Isabelle. Little more than half an hour later the last charge of the 13th Half-Brigade spent itself in the masses of its enemy. Lalande expected to die at the head of his men, but death eluded him, as it had so often, and he was captured. At 0150 a calm voice sent the last radio message from Isabelle:

"Breakout failed. We must break communications with you. We are going to blow up everything. *Fini*. Repeat *fini*. *Au revoir*."

Minutes later the circling French planes were rocked by the shock waves from exploding Isabelle.

In his jammed underground hospital Dr. Grauwin knew the end was near:

Suddenly I heard gasps and protests in the main passage and saw a long line of muddy statues—but they were moving, groping their way along the walls, trying not to disturb the poor fellows lying on the stretchers in the passage. I went closer and recognized them: they were the wounded who had still been in my shelters a couple of weeks ago. Under their layers of mud they were quite naked. "Where have you come from?" I asked.

They had come from areas which the Viets had overrun. Too severely wounded to fight, they had been returned to their units because the underground hospital was overflowing with even more seriously wounded; now they had been lying alongside the dead of their units for days. The Viets had rounded them up and sent them back to the hospital.

One of [the wounded] had a leg missing. How had he managed to get here? Another had an arm missing. Another had only one eye— he it was who only yesterday asked me if he could go back to his unit; I had operated on him only the evening before. Then men with casts on their shoulders, their chests, their legs. There was mud over everything, dressings and plaster. It got between the plaster and the skin and was bound to reach the wound underneath. In the thick of all this mud I saw eyes with a question in them: "Why is this happening? Will it be over soon?"

I felt that my mind was giving way. Was it possible that God would permit this final ordeal?

The hell of nearly two months of battle ended at 0530 on May 8 when De Castries issued the order to cease firing. Surrounded closely by a guard of Viets, he stepped from his command post into a morning so fair under a bright blue sky that it seemed nature rejoiced at the end of the slaughter. Smoke still eddied on the ground where bodies, twisted and already bloating, were dark with flies. De Castries' pale face was set expressionlessly, his red forage cap fixed levelly on his head, and smoke curled from the cigarette in a corner of his lips. And then he strolled away, a prisoner.

Dienbienphu had fallen, signaling the fall of French claims to rule in Indochina.

Yet another ordeal faced the survivors, except for some of the severely wounded who were fortunate enough to be released and evacuated to French hospitals soon after the battle. To many the infamous Death March they were forced to undergo was an even greater trial than the battle itself. About 4,000 men were killed or died of wounds at Dienbienphu and about 1,000 were too seriously wounded to be able to stand. Some 7,000, including many wounded, had to make forced marches of hundreds of miles over jungle trails to Communist prison camps; less than 4,000 of them were returned later in the year as "living skeletons." Among those who survived were De Castries, Dr. Grauwin, and Nurse Geneviève.

The Viets singled out the survivors of Dienbienphu for especially cruel treatment. Men exhausted by fifty-seven days of grueling battle had to march about ten miles a day for forty to fifty days over trails where they sank to their ankles and knees in mud. Many dragged companions or helped carry litters. The food ration for each man was one bowl of cold rice each day. One man, bereft of friends, dragged himself for miles on his hands and the stumps of his legs. Companions of a Legionnaire whose thigh was fractured at Dienbienphu carried him three hundred miles through the mountains to prison; not until two months later was his fractured thigh immobilized.

During the war in Vietnam, from 1946 to 1954, the Legion suffered 10,482 killed and more than 30,000 wounded. Of 6,328 who were captured, only 2,567 were returned alive.

When word of the fall of Dienbienphu reached Sidi-bel-Abbès on May 8, the Legion's trumpets sounded *"Aux Morts."* The ranks stood stiffly at attention as Colonel Gardy read the order of the day in a voice that shook with emotion.

"We are gathered here to commemorate the heroes who fell in that epic struggle. Let us present the honors to the flags of our units which have disappeared in battle:

301

"The 13th Half-Brigade of the Foreign Legion, its regimental service units and its 1st and 3rd Battalions;

"The 1st Battalion, 2nd Foreign Legion;

"The 1st and 2nd Foreign Paratroop Battalion;

"The Mortar Companies of the 3rd and 5th Foreign Legion, and the numerous volunteers of other Foreign Legion units dropped into the fortress during the siege. . . ."

A Frenchman, Robert Guillain, the correspondent for *Le Monde* in Vietnam, suggested in a dispatch to his newspaper why they— and all the other defenders—had been willing to die at Dienbienphu:

"Let the enemy come," said our troops at Dienbienphu, "and we'll show them." We'll show them? We'll show what, and to whom? "We'll show those who face us in battle," they said. "We'll show the enemy. And we'll show them in Hanoi. We'll show them in Saigon, the people busy sipping cool drinks on shaded café terraces or watching beautiful girls in the pool at the Sporting Club. We'll show the people of France, the people of France above all. They have to be shown. They have to be shown what their neglect, their incredible indifference, their illusions, their dirty politics have led to. And how best may we show them? By dying, so that honor at least may be saved. . . ." Our dead at Dienbienphu died, I claim, protesting, appealing against today's France in the name of another France for which they had respect. The only victory that remains is the victory of our honor.

22

The Dead Cause

Legionnaires returning from Vietnam felt at first that nothing had changed significantly in Algeria.

Life went its ceremonial way. Within the gleaming white walls of the posts the guards changed precisely as they had for a century. At inspections the white kepis and red epaulettes gleamed in long straight lines under the broiling African sun.

The ritual of lunch in the officers' mess had not changed since the days of Bazaine. First, as had been the custom for a century, they "shook the sand out of the glass." Each poured a mouthful of wine into his glass and then all rose and repeated together, "To our friends who are in the sands." Draining their glasses, they slammed them down hard on the tables. Then they sang a few lines of the Legion's slow marching song, *"Le Boudin."*

> "In the course of our faraway campaigns,
> Facing fevers and bullets,
> Let's forget, along with our sorrows,
> Death, which never forgets us . . .
> Here's the blood sausage,

the blood sausage, the blood sausage,
For the Alsatians, the Swiss,
     and the Lorrainers,
There's none left for the Belgians
     'cause they're shirkers. . . ."

All sat down, except the youngest officer who congratulated anyone present whose birthday fell on that day. Then he read off the
menu and concluded the ceremony with a shouted, *"Vive la
Légion!"*

Being French by birth or adoption, the officers usually first discussed the merits of the food and the wine and the chef. At most
of the larger Legion officers' messes in Algeria you ate as well as you
could in most Paris restaurants. Prize chefs were pampered and
guarded jealously. ("Ours was head chef at the ———— in Paris. He
lost his head one day and cut up the pastry chef a bit. Major
———— happened to be on leave and hear of it. He posted straight
into action, talked to the police and the chef. The poor fellow agreed
better five years with us than time in jail. He's quite happy now.
You see, he didn't have to bring his wife with him.")

Being men, they soon began to talk of women. ("Did you hear
what happened to that young wife of old ————'s? She left him
and got involved with a pimp in Tlemcen. When old ———— caught
up with them and found she was zigzigging half the young men in
Tlemcen, he was annoyed. But what made him really furious was
when the pimp demanded fifty thousand francs to sell her back to
him.")

Being soldiers, they talked shop. Would the Legion ever receive
atomic arms?

"Probably not, my friend. You don't burn down the house to boil
an egg. And we are the egg-boilers. Though don't tell us we were
just boiling eggs in Indochina. And I guess you can't tell the Americans who were in Korea that they were just boiling eggs either. But
that's the way the politicians—pardon, statesmen—look at it. The
Americans call these unpleasant incidents brush-fire wars, don't

they? Indochina. Korea. Brush-fire wars? Hmmm. Oh, well, what does it matter what they call them? The main thing now is to keep war small and not cut loose that big BANG!"

But, being Legionnaires, they did not discuss French politics—unless they were certain to whom they were talking. But when they were certain, they talked earnestly, even vehemently.

Gradually at first, and then swiftly, both the rank and file of the Legion realized after the defeat in Indochina that matters were changing rapidly in Algeria. Nationalism was not, after all, confined only to Vietnam where its drive had been exploited by communism. Legionnaires reflected with a curious intensity the bafflement, bitterness, despair, and hope coursing through the French Army. There were several reasons for their turbulent emotions.

In the first place, the Legion finally had become a "respectable" component of the French Army. For the first century of its existence it was not even included on the Army List of Regiments. In its centenary year, 1931, however, it finally was somewhat grudgingly given a place on the List just below the *Bataillons d'Afrique,* the notorious French penal units, and just above various colonial units and levies. It also received an inspector general, responsible for inspecting its units and reporting on them to the War Ministry. Largely as a result of its outstanding performance in Vietnam, its position was further improved in 1950 when its status was elevated to the *Groupement de la Légion Etrangère.* This, in effect, made it an independent corps within the framework of the Army and its status became somewhat similar to that of the United States Marine Corps within the defense establishment of the United States. Now, at last, the Legion finally had confounded those French elements—many of them within the Army itself—who maintained a kind of conspiracy of silence about the activities of the Foreign Legion.

Hand in glove with the Legion's improved status and prestige, however, went its disastrous military defeat in Vietnam. Its bitterness over this reflected the general rancor of the French Army, which had been overwhelmingly defeated in 1940 and then again in 1954. Still having faith in itself, the Army—and its component

305

Legion—traced its defeats to politics and public indifference. To most professional soldiers combat must be the center stage of war, and when they feel that their role is being diluted they are as outraged as temperamental actors. The Army and the Legion felt that French politicans had sold them down the river in Vietnam; the only way the Viet Communists possibly could have been defeated would have been if France had sent large numbers of conscripts—which the politician refused to do.

"Our hash is cooked in such places as Paris and Geneva," a Legion officer remarked privately. "We eat it cold wherever we happen to be. We *have* to eat it. But that doesn't mean we have to like it."

Premier Joseph Laniel tottered to a fall soon after the fall of Dienbienphu. He was succeded by Pierre Mendès-France who negotiated a peace agreement which withdrew French forces from Vietnam.

Mendès-France wrote: "We are deliberately closing our eyes to the existence all over the world, and particularly among the peoples whom we have inspired with the desire for freedom, of strong currents of nationalism." France, he said, was trying to compensate for the weakness of its colonial political institutions "by police violence. But though France may think she is preventing or slowing down [colonial] developments, she is in fact speeding them up, for where a people with any sort of education is concerned, requests for reform are being transformed into revolts."

Many officers of the Army read such statements with irritation. Was Dienbienphu "police violence"? To Legion career men, especially, anticolonialism was anathema. They were devoted "organization men," and the chief role of their organization had been to build the overseas empire. Now were they simply to watch the empire disintegrate?

It developed that, indeed, they were. The countries of the French Union were on the path to becoming the free republics of the French Community. Indochina had gone and it was evident that Morocco—for which the Legion had paid such a costly price—soon would gladly sever its French ties without any resistance on the part of

306

France. There was no political idealism and little allowance for changing world views in the mystique of the Legion. Alexander the Great's Macedonian phalanxes would have comprehended that mystique, but the ideals of Alexander were buried in the dust of antiquity. Most alarming of all, in the view of veteran Legionnaires, was the change in the nature of war itself.

Terrible as Dienbienphu had been, it also had been glorious—at least in retrospect to those steeped in the Legion's mystique. At the heart of war, to their minds, was the breakout, the last splendid charge against overwhelming odds, the triumph of honor. And it began to appear possible that there would be no more battles like Dienbienphu. Some intelligent officers argued that the battle actually had been lost *before* it began. The battle for Vietnam represented, they said, the triumph of the psychology and tactics of Mao Tse-tung as applied by the Viet Communists over the traditional military tactics of the West. But these officers won few converts at first among veteran Legionnaires dedicated to the idea of the succinct pitched battle as the only means whereby war can achieve its goals.

Legionnaires, like all soldiers, tended to blame their difficulties and failures on politics and politicians. Yet the Legion had a tradition of obedience to civil authority as old as that of the armed forces of the United States. It was surprising considering the unstable and downright schizoid nature of Government authority in France. Since 1789 France has had two monarchies, two empires, five republics, the German satellite state of Vichy, and fifteen constitutions. Despite its enervating political system, so baffling and irritating to an American or an Englishman, it has been able to lay claim to greatness. And its chauvinistic military minds always have insisted, rightly or wrongly, that the greatness of France lay in its arms.

In this mood of doubt and perplexity the Legion began its most trying and complex battle—the battle for Algeria.

On November 1, 1954, while skeletonlike survivors of Dienbienphu still were creeping back from the prison camps and awaiting repatriation, a communiqué reported outbreaks of violence at several widely scattered points in Algeria. General Paul Chérrière later wrote: "We thought at first that we faced a tribal uprising similar to those that had marked our history in North Africa. It seemed sufficient for the army to reduce some dissident local tribes and for the police to maintain order elsewhere."

What the French and their Legionnaires actually faced, however, was a long, fierce, frustrating struggle that would not end until Algeria won independence nearly eight years later. It was fought on the terms of a small, determined group of rebels and never reached the stage of a significant set-piece battle. It was war as the Communist Mao Tse-tung said it should be fought by a weak and underprivileged people against a great power. It was a reign of terror and counterterror in which civilians often were as much involved as soldiers. Its political and terrorist aspects eclipsed its tactical events; indeed, the so-called tactical battlefield was diluted into nearly every street and alley in Algeria. Before it was finished, the Legion felt that it was fighting for its home and its very existence.

The scattered violence of November 1, 1954, was the work of the Army of National Liberation (A.L.N.), the infant fighting arm of the Federation of National Liberation (F.L.N.), which had divided Algeria into six *wilaya,* or provinces, with each in turn subdivided into sectors for operations. At first the A.L.N. was a force of only some 2,000 to 3,000 poorly armed but astutely led men. Eventually it reached a strength of approximately 40,000.

In time France poured an army of 400,000 into Algeria. The mass of these were conscripts employed on guard duty and routine patrols in the face of terrorist activities. Either from ignorance or willful distortion, the French are fond of saying that the Foreign Legion—which averaged about 30,000 men during the campaign—did only its proportionate share of the fighting. The truth is, however, that a force of 40,000 to 50,000 Legionnaires and French paratroopers composed the shock troops of the campaign.

To the French conscripts, service in Algeria was a monotonous and occasionally terrifying experience. But to veteran Legionnaires,

French paratroopers, career officers of lower ranks, and the leaders of the French Army it was a dedicated crusade, a passionate adventure. Many conscripts did not care what became of Algeria, but to most professional soldiers it must at all costs be held as if it were the soil of France.

As the rebellion spread and flamed higher during 1955 it became evident that the familiar tactics the French and Legionnaires always had employed in repressing tribal uprisings no longer were effective. When a patrolling force heard of trouble in a village and went there, it almost invariably found that the troublemakers had fled. The old method of burning a few houses and taking a few prisoners no longer insured peace; it merely roused greater Moslem antagonism. Either from desire or fear of reprisal the Moslems flocked increasingly to the cause of the F.L.N.

In February, 1956, the Government of Premier Guy Mollet approved a new strategy developed by the Army and called "Pacification." This was a vast grid operation, which garrisoned every city in major strength and towns and villages in diminishing numbers. At the same time the borders of Morocco and Tunisia were sealed off to prevent the movement of elements of the F.L.N. into or out of Algeria. The Morice Line, stretching two hundred miles into the desert from the sea along the Tunisian border, was a formidable complex of barbed wire, electrified wire, mine fields, fortifications, searchlights, and automatic alarms. The defensive net along the Moroccan border, though less formidable, proved to be effective. The third phase of the "Pacification" strategy was to mark off large areas within Algeria where rebel forces were congregated—in the Aurès and Kabylia mountains, on the Collo Peninsula and in other places. All residents of these areas were removed and their buildings destroyed. Then with tanks, planes, helicopters, armored cars, and foot patrols the French and Legionnaires combed the areas daily, shooting at anything that moved.

There was yet a fourth and even more amazing phase to the "Pacification" which the French and Legionnaires pursued with passionate intensity. Since the grid system could not be extended to every remote village and hamlet, the villages were brought into the system. In one of the greatest population movements since World War II, more than one million Moslems were removed from their villages and relocated in specially constructed camps and developments near military strongholds. Some came voluntarily, seeking refuge from the rebels. But many had to be coerced. In some instances villages were bombed out. In others, their access roads were blockaded and the people starved out.

As the French began their military build-up, all units of the Legion, except one battalion in Madagascar, were grouped in Algeria. The Legion's recruitment program in Europe was intensified and training camps were established in the vicinity of Sidi-bel-Abbès where the 1st Regiment continued to function as a training cadre.

The 2nd Regiment, returning from Vietnam by way of Morocco, was sent to control sealed-off and depopulated areas of southern Oran Province. The 3rd was assigned a similar mission in the Kabylia district. The 4th, converted to a motorized regiment, took up positions in the Tunisian defensive net. The 5th had a similar mission in the Moroccan defensive net. The reconstituted 13th Half-Brigade undertook work in sealed-off areas of the Aurès. The 1st and 2nd Cavalry Regiments, equipped with heavy armored cars, patrolled the Morice Line on the Tunisian border. The 1st Parachute Battalion was expanded into the 1st Parachute Regiment and assigned to Zéralda outside Algiers from which point it made frequent forays into the mountains to the south. A new parachute regiment, the 2nd, was formed and established at Philippeville. The four motorized Saharienne Companies were recalled from their remote desert posts and began patrolling sealed-off areas of the mountains near the Sahara.

The Legion no longer could complain of inferior arms. In the final Algerian campaign it was supplied with the best weapons the French possessed. Its pay was made the equivalent of French regulars. In every respect it was a first-rate fighting organization.

Along the border nets and in isolated areas of the interior, Legion units often fought small pitched battles with groups of the A.L.N.

But in general the Legionnaires shared the frustration of French units on wide-sweeping patrols. A Legion veteran of the campaign describes the climax of a patrol in a sealed off area:

For four days our company had been on the track of a band of eighteen or twenty rebels in the mountains. They knew we were after them, of course. They struck south fast and our helicopters spotted them from time to time, but they were so dispersed in rocky country that there was no point in calling for an air strike. They feinted east, then west. For a time it seemed they had split into two groups—and maybe they had—but the tracks showed that they rejoined again. Our captain was a shrewd bloodhound who knew the terrain well. He was convinced they were headed for ———, a high craggy ridge with populated country beyond it.

Once he'd made up his mind, we resumed the march at midnight. By early daylight we were below the ridge and through our glasses made out two sentries posted on it. The captain wasted no time. He radioed for a helicopter and then for two tanks from ——— to take up positions on the farther side of the ridge. The captain said, "We'll cook this goose by noon." We moved out to left and right in squads and began working up the ridge. The captain had his command post at the base in radio contact with the helicopter, the tanks and the squads.

The rebels started down the other side of the ridge and saw the tanks waiting for them. They scattered in twos and threes, some heading east and the others west along the other side. Our lead squads went over the ridge at the double. But only one squad came within range of one group of rebels. We got three of them, stitched them nearly in half with automatic rifle fire. But fifteen or sixteen got away. So the captain folded up his command post and we started after them again.

Although elusive, the enemy was omnipresent in Algeria. As F.L.N. terrorist activities increased, Legionnaires discovered that in the new world of rising nationalism the role of the soldier may be chiefly that of a policeman. This "police" role was first thrust upon the Legion's 1st Parachute Regiment which was in the 10th Paratroop Division commanded by General Jacques Massu, a blunt, tough supporter of the right-wing colonialists.

311

F.L.N. bombings and other acts of terrorism in Algiers were climaxed by a call for a general strike protesting French rule in January, 1957. In reply the French ordered the 10th Division to restore order in the city and gave it blanket authority. Massu's plan of policing the city was thorough and ruthless.

Every man, woman, and child was registered and issued an identification card. The paratroopers surrounded the Casbah with barbed wire and set up a headquarters at the main gate linking it to the rest of the city. Mobile groups of paratroopers roaming the Casbah were in constant radio communication with their headquarters. At varying hours of day and night they cordoned off areas and made room-to-room searches for arms and suspicious persons and literature. Anyone who attempted to resist was shot on the spot. Prisoners were taken to secret places for questioning; it has been thoroughly substantiated that many of them were brutally tortured. Those who survived interrogation were sent for indefinite periods to concentration camps.

Within six months the paratroopers had destroyed the F.L.N. network in Algiers. The Moslems there lived under as strict a police state as ever existed in any totalitarian nation. Under the "block" system which the paratroopers devised one person in each family was responsible for the whereabouts of all the others twenty-four hours a day. This person was in turn responsible to a floor chief, who was responsible to a building chief, who was responsible to a block chief. In this way the paratroopers could locate any Moslem in the Casbah within a matter of minutes.

A similar system, though not as strictly enforced, was extended into most Algerian cities and towns. In rural areas the Army controlled all the basic elements of life—transportation, work, food, education, medical services. Units of the Foreign Legion did not participate in the program to any great extent, however; they remained combat and patrol forces.

The Army—and the Legion—felt that they almost had won the strange battle for Algeria, which involved control over the minds of Algerians as much as control of terrain. But the professional soldiers of the Army and the Legion in Algeria had a final and bitter lesson to learn about the nature of warfare as the means of suppressing nationalism: in a war of this nature the battle no longer was the pay-off. It was a difficult lesson for traditional military minds to comprehend. To their way of thinking, after granting full consideration to military logistics, Waterloo had been decided at Waterloo, Sedan at Sedan, Verdun at Verdun. There was a dramatic, clear-cut finality to the issues involved; that had been the purpose of battle throughout the course of history. But it seemed that the issue of Algeria could not be settled in Algeria.

The F.L.N.'s struggle for Algerian independence had kindled support and enthusiasm abroad. The Arab world was for it. Sentiment ran high in behalf of it among the emerging nations of Africa and Asia. Morocco and Tunisia, gaining independence in March, 1956, asked why Algeria should not be independent, too, and did all in their power to aid the F.L.N. American opinion, not unexpectedly, favored an independent Algeria. Within the French people themselves there was a strong division of opinion on the issue. A century previously international opinion might not have made much difference. But in the swiftly changing world of rapid communications and transportation it seemed that no nation or area could be an island unto itself.

"You cannot really understand how frustrating it all was to a soldier in the field," recalls a Legion officer who then was serving on the Tunisian border. "We Legionnaires tried to perform our duties as soldiers, but we were hampered from carrying them out effectively by forces far removed from the scene. Our task was to crush the F.L.N. So! Across the border from Tunisia comes a force of the F.L.N. We try to draw them in, but they will not be drawn. We fight and beat them back across that magic line. And then they stand there and thumb their noses at us. We cannot pursue and destroy them. If we do, there will be a big stink somewhere—at the United Nations in New York or in Paris—somewhere. And then the word would come down: *Who* crossed the magic line last night and did his duty as a soldier? Off with his head! Retire him! Let him pace some lonely village in the Pyrenees, gnawing his nails, all his professional knowledge and skill unused. Nothing worthwhile to do as he walks around a village until he dies!"

The currents and pressures swirling around the question of Algeria had caused the downfall of six French governments when De Gaulle finally returned to power and became Premier on June 1, 1958. A new constitution was approved and the Fifth Republic was born with De Gaulle as its President. Now, thought the professional soldiers of the Army, they finally had a leader who was one of their own and understood how they felt. Understand De Gaulle did, but he would not be shaken from his stand of self-determination for Algeria.

General Massu, the darling of the right-wing colonialists of Algeria, expressed the opinion of a powerful element in the Army when he publicly criticized De Gaulle's stand for self-determination. Never a politic man, Massu apparently was tricked into making his statements in an interview with a German journalist. No officer ever publicly criticized De Gaulle and survived in his career; Massu was recalled to France and relieved of command.

Massu's dismissal on January 24, 1960, resulted in an angry uprising by European citizens in Algiers. Instigated by numerous right-wing groups, they armed themselves and barricaded streets. With mounting alarm Gaullists in the city observed that the Legionnaires and French paratroopers of Massu's 10th Division made no move against the demonstrators. General Maurice Challe, commander of the Army in Algeria, warned De Gaulle that the situation was crucial and anxious days followed for the Government of the new Fifth Republic.

While the Algiers insurgents strengthened their barricades and increased their arms, the Legion and French paratroops simply stood and watched them passively. As the hours passed, the conviction grew in observers that the paratroops actually were *protecting* the insurgents. After two days of tension and negotiations, the paratroops were replaced by infantrymen rushed in from distant areas of Algeria. Although no shots were exchanged between the insurgents, and the fresh troops loyal to De Gaulle, the barricades were slowly smothered.

Many of the insurgents were allowed to slip away. The remainder were given a choice of standing trial for civil insurrection or joining the Foreign Legion to fight the F.L.N. Of the 780 who gave themselves up, the Legion found only 420 physically able to meet its standards. This group served for a few months as a separate unit attached to the 1st Parachute Regiment at Zéralda and then was quietly discharged.

De Gaulle and the Fifth Republic had survived a crisis, but in many French minds there remained the question of whether the Army in Algeria truly could be trusted. As an American journalist in Algiers remarked, "A shoe had been dropped, and people were waiting for the other shoe to follow." The tension within the Army itself was evident from the events of April 21, 1961.

That afternoon a French soldier stationed in the Kabylia district told his captain, "I've received word to go to Algiers tonight to take part in a *putsch.*"

After thinking about it for a while, the captain told his major, who told his colonel, who told his general, who sprang into a helicopter and flew to Algiers where he told General Fernand Gambiez, the new commander in chief of the combined Army, Navy, and Air Forces in Algeria.

At first Gambiez thought it just another case of hysteria. But after reflection he told Jean Morin, Delegate-General of Algeria, who called a meeting of high-ranking officers that Friday evening. Someone brought to the meeting a newsletter published by an extreme right-wing organization which said that the loyalty of the Army would be questionable after 2 A.M. on Saturday morning.

All agreed that anyone planning a military coup certainly would not announce the hour when it would occur. Nevertheless, precautions were taken; military patrols in the Algiers area were doubled and the police were alerted. Then the brass went home to bed.

Shortly before midnight the duty officer at headquarters phoned

Gambiez and told him that a transport truck company had been sighted on its way to the Legion's 1st Paratroop Regiment in Zéralda. Gambiez phoned General Bernard Saint-Hillier, the new commander of the 10th Parachute Division and a hero of the French Resistance in World War II. Saint-Hillier in turn phoned the commander of the 1st, Major Elie de Saint-Marc, to ask him what the devil was going on in Zéralda.

Madame de Saint-Marc answered the phone and said that her husband was ill. Then she added nervously that he was not home.

"Tell me, Madame," said Saint-Hillier, "is your husband up to some dirty trick tonight?"

After a moment's hesitation she replied faintly, "I fear so."

Generals Gambiez and Saint-Hillier hurried into their cars and raced toward Zéralda, twenty miles west of Algiers. On the way they saw a column of trucks approaching. Pulling to the side, they got out and stood in the middle of the road trying to wave down the column.

A Legionnaire in the lead truck, seeing them in the glare of headlights, cried, "Squash the old fools!"

The two generals leaped into a ditch and the trucks filled with armed Legionnaires roared by. Jumping into their cars, the generals turned around and passed the column which was speeding toward Algiers. As they passed they heard the Legionnaires singing, but no one fired. The generals beat the trucks to the General Delegation Building in Algiers, seat of the city's military and civic government, and inevitably the first goal in a coup. An iron grilled fence with two locked gates surrounded the forecourt of the building; before each gate a general drew himself to attention and waited.

Soon the trucks pulled up and Legionnaires, wearing their mottled combat uniforms, vaulted to the ground. Two big Legionnaires picked up Gambiez, a short, stocky man, and passed him to their officers as lightly as if he were a baby. Others overpowered Saint-Hillier and swarmed over the iron fence like monkeys. Within minutes they had seized control of the General Delegation Building.

The first question that shocked France and electrified the world was the extent of defection in the French armed forces. Of the 400,000 men under French arms in Algeria, how many could be counted on to obey the orders of the Fifth Republic? Who was loyal and who wished to turn Algeria into a lunatic colonialist bastion teeming with enemies within and surrounded by enemies without? Or was that the purpose of the coup? Did the dissidents propose to rule both Algeria and France by some military junta?

These questions must have raced through Gambiez's mind early on that Saturday morning when Legion officers hustled him into an office. A man turned slowly from a window and Gambiez gaped in consternation at General Challe. So *he* was the leader of the coup!

Challe bowed courteously and said, "Join us, General. Join and lead us."

"Never!" Gambiez replied indignantly. "Never under any conditions!"

He was led away and placed under guard.

Meanwhile about fifty officers, supported by not more than 8,000 men, most of them French and Legion paratroopers, were executing a model *coup d' état*. Not a shot was fired. Everything was accomplished by persuasion and bluff. Working on a carefully prepared timetable, the dissidents under Challe captured key buildings and positions in Algiers, Constantine, and Oran.

Their success depended on thousands of other officers and men joining them. They were sure that unit after unit would defect to them. Paris was frantic as the Government braced for civil war and an invasion by paratroopers.

As the hours passed, however, the dissidents grew more alarmed than the Government. Legionnaire paratroopers had vowed that the Foreign Legion would defect with them in a body. But the Legion did not. It remained loyal to the civilian authority of France, as did regiment after regiment which had been expected to join the coup.

Behind the coup was a new secret army organization, the *Organisation Armée Sécrète* (O.A.S.), which had believed it could per-

317

suade large numbers of French Army conscripts to join it. But the conscripts would not be budged from fidelity to the Fifth Republic. Many tried to sabotage the efforts of the dissidents, pouring water into the gasoline tanks of trucks and armor and creating so much nuisance that the O.A.S. had to expend its forces in guarding those loyal to the Government. To right-wing *colons* the O.A.S. handed out some 30,000 arms, less than half of which the Army ever recovered.

The *putsch* slowed down on Sunday afternoon and on Monday it collapsed as swiftly as it had begun.

The Government responded firmly with widespread arrests and a shake-up of commands. Challe surrendered and was brought to trial. To the annoyance of many French, the Government did not seek the death penalty, and he was sentenced to fifteen years in prison. De Saint-Marc was sentenced to ten years, and other sentences were for relatively brief terms. Before the trials the Legion's 1st Parachute Regiment and two French paratroop regiments were dissolved.

As might have been anticipated, the 1st Regiment reacted to its dissolution theatrically. Rather than let any ordinary soldiers inherit their barracks, the Legionnaires blew up their white-walled quarters at Zéralda. Then a few deserted and went underground with the O.A.S. to fight the F.L.N.

In years past the white settlers had treated the Legion contemptuously, but during the ruthless "Pacification" of Algiers the Legion paratroopers had endeared themselves to the European rightists. When the disarmed Legionnaires of the 1st rolled slowly through the Algiers streets in trucks on their way back to Sidi-bel-Abbès, men and women wept and cheered them. Pressing round the trucks, the crowds tossed red roses and bottles of cognac to them. Placing the roses behind their ears and toasting the crowds in cognac, the Legionnaires began to sing. French newspapers reported that they chanted a song Edith Piaf had made popular in Paris the previous winter. *"Je ne regrette rien, je repars à zéro. . . ."* No regrets! It must have been the idea of an imaginative reporter. Actually the Legionnaires sang *Le Boudin*.

At Sidi-bel-Abbès the Legion scattered the disgraced Legionnaires of the 1st into other units, making sure that no two of the ringleaders were enrolled in the same company.

"After that," says a Legionnaire, "we should have known that the days of the Legion and the French in Algeria were numbered. But we could not believe it. We did not *want* to believe it. We had marched and fought too long there ever to go."

But the war did end. A cease-fire agreement was reached in March, 1962, and Algeria moved toward independence.

As French units began to pull out of Algeria, a new headquarters home was selected for the Legion at Aubagne near Marseilles. It was given four months in which to collect its equipment, its relics of the past, and prepare for the move from Sidi-bel-Abbès into France.

On October 24, 1962, as the sun sank toward the green Algerian horizon, the white walls of Sidi-bel-Abbès echoed for the last time to Legion trumpets sounding retreat. The long lines stood motionless and silent as an officer paid a tribute to the Legion dead in Algeria. And then, in conclusion, he read a poem written by Captain de Borelli in tribute to his orderly, Thiebald Streibler, who had sacrificed his own life in the fighting in order to save his captain:

> And now would the French understand
> That war is tooth for tooth, eye for eye,
> And that the foreigners who are dead
> Have saved them mourning by falling?
>
> . . . If you do not know all that is past,
> And if you are not lying dead for nothing,
> If you have not died for a dead cause,
> O my poor friends, do not ask!

23

At

Aubagne

Aubagne is a drowsy town, shaded from the Mediterranean sun by plane trees. It reminds one of towns in Algeria, but it is in France —and that makes a difference to Legionnaires.

Camp de la Demande, the new administrative headquarters of the Foreign Legion, lies between gray hills and a superhighway where traffic hums to and from Marseilles, ten miles distant. Built as a rest camp for German sailors during World War II, it had changed little by the summer of 1963. Dilapidated-looking wooden barracks scattered among the brush along dusty tracks housed squads of Legionnaires. There was an air of impermanence about the camp that summer that reflected a mood of uncertainty and restlessness in the Legion. Yet it was the same Legion; there was evidence of its past everywhere. A trimly bearded officer, a man of wit and wisdom, who was a veteran though still young, was quick to point out signs of the past to a visitor.

An *ancien* of forty years service, gray beard flowing to his waist, stepped slowly from a barracks wearing wooden clogs and carrying a mop. Wasn't he rather old for active duty?

"Why no! See, he breathes, he walks, he works, he salutes, he smiles most happily. You may be too young to be a Legionnaire, but possibly you never are too old."

A man walked slowly along the track, tapping the dust with a white cane and resting a hand on the shoulder of a Legionnaire, who paced beside him while he raised sightless eyes to the blue sky of Provence. Who was he and what had happened to him?

"He is a Legionnaire. He deserted us in Algeria and joined the O.A.S. A few months later the F.L.N. captured him and burned out his eyes with hot irons and then tossed him into one of our camps. We found him crawling sightlessly on all fours. His offense in deserting merited a court-martial. But, like us, he had been trying to serve France. He had been misguided, but his heart was true to France. We're trying to obtain a pension for him. I don't know whether we'll succeed. Meanwhile he eats, he walks, he has memories, he hears music."

As never before in its history the Legion is trying to take care of its own. Twenty miles from Aubagne across the hills of Provence lies the grass-sweet village of Puyloubier where the Legion has established its historical section and a rehabilitation center for its wounded. There veterans are engaged in fashioning metals and pottery, in performing exquisite works in wood and stone, with the hope that some in time may take their crafts into civilian life. There, too, a complete and modern printing unit publishes the monthly Legion magazine *Képi Blanc*.

Of equal significance at the Legion installation in Puyloubier are its relics of the past which it brought from Sidi-bel-Abbès. The grave of General Rollet was dug up, his remains transported to Puyloubier and interred. In a chapel nearby, among other mementoes of the past, stand Legion regimental colors, splendid with honors, but growing musty in the dim light that flows through stained-glass windows.

These relics are awaiting the day when they can be moved to a new and refurbished Camp de la Demande at Aubagne.

For the Legion has plans for a new and better installation, rising from the brush and decrepit barracks it inherited. The plan is on paper, in cardboard models, in the minds of many Legionnaires. "It will happen, you have my word for it. I can't say when. Maybe 1965 or 1966. But it will happen. It will be just like this——" The officer gestured to the models and a bearded enlisted man leaned forward, staring at them intently. "Here, you see, its center will be the parade ground and the Memorial to the Dead. . . ." The Memorial to the Dead faces Africa.

Is the Legion looking too much to the past instead of to the future?

The few *anciens* still in its ranks, some of them old soldiers in their sixties and seventies, think not. They live in the past, endure the present, and care not at all about the future.

But some young enlisted men feel that the Legion is too wrapped up in its past. You can listen to them in an Aubagne brothel bar like Chez Katty to which a few tired-looking women have followed them from North Africa. You can buy the Legionnaires drinks and listen to splendid lies and striking truths.

One still cannot generalize about Foreign Legionnaires. They are as various as mankind. There is the one who says in utter sincerity, "The Legion is my love, my family, my life." And there is the one who is looking for the opportunity to desert. An officer says with a wry smile, "Everybody who wants to desert the Legion already has." But not quite; one is awaiting a friend who will pick him up by car in Aubagne, drive him to a yacht at Cannes, and sail away to Italy. Or is he only daydreaming?

And there is yet another kind of young Legionnaire today. He compares favorably to the volunteer enlisted man of nationalist armies who seeks a career in combat outfits. He is a tough young man, accustomed to hardships, who joined the Legion because of pique with his environment. He hopes to improve his lot in life and he instinctively feels that fighting is the only way he can manage to do so. He was born with a European's sense of conflict, and he knows more about the nature of the world than his father before him.

It is this kind of Legionnaire who believes that the Legion is too much concerned with the past and is not giving enough thought to the future. Basically he seeks a military purpose in a world that is largely seeking peace. He asks, "Why aren't they training us in nuclear weapons? We're professionals—not just conscripts trying to pass the time away. Where are we going?"

Neither officially nor privately will any Legion officer disclose anything about the present strength or future plans of the organization to an outsider. Its past is largely an open book with only a few pages pasted shut. But as to the future . . . Who knows? And then a shrug.

Some facts can be obtained from other sources, however. The effective strength of the Legion today is between 12,000 and 13,000 men—its lowest since the difficult days of World War II. In April, 1963, it enrolled only sixteen recruits—the smallest number for any month in twenty years. It was developed training centers on Corsica, but it has not been able to develop any important military mission since leaving Algeria.

At present it has small garrison forces at Djibouti in French Somaliland, at Diégo-Suarez in Madagascar, and Bou Sfer, Mecheria, Laghouat, Ouargla, Reggane, Colomb-Béchar, and Ain Sefra in Algeria. The small garrisons in Algeria are present by agreement with the Algerian Government and are expected to be withdrawn by 1965. Their function is to aid any Europeans in distress and they are forbidden contacts with the Moslem population. Access to and from the posts is strictly regulated by the Algerians.

The present or prospective role of the Legion within the North Atlantic Treaty Organization, if any exists, is a top secret. Late in the spring of 1963 Legion units did participate with units of the United States Marine Corps in joint maneuvers in Corsica. Afterward a Marine officer remarked, "The highest compliment I can pay the Legionnaires is that they would make first-rate Marines. I hope the French have better sense than to let such good material wither away."

A Legion sergeant in Paris put it in another way. "The Legion today," he said, "is like a beautiful young French girl who got a little drunk and fell into a garbage can. An American tourist passed by and took a look at her. 'My oh my,' he said, shaking his head, 'there's a lot of good left in this girl yet. How wasteful to throw her away. And I'd always heard the French are thrifty.' "

But the Legion has not been thrown into a garbage can and the French are, indeed, too thrifty to dispose of it.

With its experience and composition of men from many countries the Legion could be an excellent permanent police force for the United Nations. That is impossible, however, in the light of present political facts. The Fifth Republic of Charles de Gaulle shows little enthusiasm for co-operating with most of the purposes of the U.N. It would not give its Legion to the U.N., and in its present precarious financial state the U.N. could not afford to maintain a permanent military force even if it were inclined to do so.

The future role of the Legion lies, of course, with the French Army and the Government of France. The age of colonialism has ended and a new era of nationalism has begun, while the Big Two, the United States and Soviet Russia, eye each other across the ramparts of Europe. In this new era the role of European military force —either conventional or nuclear—cannot be made clear in all its details.

The Legion, awaiting its future role, can draw profitable lessons from its past. It can see that its destinies are inseparable from the destinies of France. It can see that its history reflects the impermanence of political institutions, the fact that most of man's military plans become outmoded while they still are being made. Often in the past the Legion has believed it saw the end of its road ahead only to find that it was simply another turning in the road.

Meanwhile the Legion waits. If it never should be employed in combat again, it would feel that its purpose had been defeated. Yet that defeat could be a victory for the world. For surely it would mean that man had ceased to wage war.

Acknowledgments

WRITING A BOOK OF THIS NATURE is an adventure that involves difficulties both overcome and insurmountable, journeys long and brief, and the help of friends old and new.

I wish, first, to express my thanks to officers of the French Ministry of Defense and to officers and enlisted men of the Foreign Legion at Fort de Nogent, Camp de la Demande, and Puyloubier for their courtesy and co-operation. I mention none by name for fear of overlooking one.

My thanks to my friend of many years, Joseph Dynan of the Associated Press in Paris, for numerous introductions, for important sources of information, and for sharing with me his store of experience in North Africa.

To R.L.S., who wishes to remain anonymous, for the use of a diary kept by an ancestor while serving with the Foreign Legion in Dahomey; though declining to permit use of the Legionnaire's name, he agrees with my interpretation of the diary.

To Colonel John R. Elting, the military historian on the staff of the United States Military Academy at West Point, N.Y., for a number of suggestions in my research and for sharing with me his vast knowledge of the history of the French Army.

To E.A. Weiss. Acting Librarian of the United States Military

Academy, and to his helpful staff for giving me full access to the fine resources of their library. To the ever-helpful and patient staff of the New York Public Library, and to the excellent staffs of the New Jersey Public Libraries in East Orange, Bloomfield, Montclair, and Glen Ridge, for their unfailing co-operation.

To Andreas Hindoe of Paris and George Pemberton of London for aid in tracing down out-of-print books. To Mr. and Mrs. H. Bach Nielsen of Glen Ridge, N.J., for leads to sources of information and aid in translation.

Finally, to my wife, Alma, for her unswerving devotion to the tasks of research, translation, and typing, for being the perfect travel companion, and for frequently bringing order from chaos. Without her help this book could not have been written.

C. M.

Sources

CHAPTER 1

Fire by Day and Flame by Night, Memoirs of Prince Aage of Denmark,
Sampson, Low, London, 1937.
Le Livre d'Or de la Légion Etrangère (revised edition), Paris, 1958.
France Under the Republic, The Development of Modern France by
D. W. Brogan. Harper, New York, 1940.

CHAPTER 2

The French Nation from Napoleon to Pétain by D. W. Brogan. Harper,
New York, 1957.
France by Albert Guérard. University of Michigan Press, Ann Arbor,
1959.
The Struggle for Algeria by Joseph Kraft. Doubleday, New York, 1961.
The Two Marshals: Bazaine—Pétain by Philip Guedalla. Reynal & Hitch-
cock, New York, 1943.
Légion Etrangère by Roger de Beauvoir. Paris, 1897.
L'Armée d'Afrique de 1830 à 1852 by General Paul Azan. Paris, 1936.
Histoire des Troupes Etrangères au Service de France by Eugene Fieffé.
Paris, 1854.
AGAIN: *Le Livre d'Or.*

CHAPTER 3

A History of Spain by Harold Livermore. Farrar, Straus & Cudahy, New York, 1958.

Modern Spain, 1788–1898 by M. A. S. Hume. John Murray, London, 1923.

La Légion Etrangère en Espagne by General Paul Azan. Paris, 1907.

The English in Spain; or the Story of the War of Succession between 1830 and 1840 by Major F. Duncan. London, 1877.

The Story of the French Foreign Legion by Edgar O'Ballance. Faber, London, 1961.

AGAIN: Guedalla
  Le Livre d'Or

CHAPTER 4

Raft of Despair by Ensio Tiira. Dutton, New York, 1955.

In The Foreign Legion by Erwin Carlé (pseudonym Erwin Rosen). Duckworth, London, 1910.

The Legion of the Damned. The Adventures of Bennett J. Doty in the French Foreign Legion as told by himself. Jonathan Cape, London, 1928.

Bugeaud by Marshal Franchet d'Espérey. Paris, 1938.

The White Képi, A Casual History of the French Foreign Legion by Walter Kanitz. Regnery, Chicago, 1956.

AGAIN: Azan's *L'Armée d'Afrique*
  Le Livre d'Or

CHAPTER 5

The French Army by Paul-Marie de la Gorce translated by Kenneth Douglas. George Braziller, New York, 1963.

Le Maréchal MacMahon by Louis Graudin. Paris, 1893.

AGAIN: Azan's *L'Armée d'Afrique*
  De Beauvoir
  Guedalla
  Le Livre d'Or
  Fieffé

CHAPTER 6

The Destruction of Lord Raglan by Christopher Hibbert. Little, Brown, Boston, 1961.

Histoire de la Guerre de Crimée by C. Rousset. Paris, 1878.

The Second Empire by Philip Guedalla. John Murray, London, 1922.

Florence Nightingale by Cecil Woodham-Smith. McGraw Hill, New York, 1951.

Napoleon III by Albert Guérard, Knopf, New York, 1955

AGAIN: Guedalla's *Two Marshals*
   Brogan's *The French Nation*
   Le Livre d'Or

CHAPTER 7

Much of the material in this chapter comes from the historical files of the Foreign Legion at Puyloubier, France.

AGAIN: Brogan's *The French Nation*
   Guérard
   Guedalla
   De Beauvoir
   O'Ballance
   De la Gorce

CHAPTER 8

Historical files of the Foreign Legion at Puyloubier.

Bazaine et Nos Disastres en 1870, General V. J. Palat. Paris, 1913.

AGAIN: Guedalla *Two Marshals*
   Guérard
   Le Livre d'Or

CHAPTER 9

AGAIN: Guedalla *Two Marshals*
   Palat
   Brogan's *The French Nation*
   Guérard
   Le Livre d'Or
   O'Ballance

De Beauvoir
De la Gorce

CHAPTER 10

French Legionnaire by Alfred Perrott-White. Caxton, Caldwell, Idaho, 1951.

La Pénétration Saharienne published by the French Ministry of War. Paris, 1930.

Sahara by René Lecler, Hanover House, Garden City, New York, 1954.

Sahara Story by Edward Ward. Norton, New York, 1962.

Les Touareg du Nord by Henri Duveyrier. Paris, 1864.

Black Mother, The Years of the African Slave Trade by Basil Davidson. Little, Brown, Boston, 1961.

Files of the National Geographic Society, Washington, D.C.

Historical files of the Foreign Legion, Puyloubier.

AGAIN: Prince Aage.

CHAPTER 11

The White Képi (*See* Sources Chapter 4).

Sahara Desert Escape by Anthony Delmayne. Jarrolds, London, 1958.

In Morocco with the Legion, G. Ward Price. Jarrolds, London, 1934.

In The Foreign Legion (*See* Sources Chapter 4).

The Bugle Sounds by Major Zinovi Pechkoff. Appleton, New York, 1926.

Fire by Day and Flame by Night (*See* Sources Chapter 1).

March or Die by Howard Swiggett. Putnam's, New York, 1953.

AGAIN: Legion records
Le Livre d'Or

CHAPTER 12

A Soldier of the Legion, An Englishman's Adventures under the French Flag in Algeria and Tonquin by George Mannington. John Murray, London, 1917.

The Struggle for Indochina by Ellen J. Hammer. Stanford University Press, 1954.

French Policy and Developments in Indochina by Thomas E. Ennis. University of Chicago Press, 1936.

The Chinese in Southeast Asia by Victor Purcell. Oxford University
   Press, New York, 1951.
AGAIN: *Le Livre d'Or*
   O'Ballance
   Brogan's *The French Nation*

CHAPTER 13

The Legionnaire's diary mentioned under Acknowledgments is a prin-
cipal source for this chapter.
*Memoirs of the late Captain H. Crow of Liverpool, with descriptive
   sketches of the Western Coast of Africa.* London, 1830.
A Mission to Gelele by Sir Richard Francis Burton. London, 1864.
Compagne du Dahomey by Jules Poirier. Paris, 1895.
AGAIN: Davidson
   Le Livre d'Or

CHAPTER 14

Je suis un Légionnaire by Jean Martin. Paris, 1930.
My March to Timbuktu, Joseph Jacques Joffre. Paris and New York,
   1915.
Neuf Ans à Madagascar by J. S. Gallieni. Paris, 1908.
AGAIN: Files of the National Geographic Society
   Le Livre d'Or
   Brogan's *The French Nation*
   Ward
   Historical files of the Foreign Legion

CHAPTER 15

Hell in the Foreign Legion by Ernst F. Loehndorff, translated by Gerard
   Shelbey. Greenberg, New York, 1932.
The Tiger of the Legion, Being the Life Story of "Tiger" O'Reilly as
   told to William J. Elliott. Greenberg, New York, 1930.
French Legionnaire (*See* Sources Chapter 10).
Souvenirs du Colonel Maire de la Légion Etrangère, edited by Jean-
   Pierre Dorian. Paris, 1939.
The Man Who Liked Hell by Adolphe Cooper. Jarrolds, London, 1933.
The Reluctant Legionnaire by Michael Alexander. Dutton, New York,
   1956.

The Legion of the Damned (*See* Sources Chapter 4).
Files of the New York *Times*.

<h2 align="center">Chapter 16</h2>

The French Army (*See* Sources Chapter 5).
Moroccan Drama 1900–1955 by Rom Landau. The American Academy of Asian Studies, San Francisco, 1956.
Morocco That Was by Walter Burton Harris. William Blackwood, London, 1921.
Lettres de Tonkin et de Madagascar, 1894–1899 by Louis Hubert Lyautey. Paris, 1920.
Lyautey by André Maurois. Paris, 1931.
Trois Colonnes au Tonkin by J. S. Gallieni. Paris, 1899.
AGAIN: *Le Livre d'Or*
   O'Ballance
   Swiggett
   Brogan's *The French Nation*

<h2 align="center">Chapter 17</h2>

The Letters and Diary of Alan Seeger. Scribner's, New York, 1917.
Poems by Alan Seeger. Scribner's, New York, 1917.
American Fighters in the Foreign Legion by Paul A. Rockwell. Houghton Mifflin, Boston, 1930.
Victor Chapman's Letters from France. Macmillan, New York, 1917.
The Great War by Cyril Falls. Putnam's, New York, 1959.
The World Crisis by Winston S. Churchill. Thornton-Butterworth, London, 1923.
The Decisive Battles of the Western World, Vol. III, by Major General J. F. C. Fuller. Eyre & Spottiswoode, London, 1956.
The Real War by B. H. Liddell Hart. Faber, London, 1936.
AGAIN: *Le Livre d'Or*
   O'Ballance
   Brogan's *The French Nation*

<h2 align="center">Chapter 18</h2>

Personal History by Vincent Sheean. Doubleday, New York, 1934.
Hell Hounds of France by ex-Legionnaire 1384 of the *Légion Etrangère*

in collaboration with W. J. Blackledge. Sampson Low, London, 1932.

France, Spain and the Rif by Walter Burton Harris. Arnold, London, 1927.

AGAIN: *Le Livre d'Or*
    De la Gorce
    Carlé
    Prince Aage
    Price
    Cooper
    Pechkoff
    Souvenirs du Colonel Maire
    Landau

CHAPTER 19

Je suis un Légionnaire (*See* Sources Chapter 14).

A Short History of the Middle East by George Kirk. London, 1948.

AGAIN: *Le Livre d'Or*
    Prince Aage
    Price
    Cooper
    Pechkoff
    Doty
    Souvenirs du Colonel Maire
    Maurois

CHAPTER 20

French Legionnaire (*See* Sources Chapter 10).

Sahara Desert Escape (*See* Sources Chapter 11).

The Call to Honour, 1940–1942, by Charles de Gaulle (Volume I in his three-volume War Memoirs). Translated by Jonathan Griffin. Viking, New York, 1955.

Sahara Story (*See* Sources Chapter 10).

With the Foreign Legion at Narvik by Captain Pierre O. Lapie. John Murray, London, 1941.

Unity, 1942–1944, by Charles de Gaulle (Volume II of his War Memoirs). Translated by Richard Howard. Simon and Schuster, New York, 1959.

Salvation, 1944–1946, by Charles de Gaulle (Volume III of his War Memoirs). Translated by Richard Howard. Simon and Schuster, New York, 1960.

AGAIN: Legion records
      O'Ballance
      De la Gorce

CHAPTER 21

In Order to Die by Henry Ainley. Burke, London, 1955.
Street Without Joy by Bernard B. Fall. Stackpole, Harrisburg, Pa., 1961.
Strange Company by Adrian Liddell Hart. Nicolson, London, 1953.
Doctor at Dienbienphu by Paul Grauwin, Major, Medical Corps, French Army. Translated by James Oliver, John Day, New York, 1955.
Le Monde, Paris, May 10, 1954.
"The Bloody Lessons of Indochina" by Major Lamarr McFadden Prosser.
The Army Combat Forces Journal, Washington, June, 1955.
L'Indochine en guerre by General Jean Marchand. Paris, 1955.
Files of the New York *Times, Newsweek, Time Magazine.*
AGAIN: Legion records
      Hammer

CHAPTER 22

Képi Blanc, December, 1962.
The Test: De Gaulle and Algeria by C. L. Sulzberger. Harcourt, Brace & World, New York, 1962.
Ordeal in Algeria, Richard and Joan Brace. Van Nostrand, Princeton, N.J., 1960.
War in Algeria, Tanya Matthews. Fordham University Press, New York, 1961.
Genêt in *The New Yorker,* May 13, 1961.
Algeria in Turmoil, a History of the Rebellion by Michael K. Clark. Praeger, New York, 1959.
Files of the New York *Times, Newsweek, Time Magazine.*
AGAIN: Legion records
      Kraft
      O'Ballance
      De la Gorce

334

Index

Index

Aage, Prince of Denmark, 6, 115, 248, 251–252, 253, 257
Abd-el-Kader, 18, 19, 33, 45, 48, 51, 52, 53, 235
Abd-el-Krim, 233–240, 242
Abomey, 168, 170, 178
Ailleret, Charles, 3, 4
Ainley, Henry, 281
Alexander, Michael, 196
Algiers, 13, 15, 18, 20, 45, 178, 310, 312, 314, 315–318
Alma, Battle of the, 63–67
Amilakvari, Colonel, 262, 272, 274
Andalsues, 261
Archinard, Paul, 182
Army of National Liberation (A.L.N.), 308, 310
Aubagne, 3, 4, 320, 321, 322
Auberville, Battle of, 223–224

Balaclava, Battle of, 67
Ballangen, 262
Barbastro, Battle of, 28–29

Bataillons d'Afrique, 9, 305
Bazaine, François-Achille, 18, 20, 26, 28, 29, 49, 50, 56, 58, 59, 61, 65, 68, 69, 70, 79, 85, 86, 92, 93, 94, 96, 97, 98, 100, 101, 102, 104, 108–112
Bazaine, Pepita Peña, 98, 108, 109, 110, 111, 112
Bazaine, Soledad, 58, 59, 69, 70, 79, 93, 94
Behazin, King of Dahomey, 164, 165, 166, 178
Belloy-en-Santerre, 221–222
Berg, Corporal, 91, 92
Bernelle, Colonel, 18, 23, 26, 27
Bernelle, Madame, 18, 24, 27, 59
Berthonval, Battle of, 218
Bir Hakeim, Battle of, 272–274
Bismarck, 57, 99, 104
Böegard, Baron, 14, 18
Bohlmann, Private, 254
Bolante, Battle of, 217
Bonnier, T. P. E., 184

337

Bosquet, Pierre, 57, 65, 67, 68, 93
Bouffarick, 20
Bouligny, Edgar J., 210
Bou-Zian, Sheik, 52, 53, 54
Brian, Major, 95, 97
Brogan, D. W., 8
Bugeaud, Thomas Robert, 32–33, 35, 44–45, 52, 93
Burgoyne, Sir John, 67, 102
Buschenschutz, Captain, 252–253

Camerone, Battle of, 4, 88–92
Canrobert, François, 56, 61, 63, 65, 66, 67, 68, 69, 93
Carlé, Erwin, 38–40, 42–43, 147–149, 191, 237
Casablanca, 204, 206, 232, 274
Casey, John J., 210
Chabrière, Colonel, 71, 76, 77
Challe, Maurice, 314, 317, 318
Changarnier, Nicolas, 50
Charles X, King of France, 12, 13
Charlotte, Duchess, 84, 85, 94, 97
Chartres, Duke of (Robert Le Fort), 114–115
Château-Salins, 228
Chatkoff, Herman, 210, 211
Chérrière, Paul, 308
Chott Tigri, Battle of the, 152–153
Christian X, King of Denmark, 6
Churchill, Winston, 215, 269
Collins, Harry C., 210
Collins, James Stewart, 210
Colmar, Battle of, 276
Colomb-Béchar, 190, 192, 193–195, 197, 253, 267, 323
Conrad, Colonel, 27, 28, 29, 101
Constantin, Private, 91
Constantine, 317
Constantine, Battle of, 46–48
Cooper, Adolphe, 194–195, 253
Cortier, Lieutenant, 120–121
Coulmiers, Battle of, 103

Dakar, 269

d'Alouana, Battle of, 206
Damrémont, General, 47
Danjou, Jean, 4, 72, 80, 85, 87, 88–90, 92
de Borelli, Captain, 319
de Bourmont, Comte de Ghaisne, 13
de Castelnau, General, 227
de Castries, Christian, 289, 292, 296–298, 299, 300, 301
de Galard-Tarraubes, Mlle. Geneviève, 292, 293, 298, 301
de Gaulle, Charles, 258, 265, 266, 269, 270, 271, 314, 315, 324
de Griest, Pieter, 189
de la Demande, Camp, 3, 320, 322
de Négrier, François O., 34, 151–152, 153, 154, 155, 156, 157, 181, 191
de Saint-Marc, Elie, 316, 318
de Villebois-Mareuil, Georges, 146–147
Delmayne, Anthony, 145, 267, 268
Dennery, Sergeant, 125–126
Dianous, Lieutenant, 126–132
Diaz, Porfirio, 94
Diégo-Suarez, 323
Dienbienphu, Battle of, 289–301, 302, 306, 307
Dodds, Alfred, 169, 170, 172, 173, 178
Doineau, Captain, 110–111, 112
Don Carlos, 23, 28, 31
Dong-Khé, Battle of, 286
Doty, Bennett J., 41, 197, 247
Draget, Lieutenant, 281–283
Duchesne, General, 185, 186
Dunant, Henri, 82

El Himeimat, Battle of, 274
El Madani, 125–136
Espartero, General, 26, 27
Espinasse, Charles, 77
Eugénie, Empress, 57, 83, 100, 102, 112
Eupatoria, 61

Federation of National Liberation (F.L.N.), 308, 309, 311, 312, 313, 315, 318

Ferdinand VII, King of Spain, 22–23
Ferry, Jules, 155
Fez, 206, 232, 233, 248
Flatters, Paul, 124, 125, 126
Foreign Legion
  casualties, 16, 29, 48, 50, 53, 54, 70,
    75, 82, 92, 97, 157, 178, 186,
    200, 203, 206, 215, 216, 217,
    218, 222, 225, 240, 259, 260,
    261, 270, 274, 276, 294, 301
  component nationalities, 7–8, 14–15,
    23–24, 71, 73, 77, 91, 209, 257,
    258, 260, 267, 279–280
  desertions, 6, 8, 26, 28, 37, 92, 95, 96,
    191, 192, 193, 194, 195–196, 197,
    234, 238, 239, 247, 283, 322
  discipline, 36–37, 42, 43, 141, 188–
    195
  enlistment standards, 34–35
    Algeria, 15–21, 35–56, 71–75, 113–
      115, 137–149, 151–153, 188–197,
      257–258, 266–269, 303–319
    Austria, 276
    Cameroons, 269
    China, 278
    Crimea, the, 60–70
    Dahomey, 169–179
    Equatorial Africa, 182–185
    Eritrea, 270–271
    France, 3–4; 103–108 (Franco Prus-
      sian War); 209–213, 216–228
      (World War I); 258–261, 263–
      265, 266, 275–276 (World War
      II); 320–324
    Gabon, 270
    Germany, 276
    Greece, 216
    Indochina, 154–163, 199–201, 277–
      301
    Italy, 76–82, 275
    Libya, 272–274
    Madagascar, 185–187, 202
    Mexico, 83–98
    Morocco, 193, 204–207, 231–240,
      244–245, 274

Foreign Legion (cont.)
  enlistment standards (cont.)
    Norway, 262–263
    Senegal, 182, 183, 268
    Serbia, 216
    Spain, 23–31
    Syria, 242–244, 271–272
    Tunisia, 274, 275
    Turkey, 215
  organization and strength, 14–15, 23–
    24, 25, 29–30, 76, 85, 153–154,
    209, 217, 231, 257–258, 268,
    274–275, 277, 278, 279, 280–281,
    305, 308, 310, 323
  training, 36–38
  uniforms and equipment, 15, 25–26,
    38, 74, 77, 180, 258, 268, 275,
    310, 323
Forey, Élie, 86, 92
Fort St. Jean, 33–34
Fort St. Nicholas, 34
Fort Umberto, 271
Francis Joseph, Emperor of Austria, 76,
  82, 84
Fromentin, Eugène, 114

Gallieni, Joseph Simon, 200, 201–202,
  214, 215, 224
Gallipoli, 59, 215
Gambiez, Fernand, 315–317
Garibaldi, Giuseppe, 217
Gaucher, Lieutenant Colonel, 291
Genêt, Edmond, 210, 219
Giap, Vo Nguyên, 279, 285, 286, 288,
  292
Grauwin, Dr. Paul, 291, 292, 293, 294,
  298, 300, 301
Guillain, Robert, 302

Haiphong, 154, 199, 288
Hall, Bert, 210
Hangard Wood, Battle of, 225
Hanoi, 155, 288
Herbillon, General, 53
Huesca, Battle of, 28–29

Hussein, Dey of Algiers, 12

Inkerman, Battle of, 67–68
Isabella II, Queen of Spain, 23, 31
Ischeriden, Battle of, 74–75
Isle St. Marguerite, 110, 111
Isly, Battle of, 33
Itzkovitz, Eliahu, 283–285

Jeanningros, Colonel, 85, 86, 87, 92
Joffre, Joseph Jacques, 183, 184, 185, 214, 218, 224
Juarez, 84, 93, 94, 97

Kanitz, Walter, 144–145, 190
Karaman Khan Nazare-Aga, Prince, 210, 228
Kassala, 271
Kasserine Pass, 275
Katau, Private, 91, 92
Kayes, 182, 183
Képi Blanc, 160, 287, 321
Keren, 271
Kinburn, 70
Kitchener, Lord, 215
Klems, Joseph, 234–235, 240
Koenig, Joseph-Pierre, 262, 269, **270**, 272, 273
Koto, 173, 174, 177
Kubkub, 271
Kum Kale, Battle of, 215

Laghouat, 323
Lalande, André, 298, 299
Laniel, Joseph, 306
la Ramée Marie Louise de, 8
Lebeau, Major, 27
Leonhart, Private, 91
Leopold I, King of the Belgians, 58, 84
Libreville, 270
Liddell Hart, Adrian, 287
Liesenfeld, Major, 296
Linh-Nghi, 161–163
Loehndorff, Ernst F., 188–189
London, 265

Londres, Jacques, 191
Louis XVI, King of France, 11
Louis XVIII, King of France, 12, 22
Louis Philippe, King of the French, 4, 13, 14, 15, 21, 23, 30, 31, 32, 56, 85
Lyautey, Louis Hubert, 198–201, 202–204, 206, 207, 214, 231–233, 236

MacMahon, Marie Patrice, 50, 51, 56, 58–59, 69, 74, 75, 77, 79, 93, 100, 101, 102, 105, 106, 108, 109, 110, 112
Magenta, Battle of, 78–79
Magrin-Verneret, Lieutenant Colonel, 261, 262–264, 265, 271, 272
Maine, Corporal, 91, 92
Maire, Fernand, 192–193, 226
Majunga, 185, 186, 187
Mangin, Charles, 225
Mangin, Paul, 74–75
Mannington, George, 158–159, 161
Marcollo, 77–78
María Cristina, 22, 23, 30, 31
Marrakech, 204
Marseilles, 3, 35, 320
Martin, Jean, 181, 244–245, 247
Martinez, Juan, 72, 73, 77–78, 79, 80, 81, 85
Mascara, 36
Massu, Jacques, 311, 312, 314
Maudet, Clement, 72–73, 81, 85, 87, 90, 91
Maximilian, Archduke, 84–85, 93, 94, 97, 98
M'Chounech, Battle of, 50–51
Mecheria, 323
Mediouna, 204
Melilla, 234
Menabha, 205
Mendès-France, Pierre, 306
Mentschikoff, Prince, 63, 66, 67
Metz, Battle of, 101–102, 103
Milan, Colonel, 88, 89, 90, 91
Miliana, Siege of, 48–50

Mollet, Guy, 309
Monclar, Lieutenant Colonel. *See:* Margin-Verneret
Morin, Jean, 315
Moulinier, Captain, 97
Moussiefre, Battle of, 243

Namsos, 261
Napoleon I, 11, 56, 86, 208
Napoleon III, 56, 58, 61, 65, 71, 73, 76, 79, 81, 82, 83, 84, 93, 97, 99, 100, 101–102, 112, 154
Napoleon, Prince, 65
Narvik, 261, 262, 263
Navarin Farm, Battle of, 219
Navarre, Henri-Eugène, 297
Neuville-sur-Margival, Battle of, 226
Nicholas I, Czar of the Russians, 57
Nightingale, Florence, 70

Omar Pasha, 63
Oran, 15, 23, 35, 59, 123, 169, 261, 317
O'Reilly, "Tiger," 190
Organisation Armée Sécrète (O.A.S.), 317, 318, 321
Ouargla, 124, 136, 323

Painlevé, Paul, 239
Pamplona, 29, 30
Paris, 13, 14, 104–108, 224, 260, 263
Passard, Colonel, 211–212
Pau, 31
Pechkoff, Zinovi, 149, 150, 219, 253, 254–255, 257
Pélissier, Aimable, 56, 69, 70, 93
Perrott-White, Alfred, 118–120, 190–191, 259, 265–266, 274
Pétain, Henri Philippe, 217, 224, 236, 239, 258, 263, 265
Phélizot, René, 210
Phu Tong Hoa, Battle of, 285–286
Piaf, Edith, 318
Pobeguin, Jacques, 124, 125, 126, 127, 128, 131, 132, 133–135
Poincaré, Raymond, 224

Port Lyautey, 206, 274
Port Sudan, 270
Puebla, 84, 86, 94
Puyloubier, 321

Rachaya, Battle of, 243–244
Radicorfani, Battle of, 275
Raglan, Lord, 60–61, 62, 63, 64, 65
Raisuli, Sheik, 235
Ranavalona III, Queen of Madagascar, 185, 186
Rif War, 6, 233–240
Rigault, Raoul, 107
Rockwell, Kiffin, 210
Rockwell, Paul, 210, 228
Rollet, Paul, 45–46, 224, 225, 226, 227, 228, 246–247
Rommel, Erwin, 272, 273, 274, 275
Rosen, Erwin. *See:* Carlé, Erwin
Rouen, 210
Rousset, Camille, 15

Saigon, 280, 288
Saint-Arnaud, Leroy, 47–48, 51, 56, 60, 61, 63, 64, 65, 67, 93
Saint Germain, Gaillard, 52, 53
Saint-Hillier, Bernard, 316
Saragossa, 29
Sarrail, Maurice, 242–243
Sebastopol, 60, 61, 63, 67, 68, 69, 70
Sedan, Battle of, 102
Seeger, Alan, 210, 211, 212–213, 216–217, 219, 220–223
Seriana, 51, 53
Sheean, Vincent, 234–235, 239
Sheridan, General Philip, 97
Sidi-bel-Abbès, 3, 6, 35, 36, 55, 71, 92, 103, 187, 197, 202, 210, 216, 246, 266, 279, 301, 318, 319, 321
Silvestre, General, 233, 234
Sobieski, Private, 73, 79
Soissons, 225
Solaud, Private, 249–250
Solferino, Battle of, 80–82
Somme, Battle of the, 219–223

Son-Tay, 155–156
Sorny Ravine, Battle of, 226
Stanescu, Private, 283, 284–285
Streibler, Thiebald, 319

Taghit, Battle of, 203
Tamatave, 185
Tananarive, 185, 186, 187
Tarragona, 24, 25
Taudeni, 116, 117
Taza, 206, 207, 231
Terny-Sorny, Battle of, 226
Têtu, General, 270
Thaw, William, 211
Thiers, Adolphe, 105, 106, 108
Tiira, Ensio, 37
Timbuktu, 116, 117, 183–184
Toulouse, 210
Travers, Susan, 9, 261–262, 273
Trézel, General, 18, 19
Tu Duc, 154, 155
Tuyen-Quang, Battle of, 156–157

United Nations, 313, 324

Valée, General, 47
Varna, 59, 60, 61
Vauyaillon Tunnel, Battle of, 226–227
Veracruz, 85, 86
Victor Emanuel II, King of Italy, 76
Victoria, Queen, 58, 66
Vienot, Colonel, 69
Vilain, Jean, 72, 81, 85, 87, 90
Vittoria, 26, 27

Weidemann, Corporal, 211
Wenzel, Private, 91
Wildermann, Private, 73, 81–82
Wilhelm, Bandmaster, 73
Willette, Captain, 94, 110, 111, 112
Williams, Wesley, 238–239
Wren, Percival Christopher, 9, 247

Zaatcha, Oasis of, 51, 52, 53, 54
Zéralda, 310, 316, 318